Casting About

Also by Terri DuLong

Spinning Forward

"A Cedar Key Christmas" in *Holiday Magic*

Published by Kensington Publishing Corp.

Casting About

TERRI DuLONG

KENSINGTON BOOKS
www.kensingtonbooks.com

KENSINGTON BOOKS are published by

Kensington Publishing Corp.
119 West 40th Street
New York, NY 10018

All Kensington titles, imprints, and distributed lines are available at special quantity discounts for bulk purchases for sales promotion, premiums, fund-raising, educational, or institutional use.

Special book excerpts or customized printings can also be created to fit
specific needs. For details, write or phone the office of the Kensington
Special Sales Manager: Kensington Publishing Corp., 119 West 40th
Street, New York, NY 10018. Attn. Special Sales Department. Phone:
1-800-221-2647.

Kensington and the K logo Reg. U.S. Pat. & TM Off.

ISBN-13: 978-0-7582-3205-2
ISBN-10: 0-7582-3205-5

First Kensington Trade Paperback Printing: November 2010
10 9 8 7 6 5 4 3 2 1

Printed in the United States of America

For Brian and Véronique,
with much love

1

When I passed the phone to Adam, I had no idea that the caller's information would force me to question my insecurity on motherhood. Adam and I had only been married for six months. Rather than focusing on starting a family, my time and energy had been directed toward purchasing my mother's yarn shop, Spinning Forward. I was still a new *bride,* for goodness sake, so being a *mom* was the last thing on my mind. "It's for you," I said, passing the telephone across the breakfast table while I continued to nibble on toast and update my to-do list.

"Yes, this is Adam Brooks," I heard my husband say. While silence filled our kitchen it occurred to me that perhaps I should apply for a small business loan. Sure, my mother had basically passed the yarn shop over to me before she left for Paris with Noah, but I knew that I wanted to be the official proprietor of the business I'd come to love. My mother was thrilled that my desire for ownership would keep what she worked at so hard in the family. And the week before she was to leave, we met with an attorney to sign the documents that would transfer Spinning Forward from Sydney Webster to Monica Brooks. My mother would only accept a minimal amount of money to make the transaction legal. Revenue from sales would pay the monthly lease and overhead, and continue the small salary of Aunt Dora. I hoped that even without some of the special services my mother offered, I'd keep Spinning Forward the success it had been for over three years. A bank loan would help to make that happen.

My attention reverted to the one-sided phone call.

"She what?" Adam said in a tone he used when he was upset.

I glanced up as my husband pushed his chair away from the table and began pacing around our kitchen. Apparently this wasn't a telemarketer call, as I had thought.

"Well, where is she now?" he questioned.

Anger was being replaced by concern. His brow furrowed as he raked his hand through sandy-colored hair, and I considered him the sexiest and most attractive man I'd known.

"Yes, yes, I understand that. But *you* have to understand that I have a job and will have to make arrangements. The soonest I could be up there would be Monday."

Up there? Where? All of a sudden it dawned on me what this phone call was about. Adam's daughter, Clarissa, was now eight years old and lived with his ex, Carrie Sue, in some godforsaken town in Georgia.

Adam reached for paper and a pen from the counter drawer. "Yes, go ahead," he said and began jotting down information. "Okay. I need some time to make arrangements. I'll call you back tomorrow."

Placing the phone on the table, he blew out a deep breath before sitting down across from me. "We need to talk."

Jumping up to grab the coffeepot, I refilled our cups. When a crisis happens, I'm one of those people who functions better while keeping busy.

Rejoining him at the table, it was my turn to exhale loudly. "Okay. What's up?"

"Carrie Sue was in an automobile accident the other night. She's in the hospital. No major injuries, but Carrie Sue and the driver were both drunk."

"My God, was Clarissa with her?"

"No, it's worse. Carrie Sue left her alone at the condo to go out drinking with her girlfriends. When the accident happened, she had to tell the authorities her eight-year-old daughter was alone at home. Social services got involved. That's who that was on the telephone." Adam began fiddling with the spoon on the table and shook his head. "Clarissa is in a temporary foster home. The woman on the phone said it's highly unlikely that Carrie Sue will retain custody of her. There's an emergency hearing next week and I have to be there."

Thoughts were swirling in my head. I'd only met Carrie Sue once. The summer that Adam and I began dating, we drove up to Georgia together to bring Clarissa Jo to Cedar Key for their annual month-long visit. Meeting Carrie Sue once had been quite enough. She came from a wealthy family that disowned her the moment she'd married Adam. Blond, beautiful, and bitchy, Carrie Sue had always enjoyed tipping her wrist a little too often with whatever alcoholic liquid appealed to her at the moment. Her drinking problem had contributed to the breakup of their marriage. I knew that Adam had attempted to get custody of his daughter and had been devastated when the judge ruled in favor of the mother, leaving Adam with only every-other-weekend visitation. This was compounded by the fact that two years ago, with an economy in tatters, the school in Georgia had been forced to let him go. Faced with hefty support payments, in addition to being responsible for his daughter's medical insurance, Adam had felt fortunate to be offered a teaching position in his home town of Cedar Key, Florida.

"And so . . . all of this means what?" I asked, too stupid or too stubborn to understand what was coming next.

"It means I have to go to Georgia and be there for the hearing. I've been paying support for Clarissa Jo these past four years, and I'm her legal guardian."

"Oh," was all I could manage to say.

Adam reached across the table for my hand and gave it a squeeze. "I know. This certainly came out of the blue. Having Clarissa with us full-time will be very different, but I think we'll manage."

We had discussed children when we began dating, and while we didn't say we'd never have any—we didn't agree that we would, either. Not wanting to sound like the witch from Hansel and Gretel, I let out a deep breath, squeezing Adam's hand in return. "Of course we will," I said, sounding much braver than I felt. "Of course we'll manage and everything will be fine."

My husband nodded and then shook his head. "Christ, Monica, what a loser Carrie Sue is. I'm just grateful nothing happened to Clarissa Jo alone in that apartment."

Scary news events flashed through my mind concerning children either left alone or abducted. Although I'd always felt horrible when I heard about these things, I certainly had never considered them from a parent's point of view.

"Jesus," he said, glancing at his watch. "I've got to get moving. Class starts in fifteen minutes."

Jumping up from the table, he came around to pull me up next to him.

"It'll be okay. I promise. We both need a little bit of time to digest this and we'll discuss it tonight. How about dinner at the Island Room?" he whispered into my hair.

God, his arms felt good around my body. "No, I'd prefer dinner here. Quiet and private. I'll make your favorite pasta dish."

"It's a deal. I love you, Monica. And things will work out."

"They will," I agreed, uncertain where any of us were headed.

After Adam left I put the breakfast dishes into the sudsy water to let them soak and prepared to start a load of wash—the whole time, thoughts of the phone call going through my head.

Pouring myself another mug of coffee I took it outside to the deck and curled up on the chaise lounge. Bushes of vivid red azaleas and yellow hibiscus rimmed the outer perimeter of the garden, creating a floral sanctuary.

I loved springtime on Cedar Key, when the air filled with all sorts of tropical fragrances. When I first came to the island to visit my mother and grandmother, it hadn't been my intention to stay forever. I was a Yankee girl—not Southern born and Southern bred. By the time a year had passed, I knew that a place of birth doesn't necessarily produce a feeling of *home*—because the small island off the west coast of Florida was what accomplished that for me.

At the time, I was between high-pressure jobs with top companies in Boston. On a whim, I applied for and was accepted to teach English at the University of Florida in Gainesville, which I did for a year. Adam hadn't been the only one affected by the economy—due to budget cuts, I also lost my teaching position. By that time, my mother's yarn shop on Cedar Key had become successful and I accepted her offer to handle the business Internet orders, which allowed me to slow down and literally smell the roses. Living in a small Southern town makes that easy to do.

Sitting at the computer at Spinning Forward, I glanced up one afternoon to find a tall, slim, sixtyish-looking woman waiting for me to answer a knitting question. By the time I became a teen, I'd lost interest in knitting, but seeing all the new fibers available since then had restored my love and addiction for this craft. With help from my mother and Aunt Dora, I'd learned the current knitting techniques.

But it wasn't the woman that grabbed my attention—it was the handsome, sexy, younger man standing beside her. The poor guy looked out of place and bored surrounded by cubbyholes filled with alpaca, cashmere, and myriad other rainbow-colored yarn.

She introduced him as her son. "This here is my boy, Adam Brooks," she told me with pride in her voice. "He teaches history to the middle school children right here on this island."

Tall and good-looking with sandy-colored hair, his blue eyes caught mine as he shrugged his shoulders and smiled. I think that killer smile of his sealed my fate.

"Monica Webster," I'd said, holding out my hand to him.

Adam had returned a few days later—without Mama—and invited me to dinner. As irritating as she can be, I've always been happy that Opal Brooks walked into the yarn shop that day with her son in tow.

The telephone ringing in the kitchen brought me out of my daydreaming.

"Hey, Monica," I heard my best friend, Grace, say. "Are you still coming by the coffee shop to drop off those needles for me?"

My eyes flew to the clock on the wall. Damn, I'd forgotten all about my promise from the day before.

"Yeah, I'll be there, but I'm not even dressed yet. So it probably won't be till after lunch. I'm in the middle of doing laundry and not due into the yarn shop till three."

"Okay. Not a problem. What's up? You sound kind of pooky today."

I blew out a deep breath. "I guess *pooky* would cover it. You're not going to believe this . . ."

"Honey, try me. Living on this island, I'd believe just about anything."

Despite my sour mood, I laughed. Grace had a way of doing that. Lightening up a difficult situation.

"Well, it seems like my little household of two might be increasing to three."

"What! You're pregnant?"

I let out a laugh. Maybe my statement needed clarification. "No, no. I'm not. Adam's daughter, Clarissa Jo, is coming to live with us."

"You mean, like permanently?"

"Yup."

"I thought that high-bred ex-wife of his had custody."

I proceeded to explain the car accident and social services.

"Hmm, sounds like you might be giving up the honeymoon for motherhood," Grace said.

Ignoring her comment, I explained, "Adam had to leave right after he got the call. We're going to discuss it more tonight, but he'll be heading up there next week for a hearing."

"Lord, it's always something, isn't it?"

Isn't that just the truth? "I need to get moving here. I'll be by the coffee shop before I head into work. Have a nice strong latte ready for me."

I walked into Spinning Forward to find Aunt Dora unpacking a recent delivery of yarn.

Brushing a strand of hair out of her eyes, she looked up and smiled. "Hello, Monica. Thought I'd get this unpacked for you before I leave."

Eudora Foster was my great-aunt and the sister of Sybile Bowden, my grandmother who had passed away three years before.

"Thanks," I said, heading to the coffeepot.

"Any word from your mother?" she questioned.

"She called yesterday morning. After only one month living in Paris, I'd say she's already a confirmed Francophile. She loves the apartment that she and Noah are renting in Montparnasse. Said she feels like a true Parisian—going out daily to shop at the market, the cheese shop, the butcher. I'm not sure we'll ever get her back into a supermarket when they return home next year."

Aunt Dora laughed and shook her head. "Oh, I had no doubt she'd fall in love with the fact she had a chance to actually live there, rather than just visit. What a great opportunity for Noah too. To be asked to teach painting at the Sorbonne, but he's a wonderful artist. So I bet he enjoys returning to a place where he'd lived for so many years."

I took a sip of the hot coffee and nodded. "Yeah, my mother said that his fluent French and knowledge of Paris is really adding to the joy of living there."

"Well, I'm glad to hear they're enjoying it so much. Anything else new?"

"Nah, not much going on," I told her. "Had to stop by the coffee shop to give Grace those needles she needed. Anything I need to know here before you leave for the day?"

Dora filled me in on a couple of telephone sales that would need to be put together and shipped. In addition to knitting and selling yarn, my mother had also specialized in the spinning of dog and cat fur for besotted pet parents across the country. Since I have no knowledge of spinning and no desire to learn, when I decided I wanted to own the shop, I made the decision to no longer offer that service. This was part of the reason I felt scared—I prayed I'd be able to keep the business successful.

Both Dora and I looked up as the wind chimes on the door tinkled.

I turned around to see Saren Ghetti, my grandfather, walk in with a bouquet of wildflowers in his hand.

"Saren, your garden must be bare the way you always bring me fresh flowers."

He threw his head back and laughed. "But you like them, just like your mama did before she left for Paris. Besides, I enjoy doing it. How're ya doin', Miss Monica?"

I felt his arms go around me in a tight squeeze. Although my mother and I had only met her birth father for the first time a few years earlier, we had all developed a deep love for each other. And although we had continued on with first names, rather than *Dad* or *Grandpa,* it certainly didn't diminish the tight bond that had grown between us.

"I'm doing just fine, and how about you?"

"Mighty good," he said in that Southern drawl I'd come to love. "Did any of ya hear about Robbie and Sally-Ann?"

They were one of the young couples in town, and I could tell by the twinkle in his eyes that he had some sort of gossip to share. When my mother had first moved to the island, she was astounded at the speed that news got around. Somebody had told her they called it the *coconut pipeline*.

"No, what happened?" I asked.

"Well, it seems that Miss Sally-Ann just up and left Robbie. Gone, she is." He snapped his fingers together for emphasis. "Just like that."

"My God," Aunt Dora said. "They've only been married a couple years and seemed to get along so well. Who has little Robbie Junior?"

"She left 'em with the babysitter and never came to pick 'em up. So Callie had to call Robbie, and there he was out there on his boat taking in clams. Seems Miss Sally-Ann had enough of marriage and motherhood—she's gone back home to Alabama to her mama's house. And Miss Bess, Robbie's mama, well, she's had to step in and help him out."

Aunt Dora shook her head. "What a shame. And little Robbie is barely two years old. I wonder if she'll come back? Maybe she just needed a little break."

It suddenly occurred to me that when Clarissa Jo descended on my household, it wouldn't be long before Adam and I were fodder for the coconut pipeline.

2

After I got the Alfredo sauce made for the pasta, I put together a salad and then poured myself a glass of Cabernet. Sitting at the kitchen table, I took a sip and realized I was tired. Stress has a way of draining people, and I was feeling mighty drained after the events of this morning.

Glancing around the kitchen, I smiled. I just loved our home. The house had been in Adam's family for three generations. When he returned to the island two years before, he'd had it remodeled and refurbished. With three bedrooms, three bathrooms, a great room, and eat-in kitchen, it was spacious but not overly large for two people. We'd taken the third bedroom and turned it into a studio of sorts for my knitting projects. It was really a mish-mosh of a house, but that's what added to its character. The master bedroom, bath, and an attached sitting area had been added on, so it jutted out from the side of the house. The great room and kitchen comprised the middle area, similar to cracker houses in the South, and on the other side were two bedrooms and baths. The house had been long paid for when Adam inherited it. But the killer taxes on Cedar Key, in addition to the astronomical premiums for wind and flood insurance, made these payments almost as costly as having a mortgage. Another reason why I hoped the yarn shop would be a success and help us financially.

I loved our view of the water just across the street, a large deck where we entertained and enjoyed the island air, and I loved the *feel* that the old house gave off. I wondered what it would be like to have toys taking up my space, the constant babble of a child or sticky kitchen counters from peanut butter and jelly.

The phone rang, and as I walked toward the spot where we always kept it in the base, I realized the handset wasn't there. Turning around in the kitchen, I followed the sound out to the deck and saw the portable phone sitting on the patio table. *That's odd. I don't remember leaving the phone out there when I left the house a few hours earlier.*

Pressing the button to answer the call, I heard Opal's voice and silently groaned. Today wasn't a good day for a chat with my mother-in-law.

"Monica, sweetie? Is that you? Opal here."

Her voice seemed to have an extra layer of saccharine today.

"Opal. How're you doing?"

"I'm doing just fine, sweetie. Wanted to let ya know—I think Naomi has had her fill of me for a while. So I'm headin' back to the island in the morning. Are you and Adam free for dinner Saturday evening? I'll cook up a nice seafood gumbo for all of us. How would that be?"

Oh, Lord—just what I didn't need at the moment. Opal coming back from Charleston for one of her indefinite stays on Cedar Key.

Putting aside my annoyance, I said, "That's nice, Opal, but I'm not sure what our plans are for the weekend . Adam is still at school with some activity. But I'll let him know and he can call you tomorrow evening, okay?"

"That would be nice, sugar. Now, I know I say this to you every time, but I'm not sure how long I'll be in town. But no matter. We'll see a lot of each other while I'm there. Now, you give my Adam a kiss from me and I'll call you when I get there tomorrow evenin'."

Disconnecting the line, I plunked into the patio chair and let out a deep sigh. All of a sudden there seemed to be a black cloud floating above me. Oh, don't get me wrong—I love Opal. I really do. But I can only put up with her sweetness and Southern belle demeanor in limited doses. I don't feel guilty about this, because Adam's sister Naomi admitted to me that yes, she loved her mama dearly—however, she too had to set limits with Opal staying with her. Believe me, more than once I thanked God that at least here on Cedar Key Opal had her own little cottage and didn't actually live *in* with us. Miss Opal, as the locals called her, was Miss Key Lime Pie of 1960 here on the island, and you'd think to God that now that she was pushing seventy, she'd put aside her vanity and just age gracefully. But oh no, not Opal.

"Honey, I'm home," I heard Adam call from inside the house. All of a sudden I didn't even have the strength to get up.

"Out here," I hollered.

"Hey, beautiful. Dinner smells great."

Spying my glass of wine on the table, he leaned over to touch my lips with his and said, "Good idea. I'll join you in a glass before dinner."

Returning with his wineglass, he sat beside me and massaged my thigh in a comforting gesture.

"Everything all right?" he questioned.

I took a gulp of wine and shrugged. "That depends what you mean by all right. There seems to be a lot going on. Your mother called and she's on her way back down here tomorrow. Wants to cook us a gumbo dinner Saturday evening. But other than that . . ."

Adam put his glass on the table, stood up and reached for my hands, pulling me into his arms.

"I'm sorry. All of a sudden it seems like our little love nest is being invaded, and it's all due to my family."

I felt his hand stroking my back and looked up into his handsome face. His lips caught mine and for a few brief moments I forgot about everything except Adam.

"Hey," I said, playfully pushing away. "You keep this up and that wonderful dinner won't make it to the table."

"Come on. I'll help you get it together."

He took my hand as we walked inside.

During dinner we managed to find a million other things to talk about except Clarissa Jo.

After we cleaned up and filled the dishwasher, I took his hand and led him to the great room.

"Okay, we've stalled long enough," I told him. "Let's discuss what we're going to do."

He patted the spot next to him on the sofa. "Come on. Sit next to me."

I curled up in the crook of his arm and for a few moments luxuriated in the intimacy we had together. Then it slid across my mind that these moments might be few and far between with a child sharing our home.

As if knowing my thoughts, he said, "I know we didn't plan for this to happen. Hell, we never really decided for sure if we even wanted a child of our own. So I know how difficult this is for you, Monica. I do. I wish to God that I'd gotten custody four years ago when the divorce took place."

"Well, Carrie Sue had to have her way. You told me she really had no motherly instincts. The only reason she wanted to hang on to Clarissa was because she knew how much you wanted her. It sure didn't have a thing to do with love."

"Right. It just would have made it so much easier if I'd gotten Clarissa Jo at four years old. I would have hired a nanny during the day while I was at work and at least she would have been in a stable environment. The poor kid has been dragged all over Georgia with

Carrie Sue. She never could stay in one place very long. And it kills me to think my daughter is now with some strangers. I've heard horror stories about foster care."

Christ, Monica—you really are a piece of work. Here I am concerned about the role I'll be taking on, and God knows what that little girl might be going through.

I squeezed his hand and sat up to look at him. "Well, hey, handsome, maybe we didn't *plan* to have this happen, but Clarissa Jo's your daughter. Our home will be her home, and we'll get through all of it together." I only wished I had more confidence in my mothering abilities but was grateful my voice sounded sure and strong.

The glow that filled Adam's face made me feel even more ashamed. I'm sure he spent the entire day being torn up about the situation.

He leaned over and kissed me. "It won't be easy. I know that. She'll be in school until May, and then I'll be off work all summer. I don't expect you to give up the yarn shop or anything else you might want to do."

I hadn't even thought about that. My entire life was about to do a one-eighty.

"So I'll call social services tomorrow and tell them I'll be up there for the hearing on Monday. I spoke to the school and told them what was going on. They've arranged for a substitute for next week and given me the time off."

Leave it to Cedar Key, I thought. Family was everything on this little island. I don't mean that in a derogatory way. It's just that I wasn't surprised that the school would help out in any way they could. Being an only child and growing up without any relatives to speak of except my parents, I had been taken aback when I first came to the island. Each family had tons of aunts, uncles, cousins, and relatives twice removed. And while they might not all like each other, it was obvious that a very strong familial bond existed and they fiercely stuck by one another. That was proven to my mother and me when the town found out that we were Sybile's daughter and granddaughter. They welcomed us with open arms because, well—we were technically *family.*

"Okay," I said, leaning over to kiss Adam's cheek. "So what do I need to do? Shop for toys? Clothes for her? We'll give her the guest room, right? Should we . . ."

Adam put his index finger to my lips. "Shh! You don't need to stress about this. I'm not even sure she'll be coming back with me next week—it might take longer, with paperwork and everything. I guess I'll know more tomorrow when I call them. As for toys and clothes, we'll go into Gainesville together and let her pick out what she'd like. Monica . . . are you sure you're okay with all of this?"

I looked into his handsome face and saw the concern that covered it. But beyond the concern, I saw his deep love for me, and I knew that had his reaction to this situation been any different, he wouldn't have been the man I fell in love with.

"I'm okay with it, and we'll work it out together. I love you, Adam."

His arms tightened around my waist.

Adam was on the phone with social services making arrangements to be at the hearing on Monday and I was scurrying around the house trying to get ready to open the yarn shop at ten. Aunt Dora and I took turns opening.

"Everything okay?" Adam asked as he watched me run from the great room into the bedroom and back to the kitchen.

"I can't find the blue sweater that I wore yesterday. Have you seen it?"

Adam shook his head. "No. Where'd you put it when you got home yesterday?"

"Where I always do—on the hall tree by the front door. But it's not there," I told him, exasperation coloring my words. "What did social services say?"

"The hearing is set for eleven Monday morning. They feel certain that the judge will grant me full legal custody, based on the emergency situation. The divorce papers stated that if anything should happen to Carrie Sue, custody would revert to me."

I nodded as I walked back to the great room to resume my search for the sweater.

"When do you think you'll be back?" I called over my shoulder.

"I'm going to book the Best Western in Macon for a few nights. That's just a short drive to where the hearing is. I'll drive up on Sunday, go to the hearing Monday, and the social worker said I'd be able to visit with Clarissa Jo the next day at the foster home. So we'll probably head back here Wednesday morning."

Annoyed that I couldn't find that damn sweater, I plopped on the sofa. "Is there anything special I need to do?"

"Nothing I can think of, but . . . we do need to tell my mother. She has no clue what's going on."

"Oh, God, you're right. Well, Opal is due on the island this evening and wanted to cook that gumbo for us tomorrow night. Why don't we invite her here instead? Besides Opal, maybe we should also invite Saren and Aunt Dora."

"Good idea. We don't want the family finding out about Clarissa Jo from the locals."

I glanced at the clock on the mantel and saw it was 9:30. "Well, I can't find that sweater, so I'll grab another one and then I need to get to the shop. Is your first class at ten?"

"Yeah, I'm going to get going too. So you do the inviting for tomorrow evening. Want me to grill some steaks?"

I nodded. "And I'll do up a salad with cheese potatoes. Between Aunt Dora and your mother, we'll have plenty of dessert. It's going to be warm tomorrow, so we'll eat out on the deck."

I stood in the doorway watching Adam leave and continued to ponder where on earth my sweater could be.

⁓ 3 ⁓

Even though Grace knew about the current situation with Clarissa Jo, I invited her to dinner with the family. Heck, Grace was like family anyway. We'd met a few years before, shortly after I had decided to stay on the island. And as the young kids say, we knew immediately that we were BFF—best friends forever.

At thirty-six, she was four years older than me, and we shared many common interests like reading, knitting, and our love for the island. Grace had found her way to Cedar Key from Brunswick, Georgia, ten years before. She might have been my best friend, but from the beginning there'd been a secretiveness about her that I'd never attempted to invade. She did share with me that her parents were killed in a car crash in the south of France when she was twelve years old. They had owned an antique shop in Brunswick and had been in Europe on business. Grace had been staying with her aunt when the accident occurred, and she had an older sister who'd been away at college. Following the funeral, she remained at the aunt's house in Brunswick to be raised by her. I always got the feeling that Grace came from a wealthy family and it was her aunt who had given her the money to relocate to Cedar Key and open her coffee shop on Dock Street. But the part I could never figure out was despite the close and loving relationship she shared with her aunt, Grace seldom went back to Brunswick to visit her. Almost daily phone calls had cemented their relationship since I'd known Grace. She seldom mentioned her sister, but it was obvious that they'd had a falling-out, because they were never in touch. Ten years later, her coffee shop was thriving and she'd become a savvy businesswoman—much like my mother's best friend, Alison, who owned the Cedar Key B&B. I learned quickly that the women on the island were a special breed—independent and strong, and they had what was known as *true grit*.

Grace dated off and on but had no special man in her life, which was another thing I couldn't figure out. Extremely attractive with a cloud of auburn curls that fell to her shoulders, she seemed oblivious to the admiring stares sent her way from many of her male customers. One thing we didn't share was her passion for the metaphysical, but it did create some humorous moments that got me laughing.

As I was filling the dishwasher on Saturday morning, the phone rang and I answered to hear her voice.

"Anything I can bring this evening?" she asked.

"Just yourself," I told her.

"How're you doing? Getting more used to the idea of having a rug rat around the house?"

I laughed. "You really make it sound very enticing. After I finish cleaning up the kitchen, I'm going to get her room ready. We're giving her the guest bedroom with the attached bath. Plus, it has a pretty view out to the garden."

"Yeah, true—I'm sure all eight-year-olds have a garden view on their priority list."

I realized once again how little I knew about kids. "Cripe, you're right. She won't care at all about what she sees out her window. God, Gracie, I'm not sure I can do this."

"I didn't mean to stir up your stress level again. I was only joking with you. You'll do fine. And you can always come to Aunt Gracie for advice. I've never had kids either, but we'll get through this together."

"Thanks. I'm sure I'll take you up on that."

"Hey, I have some interesting news to share. . . . There's a fellow that's been dropping by the coffee shop a lot. Very good-looking and don't laugh, but he reminds me a little of George Clooney. Sounds like a cliché, I know—but he's tall, dark, and handsome."

"Hmm, that *is* interesting. Does he live on the island?"

"No, in Gainesville, right now. Originally from New Jersey. He asked me out for dinner next week."

"And are you going?"

"Yeah, I figured what the heck. Haven't had a date in ages."

"What's he do for work?"

I heard a pause before she said, "He's a developer."

To the locals on the island, she might as well have said, *"He's a leper."*

"Okay, okay. I know . . . developers are right up there with the IRS. But he's not looking to develop here on Cedar Key."

"And you know this, how?"

"Well . . . I don't for sure. But he's working on some project in Gainesville. Anyway, it's *just* a date."

She was right, and maybe I was being a bit too hard on her. "Then I hope you have a good time and it goes well."

"So you're ready to spring the news on the family tonight? I'm sure they'll all welcome little Clarissa Jo with open arms."

"I'm sure you're right."

Opal was the first to arrive. She walked into the kitchen carrying her famous key lime pie and after setting it on the counter, leaned in to give me her requisite cosmopolitan kiss on both cheeks.

With hands on my shoulders, she pulled back and said, "I do declare, marriage certainly agrees with you. Love your new bob cut, Monica. You could use a bit more blush, though."

I laughed as I gave her a hug. Considering that Opal was known for using about an ounce too much makeup, I took her beauty tips with a grain of salt.

"Thanks for the pie," I said, putting it into the fridge. "You're looking pretty good yourself."

She waved a hand in the air as she perched on the bar stool at the counter, carefully crossing her shapely legs. Opal was a fashion plate—no doubt about it. The woman had style and didn't shy away from making people take notice. Today she was sporting a black leather skirt two inches above her knees, with black silk stockings and a mint green silk blouse that accentuated her overly bleached, chin-length blond hair.

"This is so nice to have a family gathering tonight. I love spending time with Saren and Miss Dora. Now, where is that handsome son of mine?" she questioned, looking out to the deck.

"He went to pick up Saren. They'll be here shortly."

"Hello, hello," Dora called from the hall.

Opal leaped off the stool to run toward the front of the house.

"Well, Eudora Foster, you're a sight for sore eyes," I heard Opal say in greeting. "It's been much too long since I've seen you."

I turned from slicing tomatoes for the salad to see both women walk into the kitchen.

Dora kissed my cheek and handed me a plate of her delicious lemon squares.

"Thought these might go nicely with Opal's pie."

"Thanks, Dora," I said, giving her a warm smile.

It was Dora who suspected long before anyone else that her sister had given birth to my mother. The first time they'd met, Dora admitted later, she knew in her soul that Sydney Webster was the daughter Sybile had given up for adoption, and adding to her certainty had been a segment she'd seen on *The Today Show*—two brothers in Maine, living in the same town, coworkers at the same furniture company, slowly putting together the pieces and discovering they were biological brothers.

Dora and Sybile were as different as roses and weeds. My grandmother was considered self-centered and ornery by some, but everyone was fond of Miss Dora. Sweet and easygoing, she was easy to love. Even before it was confirmed that my mother was her niece, they'd developed a very special relationship. Not until Sybile was at the end of her days did my mother and grandmother bond and come to understand each other.

"How long will you be on the island?" I heard Dora ask Opal.

"Oh, who knows." Opal's laughter filled the kitchen. "I'm just like a butterfly—flitting here, there, and everywhere. But I think poor Naomi needed a bit of a break from her mama. Not that I'm difficult to get along with, but I guess we all need our space."

Adam arrived with Saren, and Grace was right behind them, so our gathering was complete.

"Would everybody like some red wine? I have a nice Sangiovese."

I saw a bewildered look cross Adam's face.

"What's wrong?" I asked.

Standing in front of the wine rack, he shook his head. "I don't know. I'm positive I had two bottles of that wine in here. Do you know where they are?"

"No, I saw them there last night when I was checking the wine supply. That's odd."

Adam began to open kitchen cabinets while I checked the cabinets under the island in the center of the floor.

"Nothing," I told him.

Everyone sat quietly observing our search and then Saren said, "My, my. Ah, yup. That *is* mighty odd. Two bottles of wine don't just go missin'."

"Oh, Saren. Now don't go jumping to conclusions," Dora said.

Not understanding what they were referring to, I questioned, "What conclusions?"

Dora giggled. "Now, Saren—you don't honestly think that Miss Elly is here in Monica's house, do you?"

I may have neglected to mention—while most people on Cedar Key are the best in the world, many do tend to be a bit quirky. Just a tad eccentric and what we islanders refer to as *characters.* Miss Elly was a ghost that had lived in Saren's house for many years. He claimed she visited him each evening to have cognac and conversation. Now, mind you, nobody else ever witnessed Miss Elly, so of course everyone chalked it up to a vivid imagination on Saren's part. However, when my grandmother came back into his life after all those years—suddenly Miss Elly departed and never returned.

"Heck, no," he said, shaking his head emphatically. "I'm just a wonderin' if perhaps Miss Sybile has decided to pay us all a visit."

Goose bumps broke out on my arms as I recalled the misplaced telephone and the blue sweater I still hadn't found.

Opal broke the tension with her laughter. "Oh, Saren, are you still believin' in those ghosts? Well, if Miss Sybile is here with us— Adam, sweetie, find another bottle of wine and let's give a toast to her."

My husband caught the look on my face and quickly produced two bottles of Pinot Noir.

As everyone lingered over dessert and coffee, Adam cleared his throat and said, "Actually, Monica and I had some news to share with everyone tonight. That's why we wanted to have this gathering."

Opal jumped up from the table, clutching her hands to her chest. "I knew it! I knew it! You're pregnant, aren't ya, sugar?" she said, directing her happy gaze toward me.

I broke out laughing and shook my head as I caught the raised eyebrows on Grace's face.

"Ah, no. That is definitely not the news," I told four staring faces that were waiting for my verification. "I can absolutely confirm that I am not pregnant."

Like a deflated balloon, Opal sank back into her chair. "Oh. Then what *is* the news?"

Adam shot me a smile. "No, Monica's not pregnant. However, we will be expecting a child in the house. My daughter Clarissa Jo will be coming to live with us this week."

Silence filled the deck as everyone waited for an explanation.

Adam went on to explain about the car accident, Carrie Sue losing custody, the call from social services, and his trip to Georgia the next day.

Dora was the first to break the silence. "That poor little girl. Ending up in foster care. Thank goodness she has a wonderful father like you who loves her. And you, Monica, that's very loving of you to take in a child you don't know that well."

Opal jumped up again, running around the table to kiss Adam. "My granddaughter? My granddaughter's comin' here to live on the island? Lord above, I may never return to Naomi's house. A week every other Christmas and a month during the summer was never enough time for me to enjoy Clarissa Jo. Oh, Adam, this is wonderful news."

I was rather surprised at Opal's reaction. In many ways she reminded me of Sybile. Heck, that woman didn't even want me calling her *Grandma*—so I came up with the pet name of *Billie*. But Opal seemed happy at the prospect of having her granddaughter around full-time.

Saren was his usual sweet self. "Well, doesn't that just beat all. So now we'll have another female member in the family. I'm looking forward to meetin' her."

"So does this mean you've changed your mind on purchasing the yarn shop?" Aunt Dora questioned.

Adam spoke up. "No, Monica will still be the new owner. Well, unless she doesn't want that. We'll hire a babysitter for any evenings we want to go out. I know this isn't what we'd planned when we got married six months ago." He shot me a look of understanding. "But Monica has been wonderful about it. It's not going to be easy for any of us and will be quite an adjustment, but I think we'll manage."

"Of course you'll manage," Dora said. "And please, count on me for any babysitting chores. My grandchildren are all grown now and I adore being around young people."

"And you know I want to get to know my granddaughter even better," Opal told us. "She can come to the cottage and spend a few nights with me whenever she'd like."

I caught the smile on Grace's face as she winked at me and I knew she was thinking, *"See, I told you it would be fine."*

For some reason I felt teary. I should have known—I should have known that on this island, nobody goes it alone. No matter what the problem is, people pitch in to help. No, it wasn't going to be easy—but it *was* comforting to know I wasn't going to be alone.

$\iff$ 4 $\iff$

After Adam left for Georgia on Sunday, I began doing laundry and getting the house ready for Clarissa's arrival. I hadn't gotten to her room the day before, so I decided to tackle that first.

When I walked in, I let out a loud gasp. There on the bed, folded up neatly, was my blue sweater. I felt a shiver go through me as I stood rooted to the spot. After a moment, I walked to the bed and tentatively put out a hand to touch the blue wool. How the hell did the sweater end up in here? I hadn't been in this room in ages. And yet—there it was, all folded neatly on top of the spread.

As I picked it up, I suddenly became aware of a fragrance floating in the air. Gardenias—my deceased grandmother Sybile's favorite scent.

Oh, this is insane, I thought. *I'm just stressed out with Clarissa's arrival. Could I have absentmindedly put the sweater in here?* I sniffed the air, looking around the room. Two twin beds done up with white eyelet comforters and shams, a mahogany table between with a crystal lamp. Except for an antique comb and brush set, the bureau top was empty. No perfume bottles or potpourris of gardenia.

For a split second I recalled what Saren had said the day before about Sybile's spirit. I didn't believe in ghosts. There was no proof of such a thing.

Taking the sweater, I walked to the front hall to hang it up and saw Aunt Dora coming up the walkway.

"Hey," she said, through the screen. "I brought you some blue-berry muffins. Got time for a coffee break?"

"Sure," I told her, pushing open the door.

She followed me to the kitchen.

I measured coffee into the filter, my mind still on the appearance of the blue sweater.

"You're quiet today. Everything all right?"

"Yeah, I guess." I poured the water into the coffeemaker and joined her at the table. "The oddest thing just happened," I said and went on to tell her about the sweater and the gardenia scent in the room.

To my surprise, she didn't laugh or admonish me for being silly.

"Hmm, interesting."

"Interesting? That's all you have to say? I mean, I suppose I *could* have put the sweater in there—but I don't see why I would've done that."

Dora remained silent for a few minutes before speaking. "Well, you have to admit, my sister was a pretty strong personality. Who knows . . . maybe Saren isn't as silly as we think."

"So what are you saying? That you believe in ghosts?"

"All I'm saying is, the older you get—things aren't always as they seem. Sometimes we should let go of preconceived notions and just be more open to what's around us."

"Okay, so let's just say that Sybile's *spirit* is hovering around this house. What's the purpose? Why would she be here?"

"You were very close to her, Monica. You hit it off the first time you met and seemed to have a *connection*. Maybe she's here to give you a message or some comfort."

"A message? About what? And why would I need comfort from her?"

"I'm sure I don't know. Is that coffee ready?"

I got up to get the cups and turned around to face Dora. "Would you go with me into the bedroom? See if you can smell the gardenias?" That room was beginning to give me the creeps, and now I was wondering if perhaps I should put Clarissa into the other bedroom.

"Sure," my aunt said, leading the way.

We walked over the threshold and stood there for a few moments. I could no longer smell the scent. Everything seemed in order. Sunlight streamed through the windows creating cozy warmth, making me feel foolish for allowing myself to be frightened.

"I don't smell a thing," she said, looking over at me.

"I don't either. It's gone. Okay, let's just forget the whole thing."

Dora walked farther into the room. "I would imagine Clarissa will love this room. It's so pretty and feminine." She put a finger to her lips, and I knew she was thinking.

"What? Something wrong with the room?"

"No, not at all. It's beautiful, with the white eyelet comforters and matching curtains. It's just so—sterile."

"Sterile?"

"Yeah. Little girls like frills and lace, but it needs something more. Like maybe you could replace those pictures on the wall with something more little girlish."

I glanced at the framed photos of the water and pelicans I'd taken. She was right. Probably not very exciting for an eight-year-old.

"What do you suggest?"

"A theme. You know, like ballerinas or Dora the Explorer or even dogs and cats."

"Good idea. How can I do that?"

"The yarn shop's closed tomorrow. Why don't we go into Gainesville? Make a day of it. We'll get some pictures for the walls, a few throw rugs to match the theme, even linens that will appeal to a little girl. There's a lot you can do to make the room more personal. Get some stuffed animals, maybe hang a mobile in that corner. Oh, and a desk. Talk to Adam about getting her one. All little girls love to have their own desk—gives them their own space to do their homework and that kind of stuff."

I leaned over to kiss Dora's cheek. "You're a genius. Thanks. It's a date. I'll pick you up at nine and we'll hit the big city."

We walked back to the kitchen to have our coffee.

"How're you really doing with all of this, Monica?"

I shrugged my shoulders and let out a sigh. "I'm not really sure. It all got thrown at us so fast. There wasn't much time to prepare, let alone really think about it."

"You're doing the right thing, you know. Sounds like that poor child hasn't had a very stable childhood."

"When I met Adam and found out he had a daughter, I guess I never gave it much thought. She lived in another state and I knew we'd have her with us during the year for visits, but that's not the same as being a full-time stepmom. I'm still not sure how I feel about having my own children. Sometimes I think I'm more like Sybile than I realized."

"What do you mean?"

"She was very honest right from the beginning when she had my mother. Having children was not in her life plan. She never regretted giving her up for adoption. I know my mom had a hard time understanding that, but Sybile was honest about it. She lived her life on her terms, and getting married and raising a daughter wasn't part of those terms. I remember when she told my mother that not every female is cut out to be a mother—not all of us are born with those maternal genes."

"So what you're saying is you think you're lacking those genes like Sybile?"

"Could be. All I know is I have no experience with children. I was an only child. Hell, I never even babysat. It didn't interest me, and I preferred having a paper route to make extra money. I can't even recall having a special *doll* like other little girls. If I did, I don't remember."

Dora smiled. "Being a tomboy or enjoying things other than dolls doesn't mean you're not cut out to be a mother. Monica, I think you're worrying too much about all of this."

"I'm not even sure Clarissa Jo likes me. Adam and I weren't married last summer when she came to stay here for a month. I was living at the Lighthouse with my mother and only saw Clarissa Jo when Adam would invite me to go somewhere with them. I tried to talk to her, but she pretty much ignored me."

"Well, she's not going to be able to ignore you living here. She'll have to listen to you and mind you and behave. But she's been through a rough time too. Keep trying to remember that."

"That's another thing. I've never had to discipline a child. God, I've never even owned a dog that required discipline. And she'll probably end up resenting me if I have to correct her or punish her. I'll just leave that to Adam."

Dora reached across the table to take my hand. "Monica, listen to me. First of all, *nobody* gets a set of instructions, even when they birth their own babies. It's trial and error. You do the best you can and you learn from your mistakes. But you cannot put the entire burden on Adam. You'll be spending a lot of time alone with her. She has to know you and Adam are on the same page. You have to show a united front when it comes to discipline."

"Yeah, you're probably right. God, it's so incredible how one's life can change in a heartbeat."

"Don't I just know that," she said and I got the feeling she was probably recalling the day she found out that my mother and I were related to her. "Have you inquired about a bank loan yet?"

I shook my head. "Not yet, but our inventory is pretty high and I think we'll be all right for a while. I'm just concerned, though. I hope I don't lose too much income without the mail orders for the spinning."

"Well, then . . . you'll just have to get a little creative with other ways to increase your sales."

"Like what?"

"Oh, I don't know. . . . Have you considered doing knitting classes? I don't mean the weekly get-together. I mean actually offering various classes and advertising this fact, and of course, you'll charge for this. You could offer various ones—ones for adult knitters, maybe one to teach young girls to knit. Do you know if Clarissa Jo knits?"

That was only one of the many things I didn't know about Adam's daughter. "I don't have a clue."

"Well, it might be nice to have a class with girls in that age group. And even something for mothers and daughters. And you could keep them theme oriented. In other words, in August or September you could be doing a class to make a Christmas ornament or stocking and then in the spring, maybe a lightweight cotton scarf."

"You're full of great ideas," I told her.

Dora laughed. "Just don't worry about it. We'll certainly put our two heads together and come up with projects to keep the sales coming."

I prayed Dora knew what she was talking about.

5

On Tuesday I returned home from the yarn shop at 2:00, made myself a quick salad with tea, and launched into turning the sterile bedroom into a little girl's delight. Aunt Dora and I had shopped for hours and we came home loaded down with all kinds of items for a child. I had to admit, I was excited about transforming the bedroom into something more appealing for an eight-year-old.

Just as I was about to unload the bags and get to work, Grace called.

"Need some help, Mary Poppins?"

I laughed. "Sure, come on over. But be sure to bring me a double latte. I have my work cut out for me and need the energy."

"Be there within a half hour," she told me.

When she arrived, I had a few quick sips of coffee and we set to work. Pulling throw rugs, towels, sheets, stuffed toys, and assorted items from the bags, we got to laughing so hard that it struck me that this was what Christmas morning with siblings might have felt like.

"These are adorable," Grace said, holding up sets of sheets with Disney characters all over them.

"Yeah, I thought I'd go with the primary colors of the Disney theme. It'll brighten up the room a bit." Pulling out a pink stuffed angora kitten, I held it up. "Think she'll like this?"

Grace nodded. "Perfect to put on the bed."

"And I got a few stuffed dogs to go with it," I said, continuing to dig into more bags.

A couple of hours later, we stood back and surveyed our work. Sheets were on the beds, stuffed animals arranged, towels with ballerinas hung in the bathroom, throw rugs in place.

"Not bad," I said.

Reaching into the last bag, Grace pulled out wallpaper border. "Do we have to wallpaper now?"

I laughed. "No, we're finished. I got that because it was so cute with the Disney characters and I thought Adam could put it up this weekend."

"I think she'll like it," Grace told me. She patted me on the back. "You've done well."

"This was the easy part, and I know that. By the way, what the heck do kids *eat?*"

Grace smiled. "Everything and nothing. They're all different, but usually they love cereal, cookies, cakes, ice cream, candy. . . ."

"Ah, all nutritional food, huh?"

"Just think back to what you liked when you were eight."

"My mother didn't give me many choices. And when she did, it was called a treat."

"You might turn out to be a better mother than you think. Too many of the moms today let the kids call the shots. With meals, bedtime, everything."

"So you're saying I should restrict her food choices?"

Grace put up a hand and took a step back. "Hey, don't get me involved in this part of it. That's all between you and Adam."

"Ah, the joys I have to look forward to. Stay for supper with me? I have leftover roast chicken and I can do up some rice and a salad."

"Sounds good," Grace said, following me into the kitchen.

After Grace left, I was sitting in the great room relaxing with my knitting. I glanced at my watch and saw it was 8:00. Adam would be calling soon. When he'd called the night before he said everything had gone well at the hearing. The judge had revoked custody from Carrie Sue and given full custody to Adam. Carrie Sue was still in the hospital and had been informed by the social worker that Clarissa would be leaving Georgia to live in Florida. She was told that if she wanted visitation, she'd have to retain an attorney and another court date would be set. Since Adam had no contact with Carrie Sue, he wasn't sure what she planned to do.

The phone rang and I answered to hear his voice.

"Hey, sweetheart, how'd it go today?"

"Not bad. I spent the whole day with Clarissa Jo. The foster parents seemed nice, but I'll be glad to get her out of there tomorrow morning."

"How's she feel about coming here to live with us?"

"She didn't say much. She was pretty quiet most of the day. I took her out for lunch and then we did some shopping for a few new clothes and toys."

"How does she feel about leaving Carrie Sue?"

"Strangely enough, she barely mentioned her. I get the feeling that life with Carrie Sue wasn't a bed of roses. She seems to be more upset about leaving Trish behind. This is a college student who cared for her after school and, from the sound of it, many evenings when Carrie Sue was out carousing. Trish had plans the night of the accident, and that's why Clarissa was left alone. She begged me to let her see Trish before we leave in the morning, so I called her and I'm taking them both to breakfast before we hit the road."

"Good idea." Even though I wasn't sure I wanted the answer, I couldn't resist asking, "Has she mentioned me at all?"

"Not really. I brought you into the conversation a couple times, but I didn't want to push."

"Right. Well, I have her room all put together. Grace came by this afternoon and helped me. It looks great. I think she'll like it."

"That was really sweet of you, Monica. I know she'll like it. Did you go with the Disney characters?"

"Yeah, and some ballerinas in the bathroom and a few stuffed toys."

"I'll tell her all about it tomorrow. God, I'm wiped. It's been a long day."

I could hear the fatigue in his voice. "Did you have supper yet?"

"Yeah, after I dropped Clarissa, I grabbed a bite at a small restaurant. Home-style Southern cooking."

"You sound tired, and you have a long drive in the morning. Get some sleep. I love you, Adam. I can't wait to see you tomorrow."

"And how I love you, Monica. I've missed you."

I normally sleep till about 7:30, but I'd tossed and turned all night and finally got up at 6:00. After showering and dressing, I got my coffee and sat outside on the deck. Another gorgeous day on the island. We were having a beautiful April, and I sat there staring across the street to the water.

Well, I thought, this day was going to change my life dramatically. What surprised me was that my focus the past couple of days had been more on the fact that Clarissa wasn't going to like me, rather than my changed lifestyle. I just wasn't adept with children. I didn't even feel comfortable being in their company. What the heck was I going to talk to her about? I didn't have a clue what the latest movies, music, or toys were for her age group. *And how on earth does one go about learning those things?*

"Hey, Miss Monica, what are you doing out there so early?"

I looked out to the road, and there was Saren taking his morning walk.

"Come on up. I have fresh coffee."

I watched him walk through the yard to the steps for the deck. He was a marvel to me. At eighty-six, he walked every morning and was in excellent health. It's not uncommon for people on the island to live till their nineties and remain in good health till the end. I used to joke that there must be something in the water.

"You're not usually out here this early," he said, taking a seat across from me.

"Yeah, I know. Adam will be back later today with Clarissa. Guess I just couldn't sleep."

"Got lots on your mind, do ya?"

I got up to get his coffee and nodded. "Guess you could say that."

When I returned a moment later and placed the mug in front of him, he said, "Wanna talk about it?"

"I feel that's *all* I've been talking about since last week. And worrying more than talking."

"Well, the news you got was a lot to take in. Here you are a new bride and getting settled into married life, and boom—now you have a child coming to live with you. That wouldn't be easy for anyone."

"Did my grandmother like kids when she was younger? Did she do babysitting or anything?"

From the look on Saren's face, I could see I surprised him with my question.

"Well," he said, stroking his chin in thought. "I reckon she liked kids well enough. She always had Miss Dora tagging around with her. But that was her little sister, so not sure you'd call that babysitting."

When I remained silent, he said, "Oh, I see what you're gettin' at. Because Sybile gave your mother up for adoption—you're thinkin' you might be like her?"

"It crossed my mind. Yeah."

"I'm not sure that kinda stuff is passed on. If ya ask me, I think with time you're gonna do just fine."

I wished I had his confidence.

Later in the day, Dora paid me a visit. I opened the door to find her loaded down with assorted things.

"What's all this?" I asked. "Here, let me help you."

Dora placed a Tupperware container on the counter filled with her delicious chocolate chip cookies.

"I thought Clarissa might like these before bed tonight."

"Oh, Dora, that was really sweet of you," I said and realized I'd never made an attempt to bake cookies. Wasn't that what bakeries were for—but all moms baked cookies for their kids, didn't they?

She removed two gift-wrapped packages from the bags.

"And these are for Clarissa. I got her a cute pair of pajamas with Disney characters and also a Madeline doll. Every little girl should have one of those. Just wanted to welcome her proper."

I pulled Dora into an embrace. "Thank you so much for everything. I'm sure she'll love them. How about a cup of tea?"

"That would be nice," she said, settling herself at the table. "So when are they due to arrive?"

"Adam called at about two, and they were in Jacksonville, so I'd say around five."

I filled the kettle with water and put tea bags into two mugs.

"Are you excited?" she asked.

I joined her at the table. "I think I'm feeling excited *and* nervous. Dora, I just don't think I'm cut out to be a mother."

"Don't be silly. Of course it'll take time to adjust, but before you know it—well, goodness, it'll all seem so routine to you."

"I've planned roast chicken, mashed potatoes, green beans, and salad for supper. Do you think that's all right?"

"It sounds wonderful. Don't second-guess yourself. You'll be surprised to learn that motherhood is ninety percent instinct. Always listen to your gut feelings. I'm sure Adam is relieved he'll now have his daughter living with him."

I nodded. "Yeah, I think he worried about her way more than he let on to me. He knew Carrie Sue wasn't an adequate parent, but the courts today always seem to lean in favor of the mother. It doesn't matter what a loving and responsible parent the father is."

"Yes, I've heard that, and it's a shame. I imagine it'll be difficult for Clarissa, though, not to be with her mother anymore."

"Not according to Adam. Apparently Carrie Sue was a party girl most nights of the week. I guess she spent very little time with her daughter."

"Oh, that *is* a shame. Children need to know they're loved, and of course parents are the ones who should spend the most time with them. I never did agree with having children and then pawning them off on day care or other people to watch them. Now, of course, sometimes that can't be avoided—but whenever possible, I think it's the parent who should be spending the most time with a child in their formative years."

I thought about Adam saying we'd hire somebody to stay with Clarissa during the hours I was at work and he was teaching summer school classes.

"So what are you saying? I should quit the yarn shop and be here with her?"

I poured water into the mugs while I waited for Dora's answer, but none was forthcoming.

"Well?" I asked.

"Monica, dear, none of this is really my business."

"You're family," I told her. "I want your opinion."

"I just think all of this is going to be difficult enough on the girl, but no, I don't think you should be giving up your job. Have you thought about enrolling her in some of the summer activities we have for the children?"

I shook my head. "No, but I'm sure Adam will know what's available."

"The Arts Center has a wonderful program during the week, and the library always offers something for them as well. It's a few hours each day. That would give you time to be at the yarn shop, but when you finished, it would be you picking her up and taking her home. Not a stranger."

Maybe Dora was right. Plus, it would be a way for Clarissa to socialize more with the other children.

"This sounds good," I said. "I'll discuss it with Adam."

"Both parents and children need their space, but you might come to see you enjoy the time you spend alone with her."

It was certainly going to be a new experience for me, but thinking back to my childhood and the hours I'd spent with my own mother lessened my anxiety temporarily.

6

I heard tires crunch on the gravel and knew Adam was home. Should I run out and greet them? Wait for him to come in with her? I chose to walk out on the deck and watch them exit the car.

Adam got out first, walked around to the other side, and opened the passenger door. After a few moments, Clarissa stepped out. She looked taller since I'd last seen her. Sandy-colored long hair was pulled off her forehead, parted, with one braid hanging down the side. She wore colorful red slacks, a white top, and sandals. Clutched in her arm was a Raggedy Ann doll.

Adam looked up, caught my eye, and waved, which caused Clarissa to also glance up at the deck. She put her head down and followed Adam to the steps.

"Hey, sweetheart," he said, coming to pull me into an embrace. "I missed you."

"I missed you too," I mumbled, feeling awkward with a display of affection in front of Clarissa. Pushing away, I looked at her and said, "Clarissa, it's nice to see you again."

For a moment I thought she was going to completely ignore me, but then I heard her say softly, "Thank you."

"How was your drive?" I asked, looking at Adam.

"Very good. Not that much traffic. Clarissa, want to help me unload the car?"

"Oh, I'll help too," I said, not sure if I was intruding.

I followed Clarissa and Adam down the steps to the car. When he opened the trunk, I was surprised to see only one medium-sized piece of luggage, a tote bag, and one large box. For some reason, I thought she'd arrive loaded down with stuff. I had a vision of my own bedroom at her age. Between all my toys, books, games, clothes, and assorted treasures, I would have needed a moving van just for my own personal belongings.

"Right," Adam said, passing the tote bag to Clarissa. "You take this and I think we can manage the rest."

Without saying a word, she reached out for the bag and headed back toward the stairs.

"How'd it *really* go?" I asked when she was out of earshot.

"She's just so damn quiet. So don't take it personally, Monica. She hardly spoke at all the entire drive."

I nodded as I reached for the piece of luggage.

We walked into the kitchen to find her standing in the middle of the kitchen floor, looking like a lost child. Heck, she *was* a lost child.

Plastering a smile on my face, I said, "Hey, would you like to see your room? I hope you'll like it. My friend, Grace, came over yesterday and we had so much fun getting it ready for you. We have Disney characters and . . ." I realized I was babbling. "Come on. It's over this way," I said, heading toward the hallway.

Adam and Clarissa followed me into the room.

Gesturing with my hands, I said, "Here it is. Welcome to your new room."

"It looks terrific," Adam told me, looking around to take in the new items I'd added. "You did a lot of work in here."

We both looked at Clarissa, who only stood there gazing from the beds to the bureau.

"And here's your own bathroom," I told her, walking toward it.

She peeked in the doorway and nodded. "It's nice," was all she said.

I had hoped for a more enthused reaction, but considering this child had just lost all that was familiar to her, maybe I was expecting too much.

"I'll get your luggage and stuff in the kitchen," Adam said, leaving me alone with her.

I caught Clarissa's eyes move to the gifts on her bureau.

"Oh," I said. "My aunt Dora dropped those off for you today. It's a welcome present."

Clarissa gave no reaction.

"Would you like to open them now?"

"I guess," she said, with emotion absent from her tone.

"Ah, what's this? Presents already?" Adam put down her luggage and box.

Clarissa walked to the bureau and reached for one of the boxes. Ever so slowly, she began to unwrap the paper. Peeking inside, she pulled out the pajamas.

"That's from Dora?" Adam questioned. "That was really nice of her. Wasn't it, Clarissa Jo?"

She nodded, reached for the other package, and carefully removed the paper. She didn't appear to be any more enthused with the doll than she was with the pajamas.

"I have Annie," she stated.

"Annie?" I asked.

She pointed to the Raggedy Ann doll she'd placed on the bed.

"Oh," I said, not knowing what else to say. Didn't a kid have more than one doll?

"Trish gave the doll to Clarissa this morning as a going-away present," Adam explained.

I began to understand. She wanted to be loyal to Trish—so another doll wasn't wanted. Or needed.

"But maybe you could place Madeline on your other bed," he told her. "There's storybooks about Madeline, too, and we'll get you those. She's from Paris, you know."

How the heck did Adam know all of this? I began to feel like I'd been living on another planet all my life. I'd never heard of a Madeline doll.

"Okay," she said, with the same lack of enthusiasm.

"Well, I'm going to get the table set. Supper will be ready in about twenty minutes. Adam, maybe you'd like to take Clarissa for a walk across the street to the water?"

"Good idea," he said, throwing me a grateful glance.

I guess he knew me well enough to realize that I needed a bit of time to regroup. Alone.

It seemed odd sitting at the kitchen table with a young person in our presence. After a few moments, I noticed that Clarissa was simply sitting there. She hadn't picked up her fork to begin eating. I shot a glance to Adam across the table.

"Something wrong?" he asked her.

"I don't like chicken," she whined.

Great. Dora had assured me that chicken was a good choice. Strike one for me.

I jumped up from the table. Maybe Grace had been right after all. "Well, we do have some cereal, and Aunt Dora brought over cookies. We might have some ice cream. . . ."

"Monica," I heard Adam say, with an edge to his tone. "Sit down and eat." He focused his gaze on Clarissa. "I guess we're going to have to have some rules in this house. Listen, Clarissa Jo, I have no idea what or how you ate when you lived with your mother. But things will probably be different here. Monica is not a maid. She goes to a lot of trouble to make very good and nutritional meals every evening. And you will be expected to eat them. Understand?"

I now recalled hearing parents talk about how stubborn their children were and knew I was getting a preview of this very trait. Clarissa sat and said nothing.

"Did you *hear* me?" Adam asked in a raised voice.

"Yes," I heard her mutter.

"Do you like mashed potatoes, green beans, and salad?"

"They're okay."

"Then you're expected to eat that, and I want you to take at least three bites of the chicken. If you don't begin eating a little of the foods you don't care for, you'll be a fussy eater all your life."

With that, Adam picked up his fork and began eating.

Our suppertime was normally filled with conversation. Eager to share with each other our time apart, we always talked about things that had happened in the yarn shop or at school. But tonight, for the first time since we'd married, our dinner table was silent—and uncomfortable.

When we finished eating, Adam made Clarissa help me clear the table and fill the dishwasher. She didn't whine, but she didn't look happy about it.

After we finished, he said, "How about all of us take a walk downtown?"

"Sounds good," I said, punching the button to turn the dishwasher on.

Again, no response from Clarissa.

She walked between us down First Street and along Dock Street. I thought I caught a glimmer of interest in her eyes when she spied the Big Dock.

"The rebuilding of the dock was completed since you were here. Everybody goes fishing from there," Adam told her. "You and I can go fishing this weekend. Think you'd like that?"

By now I'd come to expect her one- or two-word answers.

"Yeah," she told him.

We walked along Second Street and headed back to the house—Clarissa silent the entire way.

When we got home, I backed off and let Adam deal with her bedtime. I heard him tell her since she wouldn't be starting school till the following week she could stay up until 9:00. But on school nights, bedtime was 8:00.

She walked into her bedroom, closed the door, and a few minutes later I could hear her shower running.

I plopped down on the sofa beside him. "It's been quite a day, hasn't it?"

He ran a hand through his hair and nodded. "It's not going to be easy. I know that. She's a sweet girl, Monica. She really is. I have a feeling she had full run of the house with Carrie Sue, so it's going to take a while to teach her things will be different here."

"What am I going to do about meals? I have no clue what she might like. Should I ask her?"

He thought about this for a minute. "No, not right now. Cook what you normally would. If she's at least trying the things she says she doesn't care for, then we'll see what kind of foods she does like."

Made sense to me.

After her shower, Clarissa came out to join us in the great room to watch TV—still clutching the Raggedy Ann doll. When Adam told her it was 9:00, she got up without a word and started to head to her bedroom.

"Hold on," I heard Adam say.

She turned around, a blank look on her face.

"Say good night to Monica and I'll tuck you in. Every night one of us will be tucking you into bed."

The look on her face struck me as one of surprise and a moment later, she said, "Good night, Monica."

"Good night," I told her. "Sleep well."

When Adam returned, he said, "I'd bet anything that Carrie Sue never once put that child to bed when she was home. Probably just let her go on her own."

"I think you're right. Is she okay?"

He nodded. "Yeah. Gosh, I'm beat. I'm glad I have the rest of the week off. What do you say we turn in and watch TV in bed for a while?"

After changing into my nightgown, I snuggled up beside him. He began gently stroking my inner thigh and within a few minutes, I knew he wanted to make love. I slid down onto the pillow as his lips met mine. The intensity of his kisses increased and all of a sudden I pulled away.

"What's wrong?" he asked.

"God, Adam, she's in the house. What if she hears us?" I whispered.

"Are you saying we're never going to make love again until she's grown and moves out?"

"Well, no . . . that's not what I'm saying. But, gee . . . this is her first night here and what if she comes walking in our room? What if . . ."

Adam rolled over onto his back and grasped my hand. "Unless it was an emergency, I seriously doubt that she'd just barge in here with the door closed. But I can tell you're not in the mood. It's fine," he said, leaning over to kiss me. "I love you. Ready to shut off the light?"

"Yeah."

Adam snapped off the lamp and said, "It's okay. Really. But don't think I'll let you get away with this next time."

I heard the humor in his voice. "Yes, darling," I replied in an exaggerated tone. "Guess a woman must perform her wifely duties."

His hand reached for mine and gave it a tight squeeze.

I awoke at two in the morning to a strange sound. Sitting up in bed, I listened but wasn't sure what it was. Adam was snoring lightly beside me.

Slipping into my bathrobe, I tiptoed through the house and stood in the great room. What was that noise? I realized it seemed to be coming from Clarissa's room.

Tiptoeing down the hallway, I stood in front of her door listening.

It was sobbing. That's what it was. She was crying.

Oh God, what should I do? Wake Adam? Go in and see what's wrong?

I stood there a few more minutes and the sound began to diminish. Deciding to leave her alone, I headed back to my bedroom. Climbing into bed, I lay on my side snuggling into Adam's warm body and prayed everything would get easier.

7

Adam was still sleeping soundly at seven-thirty when I opened my eyes. He'd had a grueling week and I wanted him to sleep in. Tiptoeing quietly out of the bedroom, I was surprised to find Clarissa Jo sitting on the sofa in the great room—that Raggedy Ann doll still clutched in her arms.

I'm slow to wake up in the morning. One of those people who doesn't utter a word until I've had my first cup of coffee. But I forced a smile to my face and made the supreme effort to be friendly.

"You're up early. Did you sleep well?"

Clarissa glanced up briefly and then continued kneading the doll's hair between her fingers.

"I guess."

That seemed to be her pat answer for everything. What was it with kids today? Was that all they could do was *guess?* Didn't they have strong feelings about anything?

"Your dad's still sleeping," I told her as I walked into the kitchen to prepare the coffee. "What would you like for breakfast?"

I prayed she wouldn't request some kid food that I wasn't familiar with.

"Cereal," was the response I got.

Cereal I could deal with. I began pulling boxes out of the cabinet as Clarissa wandered into the kitchen.

"We have plenty of that," I told her, lining up boxes of Kashi, Special K, granola, and raisin bran.

When she stood staring at the boxes, I knew I was in trouble again.

"Something wrong?"

"I like Froot Loops or Cap'n Crunch."

Ah, that stuff loaded with sugar that made dentists rich. I blew out a puff of air. Shit, I hadn't even had my first *sip* of coffee yet and glared at the coffeemaker, urging it to drip faster.

"Hmm, well . . . we don't have that cereal in the house. How about some eggs? Or French toast?"

Clarissa shook her head. "I like pancakes."

I could do pancakes. "Okay," I told her and saw the carafe had filled with that welcoming brown liquid. Grabbing a mug, I gratefully poured myself some coffee. After taking a sip, I said, "Pancakes it is. Give me a few minutes to get it ready."

Clarissa climbed onto the stool at the counter. With chin in her hands she proceeded to watch my movements. I wasn't used to an audience while I prepared food. As I whipped up the batter and heated the griddle, I felt like I should be conversing with her, but I had no clue what to talk about. Being with this mute eight-year-old wasn't only awkward, it was unpleasant.

After I placed the pancakes in front of her, I picked up my mug of coffee only to find it had grown cold. I added more to the mug to heat it and told Clarissa I was going outside to get the newspaper.

Stooping down to pick up the *Gainesville Sun,* I noticed Tilly Carpenter in her yard pruning her rosebushes.

"Good morning, Miss Tilly," I called over.

"Mornin'," she said and resumed her cutting.

She'd been Adam's neighbor since he'd moved in, but seldom spoke more than a few words to us. This was unusual for a Cedar Key resident. Normally, bumping into somebody was cause for a thirty-minute conversation about anything and everything. People were just naturally friendly on the island. But Adam had told me that Miss Tilly had had a tragedy involving her husband and young son about forty years ago, and since she'd retired as art teacher at the school a few years before, she'd been sinking into a deep depression that had locals concerned.

I walked into the kitchen to find Adam pouring himself a cup of coffee while Clarissa finished up her pancakes.

"Good morning, beautiful," he said, placing a kiss on my cheek.

I smiled as I joined him at the counter. "Did you sleep well?"

"Yeah, I think I was tired from the trip."

Not to mention the subtle stress that seemed to be in the air since Clarissa's arrival, I thought.

"You like pancakes, huh?" he asked Clarissa.

"Yeah, they're okay."

"You know, I was thinking," Adam said, after taking a sip of coffee, "we should have a party."

"A party?" both Clarissa and I said at the same time.

Adam laughed. "Well, maybe not exactly a party, but a gathering with family."

Good idea, I thought. "Sure. What have you got in mind?"

"We'll have a barbecue tomorrow evening. Invite my mother, Aunt Dora, and Saren. And Grace, of course. Grace is Monica's best friend," he explained to Clarissa.

"Oh," was her response.

Sounded good to me, and maybe Clarissa would be more talkative with a few people around. "I'll call them later and let them know. What are your plans for today?"

He looked at Clarissa. "Anything special you'd like to do?"

She paused for a moment and then said, "Could we take a boat ride out to Atsena Otie?"

"Sure, we can do that. They have trips out there from the City Marina, and we've never done that during your summer visits. Wanna come with us, Monica?"

An odd sensation had come over me. "I think I'll stay here," I told him. "I need to call everyone about coming tomorrow night. You two go. Clarissa will enjoy that."

Adam finished off his coffee. "Okay, I'm hitting the shower. You get ready, Clarissa, and we'll take off."

When he left the room, I looked across the counter at her. "Why'd you choose the boat ride to Atsena Otie?" I questioned.

Her eyes shot up to meet mine. She seemed hesitant to say anything and then replied, "The lady told me," before leaving the kitchen.

"So how's she settling in?" Dora questioned when I called her.

"It's really hard to tell. She barely talks at all. She's a very fussy eater. Chicken didn't work last night. I heard her crying in her room about two this morning. I don't know, Dora—I don't know if she'll be happy here with us."

"She's just a child. You have to give her a chance. This is quite an upheaval for her, and although Carrie Sue isn't the best of mothers, she is her mother. She's probably missing her. Has she mentioned her at all?"

I'd heard that before—that no matter the environment or circumstances, a child was usually loyal to the parent they lived with. "No, not a word. She isn't showing any signs of missing Carrie Sue."

"They usually don't. They hold it all inside. Has Adam considered counseling for her?"

"Not yet, but it might not be a bad idea eventually." I went on to tell Dora about our planned gathering for the following evening.

"I'm looking forward to meeting her. I'll be there."

My next call was to Opal and then Saren. Both also accepted the invitation. I glanced at the clock and saw it was after ten.

Before heading into the shower, I walked into Clarissa's bedroom to make sure she'd made her bed. I momentarily thought perhaps a hurricane had hit that part of the house and left the rest unscathed.

Piles of clothes lay in heaps on the floor. The wet towel from her shower the night before was now balled up on the carpet in the bedroom. Crumbs from an empty potato chip bag were scattered across the bureau. How the hell could a kid demolish a room in less than twenty-four hours? Walking into the bathroom, I saw toothpaste splattered across the mirror, and the tap in the sink had been left dribbling.

"Whoa!" I said to the empty room. "This is *not* acceptable!"

I slammed the door shut behind me and headed to my neat and orderly bedroom.

I saw a grin crossing Grace's face after I'd shared the events of the morning with her. "You think it's funny that she left her room like a pigsty?"

"Monica, she's testing you. I bet you did the very same thing in various ways at that age. And because of what's happened in her life, she's going to test you even more."

I passed Grace a mug of coffee and settled down on the sofa. Glancing around the yarn shop, I shook my head and let out a deep sigh. "Yeah, well, I'm not putting up with this. There's no reason for her to leave her room looking like that."

"She's getting back at you."

"For what?" I could feel anger bubbling up inside me. "What the hell did *I* do to her?"

"She's angry and resentful. What life she knew has been taken from her and she has no control over anything. From what you've told me, it seems that child was pretty much her own boss. And now she has to take orders from you and Adam. It's not going to be easy, Monica."

"No shit."

Grace reached over to touch my hand. "It'll take time, but you'll get through this."

I wished I could feel as confident as she sounded.

"I want this to work," I said. "As much for Adam's sake as Clarissa's." I couldn't bring myself to explain that my own feelings concerning Clarissa seemed to be emotionally uninvolved—and even worse, I had no explanation as to why or if this was even natural.

8

"Any ideas yet on new services you'll be offering?" Grace inquired the next day when she dropped by Spinning Forward.

"Dora suggested I offer knitting classes—the yarn would be purchased here and then I'd charge for the classes."

Grace nodded. "That's a good idea. Lots of women would love to learn to knit or take a class to learn new skills." She paused to take a sip of her coffee. "Hey, have you thought about offering a *knitting service?*"

I laughed. "You seem to forget, that's exactly what I do here. I sell yarn, patterns, and supplies."

"No, no. That isn't what I mean. I mean actually *knitting* for other people. I read something on the Internet recently—that women today are often too busy to devote time to handmade gift items. Yet they find themselves wanting to give something more personal than running into a department store or Walmart and grabbing a quick gift. The article talked about one woman up in Vermont—she had started a small business catering to baby boomers who wanted homemade jams and jellies for Christmas gifts. The business ended up growing so much she had to hire a couple other women to assist her."

"Hmm," I said, recalling that I'd heard about various women doing something like this. "Yeah, I remember seeing a woman on *Oprah* or someplace that developed her own line of personalized bath products for gifts. Not only did she make everything herself, she'd create a fancy label with the name of the product being whatever the customer wanted. She said girlfriends loved giving and receiving these because to see your own name on the label of a shower gel or lotion made it very special."

"Exactly." Grace snapped her fingers in the air and leaned forward. "I've got it," she said with enthusiasm. "Hand-knitted Christmas stockings. It would appeal to both moms and grandmothers. You could personalize them with the child's name, date of birth, that particular year—whatever they requested. Something like that turns into a family heirloom and a treasured memento."

I recalled some of the things passed on to me by my mother—hand-knitted Christmas ornaments that I could never part with. "You might be on to something. But how would I begin?"

"The same way your mother did. Develop a Web site, come up with a name for your stockings—something unique and appealing. Do lots of Internet advertising—Facebook is great for that. Send out flyers with some photos of finished ones. And like anything else, it's word of mouth. Other moms and grandmothers will see them and want one for their kids."

My mind was racing with thoughts, and I felt Grace's idea had a lot of potential.

"You're very talented with designing patterns, Monica. You could use the ones you designed last year on the scarves you made—just incorporate the pelicans and dolphins onto stockings. They even had red bows around their necks, remember? Design the child's name across the top and I think you have yourself a very popular and unique gift item."

I visualized my brightly colored knitted stockings hanging on display around the shop catching the attention of tourists. Maybe this was exactly what I needed to replace the spinning of dog and cat fur. Something that was all mine—a creative marketing idea that would keep the business successful. Extra income to offset the slow periods.

All of a sudden the enormity of the project hit me. "What if it really took off and I was swamped with orders? I can only knit so fast."

A look of disappointment crossed Grace's face. "I think you have a point. How many stockings could you realistically make in a week?"

I shrugged while pondering the question. "I suppose that depends on how large I make them. The longer they are, the more . . ." I turned around as the wind chimes tinkled and Dora walked into the shop.

"Hope I'm not interrupting. I finished the sweater for Marin and need to get more yarn for my next project."

"You knit faster than anybody I know," I told her, and as soon as I said it a thought occurred to me. "Grace and I have been sitting here brainstorming for an idea to replace my mother's spinning service. I'm definitely going to offer the classes like you suggested, but I need something else."

I went on to explain about the possibility of personalized knitted stockings.

"Oh, I think that's a grand idea! Knitting has come full circle and made a tremendous comeback. There was a time you never saw a woman without her yarn and needles, but unfortunately over the years only us diehards kept knitting. But it's enjoying a resurgence, and even women who don't have the time to knit themselves love the new fibers and items that can be handmade. Why, look at all the patterns available for scarves and shawls, and those felted handbags are very popular. I think offering a service of knitting personalized

Christmas stockings could be every bit as successful as your mother's spinning was."

"Aunt Dora," I said, jumping up to pull her into a bear hug, "I do believe you and I need to have a talk."

I got Dora a cup of coffee and settled her on the sofa beside me before explaining my idea.

"How would you feel about entering a new business venture with me?"

"Me?" Surprise and pleasure crossed her face.

I nodded. "Now, you have to promise to be honest with me. If you don't want to do this for whatever reason, I'll certainly understand. But I'm thinking these stockings are something we could do together. If I get this up and running and it actually takes off, I'm going to need help knitting the orders that come in." I paused to allow her a few moments to consider what I'd told her.

"I wouldn't be able to pay you a lot at first," I explained. "But depending on what we charged for the stockings, I'd give you a percentage of the price as your profit for the labor. And hopefully the orders would increase and I'd be able to increase your commission."

Dora shook her head and smiled, making me realize that my offer to her was pretty skimpy.

She reached for my hand and gave it a squeeze. "Monica, I'm going to tell you the same thing I told your mother when she offered me the position as assistant here. I don't need the money. I work here because I truly enjoy *being* here, surrounded by the yarn and the customers. I love to knit and my secret dream was always to own a yarn shop. Your mother provided the best of both worlds—I get to be here a few days a week and now I share the hours with you. But I'm not wearing myself out with a full-time business. Being in my early seventies—this is perfect. So yes, of course I'd love to help you launch this new venture! You're right, I do knit rapidly, so I'm always looking for new projects as soon as I finish the previous one.

And as far as paying me for my labor, for somebody that loves knitting, it would be a labor of love. I know you won't allow me to do this for nothing, but after we determine the price you'll be charging, then we'll discuss that. Agreed?"

I felt moisture burning my eyes. They say you can choose your friends but not your relatives. However, my mother and I did have the opportunity to choose and not only accept, but be accepted by her biological family, and I was very grateful for that.

Leaning over, I pulled Dora into an embrace. "Agreed," I said. "You're one in a million."

Grace had been sitting quietly across from us and now jumped up to also hug Dora. "Monica's right. You sure do remind me of my aunt Maude, and that's a compliment."

"I've got it," I exclaimed with excitement as another thought hit me. "Ewedora Stockings! That's what we'll call them. The pronunciation of your name will be the same but we'll use e-w-e, which will indicate the yarn fiber."

"Oh, my God! You're brilliant!" Grace said, pulling me and Dora from the sofa for a tight embrace.

"No, *we're* brilliant," I told them and laughed as my hand connected with hers and Dora's for a high five.

9

I was slicing potatoes for the potato salad when laughter from outside drew my attention. I'd been busy all morning with food preparations for our barbecue and had welcomed Clarissa's request to sit on the deck. The child had been moping around, yet she'd declined Adam's offer to take a ride to the Jiffy store to purchase gas for the grill.

Wiping my hands on a towel, I walked to the window to see Clarissa in the next yard talking to Miss Tilly. Cripe, I wished she'd stop bothering that poor woman.

"Clarissa," I called from the deck. "Miss Tilly is probably busy. Come on back over here."

Tilly Carpenter cupped a hand to her forehead and squinted up at me. "I'm not busy, and besides, we're having a nice chat about art."

Art? Clarissa was interested in art? "Oh . . . well, don't wander off," I told her. "And, Miss Tilly, you send her on back when she gets to be too much."

Walking back into the kitchen, I peeked out the window. Miss Tilly had thrown her head back laughing in response to something

Clarissa had said. What on earth could the child have said that brought about that reaction? She sure didn't strike me as a child possessing one ounce of humor. I stood and watched for a little while longer.

Miss Tilly was wearing what I referred to as her gardening uniform: loose-cut tan slacks, a matching blouse, and her signature floppy hat with the wide brim. Her snow white hair was pulled away from her face into a bun at the nape of her neck. Purple gardening gloves completed her outfit.

But it wasn't her style of dress that forced me to keep staring out the window—it was the genuine smile on the woman's face and her obvious interest in Clarissa Jo.

I was pulled away from the window by the sound of Grace's voice at the back door.

"Hey," she said, depositing some covered Pyrex bowls on the counter. "Here's my contribution for dinner tonight."

I walked over to see a container of macaroni and cheese and a sweet potato casserole.

"Thanks, Gracie," I said and resumed slicing potatoes. "Want some sweet tea? It's in the fridge. Help yourself."

"I see Clarissa met your neighbor."

I watched her pour herself a glass of the tea I'd made the day before and nodded.

"Any more word from this new beau of yours?" I asked.

"Yeah, he called again and we're having dinner together Tuesday evening."

"Does this George Clooney look-alike have a name?"

Gracie laughed. "Tony. Tony Rizotti."

"Hmm, an Italian lover."

"He's not my lover. Just a dinner date. But he's taken an apartment on the island, just down the street from your shop."

After I rinsed the potatoes, I turned them on to boil. "Oh, the vacant one above Noah's gallery?"

"Yeah, and I guess I'll find out how Italian he is—because he's cooking me dinner."

"Sounds like fun."

"What sounds like fun?" I heard Adam ask as he walked into the kitchen with a propane tank.

"Grace's new friend is cooking her dinner next week," I told him, leaning in for his kiss.

"Ah, I detect some romance floating in the air," he kidded her as he walked out to the deck.

Grace glanced at her watch. "Well, I'm outta here. Have to get over to the coffee shop. I'll see you about five."

"I saw Clarissa next door talking to Miss Tilly," Adam said, coming back inside. "They're sitting on the porch having a cold drink."

"Really?"

He laughed. "You sound surprised."

"Well, I am, a bit. Tilly doesn't normally bother with anybody, much less a child. And Clarissa . . . well, she's barely said ten words to us since she arrived."

I felt Adam's arms go around me, pulling me into an embrace. "Maybe this little friendship will be good for both of them."

He buried his face in my neck and began nibbling on my ear.

"Hmm, wonder how long she'll be over there?" he whispered.

Feeling the stirrings of desire, I was now sorry I'd turned him away the other night.

Kissing his mouth, I pulled back. "Not long enough for what you're thinking. Oh, that reminds me . . . we just don't seem to have any private time to talk anymore, and I keep forgetting to tell you. For three nights since Clarissa arrived, I've woken during the night to hear her crying in her room."

"I don't think that's unusual. Have you mentioned it to her?"

"God, no. That would be like intruding."

"You're her stepmom now, Monica. You have a right to intrude in stuff like that. But maybe we won't mention it and see what happens. I knew it would take her a while to adjust, and I'm sure that's part of it."

"She hasn't mentioned Carrie Sue at all. Do you think that's normal?"

Adam shrugged. "Under the circumstances, probably. I think we just need to give her some time. Let her tell us what she's feeling, rather than drag it out of her."

My own feeling was that even if we tried, dragging anything out of Clarissa wasn't going to be an easy feat.

When Clarissa returned from Miss Tilly's, she didn't seem quite as subdued. Tilly had let her borrow a book about a little girl and her dog, and it occupied Clarissa for the entire afternoon.

I had just finished the final touches on the fruit salad when she wandered into the kitchen.

"That's a pretty bowl," she said.

I smiled. "Thank you. It belonged to my grandmother. I bet you're excited about seeing your grandmother again. It's been about two months, hasn't it?"

"Yeah. She came to get me during February vacation and took me to lunch and out shopping."

"And now you'll have a chance to do that much more often with her. I know Opal's happy you're here and she'll be spending more time with you."

"Why?"

I turned from the counter. "Why? Well . . . because you're her granddaughter and I'm sure she loves you. Just like your dad does."

I hoped she didn't pick up on the fact that I didn't put myself into that equation.

She remained silent and as if on cue, I heard Opal's voice coming up the stairs of the deck.

"I'm here," she hollered. "And where's that granddaughter of mine?"

Adam came into the kitchen to greet his mother. He put a hand on Clarissa's head. "Right here," he said.

Opal looked her usual stylish self, sporting a pair of black palazzo pants and a white silk blouse.

"Oh, my. I swear you've grown two inches since I last saw you," she exclaimed. Without hesitation, she pulled Clarissa into her arms.

I almost felt bad for the child, standing there like somebody in a straitjacket, enduring all the fuss that Opal was making. I didn't miss the fact that Clarissa showed no return of affection. When Opal held her back to get a better look, I could see Clarissa appeared uncomfortable under her grandmother's scrutiny.

"You're such a beautiful child," Opal gushed. Fingering the long hair, she said, "Gorgeous. You have just gorgeous hair."

Clarissa had pulled her hair high on top of her head and secured it with a purple scrunchie.

"Oh, Adam," Opal went on. "Doncha think she looks just like you? And I might say, I think I see a tad of myself in her."

Leave it to Opal to make this about her.

The entire time Clarissa simply stood staring, not uttering a word.

Adam cleared his throat. "Well, Clarissa, say hello to your grandmother."

I saw him shoot a look to his mother that clearly said, "Tone it down a bit."

"Hello," Clarissa said, softly.

Opal pulled the child back into her arms. "I'm so glad you're with us, sweetie. It'll be so nice getting to spend all the time we want together. We're going to have such fun. You won't be missing that mama of yours at all."

"Mom." Adam's raised voice filled the kitchen.

The woman actually looked confused, not having a clue as to what she might have said wrong.

Adam walked over to put an arm around Clarissa. "Hey, honey. Wanna do me a favor and take these plastic dishes out to the deck?"

Without a word, Clarissa picked up the brightly colored plates and left the kitchen.

"What the hell are you thinking?" Adam hissed at his mother. "I will not put up with you tearing Carrie Sue apart."

Surprise covered the woman's face. "Well, I was . . . only letting her know that I'm happy she's with us now. I didn't mean to say the wrong thing."

I was positive the glistening I saw in Opal's eyes was the beginning of tears.

Adam ran a hand through his hair and let out a deep sigh. "Listen, Mom, we have to get some things straight. I know you're excited about finally getting to spend more time with your granddaughter. But I don't want you talking against Carrie Sue to Clarissa. Understand?"

Opal sniffed and reached for a napkin on the counter to dab her eyes. "Oh, Adam, she was such a *poor* excuse for a mother. You know that as well as I do."

"That may well be. But I don't want you discussing that with Clarissa. *Understand?* No matter what kind of mother she was—she *is* her mother."

Regaining her composure, Opal nodded. "Yes, okay. I understand."

Raising her fingers, she moved them quickly across her pursed lips.

"Opal, how about some sweet tea?" I asked, trying to break the tension.

"That would be lovely," she murmured.

The rest of the evening passed in a calm manner. Everyone in the family welcomed Clarissa Jo. Aunt Dora talked to her about books and games her own grandchildren had liked when they were little, but it was Saren who seemed to make the biggest impression on her.

"Yup," I heard him say. "I think you're gonna like livin' on this here island. Ever done any crabbin'?" he asked her.

Clarissa's gaze was glued to Saren's face. She shook her head with interest.

"Well, then, we'll just have to do that, won't we? I'll teach you how."

I actually saw a smile cross the child's face. This was the most animation I'd seen from her since she'd arrived.

I got up to head to the kitchen and bring out the desserts.

"She's delightful," Dora said, following me inside. "She reminds me a bit of my Marin when she was that age."

"Oh," was all I said. "Would you mind taking this out for me? I'm going to run to the bathroom."

Just as I walked back into the kitchen I heard a crash on the deck.

Running to the door, I saw Clarissa Jo standing there, with Sybile's beautiful glass bowl smashed to pieces at her feet. My carefully prepared fruit salad lay splattered, creating a still life of watermelon, pears, oranges, apples, bananas, and grapes.

"What the hell!" I screamed. Rushing forward, I yanked Clarissa back, away from the broken glass and fruit.

"It was an accident," Adam said, jumping up from his chair.

"An accident? What the hell was she doing carrying that out here anyway? That was my favorite bowl from Sybile." I bent down to start picking up glass and felt Adam's hand grip my wrist.

"Don't," he said. "You'll cut yourself."

Somebody had produced a roll of paper towels, along with a broom and dustpan.

I stood up and blew out a stream of exasperated air while I let Adam do the cleanup. It was then that I noticed Clarissa Jo had run into the house and our guests sat staring at me.

"Well, for Christ sake," I said, frustration lacing my words. "She shouldn't have been carrying that bowl out here."

Grace was the first to speak.

"She didn't drop it on purpose, Monica."

Oh, sure—stick up for the kid, I thought.

"Whatever," I snapped and returned inside to prepare coffee.

A few minutes later, I felt Adam's arms encircling me from behind.

"Grace was right," he said softly. "She didn't mean to do that."

A nasty thought crossed my mind. *Are you so sure of that?* I wondered. Clarissa knew that bowl meant a lot to me.

"Okay. Let's forget it," was what I mumbled.

I managed to get through the rest of the evening. Adam had gone in to talk to Clarissa and a little while later she emerged from her bedroom.

"I'm sorry," she said, without much conviction.

"It's okay," I told her, with the same lack of emotion.

❧ 10 ❧

By the time the following Saturday rolled around, I was more than happy for a break in the routine of the previous week.

Clarissa began school on Monday. I managed to be up with one cup of coffee ingested by the time Clarissa got up at seven. We then played the breakfast game. Did she want cereal, eggs, pancakes? And each morning, I got the same answer of "I don't care."

I swear it crossed my mind to prepare eggs Benedict, something I was certain she'd turn her nose up at. There was something about this child that could push my nastiness button and I didn't understand it.

I was grateful that Adam took her to school with him when he left and that chore hadn't become part of my job description. Wednesdays were half-days for the students, though, so I was expected to pick her up while Adam spent the afternoon in meetings.

I had switched my hours from ten till two at the yarn shop. Dora and I worked it out that I'd take Wednesdays off work and cover the shop for a few hours on Saturdays.

I was due at the shop at ten and had been grateful for the extra hour of sleep I'd gotten. Just stepping from the shower, I heard the phone ringing.

Adam was outside mowing the lawn, so I raced to grab it at the bedside. I heard the unmistakable voice of Carrie Sue talking to Clarissa.

"And so?" I heard her say. "Do you really want to stay there? Don't ya know that Mama's been missin' you terribly?"

Silence from Clarissa's end of the phone.

"Clarissa Jo, this is your mama. You're supposed to be with me. What's that father of yours gone and done? Turned you against me, I bet he has!"

My God, the woman was intimidating her own daughter. I flung my bathrobe on and ran out to the great room, where I found Clarissa holding the phone to her ear, still not saying a word. Her face shot up when she saw me.

"Give me the phone," I told her. Was that a look of relief on her face as she willingly passed it to me?

"Carrie Sue, this is Monica. You have no right to be speaking to Clarissa like that. If you want to discuss this situation, hold on and I'll get Adam."

"Don't bother!" she yelled into the phone before the loud click assaulted my ear.

I let out a deep breath. "Are you all right?" I asked Clarissa.

"Yeah."

I began to think better of what I'd just done. "Maybe you wanted to talk to her? Maybe I should have let you stay on the phone?"

Clarissa shrugged. "Not really."

Great. Just great. It looked like now we were going to start being bothered by Carrie Sue. We had enough on our plate. I didn't need her antagonizing us.

Clarissa had turned around and headed to her room. I put the phone down, walked out on the deck, and motioned to Adam to come inside.

He came in the kitchen mopping the sweat from his forehead. "What's up?"

"Carrie Sue just called and was talking to Clarissa."

I went on to explain the short conversation to him.

"Damn," he said, taking the pitcher of sweet tea from the fridge. "We didn't need this."

"You've got that right. Maybe I shouldn't have interfered. . . ."

"No, you did the right thing. Carrie Sue shouldn't have called. She knows full well that if she wants any contact with Clarissa, she has to get an attorney and we'll go back to court."

"Do you really think she wants her back?" I was beginning to get a feel for what life with Carrie Sue was like, and even with the upsets, I knew the child was where she belonged—with us.

"I seriously doubt it. It's just a ploy on Carrie Sue's part. I'll talk to Clarissa about it—try and find out how she really feels. And then we'll just wait and see what happens."

I was updating order accounts when I heard the wind chimes on the door. Turning around, I saw Polly walk in. Miss Polly owned the Curl Up and Dye, the hair salon on the island.

"Hey, Miss Monica. I dropped by to pick up that alpaca yarn you ordered for me. Is it in yet?"

"Yup, it came in the other day," I said, walking to the shelf where we kept special orders.

"So how's it going with Adam's daughter?" she asked as I rang up the sale.

"I'm not sure. It's a tough situation, and I have a lot to learn about motherhood."

Polly smiled. "Honey, my kids have been grown and gone for years, and I'm still learnin'."

"That's encouraging," I told her, passing the bag of yarn across the counter. "I feel like I've been out of the loop with island stuff. Anything exciting been going on?"

Polly placed an index finger to her lips while thinking. "Well, I probably shouldn't say anything, but . . . did you hear a big developer might be coming to the island?"

I immediately thought of Grace and her new friend. "No. What's this all about?"

"I'm not really sure, but gossip has it somebody has delusions of grandeur. Wanting to turn our little town into a high-priced resort. Fancy-schmancy shops—that sort of thing. We're a small fishing village, for goodness sake. If you ask me, it's all about greed. Plain and simple."

I had to agree with Polly. Cedar Key had its share of restaurants and small shops, but it could never be considered upscale. And that's how the residents liked it. Galleries filled with work by local artists. The Keyhole downstairs from the Arts Center, offering unique pieces of mosaic, ceramic and wood sculptures—much of it with the flavor of the island.

"Yeah, I see what you're saying," I told her. "Any talk about what in particular they have in mind?"

"Somebody mentioned something about a glitzy hotel, maybe a high-priced jewelry store, and oh, there's been talk about one of those posh coffee shops."

That caught my attention. Posh coffee shop? We had a coffee shop—Grace's place. No, it wasn't a Starbucks, but to the locals it was *home*. A place they went to socialize and relax in the comfy, deep-cushioned chairs Grace provided.

"I can't see that we need another place of lodging. We have the Island Hotel and a bunch of other smaller motels and vacation homes. And a coffee shop? Everybody patronizes Gracie's place." Even though the wooden sign that hung above her door said COFFEE, TEA & THEE, her shop was affectionately known as Gracie's Place.

Polly shook her head. "I know, I know. Well, maybe none of it will happen. Maybe it's just rumors floating around. I need to get going. I have a shampoo and set at eleven. You take care and I'll see ya soon."

I watched Polly walk out the door as an uneasy feeling settled on me. What if this time the rumors turned out to be fact? Where would that leave Grace? And could it be possible that this Tony was behind all of it?

At 2:00 Aunt Dora showed up to relieve me, and I decided to head over to the coffee shop before going home.

I walked in to see a few locals sitting inside, and a few others were sitting out back at picnic benches overlooking the water. A line of about eight people stood in front of the counter waiting for Grace to complete their orders. During the week her clientele consisted of mostly locals, but on the weekends she was always busy with tourists.

As I waited my turn, I looked around the shop. She had a perfect location right on the corner of Dock Street. Out the front door, one looked out to a view of the Gulf with the Big Dock in the foreground. Side windows also showed the Gulf with boats going in and out of the channel. The back windows looked out onto an area where Grace had arranged a few picnic tables that afforded another water view with a small bridge to the left. With the cushy chairs, a few bookcases filled with paperbacks, decks of playing cards and checker boards on some tables, the shop oozed an ambience of cozy. Mingling with the strong aroma of coffee was the pungent smell of sage and cedar that Grace usually had burning in a few incense holders. A large dream catcher dangled from the ceiling, and the soft strains of some New Age melody poured from the CD player. Just being there gave people a sense of good energy.

"Hey, what's up?" I heard Grace say as the customer in front of me left.

"Just finished at the yarn shop and I'm craving a latte."

"Coming right up," she said, reaching for my personal mug that had cabbage roses painted on the front. Most of the locals had their own cups for coffee, and we left them at the shop.

"Can you take a break?" I asked, indicating one of the empty tables outside.

"Sure. I can watch the front door from there."

She grabbed her bottle of water and followed me out.

"So how's Little Orphan Annie doing?" she asked.

I laughed. "So-so. Adam's with her. Oh, Carrie Sue called this morning," I told her and went on to explain the phone conversation.

"Hmm, you think she wants Clarissa back?"

I shrugged before taking a sip of coffee.

"Have no idea. But like Adam said, she has to get an attorney if that's what she wants, and they'll be back in court again."

"How would you feel about that? If she went back to live with Carrie Sue?"

Concerned was the first thought that came to my mind. "I don't know. Hey, how's it going with Tony? Is he a candidate for a chef on the Food Channel?"

Grace laughed. "I'd say he's close. He cooked us a delicious Italian dinner the other night. Antipasto, followed by delicious tortellini and a wonderful red wine. He even had salad and garlic bread to go with it."

"Martha Stewart, move aside," I said. "So what's his job entail? Did he tell you what he's developing?"

"Not really. We didn't talk much about work. He mentioned some project he's involved in with some other developers. In Gainesville, I think. But I didn't get the details."

Was he purposely keeping the information from Grace? Was I overreacting in thinking that he had an ulterior motive in dating her?

"Oops! Gotta go," she said, jumping up. "Customers calling."

I turned around to see two couples waiting at the counter. After finishing my coffee, I walked inside, rinsed out my cup, placed it back on the hook, and waved good-bye as Grace tended to another group of tourists.

$\begin{smallmatrix}\text{\Large \ensuremath{\infty}}\end{smallmatrix}$ 11 $\begin{smallmatrix}\text{\Large \ensuremath{\infty}}\end{smallmatrix}$

I returned home to find Adam and Clarissa at the kitchen table playing a game of Monopoly.

"Hey, honey," he said, getting up to give me a hug and kiss. "This daughter of mine is almost making me bankrupt. Wanna help me out here?"

I hadn't seen a Monopoly game since I was ten and was pretty sure we didn't own one.

"Where'd that come from?"

"My mother dropped by earlier. She had picked it up for Clarissa. Which reminds me, she wanted to know if Clarissa could spend the night with her. I think she's secretly looking forward to playing this game."

Somehow I couldn't picture Opal deep in concentration about whether she should purchase Park Place or a railroad.

"Sure, if you think she can go. Your mother will probably enjoy that." Not to mention that I'd delight in having my home and my husband back for a night.

"Then it's a done deal," he said. "Clarissa, why don't you go call your grandmother. Tell her I'll drop you off in about an hour, if that's good with her."

She walked into the great room and I could hear the beeps as she dialed.

"Honey, when I ask you something to do with Clarissa, don't put the ball back in my court."

"What do you mean?"

"When I asked you about her going to my mother's, I was looking for you to make the decision. I mean, I knew you'd say yes—but you said, if *you* think she can go. I'm not the only one making decisions in this family concerning Clarissa. She has to feel that we're united."

I recalled Dora saying something about making sure that Adam and I were on the same page. Chalk up another lesson in Mothering 101 for me.

"Yeah," I said, nodding. "I see what you're saying. I'm just not used to making decisions for another person."

I felt his arms go around me.

"You will. Hey, would you like to go out for dinner tonight?"

"Actually, I'd rather stay right here with you."

"Sounds good to me. How about I do some steaks on the grill?"

"Perfect," I told him as Clarissa walked back into the kitchen.

"Grandma said an hour is good. She's making me macaroni and cheese for supper and it'll be ready when I get there."

Macaroni and cheese? In the ten days Clarissa had been with us, I never thought to make that and couldn't resist asking, "Do you like that meal?"

"It's my favorite," she stated.

Why the heck didn't she bother to tell me that? And how did Opal seem to know this?

"Go pack your overnight bag," Adam told her. "Then we'll go."

I had just finished putting together a bowl of scalloped potatoes to go with the steaks when Clarissa walked back into the kitchen. She had a pink tote bag with Barbie on the front in one hand and the ever-present Raggedy Ann doll in the other.

She hitched herself up onto the stool and watched as I covered the casserole bowl with tin foil.

"How did Opal know macaroni and cheese was your favorite?" I blurted out.

Without hesitation, Clarissa replied, "She asked me."

"Oh," was all I could think of to say.

Adam walked into the kitchen jangling car keys. "All set?" he asked her.

Jumping down from the stool, Clarissa nodded.

"Be right back," he told me.

Clarissa turned around and paused. "Bye," she said.

"Have fun," I told her. "Have a good time."

I pushed the button on the stove to preheat the oven. Then I set about putting together a salad. All the while I was thinking about what Clarissa had said. Hell, I didn't even know if the girl had a favorite color or holiday or anything. When it came right down to it, I knew very little about Clarissa Jo Brooks.

Sitting in the lounge beside me, Adam reached for my hand.

"That was nice," he said. "I enjoyed that dinner."

"It *was* nice," I told him. But I was referring to more than the food. I had to admit it was very nice to dine with my husband alone. Just the two of us.

"More wine?" he said, getting up to get the bottle of Cabernet.

I nodded as I held out my glass for him to refill.

It was a gorgeous spring evening and the scent of lantana was heavy in the air. I glanced across the street from the deck. Boats were making their way back to the city marina before night fell. The water created ripples that seemed to go on forever.

I let out a deep sigh. "I love living here. I don't think there's a place on earth I'd rather be."

"It is pretty magical, isn't it? I've always thought so, even when I was a child. Maybe that's why I'm so happy that my own daughter will get to grow up here."

I sat up straighter in the lounge. "What do you think will happen, though, Adam? Do you think Carrie Sue will pursue the issue about custody?"

He took a sip of wine before answering. "Well, we haven't heard from her again. But knowing her, nothing would surprise me. The court rescinded her custody, so I think the best she could hope for would be visitation rights."

"What exactly did Clarissa say to you when you spoke to her about the phone call?"

"Not much, as usual. I couldn't get her to tell me if she wanted to go back to Carrie Sue or stay here. But I got the feeling she'd prefer to stay here."

"Adam, I feel really stupid saying this, but . . . I really think I'm one of those women like my grandmother. I just don't think I'm cut out to be a mother. I can't seem to get anything right. God, I didn't even know the kid liked macaroni and cheese."

He threw his head back, laughing. Unable to see any humor, I felt annoyed.

"Monica, you really *are* being too hard on yourself. It just takes time to know what she likes and doesn't like."

"Yeah, but I don't even know the right questions to ask." Wanting to change the subject, I said, "Hey, have you heard any rumors about new development possibly going on here?"

Adam nodded. "I was at the post office the other day and a few of the guys were talking about it."

"What'd they say? Do you think there's any truth to it?"

"I don't know. They said something about a developer wanting to make some major changes in the downtown area. But this has happened before and it never materialized."

When I remained quiet, Adam questioned, "Why?"

I told him what Polly had told me, and then I shared with him about the new man Grace was dating.

"So do you think this fellow has something to do with possible development on the island?"

"I don't know. I'd hate to think he's stringing Grace along, but she told me today that he hasn't said much to her about his job."

"Well, I'm sure it'll work itself out," he said, pulling me to my feet. "We have the entire house to ourselves, and I think we need to take advantage of that."

I put my arms around his neck as his head bent toward me. His body was strong and firm against mine and I felt the crush of his lips. I let myself sink into the moment as desire stirred me.

"Hmm, nice," he said, nuzzling my neck.

"Very nice," I whispered.

Taking my hand in his, he led me toward the French doors into the house.

"I think we need to have one of those nights of making mad, passionate love like we used to."

"You're a very wise man," I said, following him into the bedroom.

12

I looked up from my knitting and glanced around the great room. It crossed my mind that the scene could have come straight out of *Leave It to Beaver*.

Adam sat in his chair, feet propped up on the ottoman, reading an article in *Newsweek*. Clarissa was stretched out on the carpet, sketchbook in front of her, bringing a fairly accurate picture of a seascape to life with colored pencils. And I sat turning cobalt blue yarn into a sweater for Adam. The only thing missing was the pooch curled up in front of the fireplace.

As if she was reading my mind, Clarissa put down her pencils, swiveled around to face Adam and me, and said, "Could I have a puppy?"

"A what?" I said, shooting my glance to Adam to see his reaction.

In the almost two months that Clarissa had been with us, smiles seldom crossed her face. Not only was a smile forming, but she giggled.

"A puppy," she repeated.

Right. Something else in my life that was needy requiring my at-

tention. Things had been going along fairly well—we'd had no further word from Carrie Sue, meal choices had gotten a bit easier, and
while I won't say that Clarissa was the happiest child I'd ever met, I
felt we had settled into a routine. And now she wanted to throw a
wrench into it with a puppy?

I felt Adam staring at me. Hey, don't get me wrong—I love dogs.
I still grieved for Lilly, my mother's beautiful boxer, who we'd lost
the previous year much too young to lymphoma. But I thought my
hands were full enough at the moment without bringing a four-
legged creature into our life.

"I . . . uh . . . I don't know . . . ," I mumbled. "What do you
think, Adam?" I asked, tossing that proverbial ball right back into
his court.

"Well," he said, leaning forward in his chair. "We'll have to discuss this, of course, but it might not be a bad idea."

Might not be a bad idea? Was he nuts? So in addition to all the
other extra duties that I'd acquired, now I was supposed to do poop
patrol as well?

I'm not sure if it was the look on my face or my stumbling with
words, but Adam seemed to catch on fast that having a puppy in the
house wasn't high on my list of things I wanted.

"Puppies are a lot of work," he told Clarissa.

No shit, I thought.

An animation seemed to come over her. She made her way along
the carpet to kneel in front of Adam. Gazing up at him with a look
that matched Shirley Temple, she nodded and said softly, "I know,
and I'd take care of it." As if to seal her words, she stroked her father's hand. If I hadn't known better, I'd have said this was Clarissa
Jo's first attempt to use her feminine wiles.

"Monica is busy enough, you know. It would have to be you who
looked after the puppy, took him for a walk, taught him not to chew
things. It's a lot of work, Clarissa. Do you think you're old enough
for that?"

She looked up at Adam, and I swear that child batted her eyelashes and said, "I would. Really I would."

"Well, a puppy might be good for you. Monica and I will discuss it some more and we'll see, okay?"

Why did I feel as if "we'll see" meant "done deal"?

After Clarissa went to bed, Adam and I sat out on the deck. Even though it was June, the high humidity hadn't arrived in Cedar Key yet. We had a nice breeze off the ocean and I inhaled the scent of salt air.

"Monica, if you really don't want a puppy, we won't get one."

Sure, make me out to be the bad guy.

He reached over to touch my hand. "It's just that Clarissa hasn't made many friends here. She was only in school a month before classes ended for this year. I think she's lonely."

He was probably right. And maybe she would be responsible. After that first fiasco with her bedroom, when Adam had spoken to her she had improved with keeping it picked up.

I felt like I was being backed into a corner and let out a deep sigh.

"I hate to be the one to say no, Adam. But gosh . . . a puppy? I don't know. . . ."

"I don't want to pressure you into this, but she's turning nine in September. It might be a nice early birthday present."

"Hmm," I offered reluctantly. I turned to look at my husband's face and felt like a rat. Maybe he did know better than I did what would be good for his daughter. I guess if it was a small dog. . . .

"What kind of dog did you have in mind?"

"Oh, I don't know. We both love Winston, Ali's Scottie. What do you think would be good?"

He was right. I adored Winston. He was friendly, bright, and a true gentleman.

"Yeah," I said slowly, giving it some thought. "Scottish terriers are a great breed. Miss Polly has a cockapoo that's really sweet too. So I do think it should be a small dog so that Clarissa can handle it easily."

"I agree. Why don't you speak to Alison and Miss Polly. See if they know of any breeders and we'll take it from there."

I saw the loving smile on his face and knew immediately that the "we'll see" had definitely morphed into "done deal."

Miss Polly put us in touch with a cockapoo breeder in Ocala. I sat beside Adam as we drove along U.S. 27 and admired the gorgeous rolling hills of horse farms that I saw out the window.

I heard humming from the backseat and craned my neck around to see Clarissa holding her Raggedy Ann doll. The humming now broke out into a child's song. She was actually singing. I had to admit, since we'd told her she could get a puppy, Clarissa had seemed to border on *happy*.

"Are we almost there?" she asked, leaning forward as much as her seat belt would allow.

"Not much longer," Adam told her.

I let my mind trail off and recalled the incident that had occurred just before we'd left the house. I'd been brushing my hair in the bedroom when something shiny caught my eye on the bureau. I glanced down to see a butterfly brooch. Sybile had given it to me and I always kept it deep inside my jewelry box. Picking it up in my hand, I couldn't figure out why on earth it was on top of the bureau. I hadn't worn it in months.

When I questioned Adam, he had no idea how it had gotten out of my jewelry box. I replaced it, but thought of my blue sweater that had ended up in Clarissa's room. And added to that was when Clarissa told me *the lady* had told her about taking a boat to Atsena Otie. When I had questioned her later about who this lady was, she'd just shrugged and had given me no answer.

"Here we are," I heard Adam say, breaking into my thoughts.

A large and well-maintained farmhouse sat at the end of a long driveway.

Adam pulled up in front and had barely cut the ignition before Clarissa had unfastened her seat belt and flung open her door.

I looked at Adam and laughed. "Think she's excited?"

A middle-aged woman opened the front door and greeted us from the wraparound porch.

"You must be the Brooks family," she said.

Adam and I walked toward her with Clarissa leading the way.

"It's nice to meet you," he told the woman. "This is my wife, Monica, and my daughter, Clarissa Jo."

"Ah, and you're the one that will be choosing a puppy," she said, sending a warm smile to Clarissa.

"Yes, and I'm so excited."

The woman laughed. "Then follow me out back. That's where the kennel is."

A white clapboard building stood in back of the house. When she opened the door a buff-colored cocker spaniel greeted us.

"This here is Sally. She's the mama dog."

Clarissa put her hand out for the dog to sniff and then bent down to stroke the cream fur.

"And over here, these are Sally's babies."

We walked over to see four balls of fur tumbling and playing.

"They're eight weeks old?" I asked.

"Yup, they were born April nineteenth."

Clarissa shot a look in my direction, and I wondered if she realized that was the date she'd come to live with Adam and me.

"They sure are cute," Adam said, bending down to pat them.

Clarissa sat on the cement floor and let all four puppies crawl over her. Their wet tongues kissing her face brought forth giggles. This was such a foreign sound coming from her that I smiled and wondered if perhaps Adam had been right after all.

After a few minutes, she said, "This one. This is the one I want."

She had chosen a buff and white puppy that strongly resembled a lamb.

"And I'm going to name it Billie."

I felt a shiver go through me. *Billie?* That was my pet nickname for Sybile. There's no way this child could have known that.

"Well, now," I heard Adam say. "It might not be a boy dog."

The woman laughed. "No, I'm afraid that's a girl puppy," she said.

Clarissa stood up, cuddling the small ball of fur. "That's okay. This is the one I want. Yes," she said with determination. "If you spell the name with a *y*, then it's a boy's name. But Billie can be a girl's name too."

"You're very right," Adam told her. "So are you sure this is the pup you want?"

One look at the child and the puppy and anybody could tell it was. The dog had nestled its small head under Clarissa's chin and the look on Clarissa's face was one of pure bliss.

I was still shaken by her choice of a name for the dog and could only stand there mute while Adam produced the checkbook and paid the purchase price.

The woman went on to tell us about food and assorted other things, much of which I didn't hear.

After thanking her, with promises that we'd let her know how the puppy was doing, we headed back to Cedar Key.

Clarissa sat in the backseat, cooing and speaking softly to her new friend—while I pondered things I had no understanding of.

❧ 13 ❧

"She named it *what?*" my mother said on the phone the next morning. Despite her being across the ocean in Paris, I knew it wasn't a bad phone line that caused her question.

"You heard me correctly—Billie," I told her as I watched Clarissa through the kitchen window romping with the puppy in the backyard.

"Interesting," was my mother's reply.

"I'd say it's a bit more than interesting." When there was silence, I said, "I just don't understand it. There's no way she could have known that's what I called Sybile. Do you think it's just a coincidence?"

"Gosh, I don't know. I suppose it could be, but it does seem like an odd choice of name for a puppy."

"Now I'm wondering what Dora and Saren will think of the name."

"I'm not sure about them, but I do have to say, I think Sybile would've had a good chuckle. She loved it when you came up with that name for her."

I smiled. She was right. Sybile had made it clear I wasn't to call her *Grandma*.

"So how'd the puppy settle in last night?"

"Actually, she did quite well. I thought I heard her whimpering once, so I got up to check and I could hear Clarissa in her room talking softly to her."

I'd also noticed that for the past few weeks I no longer heard Clarissa crying during the night.

"Well, I'm glad you got her, Monica. I still miss Lilly so much. It'll be nice to have a dog in the family again."

"Yeah, Saren's all excited too. Since Precious died, I know he's missed not having a dog. He's coming over later this morning to meet . . . Billie."

After catching up on other news, I hung up the phone and stood staring out the window. Clarissa had put on the pink harness and attached the pink leash to the puppy and was having a ball running back and forth with her. I smiled. Maybe things were going to work out after all. True, I still hadn't developed any maternal love for Clarissa Jo—but at least we seemed to be tolerating each other.

Within a month, Billie had settled in fairly well. Oh, there was still the occasional piddle on the floor, but for the most part Clarissa had done well getting the puppy on a schedule. We'd been advised to crate-train Billie, and at least I didn't have to worry about the pup tearing the house apart when we were out.

I was finishing up some accounting when Dora walked into the yarn shop.

"Gosh, is it two already?" I asked, glancing at my watch.

"Just about," she said, placing her handbag in the desk drawer. "Are you picking up Clarissa at the Arts Center?"

"Yeah, she really seems to enjoy the classes. Her sketchbook is filling up."

"That's good. Has she made any friends yet?"

I shook my head. "No, I'm afraid not. She's been spending more and more time with Miss Tilly. She takes Billie over there and I hear them laughing."

"Well, you know, that's sure good for Tilly. She showed up at the Garden Club meeting last week. Nobody could believe it. She hasn't ventured out in ages. I think Clarissa is good for her."

Hmm, I wasn't aware of this.

"Once Tilly stopped teaching, it was like all the years since she lost Carl and Carl Junior caught up with her. She's been in a terrible depression. Everybody's been worried about her and we've tried everything to get her out. She told us that she's going to rejoin the Women's Club too. It's amazing."

It certainly was. *You mean to tell me that one little girl can have that much impact on an elderly woman?*

I grabbed my purse and headed for the door. "You take care, Dora. I'll see you on Thursday."

I was surprised to see Clarissa standing in front of the Arts Center with another little girl.

"This is my new friend, Zoe," she explained.

"Hi, Zoe," I said, smiling at the blond, curly-haired little girl.

"Can Zoe come home with us and meet Billie?" Clarissa asked.

This was something new for me.

"You can come, but you'll have to let your mother know."

"My mom is sick. I can call Claire from your house. She takes care of me."

When we arrived home, Zoe made the call. I remembered bringing home my own girlfriends and automatically opened the fridge to put together a snack for the girls.

Clarissa had run to release Billie from the crate to take her outside.

I put a bag of popcorn into the microwave and was pouring Pepsi into glasses when Zoe came back into the kitchen.

"Clarissa's out back with the puppy. Is your mom okay?" I asked her.

"Oh, she's not going to get better," the child said matter-of-factly. "She has cancer."

I stopped pouring to stare at Zoe. Did this mean the little girl's mother was dying? I wasn't sure what to say. "I'm sorry about that," was all I offered as she walked out the door. Gosh, that was a terrible burden for an eight-year-old. To know she was going to lose her mother. I wondered if Clarissa knew this and what she thought.

That night over dinner, I brought up the subject.

"It sounds like Zoe's mother is pretty sick," I said, watching for Clarissa's reaction.

Her face remained void of expression.

"Yeah, that's what she said."

"Her mother is Sandy Collins, isn't she? I'd heard she'd been ill," Adam told us.

"She was in the hospital," Clarissa said. "But she's back home now. Zoe doesn't have a daddy to help out, so Claire takes care of her."

Adam and I exchanged a glance and I thought it best to change the subject.

"Tell your dad about the art project you're working on."

Clarissa brightened and explained to Adam that she was going to be entering an art contest and that Miss Tilly offered to tutor her.

"That's great. We just might have a budding artist in the family."

Following supper, I was in the family room knitting a Christmas stocking. Dora and I had decided to get a head start and begin working on what we hoped would be customer requests.

"Are you yarning?" I heard Clarissa ask.

I laughed and looked up as she walked over to sit beside me on the sofa. "Am I *what?*"

"You know," she said, pointing to the stocking taking shape on my needles. "What you're doing there."

Obviously, she wasn't joking by using that term. "Where did you hear what I'm doing called *yarning?*"

Clarissa remained silent for a moment as if considering whether she'd said the wrong thing. "I didn't hear it. Isn't that yarn on those sticks?"

When I nodded confirmation, she said, "Well, then isn't what you're doing yarning? Like when you jump, it's jumping? Or you walk and it's walking?"

I was becoming more intrigued with the way a child's mind worked, especially when it came to using words, and I had to admit—she certainly had a point.

Letting out a deep breath, I smiled and wondered about the best way to explain the terminology of knitting to her. "Well, technically, you're right. This *is* yarn and therefore, I suppose the action of turning it into something handmade *could* be called yarning. But it's always been called *knitting.*"

"Oh," was all Clarissa said, but a moment later she questioned, "Why?"

Hmm, good question. "Well," I explained. "There are actually a few definitions of the word *knit,* one of which means becoming closely and firmly united, to grow together. So with the craft of knitting you can form a scarf or sweater or this stocking by interlocking loops of a single yarn by using needles. These aren't sticks. In knitting we call them needles."

Clarissa took a moment to think about what I'd just told her and then said, "Oh, I guess that makes sense. But I think I like the word *yarning* better."

I laughed and looked over to see Adam suppressing a chuckle.

After Clarissa had gone to bed, I found myself thinking about her friend again.

"Do you think Clarissa understands that Zoe's mother could die?" I asked Adam.

"I'm not sure. We haven't had any discussion about death, and Clarissa hasn't lost anybody close to her."

"It just seems unfair. That's such an adult subject—death. And yet Zoe might be faced with experiencing it. If Clarissa had questions, do you think she'd ask you?"

"Well, she's opening up more than when she first came here. I forgot to tell you, the other day she asked me if I thought Carrie Sue would be calling again or coming to visit her."

I sat up straighter in my chair. "Really? Did she act like she wanted this to happen?"

"I got the impression she didn't. I felt that Clarissa hoped we wouldn't hear from her again. She asked me if Carrie Sue went back to court, would she have to go and live with her again, and I explained that we had full custody. But she might have to spend some time with her mother if Carrie Sue wanted visitation rights. She didn't say she didn't want to see her—but she made me feel this was something she hoped wouldn't happen."

"Hmm," I said. "I'm surprised about that. I guess I've felt from the beginning that Clarissa didn't really want to even come here. That maybe she'd have preferred staying with her mother. You know, loyalty and all that. She never mentions her name though."

"All any child wants is love, Monica. I've always thought that Carrie Sue was much too self-centered to lavish any love on Clarissa. I'm more convinced than ever that the only reason Carrie Sue fought me for custody was to get back at me. Revenge for not putting up with her behavior."

"You could be right. I remember you told me that during the first four years you're the one that took over the bulk of child care. Playing with Clarissa, reading to her, taking her places."

"Carrie Sue was too involved with shopping and her spa visits. A child really cramped her style."

I felt a twinge of guilt. Wasn't that how I'd been feeling? Having a child in the house had certainly upset the balance that I'd been used to. Plans got readjusted, schedules turned upside down, and the only privacy that Adam and I had anymore was in the evening after she went to bed or when she spent a night with Opal or Dora.

As if reading my thoughts, Adam said, "How're you feeling now about having her with us?"

I felt heat sliding up my neck to my face. "Well, gosh, Adam, she's your daughter. I knew we'd have her here during the summer and some holidays. But I have to admit it's been a bit different having her here permanently. Our lives really got turned around. Some days I feel like I'm just going in circles. Keeping up with the extra laundry, trying to think of meals she'll eat. . . ." My voice trailed off, and even to my own ears it sounded like whining.

"I'm not sure it'll make you feel any better, but you're doing a great job. You really are. And I think Clarissa Jo likes you a lot."

He could have said anything else and I might have believed him—but Clarissa *liking* me? I don't think so! That child tolerated me. Just as I tolerated her. Not wanting to hurt Adam's feelings, I remained silent.

❦ 14 ❦

The next morning I answered the phone to hear a strange voice with a strong Southern accent say, "Is this Mrs. Brooks?"

"Yes," I replied, wondering if it might be the social worker in Georgia.

"Oh, good. First I want to apologize for not calling you sooner. This is Becky Stratham. I was Clarissa Jo's teacher at school."

"Okay, is there a problem?"

Her laughter came across the phone. "No, no. Not at all. Clarissa Jo was a model student, and I must say the other children and I missed her when she left. But I'm very glad she was able to relocate to live with you and her father. The reason I'm calling. . . . Clarissa Jo won first place in the art contest that the school had in April. I'm sure she told you all about it."

First place in an art contest? Clarissa hadn't uttered one word to me, but I said, "Yes," waiting for her to continue.

"It was such a shame that she had to miss school that day and not be here to accept her award. There was a nice little ceremony on the stage and all the parents attended. One child from each grade was honored for first place. And then, of course, that night her mother was in the car accident and . . . well, as you know, Clarissa never did return to school. So I have her award and would like to mail it down to her if that would be all right?"

Such an important event, and Clarissa had neglected to mention this at all. I was certain that Adam had no knowledge about the award, either.

"Oh, yes, that would be great. I know Clarissa would love to have her award, and that's very nice of you."

I gave Miss Stratham our mailing address and promised to have Clarissa send a letter to her classmates. Hanging up the phone, I wondered why she'd missed school that day, but even more important—why hadn't she shared such good news with us?

That evening I pulled Adam into our bedroom to relate the telephone call. "So did you know about this award?" I questioned.

Running a hand through his hair, he let out a deep sigh and shook his head. "Not at all. I mean, it seems like the school had a nice recognition for the students. I don't understand why Clarissa Jo didn't tell us, but I'll bring it up over dinner."

I joined Clarissa and Adam at the table and participated in the usual dinnertime chitchat.

Just before we finished eating, Adam said, "Clarissa, Monica got a phone call today from Miss Stratham. Why didn't you tell us you won first place in an art contest?"

Clarissa pushed the remaining food around her plate and without looking up said, "It wasn't a big deal."

"Of course it was a big deal, and even the school thought it was. They had a nice ceremony planned for the winners and their parents, but you weren't there. Were you sick that day?"

"No."

Adam and I exchanged a look across the table, and he went on. "You weren't sick? Then why weren't you at school that day?"

After a few moments, Clarissa said, "Because Mom wouldn't get up. I had set my alarm and I kept trying to wake her up. I told her it was the morning of the art awards, but she said she didn't feel good and the award wasn't such a big deal. She said I didn't have to be there."

Hearing those words and seeing the look on Adam's face sent a profound feeling of sadness through me. Carrie Sue hadn't thought it important enough to drive her daughter to school that morning and be present while she received a highly regarded award? My mind flashed back to third grade—I was a finalist in a national spelling bee, and I'll never forget standing on that stage and looking out to the audience to see both of my parents sitting there, beaming with pride.

"Well, it was a big deal," I heard Adam say, and I knew he was struggling with his emotions. "It was a *very* big deal. As a matter of fact, it was *such* a big deal that was why Miss Stratham called here this morning. She wants you to have your award, and she's mailing it down to you."

"She is?" Clarissa's head shot up to stare at her father as joy filled her expression.

"She certainly is," Adam told her emphatically. "And I'm so proud of you! First place in an art contest. Clarissa, you should be very proud of yourself. Not everybody has the talent that you do."

"But I love drawing," she said. "For me, it's not hard."

"That's exactly what your dad means," I said. "You have a gift, but not everybody does. When it comes to the arts, like dancing or music or writing and drawing—only certain people have been given a gift to excel in these areas, and you're one of them, Clarissa. Like your dad said, you really should be very proud. I'm certainly proud of you." As soon as I said the words I knew they were true—I felt pride for this child who so willingly accepted the neglect her mother displayed.

"And you know what?" Adam told her. "I think this calls for a celebration. How about Friday we all go into Gainesville for dinner at McAlister's, that deli you like, and then a trip to Toys R Us? How's that sound?"

Clarissa's grin lit up her face. "Oh, cool!"

* * *

After Clarissa was tucked into bed, Adam and I sat outside on the deck and resumed the conversation concerning the art award.

"Can you believe it?" he said. With Clarissa out of earshot, he allowed his anger to bubble up. "That rotten bitch! Can you believe Carrie Sue was that selfish? It meant nothing at all to her that her daughter was receiving an award. I'd bet anything that she'd been out drinking the night before—she had a hangover. That was why she couldn't get out of bed to drive Clarissa to school. How the hell can a mother have such a lack of caring and responsibility?"

I reached over to rub Adam's arm. "I have to admit that this episode really shows what a poor excuse Carrie Sue is for a mother."

"And the thing is, if that teacher hadn't called, I'm positive Clarissa never would have mentioned the art award. What kind of message does that send to a child? If her own mother doesn't care enough to celebrate and acknowledge her daughter's accomplishments, Clarissa is never taught to develop self-esteem."

I heard Adam's voice crack and knew he was having difficulty holding back tears.

"All I can say is, thank God you now have full custody. I just don't understand how a judge couldn't look at the evidence and the situation and in his heart know that you were the better parent to raise her. Divorce is never pleasant, and when children are involved it's even worse. Ideally, a joint custody is the best for children. But in a situation like this where the mother is clearly neglectful . . . I just don't get it."

Adam blew out a deep breath. "Neither do I. Hey, I'll be the first to say that in most cases, with two fit parents, a child should spend fifty percent of the time with each parent. When I lost my job in Georgia, we went back to court. I knew that without me around, it would only get worse with Carrie Sue shirking her responsibilities for Clarissa Jo. My lawyer tried, she really did. We called character witnesses who lived in the apartment building where Carrie Sue lived. They testified that she was out until all hours drinking and partying. But did that matter? Not one single bit! She had a quali-fied babysitter staying there with Clarissa."

"It's really insane. I just don't understand the law. It makes no sense, and it's *not* about what's best for the child."

Adam took a sip of sweet tea and shook his head. "No, I'm afraid it's not. Do you know that if a mother is doing drugs in the house with children present, even *that* might not be enough to take away her custody?"

"What?" Surely he was joking!

"I couldn't believe it either, but here's the kicker—if the mom is shooting up cocaine or heroin and she's in the same room as her children, as long as her back is turned to the children there's no cause to remove them from that environment. In order for that to happen, the mom has to be facing the children as she's shooting up the drugs. So yeah, it's beyond insane."

"I know enough about women's rights and the feminism of the sixties. Most of the time, women truly didn't get a fair shake back then when it came to divorce and child support payments. Hell, most states didn't even go after the fathers if they didn't pay. The mom had no choice—in order to support her children she was at the mercy of the state to provide welfare payments, and I remember my mom telling me about a few friends of hers. It was horribly degrad-ing for a woman to stand in line at the bank cashing a welfare check and taking handouts. But with preschool children, it was impossible for her to work enough to pay the rent and cover all the household expenses." I shook my head at the unfairness of it. "But I tell you what—that pendulum has swung way too far the other way. Nowa-days, fathers can be totally disregarded in many cases. Hell, until re-cently if a girl got pregnant and chose not to tell the father, he had no rights concerning that child. Look at what Sybile did to Saren."

Adam squeezed my hand. "I know, and you're so right. . . . Thank God I finally got custody of my daughter. Hopefully not too much damage was done and the worst is behind us."

✥ 15 ✥

Adam leaned across our table at the Island Room, raised his glass of wine to me, and said, "To the most beautiful wife in the world. Happy ten-month anniversary."

I touched the edge of my glass with his and smiled. During the first five months that Adam and I had been married, we'd made a point of going out to celebrate the monthly milestone. But for four months, since Clarissa had moved in with us, somehow we hadn't gotten around to continuing our ritual. I was pleased the day before when Adam informed me that he'd booked us a table so we could celebrate being married for ten months.

"I love you, Adam," I told him. "Sometimes I wonder how you put up with me."

He threw his head back laughing. "Yeah, you can be a brat—every bit as much as Clarissa, but I wouldn't trade you for anything."

I thought back to my failed relationships before meeting Adam. I still wasn't sure if the endings had all been my fault. I just knew I wasn't meant to be with any of them. Adam was my soul mate, and I knew it that first day in the yarn shop.

Halfway through our dinner two gentlemen were seated across from us. Mid forties, well-dressed, obviously businessmen.

Not intending to eavesdrop, I heard the one with dark hair say, "It's only a matter of time till I have her convinced."

"I wish I felt as confident as you do," the other one replied.

"If we drive her out, Grace isn't going to have a choice, is she?"

My gasp caused Adam's head to snap up. "Everything all right?"

I nodded and cast a glance to my right. I had never met Tony Rizotti, but I'd have bet anything that was him. What the hell was he referring to? Drive Grace *out?* The last time I'd spoken to Gracie she admitted that while marriage certainly wasn't on the horizon, she was sleeping with Tony, and it was obvious that she cared for him a great deal. Was he only using her? In order to purchase her coffee shop? Hell, it wasn't just her coffee shop—it was her residence. She lived upstairs in the one-bedroom apartment.

Overhearing that conversation put a damper on the rest of the dinner. I couldn't wait for Adam to get the check so we could leave.

As soon as we got outside, I asked, "Did you hear him? Did you hear what he said about Grace?"

Not understanding, Adam said, "Who?"

God, sometimes men could be so dense. "Those two guys sitting across from us. I'm positive one of them was Tony. The *Tony* that Gracie is dating. He said something about driving her out. I told her! I told her to be careful with a developer, but oh no, she wouldn't listen to me. And now—she could find herself right out on the street, just like my mother did when my dad died."

Adam put an arm around me as we walked toward the car.

"Honey, calm down. Maybe you're overreacting. You probably just misunderstood what was being said."

"Yeah, right, and it's gonna snow in Florida tomorrow."

I thought the best way to approach the situation with Grace was with a girls' day out. I convinced her to get somebody to cover the coffee shop for the following Saturday, telling her that we owed it to ourselves to just go have some fun for a few hours. She balked at first and then agreed it had been much too long since we'd done something like that.

"This was a good idea, Monica," she told me as I drove along SR 24 toward Gainesville.

"Of course it was. I'm usually right."

Grace laughed. "Cripe, you sound like your mother's friend Alison. So we hit the spa first, huh?"

"Yup, we're booked for an eleven o'clock appointment for a facial and pedicure and then lunch at Amelia's."

"Sounds like fun. So how're things going with Clarissa? I can hardly believe that school starts again next week."

"Well, I guess we're both holding our own. Kids are just so much work. She's talking a lot more now, that's for sure. Sometimes I long for those days when she was so quiet."

Grace laughed. "Oh yeah, I know what you're saying. They have a million questions at that age and it's nonstop chatter."

I nodded. "I'm just not used to it. I was involved in an intricate pattern with my knitting the other night, and she was going on and on about the movie that Adam had taken her and Zoe to see."

"For what it's worth, Monica, I think you're really doing well with her. Still no further word from Carrie Sue?"

"Nope."

"How would you feel if she reopened the custody suit? Do you think Clarissa would want to go back to her?"

"Well, Adam has full custody, but there's always the chance that Carrie Sue will try to claim her visitation rights." I couldn't honestly tell Grace how I felt about this possibility, but I knew I really didn't want to subject that child to Carrie Sue. "Adam seems to think that Clarissa would like to avoid going back and forth."

"That's understandable. Children thrive on stability. I was fortunate to have such a close relationship with Aunt Maude. Oh, I won't say it wasn't devastating to lose my parents—it was. But I know it would have been so much worse if my aunt hadn't taken me in. Looking back now, that stability meant everything to me."

I recalled my own secure and stable childhood and knew what she meant.

By the time we walked out of the spa, I felt like a new person. *What is it about pampering that makes a woman feel so rejuvenated?* I glanced down at my bright red nails peeking out from my sandals and smiled. Following the facial, we had the tech apply a new brand of makeup, which of course, we ended up purchasing.

Pulling into a parking spot near Amelia's, I checked my reflection in the visor mirror and then glanced at Grace.

"We look pretty damn good," I told her.

She laughed. "I'd say we qualify for *hot.*"

With our order given and a glass of wine in front of us, I decided to broach the subject of Tony.

"So how's it going with lover boy?" I said, attempting to start out with humor.

"Now there's somebody that definitely oozes *hot.*"

Great. Obviously she was into this guy, and I was probably going to burst her romantic bubble.

"So . . . things are getting serious?"

"Well, let's just say things are heating up. I like him, Monica. He's drop-dead gorgeous, has a great sense of humor, and I love being with him."

Yup, I could definitely hear a *pop* coming.

"Has he mentioned any more about his development work?"

"What? Are you doing interviews for the *Cedar Key News*? Why are you so interested in his line of work?"

"Because I've heard the rumors about a developer wanting to change things on the island—in a big way."

"Oh, and so based on these rumors, you think Tony might be involved?"

"I have a pretty good idea that he might be, yeah."

"So what? What's that got to do with me?" *Probably way more than you could imagine,* I thought. But I decided not to spill the beans quite yet about what I overheard at the Island Room. Instead, I thought it might be better to fight fire with fire.

"Hey, are you keeping him hidden for any particular reason?"

"Hidden? Don't be silly. I'm not doing that."

"Good, then how about you bring Tony over so I can meet him. Friday evening? We'll have a seafood feast on the deck."

Grace's face lit up. "Oh, that would be fun. Sure. Let me just check with Tony to make sure he's free, but I'd like you to meet him."

Don't be too sure of that, I thought.

I turned toward the sound of a car door closing to see Grace and Tony walking toward the deck.

"Hey," I hollered. "Come around back and come on up."

"Oh, they're here?" Adam said, walking out of the kitchen with a tray of cheese and crackers.

Grace got to the top of the stairs and I could see she'd taken extra care with her hair and clothes. White shorts showed off her long, tan legs, while a pink blouse brought out strawberry highlights in her bouncy curls.

She made the introductions and my first thought was that she was right—he did bear a striking resemblance to George Clooney. I was so upset with what he'd said in the restaurant, I hadn't paid attention.

"Nice to meet you," he told Adam and me. "You have a lovely place here. Great view."

Yeah, well, don't even think about scooping up this property, buster.

Everyone decided on white wine and Adam went inside to get a bottle.

"Sit down," I told them, gesturing to the patio chairs.

"Where's Clarissa?" Grace asked.

"She's spending the night with Opal. They're going to have a Disney movie marathon."

Adam came out, poured the wine, and I lifted my glass high.

"Here's to beautiful Cedar Key," I said. "May it always stay the same."

Gracie shot me a quizzical look, but only nodded.

By the time we'd finished a delicious dinner of Cedar Key clams, mullet, corn on the cob, and salad, I could see why Grace was attracted to Tony. He was a great conversationalist, was attentive to her, had fine manners—and seemed to be a born schmoozer.

"So," I said, stirring cream into my coffee. "What are your plans for development here on the island?"

Grace's head shot up, but she waited for his answer.

"Well, uh . . . I'm still not sure."

"You mean you *are* considering a project here on Cedar Key?" she questioned him. "This is the first I'm hearing about it."

"Yeah, there's another developer—a good friend of mine. We're tossing around a few ideas."

I just bet you are, I thought.

Grace sat up straighter and leaned forward. "Like what?"

Tony seemed absorbed in fingering his napkin. "Oh, it's still too early to know for sure."

He was being purposely evasive.

"You must have some idea what's being considered. Jewelry shops? Clothing stores? A movie theater?" I wasn't about to back down now.

He nodded. "Yeah, some of those things might be in the works."

"Hmm," I said and hated to do this to Grace, but she had to know the truth. "Boy, Gracie's location is prime property, isn't it?"

I saw him visibly squirm as my best friend shot me a bewildered look. Three of us sat there waiting for an answer.

When none was forthcoming, I plunged in. "Gee, that good

friend of yours? Was he the one we saw you having dinner with the other evening at the Island Room?" I hoped I wouldn't regret this. "The one that I heard you tell about *'driving Grace out'?*"

Tony's face registered surprise and then recognition. I knew he was remembering Adam and me from the restaurant.

"What?" Grace exploded. "What the hell are you talking about, Monica? Drive me out of *where?* For Christ sake, will somebody please tell me what's going on?"

Tony stood up. Taking Grace's hand, he pulled her from the chair.

Before he had a chance to say anything, I said, "Only Tony can explain that to you, Gracie."

"And that's exactly what I intend to do. Thank you for a nice dinner, and I'm sorry the evening ended on a bad note."

Without as much as a good-bye, Grace followed him down the stairs and out to the car.

I may have lost a friendship, but hopefully my friend wouldn't be losing her business and the roof over her head.

❦ 16 ❧

When a week had passed with no word from Grace, I had a sick feeling that our friendship was over. I hadn't seen her around town and refrained from dropping into the coffee shop. But worst of all was that I thought perhaps I'd been wrong to accuse Tony. Maybe I'd misunderstood what I'd heard in the restaurant, but I didn't think so.

"Monica?" I turned around to see Clarissa standing in the kitchen, a pair of scissors in her hand.

"Oh, my God!" My hand flew to my mouth. "What the heck did you do?"

Clarissa stood there just staring at me. One side of her hair was missing a good three inches. The look on her face was a mixture of fear and regret.

I ran over to touch what remained on the left side of her head. "Clarissa! Why did you cut your hair?" I screamed.

"I . . . don't . . . know. . . ."

For the first time in five months I thought for sure that tears were about to course down her face. This child had never once cried in front of me, but within a second she stepped back, swallowed, and said, "I wanted to," with defiance lacing her words.

"You wanted to?" God almighty! Adam was going to kill me. I had no clue she was in her room chopping off her hair. "What do you mean you *wanted* to? If you wanted your hair cut, why didn't you tell me? This is horrible. Your hair is gone now! What the heck are we going to do? You look ridiculous. How am I supposed to fix this?"

The silence that filled the kitchen only infuriated me more.

"I don't know," she finally said.

"Give me those scissors," I demanded, putting out my hand. "And go to your room. I'm calling your father right now to tell him what you did."

Obediently, Clarissa passed me the scissors, turned around, and left the kitchen.

I sank into the chair, shaking my head. God, this wasn't getting easier. It was getting worse. What the hell was I going to do? I glanced at the clock. Adam was still in meetings at school and wouldn't be home for another couple of hours. I shouldn't interrupt him at work. After a few minutes, I let out a deep sigh, picked up the phone, called Miss Polly—and made my first decision as a stepmom.

The moment we walked into the Curl Up and Dye, three heads beneath hair dryers glanced at Clarissa, raised their eyebrows, and looked at me with pursed lips.

"So," Polly said, tapping the back of the salon chair in front of her station. "What have we got here? Have a seat, Clarissa."

Was that a grin that Polly was trying to smother? This entire episode was about as funny to me as a tearjerker movie.

I watched Polly comb through Clarissa's hair while she nodded to herself. Everyone in town knew that Polly had a knack for cosmetology—but what we were staring at required magic.

"Okay," she finally said. "First of all, I need you to disappear for a little while."

I pointed to my chest. "Me?"

"Yes, you. Pop over to the yarn shop to see Dora. Come back in about an hour."

I let out a deep sigh. "Be good," I told Clarissa and did as Polly had instructed.

Aunt Dora glanced up at the sound of wind chimes, took one look at my face, and said, "What's wrong?"

As I related Clarissa's attempt at playing Delilah, Dora poured coffee into two mugs.

"Here," she said, passing one to me.

Was that a smirk crossing her face? Why was I missing the humor that Dora and Polly obviously felt?

"Do you think this is funny?" I said

"It's not such a major thing, Monica. Every little girl tries to cut her hair—my Marin did it when she was six, and believe me, I was as upset as you are. Age has a way of allowing us to see things differently. I bet you tried it yourself."

I had no recollection of doing such a thing.

She shook her head and chuckled. "Don't ask me why kids do that, but they do."

I took a sip of coffee. Had I overreacted? Maybe.

"Do you think she'll do it again?"

"Probably not. They usually learn their lesson."

"But if she wanted her damn hair cut, why couldn't she just tell me? I'd have taken her to Polly's."

"I think it has something to do with having control. A need to do it themselves."

"Yeah, that was really smart of her. She ended up at Polly's salon anyway."

"It's all part of them growing up, Monica."

All of a sudden I felt way older than my thirty-two years.

"How the hell do mothers survive raising kids?"

Dora laughed. "It's not always easy, trust me. But, hopefully, many years later it reaches a point where mothers and daughters actually become friends."

I wasn't so certain that would ever happen between Clarissa and me.

"Don't be too hard on her, Monica. At least she didn't cut herself."

Not once had that thought occurred to me. I still had a lot to learn about being a mother.

"Any word from Grace?" she asked.

I shook my head. "No, and I miss her."

"Why don't you pop over to the coffee shop?"

"I can't. I think she hates me for what I insinuated about Tony."

"He's bought the empty shop down the street, you know. You were being a good friend trying to steer her away from him."

"No, really? I hadn't heard that. What's he planning to do with it?"

"Have no idea. Leave it to Saren—he keeps going over there to ask questions. Tony tries to be polite to him, but he keeps telling him he hasn't decided yet what type of business will be opening."

"It should be interesting to see the end result," I said. "Oh, while I'm in here, I need more of that cobalt blue yarn. I think two more skeins will be enough to finish off Adam's sweater."

I walked over to the cubbyholes where the different yarns were kept and removed two balls.

Dora reached into a box she'd been unpacking.

"Look at this," she said, holding out the most scrumptious color of yarn. It reminded me of pistachio ice cream with a thread of pink cotton candy woven into it.

"Oh," I said, reaching out to touch the wonderful softness. "I love it. But what the heck would I make with this?"

"How about a sweater for Clarissa?"

"Are you serious? What makes you think she'd even like a hand-knit sweater?"

"I don't know for sure, but I do know it might be a nice way to break the ice between you. A lot of love goes into knitting. Each stitch just might have the ability to make your relationship together tighter."

I fingered the yarn. It *would* make a beautiful little girl's sweater. I recalled Clarissa's word for knitting—yarning—and I smiled.

"All right, let's find a pattern and I'll get enough of the yarn to complete the project."

"I really like it," Adam said that evening over dinner. He stabbed a piece of chicken with his fork and nodded. "I really do, Clarissa. But what made you decide to get your hair cut? Were the other girls in your class getting new styles?"

Clarissa shot a glance at me.

"Oh, you know how it is, Adam. A female gets sick of the same old thing. A woman's hair is her crowning glory, so they say. It's nice to have a bit of change."

My stepdaughter's head tipped down as she concentrated on her food.

I had to admit, Polly really had created magic. The new cut was adorable. Chin length and bouncy. It seemed to make Clarissa's eyes bigger and her cheekbones more pronounced.

Polly had taken me aside before we left the shop and related that Clarissa had told her that Billie got to go to the groomer for her cuts and she had just decided to try and cut her own hair.

I suppose I should be thankful that Clarissa hadn't chosen to use those scissors on Billie.

17

One of the things I loved best in college was the camaraderie among the girls. Being an only child, I hadn't grown up with sibling rivalry, nor had I enjoyed the closeness of having a sister. Gathering in a dorm room, with CDs playing, sharing snacks, and catching up on everyone's latest news was nirvana for me. Joining the other women on the island at the yarn shop for a knitting session was very similar, and I always enjoyed it.

As I worked on the intricate pattern of the sweater for Clarissa, I was glad I'd decided to keep the shop open later one evening a week so we could all gather. I loved the fact that when a woman reached a certain age, age simply didn't matter with friendship. I was the youngest one in the group, and at eighty-nine, Miss Margaret was the oldest, and yet, all of us were bound together in more ways than just a love for knitting.

"So can you believe it?" I heard Miss Polly say. "Almost got herself arrested, she did."

My head shot up and I paused with my yarn overs. "Who're you talking about?"

"Helen. Helen Thompson. The Red Hatters went to see a musical in Gainesville last week. One of the women got sick and had to cancel, so of course she had to forfeit the price of her ticket. Helen thought a refund was in order, but the theater refused. So what did Helen do? Stood there, on the sidewalk, right in front of the theater and tried to sell the ticket to other patrons. She planned to give the money back to the girl who wasn't able to go. There she stood, with her purple dress and red hat, doing *scalping*. Along comes an officer and I tell ya what—he was inches from arresting her, he was. The rest of us all jumped to her rescue and maybe twenty women were too much for him, I don't know. But he agreed to let Helen go with a warning. Can you just imagine. . . . We might have been bailing her out of an Alachua County jail."

Helen being in jail wouldn't have been funny, but all of us started chuckling at the thought of her being dragged off in handcuffs. A prim and proper Red Hatter—not very good publicity for the organization.

I shook my head. "You gals are something else. Like a bunch of teenagers."

Dora laughed. "Yeah, seems the older we get, the more daring we become."

"So what's the latest on the new developer?" Twila Faye asked.

Raylene shook her head. "I'm still not quite sure, but Harry dropped by there the other day. Seems the owner has some mighty big plans for turning the space into a fancy-dancy coffee house."

"What?" I burst out. "We already have a coffee place—Gracie's."

"Yup, but don't think that's gonna make a whit of difference to this wheeler-dealer. Harry says he thinks this guy is doing it on purpose—to force Grace out. All he really wants is the property where she's at, and she's not about to sell."

It was going on a month now since I'd heard from Grace. So I had been right when I overheard Tony that evening at the Island

Room. That rotten guy didn't care about Grace at all. It was just an excuse to try and buy her building.

"What the heck does he want her place for?"

Twila Faye piped up. "Well," she said, leaning forward over the knitting in her lap, "I heard we might be gettin' a French restaurant in Cedar Key."

I nearly choked on hearing this. "A French restaurant? Is the guy nuts?"

"Yup." Twila Faye nodded. "Real upscale, with white table-cloths, high prices, and even a chef that happens to be French."

"Doesn't that just beat all," Dora said, shaking her head. "Lived here all my life and this is the first time somebody thought about doing that."

"How can he even think to make money on such a venture?" Polly asked.

"You're right," I said. "The biggest time for merchants is on the weekends. That's when they pull in the most money from tourists. I'm not sure the locals would be that interested in paying the exorbitant prices he'll probably be charging just for a weeknight evening out."

"What's Grace say about all this?" Polly asked, looking directly at me.

"I'm sure I wouldn't know. We've had a falling-out, and I haven't heard from her in quite a while."

"Oh, that's too bad," Dora said. "I'm sorry to hear that the two of you are still on the outs. You're such good friends."

I didn't feel it was right to share all the details of the cause. "Yeah, well, those things happen," was all I replied.

"Right," Twila Faye said. "I'm sure it'll all blow over."

I wasn't so sure about that.

I walked into the house to find Adam going through files at the desk in the great room.

Leaning over to kiss his cheek, I asked, "Is Clarissa in bed?"

He nodded, absorbed in looking at some papers. "Yeah, I got her off at eight."

"What are you so involved with?"

Placing my knitting bag on the coffee table, I sat on the sofa and kicked off my shoes.

"Had a call tonight—from my lawyer."

"Oh?" I knew this was probably not going to be good news.

"Well, it seems Carrie Sue did get herself an attorney. Claims she wants what's rightfully hers—Clarissa."

"You mean she's going to fight you for full custody again?"

"No, my lawyer doesn't think so, but we can't trust anything when it comes to Carrie Sue. But she's saying she wants Clarissa twice a month and for the entire summer."

My first thought was that my days of motherhood might be coming to an abrupt halt, but my second thought was that this can't be very good for a child—back and forth so much.

"So what's the plan?"

"Well, Trina told me to make sure I have all the canceled checks from four years' worth of support. That's what I'm getting together now. They've set up a court date for the first week in November. All we can do is go to the hearing and see what happens."

"God, Adam," I said, getting up to put my arms around his neck. "I'm so sorry. Does Clarissa know about this yet?"

He shook his head and reached up to grasp my hand. "No, and I'd rather she didn't right now. She's been with us almost five months, and she's settled in well. She's doing good in school, making friends and Billie—I know for certain there's no way Carrie Sue would let her bring the dog up there during her visits."

That dog meant everything to Clarissa, and as much as I was against it, bringing Billie into our home was one of the best things we could have done. Clarissa had been true to her word and taken over much of the responsibility of having a pet.

"We'll think positive," I told him, heading to the bedroom to get into my nightgown.

Life sure did have a way of throwing out some twists and turns, I thought. A year ago I was preparing for my wedding, not thinking about children at all. And here we were with a child almost nine years old that I was coming to accept, but she could end up spending more time in Georgia with Carrie Sue than with us.

I turned around as Adam came in the bedroom.

"I turned out all the lights," he said. "Thought maybe we could just relax in here."

"Good idea. How about a glass of cognac to unwind?"

"That would be great. I'll get it."

I curled up on the sofa in our sitting room waiting for Adam to return. Although I'd been concerned about bringing Clarissa into our home, the thought of not having her for an entire summer made me feel sad. Poor Adam. He was such a great father and yet—the courts always seemed to favor the mother, as he'd said. If Carrie Sue hadn't been in that accident, Clarissa would still be with her.

"Here you go," he said, handing me a small glass filled with amber liquid.

"Here's to good things happening," I told him, raising my glass.

He nodded before taking a sip.

"Won't the court see how disruptive it would be for Clarissa? Going back and forth twice a month and then not seeing you for three months. It's not right."

"It wasn't right when they denied me custody the first time. The visitation they allowed me wasn't right. But it's not about what's right, Monica. When it comes to the court system and children, it's never been about *right*."

"Hey," I said. "Clarissa's birthday is next week. Are we going to have a party?"

Adam nodded. "She mentioned that this evening. I asked her

what she wanted and she said she already got her gift—Billie. But she said she'd like to have a few friends over for cake and ice cream."

I could do cake and ice cream, and I recalled my ninth birthday. My mother had gone all out with decorations and games and favors. I was terrible at organizing something like this and knew the one person who'd be perfect was out of my life. It was times like this that I really missed Grace. She made everything so much more fun.

"I could try and organize a party."

Adam's face brightened. "Really? I didn't want to put any pressure on you, but that would be great. I love you, Monica."

I felt his lips on mine and placed my glass on the coffee table, allowing him to slide me down onto the sofa. All thoughts of parties drifted out of my mind.

✎ 18 ✎

The wind chimes sounded at Spinning Forward and I glanced up from the computer to see Grace walk in.

Passing a double latte toward me, she said, "Can we be friends again? I'm sorry."

I jumped up to pull her into my arms. "You silly goose, you don't have anything to be sorry for. It was all me—shooting off my mouth as usual when I shouldn't have. I'm so sorry for that."

Grace squeezed me and then pulled away to dab moisture that formed on her eyelids.

"Yeah, well, you were right on. Everything you'd said was true, Monica. That lousy bastard was only dating me to soften me up and sell him my property."

I uncovered the Styrofoam cup and took a sip of the delicious coffee. "Thanks," I said. "So I take it you brought it to an end?"

Grace curled up on the sofa and nodded. "Oh, yeah. Big-time. It's a wonder you didn't hear me telling him off."

I had witnessed Grace's temper in the past, and a smile crossed my face. Good. He deserved it.

"I'm sorry. I really am sorry it turned out like this for you."

Grace shrugged. "Hey, with those George Clooney looks, he was too good to be true anyway." She brushed an auburn curl off her forehead. "And did ya hear? Did ya hear that good-for-nothing is going to open a *coffeehouse* and try to put me out of business?"

So she did know. "I heard. You know the locals will never go there, Gracie. They're a loyal bunch. You're not worried about that, are you?"

"I'm not sure. I guess only time will tell. So what's been going on in your life? How's the rug rat doing?"

I laughed. "Actually, pretty well. Settling in, and except for damn near scalping herself, things have been fairly calm."

"What?"

I proceeded to bring Grace up to date on the hair-cutting episode and also the impending court hearing.

She shook her head. "Life is just plain unfair sometimes, isn't it? I feel bad for Adam. He's done everything possible to do the right thing, and it seems to come back and bite him."

"Hey," I said, changing the subject. "I'm in the midst of planning a birthday party for Clarissa for next week. Any chance you could help me? I'm not sure I have a clue how to entertain ten little girls."

Grace laughed. "Ah, that's my specialty. Let's see, it might be too late to get the Chippendales, but I could possibly arrange for Johnny Depp to make an appearance."

"Yeah, right—nine-year-olds probably don't even know who Johnny Depp is."

"Sure they do. *Pirates of the Caribbean* and all that. But yes, I'd love to help you plan the party. Do kids still play Pin the Tail On the Donkey? Only kidding—I'll speak to some of the moms who come in the coffee shop."

"You're a lifesaver. Thanks, Gracie." I got up from the sofa and ruffled the curls on the top of her head. "And thanks for being such a good friend. I'm glad we're speaking again."

"Me too," she said, walking over to inspect a recent arrival of yarn. "I need a new knitting project to keep me busy."

I picked Clarissa up at school and when we got home, she released Billie from the crate and took her into the yard.

After making myself a cup of tea, I began sorting clothes in the laundry room and could see Clarissa had perched on the stool in the kitchen to begin her homework.

"Monica?" she hollered.

"Yeah?" I said, walking back into the kitchen.

"Do you think I'll ever have to go and stay with my mother again?"

Her question took me by surprise. I was expecting something along the lines of a math problem.

"Well, uh . . . I don't know. Why?"

She was silent for a moment and then said, "Because I like it here."

She did? I mean, yes, she had a nice room and a nice home, not to mention a loving father. But I'd often wondered if she really *liked* being with us.

"And your dad is thrilled to have you here."

"So will I have to go back and stay with my mom?"

I pulled up a stool to join her at the counter. "I honestly don't know, Clarissa." Did I have a right to ask the child if she missed her mother? "Your dad has full custody of you now."

"Yeah, but I know my mother. She always wants what she can't have."

How did a child of almost nine have such insight?

"Well, if she goes to court, she does have a right to see you. You know, for visitation on weekends and during the summer. It might be nice to go back to Georgia and visit with her for a while, don't ya think?"

Clarissa remained silent and then reverted to that phrase I hadn't heard in a while, "I guess."

I left her to finish up her homework while I peeled potatoes for supper. Then I grabbed my latest Fern Michaels novel and headed to the great room.

"I'm going to lie down on the sofa for a little while to read. Do you need any help with anything?"

"No, I'm okay," she told me.

I must have dozed off because I opened my eyes to see the book propped on my chest, and the clock on the mantel told me it was already 4:30. Yawning, I stretched and stood up. Clarissa wasn't at the counter. Her books were neatly piled up beside her backpack. Walking to the other side of the house, I could hear her talking to Billie in her room.

I walked toward my bedroom and my nasal passages were assaulted with the fragrance of Douce Amère—a very expensive perfume my mother had gotten me on one of her trips to Paris. What the heck? Stepping over the threshold, I saw a puddle in the middle of my bureau. It appeared to be effectively leaving an oval stain on the oak wood. I ran to pick up the bottle and found that not a drop was left.

Anger coursed through me. I never minded letting people borrow my things—but it had always irked me when somebody touched items without asking. And this time, a much-loved perfume was gone.

Grabbing the bottle, I went running through the house to Clarissa's room. Pushing open her door, I stood with the evidence raised above my head. "Did you do this? What were you doing in *my* room touching stuff that didn't belong to you? You have no right to touch my things!"

Clarissa scooped up Billie and backed away toward her bed. "I just wanted to smell it. I didn't mean for it to fall over and spill."

"Well, it did!" I screamed, feeling myself losing control. "It did, and you've ruined the wood on my bureau. Not to mention the fact that it was a very special perfume from my mother."

I spun around to see Adam standing in the doorway, pausing long enough to see the look of concern on his face. Then I pushed past him and raced to my bedroom, slamming the door.

Plopping on the bed, I burst into tears. I wept for the lost perfume, but I also cried for my terrible behavior. I just wasn't cut out to be a mother. Taking care of a child and all that went with it was something I couldn't seem to learn. But dammit, Clarissa had no right coming in and touching my personal things.

About ten minutes later, Adam opened the door and came over to the bed.

"Are you all right?"

I sat up, rubbing my tearstained eyes. "No, I'm not all right. I haven't been all right for months."

Sitting down beside me, he reached for my hand. "I'm sorry I've done this to you—turned your life upside down as a newlywed. But you didn't need to scream at her like that." I thought he'd come in to make me feel better, and here he was admonishing me?

My temper flared again and I jumped up to begin pacing the room. "What exactly do you mean by that?"

"What I mean is," he said, with an edge to his voice, "is that you were out of control. That's no way to deal with a child. She didn't spill the perfume on purpose, Monica. You should have calmed down before talking to her about it."

"Oh, well, excuse me! I must have missed that lesson in Mothering 101. She had no right coming in here and touching my things. If she'd stayed out of here, none of this would have happened. You didn't even know about her cutting her own hair. I covered for her—let you think it was her idea to get her hair cut. And this is the thanks I get? You're taking her side?"

"Monica, it's not about sides."

I could feel the tears coursing down my face. "Oh, it's most definitely about sides," I said, reaching into the closet for my overnight bag.

"What're you doing?"

Throwing in my night gown, a robe, underwear, and few other things, I said, "I'm packing, that's what I'm doing."

"Oh, running away like you did all those times before?"

I felt like a vise had gripped my heart.

"Monica, just because we're having an argument, running away isn't going to solve this."

I knew that anything I said at that moment I'd probably regret for the rest of my life. Grabbing my knitting bag, I headed to the front door.

"I'll be at Gracie's," I tossed over my shoulder.

19

The aroma of coffee and sunlight caused me to open my eyes. For a moment I felt disoriented and looked around the room. I was on Grace's sofa bed in her living room. All the heartache of the night before came rushing back. I'd thought for sure that Adam would have called and coaxed me back home, but that hadn't happened.

I felt something soft rubbing against my arm and saw that Grace's huge black and white cat was curled up beside me. Turning over, I began stroking his fur and realized perhaps I shouldn't have had that last martini the night before. My head was pounding.

Swinging my legs to the side of the sofa, I got up tentatively and stretched. I definitely needed aspirin.

Making my way to the medicine cabinet in the bathroom, I saw the note on the table that Grace had left for me.

Aspirin in medicine cabinet. When you're up to it, come downstairs for fresh coffee and muffins. Love—Gracie

She was such a good friend. I knew she was tired, but she'd stayed up with me till almost two in the morning listening to me bitch and complain.

Walking back into the kitchen, I poured myself some water, downed the aspirin, and saw it was 12:30. God! I hadn't slept this late in months. Of course, my normal bedtime wasn't 2:00 A.M. either.

Before heading to the shower, I checked my cell phone. No message from Adam.

"Ah, decided to join the living, huh?" Grace said as I walked into the coffee shop.

"I'm sorry I kept you up so late."

"Not a problem." She passed me a cup of strong coffee. "What're friends for?"

I smiled before taking a sip. "You're the best."

"Any word from Adam?"

"No. Nothing."

Grace remained silent.

"He hasn't been in touch with you, has he?"

She shook her head. "Not a word."

"Hmm," I said, as I sat at one of the tables to look through the *Cedar Key News*.

Grace came over to join me. "You know, you just might have to bite the bullet on this one."

"What do you mean?"

"You might have to put your stubborn streak aside and be the first one to make a move."

"Me? Go crawling back to him? I didn't do anything wrong."

Grace said nothing.

"Did I?" I questioned, an uneasy feeling settling over me.

"You weren't wrong to be angry, Monica. But . . . I think you could have handled it all differently. She *is* only eight years old. I have to agree with Adam—Clarissa didn't spill the perfume on purpose. It was an accident."

I blew out a deep sigh. "Well, yeah. . . . I know that. But . . ."

"That's why being a parent is so damn hard. She was wrong to be touching your things, but your reaction was as childish as Clarissa's behavior. If you'd waited until you'd calmed down, you could have explained to her why she was wrong and then passed out a punishment to her. This way, nothing got accomplished."

Maybe Grace was right. Obviously losing my temper and screaming like a banshee had only escalated the entire episode. And here I was, alone without Adam.

A couple of hours later I walked into my empty house. Billie was in her crate, and at the sight of me her tail began wagging as she whimpered for my attention.

"Come on," I said, clipping on her leash to take her in the yard. "You probably hate me too, but I'll take you out to pee."

When we came back inside, I wandered into my bedroom. The subtle scent of the perfume still lingered in the air but the mess had been cleaned up. Adam had placed a lace doily over the stain where the wood had been scarred.

I walked into the kitchen and prepared myself a cup of tea. Waiting for the water to boil, I wondered if this was the reason Sybile had given up my mother at birth. Raising a child was just too tough for her.

My head turned to the sound of Adam and Clarissa coming in the back door.

If Adam was surprised to see me standing in the kitchen, he showed no sign. Clarissa stood beside Adam, a look of apprehension on her face. Nobody spoke for a few moments.

"I'm back," I said, knowing this was obvious.

Adam nodded and placed his backpack on the counter. Clarissa did the same thing, taking her cues from her father.

"I . . . uh . . ." I cleared my throat. "I'm sorry everything hap-pened the way it did yesterday." Still no response from my husband or stepdaughter. I looked directly at Clarissa. "I shouldn't have screamed at you the way I did. It was wrong."

I saw Adam shoot a look to his daughter with raised eyebrows, waiting.

"I was wrong to touch the perfume," she said, glancing at Adam, before going on. "I shouldn't have been touching your things and I didn't mean to spill the bottle. I'm sorry."

I folded my arms across my chest and nodded. *Now what?* I wondered.

"We need to have a family discussion," Adam said, going to the stove to shut off the boiling water. Reaching for another cup, he prepared the tea and looked at Clarissa. "Would you like some Gatorade?"

She nodded and took a seat at the counter.

After placing the drinks in front of us, Adam sat down.

"What happened yesterday was unfortunate. I know how much that perfume meant to you, Monica. Clarissa has agreed to save up all her allowance money and send it to your mother in Paris so she can purchase another bottle for you."

Well, that seemed fair.

"I'd asked Clarissa what she thought her punishment should be in addition to replacing the perfume. She mentioned her birthday party. But I think giving up her party might be a little too extreme. You're her stepmother, Monica. What's your opinion?"

Cancel her party? That *did* seem a bit rash.

"Well, yeah. . . . I agree with you. I think Clarissa should have her party as planned. But I think she should give up her PlayStation Portable for a week." Where on earth had that decision come from? Maybe I was getting the hang of this mother stuff after all.

I caught the look of distress that crossed Clarissa's face. She loved playing with that toy and did so as much as she could.

"Well?" Adam said, looking at his daughter.

Clarissa slowly raised her bowed head. "Yeah, all right," she replied reluctantly.

"Go into your room and bring it out here to Monica. She'll return it to you in one week."

When Clarissa left the kitchen, Adam came and stood in front of me. Taking my face in his hands, he said, "I missed you last night. I missed not having you next to me. I'm glad you're back."

"I'm glad I'm back too. And, Adam . . . I love how you love me."

20

The morning of the birthday party I was filling paper cups with nuts and candy when Dora showed up with the cake she'd created.

"Oh, wow, it's gorgeous," I said, holding the back door open.

She placed the box on the counter and stood back to admire her work.

"It is kinda nice, isn't it?"

Walking closer to inspect the pale pink cake with ribbons of rose-colored frosting and small white flowers, I nodded. "Clarissa will love it. Look at the little dog. It looks just like Billie, and the little girl holding the leash looks just like Clarissa. You're amazing, Dora."

She smiled and waved her hand in the air. "What time does the gala event begin?"

"At four. First a barbecue, then the cake and ice cream, and then she'll open her gifts."

"Oh, I almost forgot. I have her gift in the car. I'll run out and get it."

Dora returned with Opal behind her.

"Hey, sweetie," she said, coming over to plant a kiss on my cheek. "Oh, my, will ya look at this cake. Dora, I swear you should open a bakery on the island. Isn't that just the cutest thing? Where's the little birthday girl? I have her gift here."

"Clarissa should be right back. She took Billie for a walk. Would you both like some sweet tea?"

"I have to go open the yarn shop," Dora said. "But you be sure to wish Clarissa a happy birthday for me."

"I will, and thanks so much for the cake, Dora. I really appreciate it."

I poured two glasses of tea and joined Opal at the counter.

"So how's everything going?" she asked. "Any further word from that wretched Carrie Sue?"

"No. The court date is set for early November."

"Well, no judge in his right mind would award that woman custody a second time. That's all I have to say. Clearly, Adam is the best parent to raise my granddaughter."

I had to agree with her on that.

"Oh, before I forget," she said. "I know your birthday and anniversary are the end of October. I'm still going to be here on the island, so I want you to know that I'm offering up my babysitting services. The two of you need to get out and celebrate. Now, I know it's none of my business, but I think you should go away somewhere for a few nights. Be alone for a while."

That had a definite appeal to it. Just Adam and me.

"That's so nice of you, Opal. I'll speak to Adam and we'll let you know."

"Let me know what?" he said, coming into the kitchen.

"Your mother just offered to take Clarissa in late October so we can go away for a few nights to celebrate our anniversary and my birthday."

"That's a great idea. Thanks, Mom. And yes, we'll take you up on it."

"Really?" I said, welcoming the thought of a romantic interlude.

"Yeah, how about Amelia Island? You've never been there and I think you'll like it. It's only about a three-hour drive from here."

"Sounds perfect. It's a deal and thanks, Opal."

"It'll be my pleasure. I sure do love spendin' time with that granddaughter of mine."

It was easy to see she enjoyed Clarissa, and Clarissa always looked forward to spending time at Opal's house. I was convinced there was a part of Opal that had never grown up, and Clarissa had a way of pulling out that child within her.

"Dora did a super job with the cake, didn't she?" Adam said, leaning over to inspect it.

"Yeah, she has all kinds of creative talents."

"Well, I have to be moseying along," Opal said, jumping off the stool. "Have myself a spa appointment in Gainesville at noontime. Now, if I could just find myself a beau who'd appreciate my assets, I'd be all set."

I laughed. "Opal, you're too much. You'll be back later for the party?"

"Wouldn't miss it for anything."

With Grace's help I managed to throw a successful party for my stepdaughter, and with her ingenuity we managed to keep them entertained with games and fun. Clarissa seemed happy to be the center of attention and I was impressed with the sincerity she demonstrated in appreciation of her gifts. She had a knack for making each girl feel the gift she'd chosen was extremely special.

Adam walked out to the deck and passed me a glass of white wine.

"I think you earned this," he said, pulling up a lounge beside me. "It was a great party, Monica, and I know Clarissa loved it."

"Yeah, I think she did," I said, smiling. "Is she still in her bubble bath?"

He laughed and nodded. "I just hollered in to her. Told her she'd better be careful or she'll come out looking like a prune."

"She really loved all those French bath products my mother sent her." I took a sip of wine and sighed.

"Something wrong?"

"I guess I'm just surprised that Carrie Sue didn't acknowledge her birthday at all. No card, no gift, not even a phone call."

"I think that's why this party meant so much to Clarissa. It's the first time in four years she's had one. But you're right—there she is moaning about wanting more custody rights, and she doesn't even remember her daughter's birthday."

"I wonder what Clarissa thinks, though. I mean, for your mother to forget your birthday—that borders on abandonment."

"That's why I feel she likes it so much here with us. She just wants to be part of a family, and we've given that to her. She hasn't said anything to me about Carrie Sue, and I feel it's better not to mention the subject."

"I know—even with the incident over the perfume and her punishment, I do get the feeling she'd rather be here with us."

"Parents are supposed to guide and protect their children. Disciplining them is part of the deal. Deep down inside, kids know that. When they're left to flounder on their own, like Clarissa was with Carrie Sue, it makes them feel lost and uncertain. Children learn by example. She might not like the punishment, but I'd bet anything she understands it. She knows I love her, and that's all that matters."

I hadn't discussed it with Adam, but I wasn't so sure that I *loved* Clarissa. Those maternal instincts still weren't surging inside me. Maybe they never would. Maybe this was the best I could hope for—a neutral relationship where we tolerated each other. My thoughts were interrupted by her voice in the doorway.

"Monica?"

"Yeah?" I looked over as she walked onto the deck, clad in her new Dora the Explorer pajamas and matching slippers, with Billie trailing behind her.

"Thank you for my party."

"Oh," I said, taken by surprise with her gratitude. "I'm glad you enjoyed it."

"I did. All the girls said it was the best party they'd ever been to."

I smiled. "It *was* a fun time. I enjoyed it too."

"I'm ready for bed now, Dad," she told Adam.

"Okay, birthday girl," he said, getting up and following her into the house.

I couldn't help but wonder if Clarissa thought it odd that I'd never offered to tuck her into bed. She always said good night to me, but we didn't exchange any hugs or kisses at bedtime like she did with Adam. It was like we had an invisible wall between us—a barrier that prevented us from getting too close.

✎ 21 ✎

Sipping my coffee, I glanced at Adam and Clarissa across the breakfast table. Had it only been six months since we received the phone call from social services? It was beginning to feel like Clarissa had always been a part of our life.

"So what's your plan for today?" I asked them.

Clarissa's face broke out into a smile. "Miss Tilly said she'll take me to paint plein air today. That means painting outdoors, you know."

I saw Adam grin. "Does it? My goodness, you're beginning to sound like a professional artist."

"Oh, Miss Tilly says I'm an artist-in-training," Clarissa said, with pride in her voice.

"What is it that you'll be painting outdoors?" I inquired.

She hesitated for a second and then said, "I can't tell you. It's a surprise."

Must be something for Adam, I thought.

"And what are you doing today?" I asked him.

"Well, you'll be at the yarn shop for a few hours, so I think I'll take a drive into Chiefland and get those rose bushes you wanted to plant."

"Great. We can do that later this afternoon when I get home."

"You didn't forget about my sleepover tonight, did you?" Clarissa asked.

I shot a glance across the table to Adam. Sleepover? Oh God, it *was* Saturday, and I now recalled she'd planned to have a few girl-friends spend the night.

"No, no . . . I didn't forget," I told her. "What time will they be here?"

"Dad said we could do a barbecue, so they're coming over around six."

"Just some hamburgers and hot dogs," Adam said. "Nothing special."

"Right. Well, I'll be home from the shop around two, so I can do up a batch of macaroni and cheese to go with it."

"Oh, goody. I love macaroni and cheese." The smile on Clarissa's face confirmed this.

"Okay," I said, getting up from the table. "So that's all set, and I'm headed to the shower."

I was just finishing up the salad I'd brought for lunch when the phone rang.

"Spinning Forward," I said.

I had finally gotten myself to the bank a few weeks before, so I was happy to hear the bank manager's voice.

"Monica, I'm pleased to let you know that your loan has been approved."

"Oh! Wow! That's terrific! That'll really help with some new ideas that I have. Thank you so much."

"It's our pleasure doing business with you. You can stop by on Monday to sign the final papers. Let me be the first to congratulate you on being the official new owner of Spinning Forward. I hope your business will be very successful."

"Thanks. See you on Monday."

Hanging up the phone, I turned around to see Grace coming in the door.

"Hey," I said. "What's up?"

"What's up is that good-for-nothing-scoundrel has a huge sign in front of his shop announcing the opening of his posh *coffee café* for next week."

"He's finished with the remodeling?"

Grace went to the table in back of me to pour herself a cup of coffee.

"Apparently so," she said, flopping onto the sofa.

"He *is* a rat, but I tend to doubt that his business will interfere with yours, Gracie."

"Don't be too sure of that. I heard he has a ritzy atmosphere in there. Leather sofas and chairs and he's offering free Wi-Fi. He also hired somebody who's going to make quiches and Cuban sandwiches at lunchtime."

Hmm, this guy was determined to pull in the customers.

"Well, I have difficulty seeing any of the locals going to such a place. That's not their style. They love your place because they just sit around and enjoy the good coffee and sweets with the conversation."

"That might be, but I have a sick feeling that I'll be losing all of my tourist customers on the weekend."

"There must be something we can do."

"Short of burning the place down, I don't know what that might be."

I laughed, but I hoped that Grace was only making an attempt at being humorous.

"Well . . . we can . . . I know! We can boycott the place. You know, gather together a bunch of the locals and walk past there with picket signs."

Now Grace was laughing. "Oh, right. And we'll all end up in the Levy County jail."

"Not necessarily. Nonviolent protests aren't against the law."

Grace plunked her coffee cup onto the table and jumped up. "Wait! I have an idea. I can have some T-shirts made up. You know, stuff like 'Don't Support Developers' and 'Locals Rock at Grace's Place.' I'll pass them out free to my customers to wear around town on the weekends." She began pacing back and forth across the shop. "Oh, and I know. . . . I can turn my place into a sixties-style coffeehouse with authors visiting and poetry readings, even some music."

Maybe she was on to something. "Might not be a bad idea. If you could contact some Southern writers, they just might be willing to come here to do readings and sell their books. You play the guitar. Why not drag it out and have some folk music to offer your customers?"

She ran toward me, hand lifted in the air for a high five. "I can do this. Thanks for your suggestions. This just might work and push Mr. High and Mighty right off this island."

I laughed as my hand made contact with Grace's. It wouldn't be easy, but I had a feeling that Grace had the tenacity to pull this off.

"Oh, hey! The bank just called. I got the loan."

Excitement covered Grace's face. "That's great, Monica. I'm so happy for you. You've now officially joined the ranks of us businesswomen. You go, girl!"

I hope so, I thought. *I hope that even with a shaky economy I'll be able to stay afloat.*

Adam and I sat on the deck watching the girls toast marshmallows on the grill. Laughter and giggles filled the backyard and it occurred to me that children really did know how to enjoy the simple things in life. It made me wonder how we seemed to lose that ability on our way to adulthood.

"They're having fun, aren't they?" Adam said.

"Yeah, that was a good idea you had. I'm thinking when they're finished maybe I'll bake some cookies with them. They'll probably want a snack later tonight."

I felt Adam reach for my hand.

"You're getting into this mothering, aren't you?"

The look of love on his face was difficult to miss, and I smiled. "Oh, I don't know about that. But . . . I guess you could say I'm trying."

When the girls finished roasting marshmallows, they joined us on the deck. I realized I enjoyed hearing their conversations about school projects, television shows, and childish tidbits of gossip. I thought back to my own childhood friends and was sad that over the years I'd lost touch with all of them. I'd always envied my mother her relationship with Ali—a friendship that spanned almost forty years. I felt even more grateful to have Grace in my life.

"Did you say we're going to bake cookies?" Clarissa asked.

"I did. Would you girls like to help me?"

"Can we lick the bowl after?" Kathryn questioned.

"You're not supposed to ask that," Zoe informed her.

I laughed and headed inside to the kitchen. "Come on, and yes, I think some bowl licking can be arranged."

Following Aunt Dora's recipe, we managed to get the cookies into the oven. The girls assisted in the cleanup and I noticed Zoe had been unusually quiet since she'd arrived.

"How's your mom doing?" I asked her.

When I saw the sad look across her face, I was sorry I'd inquired.

After a moment, Clarissa said, "She isn't very good. They might have to have hops spits come to the house."

For a second I didn't understand what she was saying. "Oh . . . you mean hospice?" I said and saw Zoe nod.

That wasn't a good sign at all.

"And Zoe might have to leave Cedar Key to go live with her dad up north," Clarissa explained.

Geez, this seemed to be a huge burden for such a little girl. I felt my heart tug at the sorrow this child would be facing, and I knew Clarissa would miss her best friend a lot.

"I'm sorry to hear that. Zoe, I want you to know that if you do have to leave . . . you'll always be welcome to come and visit us. If your dad is agreeable, we'd love to have you stay with us during school vacations."

Zoe's face shot up to stare at me. "Really?" she asked hopefully. "Because when I spoke to my dad on the phone, he did say that. He said I could always come back here to visit."

"Of course you can," I reassured her. "Now why don't you girls get into your pajamas, and by then the cookies will be cool enough to eat."

Adam walked in from the deck. "I heard that conversation. That was nice of you to extend an invitation to Zoe."

"It's going to be really tough on both her and Clarissa. It's not right at all that children have to go through adult sorrow."

"I know," he said, pulling me into an embrace.

I got up during the night and was headed to the kitchen for a glass of water when I saw the light still on beneath Clarissa's door. The clock on the mantel said 2:05, and the girls were still awake.

Tiptoeing toward the bedroom, I heard soft murmuring and put my ear to the door.

"You're very lucky," I heard Zoe say. "Even though your real mama didn't want you, your daddy's new wife is very nice to you."

This didn't sound like a nine-year-old conversation to me.

"I know I am," Clarissa said. "I'm not sure Monica likes me, but she's never mean to me. Maybe your daddy's wife will be nice to you too."

"I don't think so," Zoe replied. "She doesn't like any children. I could tell when I visited them last time."

"It'll be okay, Zoe. We'll always be friends, and when we get grown-up, you can come back here and live forever."

"I wish I was going to live with somebody like Monica. I like her."

I heard a moment of silence before Clarissa replied, "I like her too. A lot. I just don't think she knows that yet, but I'd be very sad if I had to leave her and my dad."

I felt a lump forming in my throat as I quietly backed away from the door.

‏≈ 22 ≈

On Monday I knew I had the beginning of the head cold that was floating around the island. Everyone who came into the yarn shop seemed to be sneezing and coughing, and by Wednesday morning, I had managed to have a full-blown case of an upper respiratory infection.

Adam came into the bedroom to kiss me good-bye before leaving for work.

"Don't get too close," I warned, turning my head.

"Will you be okay here all day? Maybe I should call Dora and have her take you into town to the doctor."

"Nah, I'll be fine," I told him, reaching for a tissue as another sneeze escaped me. "I'm taking Tylenol and cough syrup. It just has to run its course. I don't want you and Clarissa catching it, though."

"Do you want me to cancel my meetings this afternoon? Clarissa will be home at noon. Half a day today for her."

"No, don't do that. I'm okay to get up and get her lunch. She'll be occupied doing her homework until you get home."

"Okay," he told me, leaning over to kiss the top of my head. "Now stay in bed and rest. I'll be back by four."

I heard the door close as Adam and Clarissa left and turned over to snuggle into my pillows.

When I awoke about ten, I felt a little better and decided to tackle the laundry that had piled up over the weekend. I fixed myself some soup and tea, loaded the washing machine, and crawled back into bed.

I felt myself being pulled from a deep sleep to the sound of my name. Opening one eye, I saw Clarissa standing at the foot of the bed, a worried expression on her face.

"What's wrong?" I asked, struggling to sit up.

"There's somebody here to see you."

I glanced at the clock on the night table and was shocked to see it was 2:00.

"Why didn't you wake me when you got in from school?" I asked, sticking my arms into the sleeves of my bathrobe. Not bothering with slippers, I followed Clarissa into the kitchen where I found myself slipping to my butt on the tile floor.

Wetness was saturating my bathrobe and nightgown as I sat in about two inches of soapy water. What the hell! Trying to get my bearings, I glanced around the kitchen and realized the washing machine had overflowed. Attempting to stand up, I surveyed the room to see the counter covered with spilled cereal, crumbs of toast, empty cheese wrappers, and globs of peanut butter and jelly. It was then that I saw the unfamiliar woman standing just inside the kitchen door.

Dressed in a drab gray suit, arms folded across her chest, the expression on her face reminded me of somebody that had just sucked on a lemon.

"Monica Brooks?" she inquired without an ounce of pleasantness. I could only nod stupidly.

"I'm with the Department of Children and Families in Gainesville."

Oh shit, was my only thought.

"I'm here today to do a spot check on the living conditions of Clarissa Brooks." Now looking like a foul odor was assailing her nostrils, she pointedly looked around the kitchen.

"Oh . . . oh, well, I'm really sorry for this mess." It was then that I saw Clarissa flattened against the sink, the worried expression on her face having turned to pure panic. "I'm sick with a cold—I've been in bed all day. . . ."

"Obviously," the woman sniffed.

If I thought things couldn't get any worse, I was wrong. It was at that moment that Billie must have realized we had a stranger in the house. The dog came running from Clarissa's room charging directly at the social worker, barking with a ferociousness that brought to mind a pit bull. The woman took a step back, but that didn't deter the dog.

"Billie!" both Clarissa and I screamed at the same time. "No!"

Clarissa sloshed forward in the water to scoop up the ball of fluff turned guard dog.

"Oh, gosh, I'm so sorry," I attempted to say, but by then the woman had her hand on the doorknob.

"Tell Mr. Brooks I'll be phoning him tomorrow," was all she said, and with that the slam of the door reverberated through the house.

Standing there, I glanced around the kitchen once again trying to figure out what had just happened, and my gaze caught Clarissa's face. She stood with Billie in her arms, her expression a map of worry, looking like she was ready to burst out crying any second. This was the closest I'd ever seen the child to tears.

The entire scene quickly replayed in my mind, and despite the possible seriousness of the situation, I began giggling. The giggles turned to genuine laughter over which I had no control.

Clarissa's face transformed from fear to surprise to doubt and within a few seconds her laughter joined mine in the kitchen. Two females unable to control the silliness, and it was in that moment that something shifted deep inside of me. I felt a bond, a connection with this child. I padded through the water to where she was standing and put my arm around her shoulders as our giggles began to subside.

Clarissa looked up at me as concern returned to her face. "Are we in trouble?"

"Probably," I said, not at all sure.

That was when her flood of tears came to the surface and I felt terrible for being so glib.

I turned her around to face me as tears poured down her face. "No, no. It'll be okay. Really."

"Are you . . . sure?" she asked between hiccups. "Will she make me go back to live with my mother?" Fresh tears poured forth. "I don't want to leave here like Zoe has to."

Pulling Clarissa into my arms, my first thought was how good she felt there. Trying to soothe her, I said, "No, don't be silly. You're not going anywhere. This was just a misunderstanding. We haven't done anything wrong . . . except to flood the kitchen."

This brought forth another hiccup followed by a giggle.

"Really?" she asked, doubt still lingering.

"Really," I told her. I kissed the top of her head. "But . . . can you tell me how this happened?"

Clarissa slowly moved away from my embrace. "Well, I knew you were sick and didn't feel good. So when I came home from school, I checked on you and you were sleeping. I didn't want to wake you, so I tried to make myself some lunch. Then I saw you were doing laundry. I put the clothes that were in the washer into the dryer and did the other load—but I must have done something wrong, because all the water came out and then that woman knocked on the door—and I didn't know what to do."

I smiled. "You did just fine, and I promise you everything will be all right. Now, maybe you can get the shop vac from the closet and we can clean up this mess."

Clarissa threw me a look of gratitude that I swear went all the way to my soul.

"Well," Adam said later that evening over dinner. "Sounds like I missed quite a fiasco here. From the way you've described that woman, she sounds like one of the characters at the orphanage in *Annie.*"

Clarissa and I exchanged a grin.

"She wasn't very nice at all, Daddy. Monica and I hadn't done anything wrong, and she was nasty. Are we in trouble, though?"

Adam reached over to take his daughter's hand. "Absolutely not. You're right. Neither of you did anything wrong. She'll call me tomorrow and we'll get this all straightened out. You're not to worry about it anymore."

"But . . ." Clarissa pushed food around on her plate before going on. "Can she make me go back to live with Mom in Georgia? I don't want that to happen."

"She can't do that, Clarissa. I have full custody of you. You do understand, though, if your mother wins visitation rights—well, that means you might have to stay with her one weekend a month."

"I'll have to go up to Georgia?"

Even a child could understand the foolishness of it all.

Adam nodded. "Yes, but we're not sure that'll happen." He paused for a moment before going on. "Clarissa, she *is* your mother. Are you certain you don't want to spend any time with her? I don't want you feeling like you have to choose between us. Your permanent home can be here with us, but I don't want you feeling guilty about loving your mother."

Her head shot up to stare at Adam and without a moment's hesitation, she said, "But I don't love her. I don't feel like I even *know* her. We hardly ever spent any time together. I was always with Trish."

I caught Adam's gaze and instinctively knew that everything I'd ever heard about parenting was true. It wasn't the gifts or monetary things a parent gave to a child that counted—it was something as simple as quality time and most of all, love.

❦ 23 ❧

Dora had planned a combined birthday and anniversary dinner at her home for me and Adam. I'd come to realize that in our family these types of gatherings were very important. Any excuse would do for a few generations to get together.

By the time Adam, Clarissa, and I had arrived, Saren, Grace, and Opal were enjoying a glass of wine.

Kisses and hugs were exchanged as Dora brought out Saren's famous mullet dip with the other appetizers.

"So y'all are headed to Amelia Island tomorrow?" Saren questioned.

"Yes," I told him. "It'll be nice to have a little getaway for a few days."

"And I'm looking forward to spending time with my granddaughter again," Opal said. "I've even come to love that little pooch of hers."

"Well, from what I heard, you've got yourself quite a little watchdog there," Dora told her.

"Everything turned out okay with that social worker, didn't it?" Opal questioned.

I nodded. "Yes, Adam handled it. She said they'll be back. I'll just make sure Clarissa's not doing the laundry the day she returns."

Clarissa laughed, and it made me feel good to see the worry had vanished from her face after Adam's talk with her.

Following a feast of seafood, cheese grits, homemade biscuits, and black-eyed peas, Dora brought out an elaborate cake that she'd made.

"Oh, this is gorgeous," I told her as I stood up to inspect her detailed work. She'd baked a rectangular carrot cake that had been divided with a frosting of lavender lilacs. One half had two red hearts entwined with *Adam & Monica* in script, while the other side read *Happy Birthday, Monica* in flowing blue.

"Blow out the candles," Dora said, "And then it's time for gifts."

"You guys help me," I told Adam and Clarissa, and together the three of us puffed out the flames.

"Birthday gifts first," Opal said, stacking the table with assorted boxes and gift bags.

"Wow, I love birthdays." I reached for the first box, unwrapping it to find a beautiful white shawl in an intricate pattern made by Dora. "This is just lovely. I'll wear it to dinner while we're away. Thank you."

Next were recent releases by Fern Michaels and Elin Hilderbrand from Saren.

"Your mama told me you might like those."

"Oh, I will," I said, leaning over to kiss his cheek. "Thank you."

I reached for a brightly colored mint green gift bag. The tag read *Mom & Noah*.

"Your mother had this mailed to me a few weeks ago," Dora explained. "She said it gave her another excuse to shop in Paris."

I laughed, and reaching inside, pulled out a beautiful pale blue silk nightgown and matching robe. Holding it up to admire, I said, "Oh, I just love it. It's perfect to take on our little getaway." I looked up to see the grin on Adam's face and sent him a wink.

I reached for Grace's gift and opened a rectangular box to find a gift certificate to our favorite spa in Gainesville.

"I figured we needed another girls' day out," she said.

I waved the paper in the air. "Oh yeah . . . I never turn down a day at the spa."

Opal's gift was a bottle of Magie Noire—Black Magic, another of my favorite French perfumes.

"And from me," Adam said, passing me a small box.

I opened it to find a slim gold chain with a small circular gold disc. Three birthstones had been embedded into the gold—mine, Adam's, and Clarissa's.

"Oh," I gasped, looking at Adam. "This is just gorgeous. Look, Clarissa, all three of us."

She came to stand beside me and inspect the piece of jewelry. "Do you like it? I helped Dad pick it out."

"I love it. I just love it. What a thoughtful gift." I handed it to Adam to clasp around my neck. Reaching up, I touched the coolness of the gold disc and fingered the stones. "Thank you so much to both of you."

"Oh," Clarissa said, running to bring me another gift. "This one is from me. Just me."

I raised my eyebrows and looked at Adam. He nodded and smiled.

I removed the birthday paper to find an 8x10 canvas of an exact replica of the Lighthouse. Moisture blurred my vision as I glanced at Clarissa. "*You* did this?"

Excitement covered her face. "Yes. . . . Well, Miss Tilly helped me a lot, but I really did most of it. Do you like it? We thought it would be nice to paint your grandmother's house."

I was speechless. It was an incredible gift, but what touched me even more was the fact that all those days she was off painting with Tilly, she wasn't making something for Adam—it was for *me*.

"Oh, Clarissa," I said, reaching out to pull her into my arms.

"It's stunning. Of course I love it, and I'll always treasure it. You have such talent."

"Ah, yup, must take after her great-grandfather," Saren said in his slow drawl, bringing forth a round of laughter.

"This was the best birthday I've ever had. Thank you, all of you, so much."

"And now the anniversary gift," Dora said. She passed an envelope to Adam and me.

"You open it," I told him.

He removed a piece of rectangular paper, glanced at it, and said, "Oh, wow," passing it to me.

I read the embossed paper—a four-night stay at the Partridge Inn in Augusta, Georgia.

"This is for us?" I looked up at five smiling faces.

"Ah, yup," Saren said. "All of us, we chipped in."

"It was your mother's idea," Dora explained. "She thought it might be nice for the two of you to get away more often. She booked you for early December. Thought you could do some Christmas shopping while you're up there."

I smiled. "My mom and Noah have been there many times, and I know they loved it—both the town and the inn. They said the inn is lovely with a lot of Old World charm. Thank you for being a part of this great gift." I was excited at the thought of another getaway with Adam. "Oh, but can you get a couple of days off work?" I asked him.

"That really was very nice of all of you," he agreed. "And yes, I have a few personal days I'll use. I've heard Sydney and Noah rave about this place, especially the Riverwalk, so I know we'll definitely enjoy it."

"And, Opal," Dora said. "If you're not here in December, I'd be more than happy to have Clarissa stay with me."

"Well, now, I guess that just gives me reason to stay a bit longer," she told us.

"What a great birthday and anniversary. This family really is the best."

"I coulda told ya that," Saren said with a chuckle.

"Time for the cake and ice cream." Dora got up to get dessert dishes from the kitchen.

I looked around at all the people I loved and felt a brief ache that Sybile was missing. She would have enjoyed this get-together. I missed her feisty ways and gravelly voice, but I also felt fortunate to have known her in the time I did. I strongly felt her presence and wondered if it was really possible that some souls lingered in our midst.

❧ 24 ❧

There's something about waking up in a hotel room, without an alarm clock or a need to be anywhere in particular, that gives me a sense of freedom. I turned over to find Adam curled up beside me still asleep.

Today was our last day on Amelia Island. We'd be heading back home tomorrow. It was wonderful spending two days here, with no interruptions in our conversations, no commitments to think about, doing what we wanted when we wanted. But I was ready to head back to my own little island.

It had been a good idea, though, to take the time to just be a married couple again. During the past six months, I'd almost forgotten what that felt like. I didn't feel any jealousy toward Clarissa, but she did consume a lot of Adam's time, and it made me feel special to have his undivided attention for a few days.

"Mornin', beautiful."

I felt Adam's hand slide across my body and I shifted to snuggle into his arm.

"Good morning, handsome. Did you sleep well?"

"Perfect. What time is it?"

I glanced at the watch on my wrist. "Eight-thirty. This has been a nice change from getting up at six."

"I know, and we get to do this again in about five weeks."

"I wish you didn't have to travel up to Georgia next week for that hearing."

"I do too," he said, now stroking my breast. "But we don't need to think about that right now."

"You have something else in mind?" I felt the stirring of desire.

"As a matter of fact, I do," he told me, sliding his hand between my thighs.

Being alone in a hotel room with the man I loved created another sense of freedom—the freedom to enjoy the luxury of being Adam's lover.

"Everything okay at home?" I asked Adam as he flipped his cell phone closed.

He nodded and took a sip of coffee. "Fine. Opal's having fun playing grandmother again. They're going to have breakfast and then take Billie to the park."

I laughed. "That dog adores her. I'm glad we got her for Clarissa."

"My Mom said they're invited to Dora's for supper tonight and Billie gets to go too. She's made herself part of the family."

I looked around the restaurant at other people having breakfast. Some couples alone, but a few with children.

"We *are* a family, aren't we?"

A look of surprise crossed Adam's face. "Of course we are. Did you have any doubt?"

I pushed around the scrambled eggs on my plate. "No . . . not really. It's just that I wasn't ever sure that Clarissa would feel at home with us, but I think she does. She doesn't want to have to be with Carrie Sue."

"I know. There isn't a thing I can do about it, but she might have to travel to Georgia once a month to stay with her. It doesn't seem right uprooting a child like that, but we both know most of the time the court doesn't do what's *right*."

"After that episode with the social worker, I feel that Clarissa and I have gotten closer. I can't explain it, but it's like something changed inside me. Do you think that's possible?"

Adam reached across the table for my hand. "I think it's absolutely possible. People change, situations change—sometimes for the good."

I still wasn't sure I could go so far as to say I *loved* her, but I felt a distinct fondness growing inside me. "Do you think that's what happens when women are pregnant? Maybe they're not all that excited about the idea of a baby at first—but then with time, this . . . this attachment grows?"

"I think that could be true, and the same goes for a guy. You have to realize he isn't even the one that carries that baby for nine months, and yet a love and a bond somehow develop."

I knew Adam must have experienced this when Carrie Sue was pregnant with Clarissa. "Do you remember when you felt that way? The exact moment that you knew you loved your daughter? Was it before she was born?"

Adam thought for a few moments and nodded. "Yeah, I know it was long before she was born. But I can't tell you precisely when. I guess . . . it just happened. But when it does—there's no turning back."

I wondered if I would ever experience that fierce love that a parent has for a child.

A little girl crying on the other side of the restaurant drew my attention. A couple in their thirties was trying to console the child, who looked to be about four. A middle-aged woman with white hair took the girl in her arms.

"It's okay, sweetie," I heard her say. "I'll see you again soon. When Grandpa gets better, we'll come to visit you."

This didn't seem to comfort the child as her sobs grew louder. "But . . . I . . . don't . . . want you to leave. I'll miss you."

I glanced across the table at Adam. It was heart wrenching to see a child filled with such despair, and I felt moisture burning my eyes. I now wondered if a child would ever love *me* as deeply.

We spent the rest of the day walking around in the downtown area. I loved the shops that dotted Centre Street, and we took the time to browse.

My eye caught the sign of Books Plus. "Oh, let's go look in there," I told Adam.

Walking into the independent book store reminded me of some that I'd visited as a child. A large, well-lit space greeted customers on entering. Displays and shelves were lined with books. I saw that one entire wall offered books by local authors or about Southern culture. Cushy chairs invited patrons to sit awhile as they browsed.

"What a great, cozy feel this place has," I said.

"Yeah, every time I ever visited here I couldn't resist stopping in."

My attention was drawn to the back of the store. A gazebo with comfy cushions beckoned for children, and I found myself heading in that direction. Surrounding the gazebo were walls of children's books. Everything was so colorful and brightly lit.

I got lost in all the wonderful books available for girls ages seven to ten.

"Find anything interesting?" I heard Adam say.

"Yeah," I said, holding out my arms loaded with books. "Look at these."

He smiled and looked at me with raised eyebrows. "Books about ballerinas and little girls with dogs? Shopping for Clarissa?"

I felt a grin crossing my lips. "Yeah, I couldn't resist. Do you think she'll like these?"

"She'll love them."

Walking out of the shop, clutching the bag in my hand, I realized this was the first time I had left a bookstore without a purchase for myself.

Across the street at the Christmas Shop, we found some adorable ornaments for our tree. Each one had our name painted on the front, and we also got a dog-shaped one for Billie.

"Where to now?" Adam questioned.

"Afternoon coffee would be good," I suggested.

"Great idea," he said, taking my hand and heading toward a coffee shop farther down the street.

I grabbed a table outside while Adam went in to order. Looking up and down the street at pedestrians, I let out a sigh. Couples strolling past holding hands, mothers pushing baby carriages—I liked this town, and it felt good just being here.

"Here ya go," Adam said, placing a cup of coffee in front of me.

"Thanks. I'm so glad we came here, Adam. I like it a lot."

"I thought you might. It's a fun place to visit and has a nice small-town feel to it. Will you be sorry to go home tomorrow?"

I shook my head. "No. Not in the least. This has been great, but I'm afraid my heart belongs to Cedar Key." I took a sip of coffee. "And that still surprises me."

"What do you mean?"

"I remember when my mother moved there. I just couldn't understand how she could leave the Boston area for some island off the coast of Florida. But then . . . I visited, and it didn't take long for me to figure it out. I guess I'm more like my mom than I ever thought. We're both Yankee girls—and yet, there's something about these small Southern towns that feels like home."

"I know what you mean. I think it could be that people up north have just become too busy. We really do have a slower pace here in the South. And when you slow down, that gives you time to appreciate what's around you."

* * *

"I'm so glad you booked here," I told Adam as we sat in the brick courtyard enjoying an after-dinner drink. A sprawling 350-year-old oak tree created a canopy above us as camellia bushes filled the evening air with their scent.

"The Florida House Inn is one of the popular places to stay here. I thought you'd like it."

"Do you think there's a ghost here?" I asked him, unsure where that thought had come from.

He laughed. "Are you still thinking your grandmother's ghost is at our house?"

"I don't know what to think, Adam. You have to admit it's pretty odd that Clarissa named her dog Billie, and how about that *woman* she said told her things? What woman is she talking about? How would she even know about Atsena Otie?"

Adam remained silent.

"I think Dora thinks it's possible. She feels that Sybile might be hanging around to give me a message or tell me something. That's creepy, isn't it?"

I felt Adam place his hand on my thigh.

"I've always felt that most anything is possible, Monica. I can't say I actually believe in ghosts. I've never encountered one—but then again, who's to say for sure. Maybe Dora's right. Maybe Sybile does have something to share with you before she can be at rest."

I placed my hand on top of his. "I just wish the hell I knew what it is she wants me to know."

❦ 25 ❧

"Here ya go," Grace said, walking into the shop loaded down with shopping bags.

I jumped up to help her. "What have you got there?"

"What I hope will put Mr. High and Mighty out of business. T-shirts."

She removed a neon pink one from the bag. Across the front, in bold, black letters, it said **Support Grace's Place** and, below that, **Not Developers.**

I smiled as I turned it over and saw a large mug of steaming coffee on the back.

"You *will* wear it around town and especially in front of his shop, won't you?" she asked.

"Of course I will. Do you think this will help?"

"Well, I'm thinking it'll stir up some conversation, and conversation is good. What I'm hoping is that tourists will stop to question what it all means and then all of us can give them our spiel. About how he purposely opened that place to put me out of business because what he really wants is *my* property."

"Makes sense to me. When are we doing this?"

Grace reached into a tote bag and produced a spiral-bound notebook. Flipping through pages, she said, "Well, people are signing up to do shifts. I could use you on Sunday from two till four."

I grinned at her organization. "So I just walk around downtown for two hours?"

"It wouldn't hurt to actually pop in there and get right in his face. That way customers will definitely see your T-shirt, and of course you'll go out of your way to make sure they do."

"Okay. Have you got one in there for Adam and Clarissa?"

Without hesitation, she whipped out a large size in bright orange and a children's size in a putrid shade of lime green.

I laughed as I reached for them. "You haven't left a stone unturned. Lots of people signed up?"

"More than I would have thought. Opal will be out tomorrow, and even Saren and Dora agreed to join her."

Yup—no doubt about it. Small-town people stuck together.

"So when's Adam leaving for Georgia?"

"Monday. The hearing is Tuesday afternoon."

Grace went to pour herself a cup of coffee. "Any word if mother of the year will be there?"

"Since she's the one that instigated all of this, I would imagine she will be."

"Do you really think she's interested in Clarissa?"

For the first time, I could honestly say, "No. Not in the least. It has more to do with her pride and winning. She's not about to let Adam come out on top."

Grace shook her head. "Nice. Instead of being more concerned what's best for the child. Oh—did you hear Sandy passed away last night?"

"Oh, God. Zoe's mom? Do you think they'll tell the kids in school today?" How would Clarissa deal with this? Not only the death, but with the loss of her best friend.

"Probably. I feel bad for Clarissa. It's not going to be easy when Zoe moves up north."

"I know." I glanced at my watch. "I'm going to close up a little early. I want to make sure I'm at school to get her when she comes out."

I could tell the moment I saw Clarissa's face coming out the front door of school that the children had been told.

"Are you all right?" I asked as she walked toward me.

"Yeah," she mumbled, falling in step beside me.

"Grace told me that Zoe's mom passed away. I'm so sorry."

"I am too. Zoe wasn't in school today. I wonder if she'll ever be back."

We headed down G Street toward home. "If she doesn't return to school, I know she'll be in touch to tell you good-bye before she moves up north."

Clarissa looked up at me. "Do you think so? I wanted to give her something."

"Yes, I do. If you don't hear from her, maybe you could call her next week."

Clarissa remained silent for the rest of the walk home.

When we walked in the door she greeted Billie and then took her out in the yard. I watched them from the kitchen window and knew this was very difficult for Clarissa. Losing a friend at any age isn't easy, but a childhood friend must be especially hard. I wondered what Clarissa was thinking and wished there were something I could do to make her feel better.

After spending some time in the yard, she came inside and without saying a word went straight to her room with Billie tagging along behind her. I heard the door close softly.

I was preparing to stuff the chicken for dinner when the front doorbell rang. Walking along the hallway I saw a strange woman standing on the porch—dressed in a suit, briefcase in hand, looking official. Oh God, this was my reprieve—the social worker.

I opened the door with a tentative smile. "Can I help you?"

"Yes, I'm Shelly Conway, a social worker with the Department Children and Families. Are you Monica Brooks?"

I nodded as I opened the screen door to let her in. This was a different one from the last time. I wasn't sure if this was good or bad. "Yes. Come on in."

"Thank you. Is Clarissa Jo also here?"

"She is. She's in her room. I'm afraid she got some disturbing news today. Her best friend's mother passed away last night."

An expression of genuine sorrow crossed the woman's face. "Oh, I'm terribly sorry. I'm sure this isn't a good time for her, but would it be possible to ask her a few questions?"

"Sure," I told her, leading the way into the kitchen. "If you'll wait here, I'll get her. Would you like some coffee or sweet tea?"

"Thank you, but no."

I headed to Clarissa's room and was grateful that at least this time my house was in order. Knocking on the door, I heard Clarissa holler, "Come in."

I explained that a social worker was here and needed to talk to her.

"Okay," she said and followed me to the kitchen.

"Hello," the woman told her. "I'm Miss Conway with the Department of Children and Families. I'm very sorry to hear about your friend's mother."

"Thank you. Zoe will have to move away now," Clarissa told her, settling herself into a chair at the table.

"Oh," Miss Conway replied, shooting a glance to me. "Why is that?"

"Because Zoe's parents were divorced, and now she'll have to go live with her dad and his wife up north."

"I see." The social worker nodded in understanding. "I imagine that's going to be very difficult for you when she leaves."

"Oh, it will be. I'm going to miss her a lot, but her dad said she can come back here for vacations to stay with us."

"That will be nice. I'm sure you'll both enjoy that. How would you feel if you had to move away, Clarissa?"

A look of concern crossed my stepdaughter's face. "Do I *have* to?"

"No, no," Miss Conway assured her, reaching across the table to pat Clarissa's hand. "No, I'm just wondering what your thoughts on that might be. Your mother lives in Georgia. Would you want to go back there to live with her?"

Without a second's hesitation, Clarissa said, "No. I like it here. Besides, my mother doesn't like dogs and I wouldn't be able to take Billie—and Billie would miss me an awful lot."

Miss Conway smiled as she glanced down at Billie curled up at Clarissa's feet.

"How are you doing in school? Do you like going to such a small school?"

"Yes, I like it a lot and I'm getting straight As. My dad teaches history at the school, you know."

"Yes, I did know that, and goodness, you're a great student. I'm sure your dad is very proud of you."

"He is."

A grin crossed Miss Conway's face. "So what is it that you like here? Do you have lots of friends? What do you do on the weekends?"

"Well, Zoe is my best friend—she always will be, but yeah, I have other girlfriends. I like being here with my dad and my grandmother." She paused for a fraction of a second. "And Monica. We do fun things together like going for walks and playing games and I get to have sleepovers with my friends."

"Didn't you do those kinds of things with your mother?"

I swear Clarissa looked at the social worker as if she had two heads.

"No, never," she said, emphatically. "My mother is always busy. She doesn't have time to play games with me, and I was never allowed to have sleepovers because she went out most nights and she said Trish couldn't be paid to watch all of us."

Miss Conway was writing into a blue notebook. "I see," she said and continued to write some more. "And Trish? Is this the nanny who cared for you when your mother was gone?"

"Yes. She was very nice to me. Sometimes she'd read to me and we'd play games."

"How about school? Did you get straight As at your other school too?"

Clarissa bent her head for a moment, looking like she wasn't sure how to answer. "No," she replied softly. "I didn't. I knew I could because I'm smart, but I didn't try very hard, except in art."

"Why was that?" Miss Conway questioned.

"Because nobody really cared."

Miss Conway capped her fountain pen, replaced the notebook in her briefcase, and stood up. "So—would I be correct in saying that you're very happy living here with your dad and Monica?"

A huge smile crossed Clarissa's face. "Oh, yes," she replied excitedly. "I'm very happy here. I don't ever want to leave—not even when I get to be a grown-up."

Miss Conway laughed and looked at me. "I think I have all of the information I need. Thank you so much for your time—both of you. And, Clarissa, you make sure you keep in touch with Zoe. Childhood friends are very special."

She turned to leave the kitchen and I followed her to the front door.

"Thank you again, Mrs. Brooks. The hearing is scheduled for next Tuesday up in Georgia, and I'll be faxing my report to the court there by tomorrow."

Without any indication as to what that report might say, she opened the door and headed to her car.

I walked back into the kitchen to find Clarissa giving a dog biscuit to Billie.

"Do you think we did okay this time?" she asked.

I smiled. "I think *you* did pretty darn good."

❦ 26 ❦

For a Tuesday, the yarn shop had been more crowded than usual. Dora was kept busy doing purchases while I tended to orders from the Internet. Within a week of developing my Web site, orders were already beginning to come in for Ewedora Stockings. I was glad that Dora was so motivated and thrilled that she was such a rapid knitter. I had put up posters in the window for knitting classes to begin after the first of the year and was pleased to see that so many people were interested.

"Whew," she said as a group of four women left the store loaded down with bags of yarn. "I swear somebody drove a bus onto the island this morning."

Laughing, I pushed my chair away from the computer. "Yeah, we've done record business for a Tuesday. There were quite a few mail orders too. How about some coffee?"

"Sounds good," Dora said, settling on the sofa.

I measured coffee into the filter and poured water into the machine. Within seconds the aroma of freshly brewing coffee filled the shop.

"Any word from Adam yet?" Dora asked.

"Yeah, he called last night when he arrived at the hotel." I glanced at my watch and saw it was 2:30. "The hearing should be going on now."

"I sure hope it works out the way you want it to. Doesn't seem right to make a child leave her home once a month to travel up to Georgia. And how's she supposed to get there?"

"I've wondered about that myself. Adam will probably be forced to drive her."

"Land sakes alive, that's just plain nonsense. All that driving back and forth."

I nodded. "Yup, but that's just what might happen."

"How's Clarissa feel about all of this?"

I pushed a strand of hair behind my ear. "Well, I think she made it pretty clear to the social worker that she'd much prefer to stay here full-time. I'm not sure that'll count for anything."

Before Dora could respond, the wind chimes tinkled and three more women walked in the door.

"So much for a coffee break," I heard Dora say under her breath.

I smiled as I poured a cup for both of us and joined her on the sofa.

The women looked to be in their sixties, and each one headed toward a different type of yarn filling the wooden cubbyholes.

I took a sip of coffee and picked up the sweater I was trying to complete for Clarissa. So far I'd managed to keep it a secret from her, but that meant working on it only at the shop and not at home.

"Oh, look at that," one woman exclaimed, walking toward me. "That's just gorgeous. Do you have any of that yarn here?"

"We do," I told her, pointing to where it was kept.

"Oh, look at this," another woman said, holding up a luscious shade of cornflower blue. "Perfect for the scarves I want to make."

"And I found the cashmere I was looking for," the third one said. "Don't ya just love this peach color? It'll make a beautiful vest for me."

I smiled. What was it about yarn and the unlimited colors and textures that drew women like a shoe sale? All I knew was that once I picked up those needles again a few years ago, I was as addicted to the stock available as I was to the actual process.

"And what's this?" one of them said, spying a photo of two finished Ewedora Stockings. "That's right, I'd heard the owner did this," she said, turning around to look at me. "Are you the owner?"

"Yes," I said, feeling a sense of pride. "I recently bought the shop from my mother, and I'm specializing in Ewedora Stockings—personalized with a Christmas theme. And this just happens to be Aunt *Dora,* my partner."

"Oh, my goodness—well, I just have to have two of these made. My grandson, Jason, just turned three, and we have a new grandbaby due in February. My first granddaughter. What a wonderful keepsake these stockings will be. Do you think I could have them by next Christmas?"

"Absolutely," I told her, getting up to get an order sheet.

After taking down the required information, she said, "I just live in Ocala, so I try to get here at least once a month. Your mother did spinning of dog and cat fur, but I don't have any pets. But these knitted stockings—I simply don't have the time to do something as involved as this. I'm limited to scarves, so it's wonderful that you're now offering this service."

When the women had finished browsing and had their purchases lined up on the counter, Dora tallied up their sales, and it was then that one of the women caught sight of my T-shirt.

"What's that all about?" she questioned. "I noticed a lot of people wearing those around town today."

I explained about Grace's coffee shop and the opening of the posh one down the street.

"You mean to tell me that this guy *only* opened his shop to run her out of business?"

"I'm afraid so," I said, filling a shopping bag with yarn.

"Well, that's terrible. I've been going to Grace's place since I started visiting the island. You can bet I won't step foot inside his doorway."

"We appreciate your support," I told her.

"And why are there so many for-sale signs on the houses around the island now?" another woman asked.

"Pretty much it's because the taxes have gone sky high. The locals just can't afford them anymore and they're being forced out."

"I'd read about that in the newspaper," her friend said. "It's not right. These people work all their life to own their homes free and clear—and then they're pushed out because of taxes they can't afford? It's not right at all."

"No, it's not," I said. "And the thing of it is, sure, many live on waterfront property, but it's not a *luxury* to them. It's their livelihood. They make their living fishing and clamming, just like all the generations before them."

"Well, I sure hope this developer is the one who ends up leaving the island," the woman said, reaching for her bag of yarn. "That's what happened to so many lovely little towns in Florida. Big developers came in, put up skyscrapers and fancy hotels, expensive restaurants and shops, and before you knew it, all the charm of those small towns was gone. That's why we love coming here to visit. People are still friendly and it still looks and feels like old Florida. So I say good for you for not wanting to change things."

"Right," the woman in the middle said. "We'll definitely support you, and we'll tell all our friends who come here to visit to stay away from that new coffee shop in town."

"Yeah," said the third woman. "Maybe he'll get the hint and realize that there are still some people who care more about the history of a place and the longtime residents than something that doesn't belong here in the first place."

I grinned at the passion the women had displayed. "Well, thank you very much, and I'll be sure to tell Grace what you said."

"Oh, we're headed over there now for coffee. We'll be sure she knows," one of them said as they walked out clutching their treasured yarn.

Dora looked at me and smiled. "I'm thinking Grace just might win this after all. She sure is determined."

"She is," I said and wondered if determination really did win in the long run.

That evening over dinner I noticed that Clarissa seemed a bit more animated from the week before. There had been no funeral for Zoe's mother—probably because of the cost. She had a cremation, but nothing more.

"Zoe was in school today," she now told me. "She said she's leaving during our Thanksgiving break to go up to Baltimore."

"Well, that's good. At least it gives you a few more weeks together."

Clarissa nodded. "Yeah, and she said her father will talk to Dad about her coming to stay here the week after Christmas. Then we can see each other again. Her dad said she can fly right into Gainesville."

"Oh, that *is* good. Of course we'll go and pick her up. I know you'll miss her, but at least you can still see each other."

I wondered what it would be like for Zoe going from a small town with relatively no crime, a small school where everybody knew her, to a large city where it was easy to get lost in the shuffle, and I was grateful that at least her father would allow her to return to the island for visits.

I had just finished loading the dishwasher when Clarissa walked into the kitchen holding her Raggedy Ann doll. A look of apprehension was on her face.

"Something wrong?" I asked.

"I was just wondering . . . do you think—it would be all right if I gave Annie to Zoe?"

Part with the doll that had meant so much to her? "Well . . . yeah, it's your doll. You can do whatever you want with it. But why? I thought you loved Annie."

"I do, but I love Zoe too, and I know it's going to be hard for her living up there. I thought maybe Annie could keep her company— like she did me when I first moved here."

I wasn't used to such unselfishness in a child and was touched that Clarissa thought to do this. "I think that would be an incredibly sweet thing to do. But are you sure you won't miss the doll?"

"Yeah, I will . . . but I have Billie now, and she keeps me company. I think Zoe might need Annie more than I do."

I shook my head. It amazed me how much could be learned from children if we just paid attention.

"I think Zoe will love Annie, and having her might make her feel a little bit closer to you too."

"That's what I was hoping," she said, walking out of the kitchen.

Just as I was getting Clarissa to bed Adam called.

"How'd it go?" I asked.

"Good news and bad news. Let me talk to Clarissa first before she goes to bed and then I'll tell you all about it."

Clarissa talked to her dad for about ten minutes and then passed the phone back to me.

"Call ya right back," I told him.

I gave her a hug and tucked her into bed, which now seemed like such a natural thing to do. Then I called Adam back.

"So what's the deal?" I said.

I heard a deep sigh come across the phone line.

"Well, we kinda sorta won. The judge ruled that it's not in the best interest of the child to be traveling back and forth once a month to Georgia. Of course, that brought forth buckets of croco- dile tears from Carrie Sue. However, the judge went on to say that if the mother could get herself to Cedar Key, the permanent residence of Clarissa, then she would grant her visitation twice a month."

I gripped the phone tighter. "*What?* Are you saying that Carrie Sue is moving to Cedar Key?"

"Well, I'm not saying that for certain—but . . . yeah, she has the option to do so, and if she does, then she'll have visitation with Clarissa. But, honey, I seriously doubt that Carrie Sue's going to be willing to come to the island to live."

"And I seriously doubt that *you* fully understand a woman determined to get her own way. Oh, Adam, what the hell have we gotten ourselves into?"

"Monica, please don't worry. It'll all work out."

"How was it left? Did Carrie Sue speak to you after the hearing? Did she say what her plans were?"

"No. I have no clue what she's planning. All she said was that she'd be in touch, and she left the courthouse with her attorney."

Great. Just great. This was exactly what I sure as hell did not need—the ex-wife coming to live in the same town.

✎ 27 ✎

Adam arrived home on Wednesday afternoon, and he looked beat. I attempted to be cheerful for his sake, but it continued to loom over me that shortly I could be bumping into Carrie Sue everywhere I went on the island. It did make me feel somewhat better to know that at least Clarissa wasn't going to be transported back and forth across the border like Florida oranges.

Clarissa and I greeted him at the door with hugs and kisses.

"I missed my girls," he said. "It's good to be home."

We'd decided to wait till he got back to explain the current situation to Clarissa.

"Just made some coffee," I told him, heading to the kitchen.

"Sounds great. Let's sit out on the deck."

I put the filled cups on a tray along with a glass of Pepsi for Clarissa.

"Okay," he said, after taking a sip from his cup. "We really did win," he told his daughter and then went on to explain that Carrie Sue did have the right to move to Cedar Key, and if she did, then she had visitation twice a month.

"So I still have to go with her?" Clarissa questioned.

I honestly thought she'd be happier with the fact she didn't have to leave once a month, but it was apparent she'd have preferred no contact with Carrie Sue at all.

"Well, yes, you do. If she moves here. But, Clarissa, I'm not sure that will happen. Even if it does, you'll be right here on the island, and it's only for two weekends a month. Now, that's not so bad, is it?"

"Guess not," was all she said, with her head bent down.

Adam looked at me with raised eyebrows. "I know this is tough," he told her. "But maybe you'll like being with your mother again. You haven't seen her for seven months."

"What am I supposed to *do* with her?" she asked.

I had to give this kid credit—she was mature beyond her years.

"Well, uh . . . maybe she'll take you into Gainesville shopping or for lunch. Mother-daughter stuff."

"She never did that kind of stuff when I lived with her."

I saw Adam suppress a grin. "Right. Well, hey, let's not worry about it now. It might never happen. Okay?"

"Okay," she said, softly.

During supper Clarissa chatted away about Zoe and the need for Adam to speak to Zoe's father.

"I will," he assured her. "I promise."

"Why don't you tell your dad what you're giving Zoe for her going-away present?"

She looked at me with a grin. "Raggedy Ann," she told him and went on to explain why.

"That's really nice of you, Clarissa, but are you sure you want to part with her?"

She nodded. "Yup. I want Zoe to have her now."

I saw the emotion that passed over Adam's face, and I was beginning to realize that kids had a way of bringing out our softer side.

While Adam and Clarissa cleaned up, I called my mother to bring her up to date on our news.

"That's wonderful. Oh, I'm so glad that poor child won't have to be bounced back and forth. I bet Opal will be thrilled too. But I wonder how she's going to deal with bumping into her ex-daughter-in-law downtown?"

"Hmm, if it happens, it should be interesting. Gosh, with all the excitement about Clarissa, I almost forgot to tell you . . . The bank approved my loan, and now I really feel like the *official* owner of Spinning Forward. This money will enable me to purchase more stock to build the business."

"Oh, Monica! That's great. Congratulations."

"Are you sure you don't mind?"

Sydney's laughter came across the phone line. "Mind? Why would I mind? I wanted to *give* you the shop. Believe me, I'm thrilled you're taking it over. It was great while I had it, but my life has moved on now, and a huge part of that includes being with Noah. So I couldn't be happier for you, and I wish you much success."

"Thanks, Mom," I said, and went on to give her an update about Ewedora's Stockings. "So I'm hoping this little venture will make up for the lack of orders with spinning dog and cat fur."

"It's a great idea! I have no doubt it will be very successful."

"Yeah, orders are already coming in, and I've set up the Web site for mail orders just like you did for the spinning. It was a good time to begin this because we'll have almost a full year before next Christmas. Speaking of which, what are you and Noah doing for Thanksgiving?"

"Actually, we've been invited to an American couple's home just outside Paris. The fellow works with Noah at the Sorbonne, and they've invited a few couples to celebrate an American Thanksgiving. How about you? Going to Dora's?"

"Yes, and you know her—she thrives on having a full house. So it'll be me, Adam, and Clarissa. Dora also invited Saren, Opal, and Grace. Marin is going to South Carolina to be with Andrew's family. It'll be fun having a child around this year."

My mother laughed. "If you think Thanksgiving will be fun, wait till Christmas. Kids really *do* make Christmas."

"I'm looking forward to it."

I crawled into bed beside Adam, grateful to have him back home. With any luck, he wouldn't be returning to Georgia again for custody hearings.

"I missed you," I told him, snuggling into his shoulder.

"I missed you too."

He shifted to look at me.

"Monica, I don't want you worrying about this. I just can't picture Carrie Sue coming here to live. Hell, she never once wanted to come *visit* here when we were married."

"Really?" That was encouraging.

"I tried many times to get her to come down. She said there wasn't a thing on this island for her. She *is* high maintenance—I don't think she could survive here without her hair salons and spas and high-class shopping."

Maybe Adam was right. Maybe I was worrying for nothing.

"I spoke to my mom this evening." And I went on to tell him how she and Noah would be spending Thanksgiving.

"That sounds like fun, but I'm sure it'll be a nice time at Dora's house."

"Oh, yeah. I remember my first Thanksgiving on the island. My mom did it at the Lighthouse. We had quite a few people there—I know Marin and Andrew came that year with their sons. It was a lot of fun. All the old stories going around the room—everybody recalling something from the past."

"I bet Saren won for the best storyteller," he said, massaging my arm.

I smiled. "Yeah, he sure can come up with some great stories from years ago. You know, I just realized—we're building our own stories, aren't we?"

I felt him nod. "That's what families do. All the events, all the times spent together, they all turn into great stories years later. I'm glad Clarissa's going to get to grow up on this island. I want her to experience that true sense of family with all of us."

"I agree. It's a great place to raise a child, and she does love it here, doesn't she?"

"I always thought she would. Looking back over these months, we've had our ups and downs, but overall, I think she settled in real well."

I only hoped that Carrie Sue wouldn't show up and upset our apple cart.

"Hey," I said, feeling Adam's hand slide between my thighs. "I thought you were tired from that long drive."

"You foolish woman—I'm never too tired for you," he whispered, pulling me into an embrace.

28

Sitting in *my* yarn shop looking around at the other women, a warm feeling came over me. Being able to get together with my best friend, great-aunt, and other close women from the island filled me with gratitude. In such a mobile world, so many families and loved ones lived apart, many times only seeing each other at weddings or funerals. It was a special feeling to know that everyone I felt closest to was no more than a twenty-minute walk away, and even though my mother was across the pond, it was only temporary and she was only a phone call or e-mail away. There's a lot to be said for that.

"So then what'd she do?" I heard Twila Faye ask Polly.

"She said, 'Well, if y'all can't get my hair this shade of red, then I'll just wait and get it done when I'm back home in Atlanta.' Honey, there was no way I was sending her out of *my* shop looking like a fire engine."

Laughter broke out in the room.

I was working on the sleeves of Clarissa's sweater and had to admit it was looking pretty good. I glanced over at the afghan that

Twila Faye was making for her granddaughter. Strips of lavender and pink. Dora was doing an intricate cable pattern on a sweater she planned to give Saren for Christmas, and Polly was attempting her first pair of socks.

"Okay," Dora said, putting down her knitting. "Everyone ready for coffee and pastry? Break time."

I got up to help pass out mugs of coffee along with the delicious lemon squares Dora had contributed.

"Heard from your mama lately?" Twila Faye asked.

I nodded and brought everyone up to date on her latest Parisian escapades.

"You think she likes it better than here?" Polly questioned.

"Not *better*. No. This island and Paris are her two favorite places in the world. But they're both different. And she loves them for different reasons—but they're both in her soul."

I smiled. I had to agree with my mother. I'd been to Paris years before she had gone, and it had the same effect on me. I loved it just as much as Cedar Key—but in a different way.

"So, Grace," Dora asked. "Are you managing to run that other coffee shop into the ground?"

"I'm not sure about that, but I do know that so far my weekend business hasn't suffered at all."

"That's great." Twyla Faye pointed a finger in the air. "That man will learn—y'all don't fool with us Southern women. When we set out to do something, we do it. There's no backing down for us. I reckon he'll find out soon enough he'd do better to mosey on outta here."

This brought forth more laughter.

"Hey," Polly said. "Did y'all hear about Nina and Carolyn from the Garden Club going to Vegas?"

"Yeah, I knew they were out there last month," I said. "Why? What happened?"

Polly chuckled. "Well, this is a good one. Seems Nina thought it might be a good idea if they visited one of those . . . houses of ill re-pute on the outskirts of town."

Twyla Faye leaned forward. "Lord above, are you serious?"

"Yup." Polly shook her head, trying to control her laughter. "They went out there one afternoon and actually got a tour from the madam."

"I never knew they gave tours," Twila Faye said. "What all did they see?"

"Well, Carolyn said it was a nice-looking house. Well main-tained. In the front room there was a silk sofa—for the men to sit. The women parade out and the *customers* choose which woman they'd like to hire."

"And this is all legal out there, right?"

Polly nodded. "Yup. Nina said the house was circular and lots of rooms ran off the main one. That's where they service the men. And then out back, there was a swimming pool and little cabanas, like small cottages. The madam told them men can hire those with a woman for the entire night, to the tune of fifteen hundred dollars."

"Lord above," Dora said. "There's some serious money in that profession."

"Carolyn said the madam was just twenty-six—drop-dead gor-geous. Real Hollywood material. So Carolyn asked her why she was in that line of work and did her family know. The girl told her she'd gone to Vegas initially to work as an executive for a large company and her family thought that's what she was still doing. She's college educated and everything. Said there was no way she could afford to live on her salary. So she was doing this strictly for money. Told them she was working a few more years and then she was retiring. Imagine that." Polly took a sip of coffee and began chuckling again. "But the best part of the story is the girl told Carolyn and Nina they should consider joining her business."

"What?" Twila Faye could barely contain her shock. "You can't be serious!"

"Yup—the girl told them that middle-aged women have become very popular in that line of business. Seems some men have a mother complex or some such thing and they prefer to be with women over fifty."

Laughter filled the yarn shop.

"Cellulite and all?" Grace questioned.

"Guess so," Polly said. "Hey, now there's a great trip for us Red Hatters. Out to Vegas."

Dora laughed. "Right. For a vacation or to work?"

A smirk formed on Polly's face. "Well, now—maybe we could work in a bit of both."

"Leave it to Carolyn and Nina to go checking out a place like that," Grace said, still laughing. "You gals are worse than teenagers."

"Hey," Polly told her. "Age is simply a number. Having fun keeps ya young."

"Very true," Dora agreed. "And I agree that laughter really *is* the best medicine."

"See what we have to look forward to," Grace told me, a grin covering her face.

I nodded. "Yup, we have some pretty good mentors here to learn from."

The conversation then turned to Adam and Carrie Sue.

"Oh, I can't picture somebody like that coming to live on the island," Twila Faye said after hearing my update.

"Yeah, that's what Adam seems to think too. I just hope you're right. I mean, at least Clarissa would still be right here if she had to visit her, but—from what I've heard about Carrie Sue, well . . . it would be awkward, I think."

"I agree with Twila Faye," Dora said. "Not everybody could live on our island. And during all my years living here, I've come to see it's pretty much black or white. You either love it or you hate it. There's no in between. A lot of people couldn't live in a town without a doctor or pharmacy, not to mention a movie theater or fancy shopping."

Grace laughed. "Right. All the reasons why *we* love it."

I joined her laughter and nodded. "True. Well, I'm just hoping she'll stay up there in Georgia. Besides, Clarissa doesn't seem very fond of getting together with her mother."

"And there has to be a valid reason for that," Dora replied. "I've always said that young people are an excellent judge of character."

Although I was no expert on children, I felt Dora was correct.

$\approx$ 29 $\approx$

I was on the back steps tending to my potted periwinkles when I heard the phone inside ringing. Dashing into the kitchen, I neglected to shut the door behind me. In a flash, I saw Billie bolt past with one of my Manolo Blahnik high heels in her mouth. Letting the answering machine take the call, I turned around and headed down the stairs in pursuit of Billie.

Before I knew what was happening, I felt myself flung forward with no way to break my fall. I landed at the foot of the stairs dazed and in pain.

"Oh, God," I said, reaching down to touch my already swelling ankle. Looking around the yard, I realized that Billie had gone. She'd never been loose or off her leash.

"Clarissa," I yelled, hoping she'd hear me in her room.

The pain was too intense for me to stand on my own.

Clarissa appeared at the top of the stairs and gasped. "Monica, are you all right?"

Why do people always ask dumb questions in these situations?

"No," I spat out between clenched teeth as the pain intensified.

"I'm *not* all right. Billie grabbed my shoe and took off and I can't stand up."

Without saying a word, Clarissa spun around and went back into the house. I heard the front door slam and realized she was taking off to find that stupid dog rather than helping me.

I slid to the first step, holding on to the railing, hoping I'd somehow be able to make it up the stairs.

A moment later both Clarissa and Miss Tilly came running from the side of the house.

"Gracious me," Tilly exclaimed. "Oh, you poor dear."

My guilt was now more intense than the pain in my ankle. Here I was thinking Clarissa had abandoned me and she'd run for help.

"Here," Tilly said, "You grab the railing and lean on me. We'll make it up the stairs."

"Can I do anything?" Clarissa asked, her face covered with fear.

"Yes, sugar," Tilly told her. "Get some ice cubes from the freezer and get them all wrapped up in a towel."

Following Tilly's instructions, I leaned on her arm while my left hand gripped the railing. Slowly, we made our way to the top and into the kitchen. Still leaning on her, I shuffled to the sofa, where I collapsed in relief.

"Here," Clarissa said, passing the towel to Tilly.

"Oh, my, you have quite a bruise here," she told me, placing the freezing mound on my ankle.

I winced from the cold, but within seconds a welcome numbness encircled the injured area.

"I don't think it's broken," Tilly said. "Just a bad sprain, I'm sure."

As the pain began to subside, I remembered Billie.

"Oh, Clarissa, did you find Billie?"

She shook her head and I saw the sparkle of tears fill her eyes.

"Get me the phone. I'll call your dad at school. He should be about finished with his meetings now and can go look for her."

When I explained the situation to Adam, his first words were, "Are you sure you're okay? Maybe we should take you into Chiefland to see a doctor?"

"No, I think it's just a sprain. But Billie has disappeared. You need to look for her on your way home."

"I'm leaving now. Tell Clarissa I'll find her."

Disconnecting, I saw the worry on Clarissa's face. "He's leaving right now. He'll find her."

"But . . . she's never been loose. She's not used to cars and stuff."

My fear exactly. "Yeah, but people on the island are careful with loose dogs. Besides, our speed limit isn't above twenty." Somehow, I knew this was no comfort to her.

"Thank you so much for coming to the rescue," I told Tilly.

"Oh, it was this young lady here who did that. She had the presence of mind to come and get me."

I nodded. Yeah, maybe at the cost of losing her beloved dog.

"How about some tea, Miss Monica?" Tilly was already heading into the kitchen.

"Thanks," I said and wished I could get out there myself to search for Billie.

An hour later Adam returned home—without a dog.

Opal found out about my spill down the stairs and insisted on coming over to prepare dinner for us.

Reclining on the sofa, my ankle propped on pillows, I could hear her working away in the kitchen. The aroma of meat loaf drifted out to me. Glancing at the clock on the mantel, I realized Adam and Clarissa had been gone almost two hours searching for Billie. I prayed they'd return home with the dog.

A few minutes later I heard the front door open and saw them enter the great room. I could tell by the look on their faces that Billie had not been found.

"Nothing?" I questioned.

Adam shook his head as Clarissa headed to her bedroom.

"God, we looked everywhere. Downtown. Out by the airport. Drove out to Jernigan and the other end of the island. Nothing."

Fear gripped me as I began to face the fact that we might never see Billie again. What would this do to Clarissa? First she'd lost her mother, then her best friend, and now—the most important thing in the world to her. A child could only deal with so much loss.

I let out a deep sigh. "I'm so sorry, Adam. I'm so sorry this happened."

He came to sit beside me, taking my hand. "It wasn't your fault, Monica. It was just one of those things."

And just when Clarissa and I were beginning to possibly forge a relationship, this had to happen. "She'll never forgive me. It was me that had the back door open."

"Don't be silly. She knows it was an accident. You didn't mean for Billie to get loose and run away."

Just like she didn't mean to spill my perfume bottle? Or cut her hair? Or let the washing machine overflow? And how forgiving had I been? I couldn't blame her if she hated me. Making it even worse was that maybe if she'd run out of the house immediately, she could have caught Billie. But no, she ran next door to get help for me. The term *wicked stepmother* was beginning to take on a whole new meaning.

"No luck?" I heard Opal ask and glanced up to see her in the great room.

"I'm afraid not," Adam told her.

"That poor child must be devastated. I made up a small bowl of macaroni and cheese for her with the meat loaf."

Leave it to a grandmother to soothe a child's pain with comfort food.

"I'm not sure Clarissa feels like eating, and I'm not going to force her tonight," he said, heading toward her bedroom.

"Dinner's all ready. Do you need some help getting to the table?" Opal asked.

I shook my head as I slid to the edge of the sofa. Grabbing the arm, I pulled myself to a standing position. "No, I can manage. Thanks." In all honesty, food was the last thing I wanted but I didn't want to offend Opal, so I limped my way to the kitchen table.

Adam came in and sat beside me a few moments later. "No," he told us. "She's not hungry right now."

"Poor baby," Opal said, passing a bowl of mashed potatoes. "Well, all you have to do is zap that mac and cheese in the microwave later if she wants it."

I pushed green beans around my plate. "Is there anything else we can do?"

"Beyond putting the word out that Billie is missing and passing out flyers with her photo, I can't think of anything else. She has her tags on with Clarissa's name and phone number."

And yet, the telephone remained silent.

"Is everything all set with Dora for Thanksgiving?" Opal asked, which I'm sure was an attempt to lighten the dinner conversation.

I nodded. "Yeah, she's been cooking up a storm. Making her famous pies and chutney. I want to bring something, but I'm not sure what. Are you making your key lime pie?"

"Yup. That's my signature dessert. Adam said you're bringing some wine. Why don't you do up a trail mix to nibble on?"

"Hmm, that's a good idea," I said as the telephone rang, causing me to jump.

Adam got up to answer and I prayed it was good news about Billie, but I heard him say, "Hi, Sydney. Yeah, she's right here."

I took the phone, "Hi, Mom."

"Monica, Miss Tilly called Dora, who called me about your fall down the stairs. Are you okay?"

That coconut pipeline again—it even reached all the way to France. "Yes, I'm fine. Just a little sprain. Opal's here and she made supper for us. But Billie's gone. She scooted out the door, and I fell trying to catch her."

"Oh, no! Poor Clarissa must be so upset."

"She is, and I feel just horrible. Adam took her all over the island and they can't find Billie."

"Geez, where the heck can she be? She's so attached to Clarissa, it seems odd that she'd just run away. And it must be getting dark there now."

That thought had already crossed my mind. Tough enough to try to locate a lost dog during the day—but darkness made it almost impossible.

"Well, listen," my mother said, "it's certainly not your fault. I feel confident that Billie will turn up. Keep me posted."

"Thanks, Mom. I appreciate it."

"Monica, keep that leg elevated to decrease the swelling. You might want to take some Tylenol also for the inflammation and pain."

I smiled. Once a nurse, always a nurse.

"Will do," I said, hanging up.

Somehow we managed to get through the rest of dinner. Adam and Opal instructed me to resume my spot on the sofa while they cleaned up the kitchen. Adjusting a pillow under my leg, I was aware that Clarissa remained behind her bedroom door.

"Honey, I'm going to drive my mom home," Adam said, coming over to plant a kiss on my cheek. "Can I get you anything?"

"No, I'm fine. Thanks."

I wondered if maybe I should go and check on Clarissa. Damn, why did this have to happen? And what would we do if Billie was never found? I glanced up to see Clarissa walking slowly toward me. If it was possible, I thought she looked even more lost and dejected than the day she'd arrived at our house.

"Oh, Clarissa, sweetheart," I said, instinctively reaching my arms out toward her.

She came to sit beside me, allowing me to encircle her. Her face was splotched with red marks that told me she'd been crying continuously behind her closed door.

I tightened my arm around her. "I am *so* sorry that Billie ran away." And in that moment my stomach lurched and I felt an unfamiliar gnawing. I knew it wasn't due to skimping on dinner. It was deeper than that. Feelings of pain combined with fear—a feeling that seemed to match the look on Clarissa's face.

"I know it wasn't your fault, Monica."

The child's voice was muffled against my chest and without any warning I felt tears on my face.

"But I'm so worried about Billie," she sniffled. "Do you think maybe she's hurt? Or that she really wants to come home but just doesn't know the way? She's not a big dog and she's never been out on her own."

Making an attempt to compose myself, I said, "No, she's not a big dog, but she's extremely bright. Just like you are. You know what I think? I think Billie wanted a bit of an adventure. You know how dog friendly she is. I think once she got loose she thought she'd do some visiting. And I bet she's just making the rounds all around the island. That little stinker has us worried sick—and she's probably having a grand ol' time."

Clarissa pulled away to look directly at me. "Maybe," she said with hesitation. "I just miss her so much and I want her to be okay."

A fresh flood of tears coursed down her face and I felt utterly helpless. There wasn't a thing I could do to take away this child's anguish—anguish that I felt every bit as deeply.

❦ 30 ❦

I had heard the phone ring once in the distance and then snuggled back into my pillow. After tossing and turning all night with worry for Billie, I welcomed the sleep. But a few minutes later I felt like I was being bounced on a trampoline and opened my eyes to see Clarissa's joyful face.

"We found Billie! We found Billie," she cried, jumping up and down on the bed.

Struggling to sit up, I saw Adam leaning against the doorway, a huge smile on his face.

"Oh, my God! Really?" I exclaimed as Clarissa's arms went around my neck.

"Yes, really," she confirmed, giving me a tight squeeze.

Wiping sleep out of my eyes, I wasn't sure whether to laugh or cry with happiness.

"Henry Talbot just called. Seems he heard Billie whimpering at his back door at two this morning. He didn't want to call then, so he took her in and gave her a bite to eat."

"What on earth was she doing in Henry's yard? That's only a few streets from here. I wonder why she didn't come home."

"Because she was having too much fun digging up Henry's rose-bushes."

I swung my legs to the side of the bed. "Oh, no!"

Adam laughed. "Yeah, got her in a bit of trouble. I told Henry we'll replace all of the bushes that were damaged and even plant them for him. Won't we, Clarissa?"

She nodded emphatically. I think if Adam had said she had to re-paint Henry's entire house inside and out, the child would have been agreeable in order to get Billie back.

"We're going over to get her, but I want to see how your ankle is today."

Sticking my leg out in front of me, I turned my foot to the right, then the left. No pain. Putting a hand on the night table, I stood up and gingerly put weight on both feet. No pain. Just a slight discomfort.

"Much better," I told him. Then I walked to the bathroom and back. "Definitely better."

"That's good. Okay, then I'll take Clarissa and we'll go collect that naughty pooch. We shouldn't be very long."

Clarissa started to follow Adam out of the bedroom, then turned around and came back. Throwing her arms around my midsection, she said, "You were right, Monica. Billie was just having an adventure. I'm so glad you knew that."

I watched her go through the door as I stood there trying to absorb what she said. Of course I didn't know that Billie would be okay. I was scared to death we might not see her again. But somehow I guess that wasn't what I conveyed to Clarissa. Instead I had reassured the child, made her feel better. In that brief moment, I began to realize that was a small part of being a mother. What surprised me was that I had done it unknowingly. Without even thinking about it. Like it was *natural*.

Smiling, I headed to the bathroom to brush my teeth. My eyes flew to the vanity—where Sybile's butterfly brooch sat. The small crystals glimmered from the sun streaming through the window. I gripped the doorknob to steady myself. What the heck was that doing in here? It had been safely tucked away in my jewelry box from when I'd found it on my bureau. There was no way Adam or Clarissa would have put it in the bathroom. This was becoming beyond eerie. I didn't have a clue what it could mean, but I knew somebody who might.

Walking to the bedside phone, I dialed Grace's number.

"Have you got a sec?"

"Sure," she told me. "What's up?"

"Is there any significance for a butterfly? Why would somebody want a necklace or something with a butterfly on it?"

"Change."

"What do you mean, change?"

"Butterflies represent change. Growth. Transformation. Many people relate strongly to butterflies on a spiritual level. They begin in a cocoon and then emerge beautiful and different from how they started."

"Hmm," I said, now finding a connection to Sybile. Once Sybile acknowledged she had given birth to my mother, she began to change. She attempted to build a relationship with both my mother and me. She also made amends with Saren and spent her final days receiving his love and loving him in return.

"Why?" I heard Grace ask on the other end of the line. "Why do you want to know about butterflies? Oh, is Sybile moving her brooch around on you again?"

"I don't know. It's all so silly, but I just found it on the vanity in the bathroom. When I know darn well it was in my jewelry box. This is crazy."

Grace chuckled. "Maybe not. You just don't believe in those things, Monica. I've tried to explain to you about another dimension, but you're too logical to even consider something like that."

"You're right, I am." Wanting to change the subject I said, "Hey, we found the wandering Billie."

"Oh, thank God. Is she all right?"

"Yeah, she was in Henry Talbot's yard digging up his rosebushes. Adam and Clarissa have gone to get the little minx."

"Uh-oh. I'd say poor Billie is in the doghouse. Literally."

I laughed. "Yeah, well, I'm just glad we have her back. Poor Clarissa was so upset. I'd better go. They'll be back with her shortly."

After hanging up the phone, I walked back into the bathroom. The brooch still sat on the vanity. I stretched out my hand to pick it up, almost afraid it would disappear into thin air. But it didn't. I folded my fingers around the brooch and felt distinct warmth emanating from the crystals. Walking to my bureau, I then lifted the cover on my jewelry box and placed the brooch inside.

Clarissa walked into the kitchen clutching something that resembled a filthy stuffed toy that had been rescued from a trash bin. It took me a second to realize this ball of fluff was Billie. Her normally groomed, beautiful buff-colored fur was between gray and ebony. The crisp and clean scarf she always wore around her neck was missing. And it appeared that in twenty-four hours she'd developed snarls in her curls. But her little tail was wagging with excitement, clearly delighted to be back in Clarissa's arms

I suppressed a giggle. "Into the laundry room," I said, pointing the way. "My God, she's a mess."

"Yeah," Adam said, filling the laundry sink with warm water and dog shampoo. "I'm afraid Billie had quite the night on the town."

"The little hussy." I was grateful she'd been spayed the month before and at least didn't return home *in the family way*.

"What's a hussy?" Clarissa asked as she submerged Billie into the soapy water.

Adam laughed. "A woman of questionable behavior. I think that would describe Billie's venture from home."

I shook my head as I headed back to the kitchen for a much-needed second cup of coffee.

Within a few hours, due to Clarissa's diligent care, Billie was looking more like her old self. Bathed, blown dry, and brushed, she was sporting a clean pink scarf with red hearts. She was also exhausted from her ordeal and curled up on the sofa.

I was putting the finishing touches of cream cheese frosting on the carrot cake I'd made when Clarissa wandered into the kitchen.

"I'm so glad Billie came back before I have to say good-bye to Zoe this afternoon."

So was I. Zoe and her dad were due to stop by so the girls could have a final farewell, and I had dreaded Clarissa experiencing that in addition to the loss of her precious dog.

"I know," I told her. "They should be here shortly."

"As soon as she leaves, I'm going to send her an e-mail."

I laughed. "You have to give her time to get to the airport and take the flight to Baltimore."

The doorbell rang and Clarissa went running.

Walking into the foyer, I saw a tall, slim man who resembled Zoe shaking hands with Adam.

"Hi," he told me, extending his hand. "I'm Rick, Zoe's father."

"Monica. It's nice to meet you. Come on in," I said, leading the way to the great room. "How're you doing, Zoe?"

"Good," she said. "I'm so glad Billie's back home." She went directly to the sleeping dog and gently stroked the top of her head.

I smiled. "Yeah, we are too. Have a seat, both of you."

"So are you flying out of Gainesville this evening?" Adam asked.

Rick nodded. "Yes, our flight's at seven-thirty. I think we've tied up everything here."

"Don't forget," I told him, "we'd love to have Zoe during a vacation week or during the summer."

"That's really nice of you. I know how difficult all of this is for her, so she'll love coming back to visit Clarissa."

The girls had gone into Clarissa's bedroom to spend some quiet time together.

"She's a brave little girl," I said. "Clarissa is going to miss her a lot. But I'm sure they'll keep in touch frequently. Between e-mails and phone calls."

We discussed where Zoe would be going to school, and I learned that she'd be living in a suburb of Baltimore and that made me feel a little better. Rick explained it was a medium-sized town with lots of activities for children and he felt that in time his daughter would settle in.

A half hour later the girls wandered back into the great room, and I noticed that Clarissa had Annie in her arms.

"Oh, have you given Annie to Zoe?"

Before Clarissa could answer, Zoe spoke up. "That was really nice of Clarissa to offer, but . . ." She shot a look to her father. "I wasn't sure if I was supposed to say anything, but I told Clarissa about Julie."

Adam and I exchanged a bewildered look.

Rick smiled. "No, that was fine, Zoe." Looking at Adam and me, he said, "My wife is pregnant."

I thought she didn't like kids, but managed to say, "Oh, that's great." Judging from the look on Rick's face, he seemed pretty pleased to relate the news. "When is she due?"

"In April. It's a boy."

Zoe's face beamed with excitement. "I'm going to be a big sister," she informed us. "So it's really nice of Clarissa to want to give me Annie to keep me company—but pretty soon I'll have a baby brother."

"That *is* exciting," I told her, but I didn't miss the lack of expression on Clarissa's face.

"Well," Rick said, standing up. "I'm afraid we have to get going,

Zoe. We don't want to miss our flight." He turned toward Adam and me. "Thank you so much for having us over. This really is a great little town. I'm thinking after the baby arrives maybe we'll plan a family trip to stay on the island for a vacation."

"That would be great. I'm sure the girls would enjoy that."

I watched as Clarissa and Zoe hugged, amid promises to always be best friends.

Clarissa stood at the door, Annie clutched in her arms, long after Rick and Zoe had pulled away from the curb.

Great. Just great. I had a feeling that Annie had served her purpose but would no longer provide comfort for Clarissa. I only hoped that Billie would fill the void she might be feeling. Because a baby brother or sister in our house was out of the question.

❦ 31 ❧

The reflection in the mirror met with my approval—black slacks and a burnt orange pullover sweater. I'd found the sweater tucked away in my drawer and immediately remembered my mother had made it the Thanksgiving I was in college. Two single rows of cables twisted down the front, while each sleeve had a thick cable running from shoulder to wrist.

"You look nice," I heard Clarissa say and turned around to find her standing in the bedroom doorway.

"Well, thank you, and so do you." She was wearing a tan wool skirt that fell to her ankles, topped off with a cream-colored turtleneck.

She stroked the soft alpaca of my sweater. "That's so pretty. Did you make it?"

"No, actually, my mother did. Many years ago."

"I want to learn to yarn," she informed me. I smiled again at the term she insisted on using. I was surprised with her request, but I was also surprised that her animation had seemed to return. She'd been exceptionally quiet since her farewell with Zoe. I wasn't sure if this had been attributed to the loss of her friend or the fact that Zoe was getting a baby brother. But teaching her to knit appealed to me a lot more than a baby in the house.

"Really? You'd like to learn to knit?"

Clarissa nodded. "Yeah. My friend, Chelsea—her mother makes quilts, and she's teaching Chelsea how to make one."

I got the feeling that Clarissa regarded this as a mother/daughter experience, and this also surprised me. My own mother had taught me to knit when I was about Clarissa's age. I recalled the many afternoons sitting beside her on the sofa, clumsily holding needles while attempting to knit and purl. They were hours spent developing a closeness that remained solid long after I lost interest in knitting.

"That might be fun," I told her. "I think I was about ten when my mother taught me. Once I got into college, I didn't knit for ages. But then a few years ago, I picked up needles again, and it's something you really don't ever forget."

"What can I make? A sweater?"

I laughed. "Well, sure, eventually you can. But we need to start you off with the basic things—learning to cast on, knit, and purl. As soon as you catch on to that, you can make yourself a scarf. Those are pretty simple and they work up fast."

"Can I pick out my own yarn?"

"Absolutely. That's part of the fun of knitting. So many different colors and textures to choose from. Tell ya what—you're off school tomorrow, so we'll go over to the yarn shop and get you everything you'll need."

"Oh, good. Wait till I tell Chelsea in school on Monday."

I got the feeling that Clarissa wanted to be like the other girls—have a mother figure at least. Somebody she could talk about doing things with and it was pretty obvious that person wasn't Carrie Sue.

"All set?" Adam asked, walking into the bedroom.

"Guess what, Dad? Monica's going to teach me to yarn tomorrow."

"Well, that's great. Now we'll have two knitters in the house. I'll have more sweaters and scarves than I know what to do with."

I caught his smile and wink, knowing this news pleased him.

"Okay," I said. "We'd better get moving. Aunt Dora won't be happy if we're late for Thanksgiving dinner."

The aroma of turkey and pumpkin pie filled Dora's house as we walked in the back door to the kitchen.

"Sure does smell good in here," I told her, planting a kiss on her cheek. "Happy Thanksgiving. What can I do to help?"

"And to you as well. Ah, let's see. Until ol' Tom comes out of the oven and the vegetables are ready to get into bowls, I think we're all set for a little while. How about a glass of wine for you and Adam? And Clarissa, some apple cider?"

Taking our glasses, we walked into the great room to greet the other guests.

"Happy Thanksgiving," I told everyone, raising my wineglass.

"There's my granddaughter," I heard Saren say and turned around to give him a hug.

"You're looking mighty dapper," I told him.

The only time I saw Saren without his Eagles cap was at holiday gatherings. He was sporting a crisp white shirt, blue suspenders, and a matching blue bow tie.

"I reckon it's kinda nice to get dressed up now and again."

I smiled as I went to join Grace on the sofa. She'd accepted our invitation, rather than go to Brunswick, explaining that her aunt would be joining friends for the day. "How's it going?"

"Pretty good. No news is good news, I'd say. And I haven't heard anything new from Tony, if that's what you mean."

Maybe he realized it was a hopeless cause to try to get her property. I took a sip of wine and nodded. "He probably figured out both he and his French restaurant aren't wanted on this island."

"Well, according to my tarot cards, my business looks secure. So I'm not too concerned."

I laughed. "Do you still read those silly things?"

"Monica, Monica, you need to be more open. I still say you should let me read your cards. It can be very helpful with events in your life."

"Oh, right. And I suppose a year ago right now you could have predicted that Clarissa was going to come and live with us?"

Grace shrugged, tossing her auburn curls over her shoulder. "You just never know what will turn up in the cards. How about right before I met Tony—the cards told me that somebody tall, dark, and handsome would be coming into my life."

"And did they also tell you what a jerk he'd be? Trying to steal your property from you?"

Grace was prevented from answering when Dora appeared in the doorway.

"I will now take the offer of some help getting food onto the table," she told us.

I got up from the sofa to follow her into the kitchen.

"Whipping the potatoes is my job," Grace said.

"And I'll do the carrots and squash," I chimed in. "Adam offered to carve the turkey."

Within a short time, we were all gathered around the large dining room table. As we took our seats, Dora stood at the head and told us, "If you'll hold hands, I'll say the grace."

Clarissa slipped her small hand inside of mine and I realized this was the first time we'd held hands. It felt secure and oddly comforting. Natural—like we'd done this a million times before. Adam grasped my other hand and I gave both hands a squeeze.

"Dear Lord," Aunt Dora said, "thank you for this beautiful day on Cedar Key. We all have much to be grateful for—our good health and kind neighbors. Thank you for my loving family and friends here with me today as we share this wonderful meal. Amen."

"Amen," everyone chorused.

"Miss Dora," Saren said, glancing around the table. "You sure 'nuff look like you outdid yourself with all this cookin'.'"

"All the women pitched in. Grace made the sweet potato casserole, Opal baked her famous key lime pie, Monica brought a pecan pie, and she and Clarissa came over yesterday to help me make the stuffing. So all of us contributed."

"And all of it looks great," Adam said, passing a platter of turkey.

Saren looked across the table at Clarissa as he helped himself to cranberry sauce. "Is that scamp Billie behaving herself now?"

Clarissa smiled. "Yeah, I think she learned her lesson. She won't let me out of her sight. I don't think she'll leave home again."

"Ah, yup," Saren replied. "Sometimes a woman's gotta do what a woman's gotta do. Get that wildness outta her."

This brought forth laughter, and no doubt Saren was thinking of Sybile.

"Are you all packed for Augusta?" Opal asked me.

"No, not yet. We're not leaving for two weeks. But I'll be ready."

"And Clarissa and I will have a busy weekend. The Arts Center has an exhibit on Saturday evening that we'll go to. And she's going to accompany Dora and me to the Christmas party for the Historical Society."

"I'm going to be yarning too," Clarissa informed everyone.

"You mean knitting?" Dora said, with surprise.

"Yes," I explained. "She asked me this morning if I'd teach her. She loves this sweater, and I think it whetted her appetite to learn."

"That's wonderful," Dora said. "With all the different yarns available now, Clarissa, you'll really enjoy it."

"Oh, you will," Grace told her. "I'm so glad you've decided to learn. I think it's something you'll always enjoy. Women have been knitting for ages, and I've always felt it's one of those things that bonds us together."

She was right. There was something special about a group of

women talking and laughing while sharing their creativity with patterns and yarn.

"Monica said we'll go to the yarn shop tomorrow and I can choose whatever I want to make a scarf. If I get really good, maybe I can even make a sweater for Billie."

Dora laughed. "We have lots of cute patterns for doggie sweaters. I'll be at the shop tomorrow, so you come on by and we'll get you all squared away."

Following dinner and the cleanup, all of us gathered in the great room with coffee and dessert.

Nibbling on Aunt Dora's pumpkin pie, I glanced around the room. Everyone was talking and laughing, enjoying each other's company. If my mother hadn't relocated to Cedar Key after my father died, I wondered where we'd both be. I know for certain that I never would have come to this small island. Heck, I had never even visited before my mother moved here. That would mean I'd never have met Adam. I looked over at him on the sofa, Clarissa encircled in his arm. I wouldn't have met Sybile or Saren either—my grandparents. My glance strayed to Saren, who was laughing at something Clarissa had said. And Aunt Dora—who really seemed to be the glue holding us all together. I saw Grace in a deep discussion with Opal. I'd never had a best friend like her. Sometimes she drove me crazy with her New Age behavior, but I loved her dearly. She had grown to become more like a sister to me.

Yes, I had a multitude of things to be thankful for, and coming to Cedar Key had made it all happen.

✂ 32 ✄

True to my word, Clarissa and I were at Spinning Forward shortly after Aunt Dora opened the door on Friday morning.

"Well, if it isn't our novice knitter," Dora said as we walked inside. "I imagine you're here to choose your yarn?" she asked Clarissa.

"Yes. Monica said I should start with a scarf."

"Good idea. It'll work up fast and be something you'll be proud to wear. Okay, first things first. Will she be doing a simple stock inette stitch?"

I nodded. "Yeah, I think that's the easiest to start with, and she'll get good practice with her knit and purl rows."

"Right. Well," Dora told Clarissa. "Now you get to choose your yarn. So why don't you browse and see what you'd like. That's half the fun of knitting. Picking out a yarn you love."

Clarissa wandered over to the cubbyholes and began fingering various skeins of fiber.

"How's the sweater coming that you're making for her?" Dora whispered to me.

"Not as good as I'd like. I can only knit when she's not around, so she won't see it. I'm hoping to get it about finished while Adam and I are in Augusta."

"Makes it difficult trying to keep a secret. Are you working on anything else?"

"Actually, no, and I have a great pattern for a diamond leaf scarf, which makes it look lacey. I think I'll make it for Grace for Christmas, so I need to get some yarn today too."

I walked over to the cubbyholes and found Clarissa holding a skein of the popular fake fur yarn.

"I like this," she told me.

I glanced at the bright neon purple ball in her hand. "Hmm, that might not be the best choice to start with. It's very thin yarn and a bit tricky to work with when you're just learning." My eye went to the display of Patons medium-weight yarn and I spied skeins of a gaudy color of grape. "Ah, maybe something from that table over there would be good."

Sure enough, Clarissa went directly to the purple yarn. "This?" she asked, holding it up.

"Perfect," I said.

"Okay," Dora told Clarissa. "You have yourself some nice medium-weight yarn. Now needles. I think maybe a size nine would be good for her to work with. What do you think, Monica?"

"Yes, very good. Not too small or too large. A nine is comfortable to hold. Oh, and we'd better get two skeins of the yarn. One to practice with before she begins the scarf."

"Good idea," Dora said as she looked for a pair of size 9 needles. "Wood is probably better for a beginner. Not as slippery as some of the others."

I returned to the cubbyholes and found some luscious Bonsai yarn in shades of black, gray, and silver that would be perfect for the scarf I'd make for Grace.

"Okay, anything else?" Dora asked as I placed my yarn on the counter.

I glanced around the shop. "Would you like one of those to hold your knitting supplies?" I asked Clarissa, pointing to medium-sized canvas tote bags in various colors.

"Do you have one?"

"I do. They're made at the Canvas Shop out on Twenty-four. Julie did a great job. Mine has a zipper and my initials monogrammed on it. I purchase them to sell here for knitters, and we can have Julie put your name on it."

"Okay, I'll get one," Clarissa said, walking over to choose a bright purple tote.

I laughed. "I guess it's safe to say purple's your favorite color, huh?"

Clarissa nodded. "Oh, yes. I love purple."

"Okay, Dora. I think we're all set."

She totaled up my sales and then put Clarissa's yarn and needles into the tote for her to carry.

I reached for my small shopping bag of yarn. "Thanks, Dora."

"You gals have fun knitting. Is that how you plan to spend the afternoon?"

"Yup. We'll have lunch and then I'll teach Clarissa the age-old craft of knitting."

"Are we ready yet?" Clarissa asked as I finished up the lunch dishes.

"Just about. Let me make myself a cup of tea and we'll be all set. How about some hot chocolate for you?"

"Yeah, that sounds good. I'm going to take Billie out now so we won't be interrupted doing my lessons."

I laughed. She was certainly into learning the knack of knitting.

"Okay," I said, sitting on the sofa with Clarissa pressed tight against me. "First, you have to learn how to cast on. That means getting your stitches onto the needle. There are various ways to do it, but I'm going to teach you the knitting-on method."

I proceeded to show Clarissa how to knit a stitch, leaving the original one on the needle, and then inserted my left needle up into the new stitch from the front. "See, then you have to slide that stitch back onto the left needle and pull the yarn to tighten it. So now we have two stitches and we just keep doing this until we have the amount of stitches required in the pattern. Here, you try," I said, passing her the needles.

Straightening her back, she took the needles in her hands. Inserting the right needle into a stitch on the left, she hesitated for a moment. Then she took the yarn to loop around and confidently cast on another stitch.

"Bravo! I think you're a born knitter."

Her face beamed with pride. "Do you think so?"

"I do. Okay, I'll watch while you cast on about twelve or so stitches and then I'll show how to knit a row."

I was surprised at Clarissa's dexterity. I remembered being all thumbs when I'd first learned to knit. But she had good control of the needles and continued along.

"Excellent. Now I'll show you how to knit a row."

I did a few stitches and then passed the needles to her. Again, although slow, she had caught on well.

"Tell you what. You keep knitting a few more rows and I'm going to cast on my stitches and begin working on the scarf for Grace."

I took a sip of tea and then began my own project. We worked along in silence for a while. I stopped to inspect her work.

"Very good, Clarissa. I think you're ready to learn to purl. When you master that, you'll be ready to start your scarf."

After watching me for a few minutes, she said, "Oh, this is just like knitting, except it's the opposite way of putting in your needle."

I smiled. "Exactly," I said and caught the fact this was the first time she'd referred to it as *knitting*. "Here, now you try."

I watched her complete a row. No doubt about it. This child was catching on extremely fast.

"Terrific! Do a few more rows of purls and then you can begin your scarf."

I resumed my own work. "How's Zoe these days?" I asked.

"Oh, she's good. I got an e-mail from her last night."

"Sounds like she's settled in pretty well at her dad's house."

Clarissa paused for a moment to inspect her row. "She has. She likes it there a lot. She has a really nice bedroom—almost like mine, she said, and Julie is very nice to her."

"Oh, that's great. I'm so glad to hear that."

"Yup, and they're going to have this thing for Julie—something to do with rain or water or something—and Zoe gets to be there too and she's pretty excited."

I laughed. "Oh, you must mean a *shower*. A baby shower."

"What's that?"

"Well, it's a party for a woman who's going to have a baby. Everybody brings gifts and there's usually food and cake. It's a celebration to welcome the coming baby."

I glanced over at Clarissa and realized she'd put her knitting in her lap.

"No wonder Zoe's all excited. That sounds like fun. She said it's going to be at a restaurant."

"When are they having it?"

"In February, because the baby's coming in April and Zoe said they have to get the room all ready for her brother."

She remained silent for a few moments and then said, "We have an extra bedroom here at our house."

Concentrating on my knitting, I mumbled, "Yeah, we do."

"Well, don't you ever want to have a baby shower, Monica?"

Thrown completely off guard, I was at a loss for words. Was she telling me that she wanted a baby brother or sister too?

"Oh . . . um . . . your dad and I aren't sure about that. We've . . . only been married a little over a year. But . . . um . . . who knows."

Who knows? Where the heck did *that* come from?

❧ 33 ❧

I awoke a few days later feeling nauseous. Oh, no, was I catching a flu? I stretched my hand across the bed to find it empty. Carefully turning onto my side to reduce motion, I saw the bedside clock read 7:10. Why hadn't Adam gotten me up? It was then I heard the sounds coming from the kitchen—dishes and silverware being rattled. He was tending to Clarissa's breakfast this morning.

Swinging my legs to the side of the bed, I sat for a few moments willing the nausea to disappear, with no effect. Great! Just great! I must have picked up some bug, and we were due to leave for Augusta in ten days.

I slowly stood up, taking huge, deep gulps of air, and made my way to the bathroom. Mouthwash made my mouth feel better, but not my stomach. Letting hot water pour over the face cloth, I took another deep breath and then held it to my face. A little better.

Getting into my robe, I made my way to the kitchen to find Adam and Clarissa seated at the table eating. The aroma of coffee caused me to grip the door frame as another wave of nausea enveloped me.

Adam looked up with concern on his face. "Are you okay?"

I pursed my lips together, refusing to give in to my rolling stomach. "I don't think so," I said, making my way to a chair. "I think I've caught a bug or something."

"How about some coffee and toast?" Adam asked, jumping up.

I shook my head. "No. But a cup of tea might settle my stomach a bit."

Within a few minutes, he placed a steaming mug in front of me.

"There's nothing on your schedule for today, right? You need to spend the day in bed."

"That might not be a bad idea," I said, tentatively taking a sip of the hot liquid. "Will you get Clarissa after school?"

"Not a problem. Come on, let's get you back to bed."

"Have a good day, Clarissa," I told her, while Adam reached for my arm to help me up.

"I hope you feel better," she told me as I made my way back to the bedroom.

Adam got me settled in bed, surrounded by pillows, magazines, and my cup of tea.

"Are you sure you'll be okay? I can call my mom or Dora to come and stay with you."

"Don't be silly. It's just . . ." Another wave of nausea grabbed me. "Just a little stomach flu."

He kissed the top of my head. "Okay, well, if you need anything call the school. We'll be home by two-thirty. I love you."

"Love you too."

Two hours later I was bored leafing through magazines and realized the nausea had subsided. I decided I'd probably feel even better if I took a shower and got dressed.

Wearing a pair of comfortable sweats, I walked into the kitchen and looked around. Adam had done up the breakfast dishes before they'd left. The thought of food didn't interest me in the least, but I thought another cup of tea might keep the nausea away. Turning on the kettle to boil, my eye caught the calendar—*December 1*. Decem-

ber first already? Wait a sec. . . . I flipped the page back to November and scanned the little blocks. No "p" written in ink. I always
kept track of my periods this way. Had done it for years. I must have
forgotten with the excitement of Thanksgiving. I then flipped back
to October—there was the tiny "p" written in a block for October
28. And according to my usual twenty-eight days that I'd main-
tained since age eleven, I was due November 25. Six days ago! I was
six days late? This had never happened before. Ever. I was on the
pill, for God's sake. I couldn't be . . . I couldn't even bring myself to
think the word.

The whistling of the teakettle filled the kitchen. Walking over
like an automaton, I turned off the burner and placed the kettle on
a cork pad. Standing by the counter, I shook my head. This is crazy.
I simply *couldn't* be pregnant. Could I?

As usual, I knew only one person could help me figure out my
dilemma. I dialed Grace's number and explained I needed to see
her.

"You want me to come over there?" she asked.

"If you could. I'm not feeling very well. I hate to make you do
this, but it's pretty important."

"Twila Faye is right here. She can cover the shop for me for a
while. I'll be there within twenty minutes."

How did any woman get through life without a best friend?

"Okay, now let me get this straight," Grace said, bringing her
cup of tea to her lips. "You actually think you might be pregnant?"

"I know. It's crazy. I'm on the pill. How could I be? But . . . I'm
six days late and I woke up this morning with horrible nausea. I
thought I had a bug, but . . . I just don't know."

"Well, I hate to tell ya, girlfriend, but there's plenty of babies out
there that can attest to the fact that sometimes that pill fails."

"Yeah, but that's if the woman forgets to take it or whatever. I
didn't do that."

"I really hate to break your bubble, but I've heard of cases where the woman insisted *she* didn't forget to take them either. Didn't skip one day and yet—nine months later she has a bouncing baby."

"Oh, Lord! Do you think? Do you think it's possible?"

"Anything's possible."

I took a sip of the tea that Grace had prepared, momentarily distracted as I savored the pungent taste. "What's this? It's good."

"Lavender. It's an herbal tea and good for relaxing. I brought it from the coffee shop. You sounded a bit stressed on the phone."

"Well, Christ, can you blame me? Here I am, going along doing what I'm supposed to be doing, and wham—out of the blue, I could be pregnant?"

Grace let out a deep sigh. "Monica, would that really be so terrible?"

Anger came over me. "Well, how the hell would you know? You've never been pregnant."

Grace remained silent for a few minutes and then softly replied, "Actually, I have been."

My head shot up to look at her and I knew from the expression on her face that she was serious. "What?" I whispered. "You never told me."

She nodded. "I know. I seldom talk about it. It was ten years ago. I was involved in—a relationship." Staring down at her mug, she went on. "I was almost four months along—and I had a miscarriage."

"Oh, Gracie." I reached out to grasp her hand. "I'm so sorry."

"Well, you know," she said, "I've always felt those things happen for a reason. I'd already seen an OB guy and was taking very good care of myself. In all honesty, it certainly wasn't planned. I was one of the women who forgot to take my pill for a few days." She paused and ran a hand through her auburn curls. "I don't even know if it was a boy or a girl. I didn't want to know. It was over. There wasn't a thing I could do about it."

Despite her attempted bravado, I detected regret in her tone. "But Gracie, you're healthy and only thirty-six—it's not out of the question for you to have a child."

She laughed, lightening the mood. "Hey, sweetie, you forget there's another part to this equation. A man. And at the moment, I'm fresh out of those."

I joined her laughter and nodded.

"But you," she said. "Hell, Monica, you have a husband that absolutely worships the ground you walk on. Adam adores you. Would it really be so bad if you're pregnant? How do you think Adam would feel about it?"

Even without a recent discussion on the subject, I instinctively knew Adam would be over the moon. But he knew my reluctance to having a child and had always been willing to support that decision.

I shrugged. "Probably happy."

"I think you're right. Look how great he is with Clarissa."

"Hmm . . ." was my only response.

"And I never thought I'd say this, but you're turning into quite a good mother to her as well."

"Oh, I don't know about that. . . ."

"I do. Look how far the two of you have come since she arrived here in April. You're developing closeness, and you know she loves being here with you and Adam. Remember when Billie was lost? You told me you couldn't believe how you felt her pain—you said it was something you couldn't even describe, but it tore *your* heart out to see her so miserable."

It did, and that emotion had totally surprised me. I had never experienced anything like that for another person before. And the first time she hugged me, sobbing in my arms over the loss of Billie— how natural that had felt.

Leave it to Grace to make me feel better. By the time she left and Adam and Clarissa walked in from school, my nausea had completely disappeared and my emotions were calmer.

I had decided not to mention any of this to Adam. I still needed some time to absorb myself what could be happening.

For the next three mornings, I awoke again with the same nausea, only to have it disappear by midday. I still let Adam think it was some kind of bug I'd caught while I tried to figure out what my next step would be. I had decided that if nothing happened by the time we arrived in Augusta, I would purchase a pregnancy kit and share my suspicions with Adam. We could discover the news together.

But that wasn't to be—on the fourth morning, instead of the familiar nausea, I awoke with the distinctive cramping in my lower abdomen, knowing full well there would be no pregnancy kit.

I stayed in bed allowing the cramps to roll over me as I considered the strong sense of letdown I felt. A sense of loss for something I never had—I hadn't been pregnant at all. For whatever reason, I'd simply been late. But for the first time in my life, I had given serious thought to the possibility of bringing another life into the world.

I glanced over at Adam, soundly sleeping beside me. His handsome face was covered with peacefulness and I reached out a finger to stroke his cheek, causing him to stir. I felt a surge of love move through my body as I thought about creating another human being that would be a part of both Adam and me and the love that we shared.

There would be no pregnancy test while we were in Augusta— but there would definitely be a serious discussion with my husband.

❦ 34 ❦

I was in the bedroom, humming to myself and choosing various clothes to take on our trip. Adam and I were leaving for Augusta in four days and I was exceptionally excited.

Having time alone with Adam was something I'd probably always welcome, and it had nothing to do with Clarissa. I had come to truly enjoy her company and having her with us, but I'd also come to understand that all couples need their quiet time together. Four days and nights would provide us plenty of time for the discussion I had planned, and I knew I'd enjoy the Christmas shopping in a new area to explore.

Trying to decide between a navy or light blue pullover, I heard the doorbell ring, which caused Billie to go running and barking in her *protection* mode.

Laughing, I walked toward the front door. "Billie, hush. We're not being invaded."

I opened the door and was so shocked to see the woman standing on my porch, I felt light-headed and couldn't speak.

"Well, hi, Monica. It's me, Carrie Sue. Surely, you remember me?"

I gripped the door frame and nodded. "Yes. Yes, I remember

you." Although in all honesty, she had aged since I'd last seen her. Still extremely attractive, but telltale lines had formed at the corners of her eyes. Blond hair was fashionably styled—chin length, with bangs that didn't quite cover lines in her forehead. Makeup so perfect, it could have been applied by a top consultant for Lancôme. Definitely still attractive—in a cheap sort of way.

"Well, are y'all gonna invite me in or make me stand out here on the porch like a dog looking for shelter?"

I found my voice and replied, "I don't know, Carrie Sue. What is it you want? Adam and Clarissa aren't here."

She threw her head back laughing and adjusted the large malachite pendant hanging around her neck. "What do I want? Well, I want my *daughter,* of course. Where *is* Clarissa Jo?"

I did have to marvel that somebody who called herself a mother had no clue that on a Monday afternoon at 1:00, her daughter would be in school.

Which was exactly what I told her. "And besides," I added, "you can't just show up here out of the blue and expect to see her. You have to discuss this with Adam."

"I don't think there's much to discuss. I got myself a lawyer, went to the judge, and I have the papers here to prove it." She patted the black Gucci bag hanging from her shoulder. "I have visitation every other weekend."

My greatest fear was becoming reality. Was she serious or just trying to pull one over on us?

"Look, I'll call Adam at school and let him know you're here, but I'm not letting you in until he gets here. So come back in about an hour. Sorry," I told her, closing the door in her face.

My legs were trembling as I leaned against the back of the door. Taking a deep breath, I ran for the phone.

Within twenty minutes of my call to Adam, he walked in the kitchen door, Clarissa at his side.

Coming over to hug me, he said, "You okay?"

"I'm not sure. She said she'd be back in an hour."

"Mama's really here?" Clarissa questioned, with a worried expression on her face. "Will I have to go with her?"

Adam ran a hand through his hair, kneeling down in front of his daughter. Placing his hands on her shoulders, he looked into her eyes. "I'm not sure what's going on. But I do know you won't be leaving Cedar Key for any visits with her. The judge made that very clear at the hearing. But yes, you might have to visit with her on the island, and that's only every other weekend. We'll figure it out," he told her, standing up and taking a deep breath.

"How about some hot chocolate, Clarissa?" The poor child needed more than a comfort drink, but I thought it might help.

"Okay," she said, leaning down to pick up and cuddle Billie. "Come on, girl. I'll take you out."

She clipped on Billie's leash and went out to the yard.

Filling the kettle with water, I felt Adam's arms go around my waist.

"We'll get through this. We will," he said, nuzzling my neck.

"I know, but it's just not fair to Clarissa. She's settling in so well here with us."

"I can hardly believe Carrie Sue actually has come to Cedar Key. I have a call out to the lawyer. We'll be able to find out if she's telling the truth about legally asserting her visitation rights."

Clarissa walked back in the kitchen, unclipped Billie, and hung the leash on the hook by the door. As she plunked into a chair, I couldn't help but think she resembled that child who had come to live with us almost eight months before—sad and unhappy.

Just as I poured water into the mug of hot chocolate, the doorbell rang. I swung around to see Clarissa looking at me with uncertainty. She reached down to scoop up Billie and prevent her from running to the foyer.

"I'll get it," Adam said, walking to the front door.

"Well, hello, sweetie." A Southern drawl filtered back to me in the kitchen. "I must say, you're lookin' mighty good these days," I heard Carrie Sue tell Adam.

"Come into the kitchen," he told her without an ounce of friendliness in his words. "We need to get to the bottom of this."

I heard her high heels tapping across the tile floor as she followed Adam and turned around from the counter to see her enter the kitchen. Although Clarissa sat right there in plain sight, Carrie Sue's gaze panned the kitchen, taking in the antique oak table, fashionable appliances, and designer decorating. Finally, I saw her eyes drift to Clarissa.

Walking to her daughter, she drawled, "Well, sugar, it's been much too long since Mama's seen you. Look how you've grown." Quickly pecking Clarissa's cheek, she then exclaimed, "What on earth is *that?*" pointing to Billie in Clarissa's arms.

"It's *her* dog," Adam informed his ex-wife.

"Oh, well, you know I'm allergic to those things," she said, raising a hand to her nose as if to catch a sneeze.

"You're no more allergic to dogs than I am." Adam pulled out a chair and sat down. "You just don't *like* dogs. So get over it. The dog stays exactly where she is. If you want to discuss this situation, then sit."

Carrie Sue's eyes grew wider and she opened her mouth as if to say something, clamped it shut, and then sat in a chair beside Clarissa at the table.

I did the same, taking the chair next to Adam. My husband was showing me a side of himself that I wasn't familiar with. Normally easygoing and soft-spoken, he now exhibited an assertiveness that bordered on aggressive.

"Okay, what exactly is all of this about, Carrie Sue?"

"What it's about," she said, reaching into her bag, "is . . . oh, do y'all mind if I light up a cigarette?"

"Yes!" both Adam and I exclaimed.

"Yes, we do mind," Adam told her. "Monica and I are not smokers, nor do we allow smoking in our house."

Carrie Sue raised a hand and shrugged. "Okay, okay. Just thought I'd ask." Pulling papers from her bag, she passed them to Adam. "Exactly what this is about is about a *real* mother claiming the right to seeing her daughter."

I caught the nasty glance she shot in my direction and watched as Adam scanned the papers in his hand. I looked across the table at Clarissa, who hadn't uttered one word, but still sat there clutching Billie in her arms.

After a few moments, Adam passed the papers back to Carrie Sue. "These seem to be in order, but I'm not agreeing to anything until I have my attorney check it out. And anyway, what are your plans? You live in Georgia. You mean to tell me you're going to drive down here every other weekend to spend time with Clarissa?"

I swear the smile that covered Carrie Sue's face was an exact replica of the Cheshire cat's. "Don't be silly, Adam. Of *course* not. That would be foolish." She paused for a second before stating, "I'm living here on Cedar Key now. If my daughter is here, then this will be my new home."

Feeling like I'd been punched in the stomach, I heard Clarissa gasp, "You moved *here?* Why?"

"Yes, Carrie Sue, *why?*" Adam repeated, ice lacing his words.

Tossing bangs off her forehead, she calmly replied, "I just told you why—to be with my daughter. I've gotten myself a condo over at Fennimore Mills. A two-bedroom, and plenty of room for Clarissa to stay with me."

Yup, my worst nightmare was suddenly materializing. You mean to tell me I now had to live in the same town as Adam's ex? Bump into her wherever I went? As the *poor me* attitude began to descend, I looked over at Clarissa and felt instant shame. The poor child looked like she'd been hit by a Mack truck—her face was pale, her eyes wide and uncomprehending, and her fingers kept kneading Billie's fur—but she remained silent.

"And what do you plan to do here, Carrie Sue? You're only going to have Clarissa every other weekend. What do you plan to do the rest of your time here?" Adam's voice had noticeably risen.

"Do?" she questioned. "Why, I don't rightly know. I saw that you have a beach—I've always liked sunbathing."

I just bet, I thought. *And probably wearing practically nothing.*

"And . . . well . . . I hope to make some new friends," she went on, irritation creeping into her voice. "Actually, that's none of your business, Adam. I seemed to find plenty to do in Georgia and I have no doubt I'll do the same here." Standing up, she straightened the short, black corduroy jacket she wore.

It was then that I assessed the rest of her outfit. I had been so focused on the problem at hand, I hadn't given much interest to what she was wearing. But now I could see the jacket and white silk blouse were definitely Ralph Lauren. The charcoal gray slacks were probably Armani, and glancing down at her stylish high heels, I would have bet anything they were Prada. All those years living and working in Boston had developed my sense of fashion. *Oh sure,* I thought, *she's going to fit right in here on Cedar Key*—where our normal attire was either jeans or shorts, depending on the weather. The old saying, *a fish out of water,* was going to take on a whole new meaning for Carrie Sue Brooks.

"And so," she said. "The judge has granted me visitation with Clarissa this coming weekend. I'll pick her up after school on Friday. Understand?"

Adam also stood up. "What I understand is—nothing will happen until my attorney gets back to me. Leave me a number and I'll call you when I hear something."

Carrie Sue reached in her bag, whipped out a card with a Georgia peach and a phone number, threw it on the table, and flounced out of our house.

❦ 35 ❧

The three of us looked at each other as the front door slammed shut. All of what had just transpired astounded me, but what really overwhelmed me was the lack of affection or interest Carrie Sue displayed toward Clarissa. Not even a good-bye.

"Now what?" I heard her say, looking up at Adam and me.

He shook his head. "I'm as confused as you are, Clarissa." He walked around the table and pulled her into his arms. "But I tell you what, you're not going anywhere until I know for certain the judge agreed to this and until I go and check out where she's living."

"You mean I really have to go and stay with her?"

I heard the plaintiveness in her voice. This was so damn unfair. Why the heck did a child have to go somewhere she clearly didn't want to be?

"We might have no choice," Adam told her. "But let's wait and see what Trent says when he calls. And in the meantime, I think the three of us deserve a nice dinner out. How about the Island Room?"

This brought a smile to Clarissa's face. "Really?"

"Yup. Why don't you go do your homework now and we'll go about six."

She walked out of the kitchen with Billie trailing behind her.

I went to Adam and put my arms around his neck. "I can hardly believe this is happening. She doesn't even want to go, Adam. It's not right. And Carrie Sue—my God, she didn't even talk to Clarissa. Showed no interest whatsoever. Why the hell is she doing this?"

"Because that's how she is. Always has been. Everything is about *her*, certainly not what's best for her daughter. Although I must admit, I seriously had my doubts that she'd actually show up here."

"And you were right—what on earth will she find to occupy her time?"

"Well, she doesn't have to work, so that eliminates that. She's set financially. We have a fair number of watering holes in Cedar Key."

I pulled back from his embrace to look at him. "Are you serious? You think she'll spend her time drinking?"

Adam let out a deep sigh. "It's what she does best, Monica."

The phone rang and I let Adam get it, hoping it was the attorney. "Hi, Trent," I heard him say.

I decided to go check on Clarissa and see if she needed any help with her homework. Her bedroom door was closed, but I could hear her talking softly. She didn't have a friend in there. Who was she talking to? I tiptoed closer and put my ear to the door.

"How do you know it will be okay?" I heard her say. Then silence. "Yes, I can be strong, but I still don't want to have to stay with her." Was she on the phone? No, she couldn't be. Adam was using the line. "I know, but . . . I just want her to go away. We don't need her here," she said. Was she talking to herself? "You will? You'll go with me whenever I have to go there? You promise?"

"Monica?" I heard Adam call, causing me to jump away from the door.

"Yeah?" I said, walking back to the kitchen.

"I'm afraid it's all legal. Carrie Sue *did* get herself a lawyer, they went to the judge, he signed the visitation papers for every other weekend—and it begins this Friday."

"Shit! Oh, no!" I said as it finally dawned on me that we were due to leave for Augusta Friday afternoon.

"I know. Augusta. Well . . . we could still go." His hesitation was obvious.

Without even thinking, I blurted out, "Are you crazy? Of course we can't go! And *not* be here all weekend in case something happened. No way. We're not going." I was emphatically shaking my head.

Adam walked over and pulled me into his arms. "I am so, *so* sorry. I know how much you were looking forward to this, and so was I." He kissed the top of my head. "Maybe after we get Clarissa situated, we could leave on Saturday morning instead."

I pulled away to look up at him. "Absolutely not. Like I said, we need to be here. What if something happened? Carrie Sue's about as responsible as a four-year-old."

Adam laughed. "You've got that right. Oh, Monica, I still feel so bad about all of this."

"Don't," I told him. "It's okay. Really. We'll reschedule and go in March during spring break. How's that sound? My mom said Augusta is spectacular in March with all of the dogwoods and azaleas in bloom."

He pulled me back into a tight embrace. "Do you know how much I love you? You are one incredible woman and everything to me."

"I do know how much, Adam, because I love you back in the same exact way."

Wednesday afternoon I was sitting in Grace's coffee shop nursing a latte waiting for her to finish up with a few customers. The last one walked out the door and she joined me.

"So, wanna talk about it?" she asked, pulling up a chair across from me.

"There isn't much more to say. I've told you everything. Carrie

Sue showing up on our doorstep, Trent confirming she does have visitation rights and she's living at Fennimore Mills."

Grace shook her head. "What a pisser, huh? And you've definitely canceled your Augusta trip? No wonder you're feeling down in the dumps."

"I'd feel much worse if we went, knowing that poor kid was stuck with Carrie Sue for the weekend and we were a seven-hour car trip away if something happened."

Grace reached across the table and gave my hand a squeeze. "Well, it's still nice of you to cancel, but I do agree. She's such a loser. God only knows what could happen. Does that woman have no brains?"

I smiled. "After seeing her in action the other day, I'd say she's probably a quart low."

"How's Clarissa dealing with all of this?"

"So-so. She doesn't want to have to spend those weekends with Carrie Sue and she shouldn't have to be going through something like this at her age. Cripe, now I think she's developed an imaginary friend."

"Why's that?"

I told Grace about eavesdropping on Clarissa's conversation.

"Did you ask her about it?"

"No, because I'm really not sure what the heck is going on. Do you remember when she first came here and told us she wanted to go out to Atsena Otie on the boat? And then, out of the blue she decides to name her dog Billie? It's just weird. All of it."

"What're you saying? Are you beginning to think it might be your grandmother's spirit after all?"

I took a sip of coffee. "I'm not sure what to think, Gracie. I know you believe in those things. I just never have. But it sure seems odd—after Clarissa came out of her bedroom, she didn't seem as upset. Certainly not happy to learn she had to go to Carrie Sue's this weekend, but it was almost like she'd resigned herself. I heard her say to whoever she was talking to that they'd go with her, and she made whoever that was promise."

"Maybe it *is* Sybile, Monica. Maybe ol' Sybile is hanging around because she still has some things to do and she needs to make sure you're in a good place before she can continue on her journey. And don't forget, children have amazing psychic abilities. Unfortunately, most of us lose these as we get older, but children are very open to these types of experiences."

For the first time I didn't argue or tell Grace she was foolish. Not so much because I believed her, but because I honestly didn't know what was going on. And for the first time, I also began to wonder if my best friend had a psychic ability she'd chosen not to share with me, in addition to other things about herself.

"Oh, geez," she said. "So now you won't have the privacy to talk to Adam this weekend like you'd planned."

"Well, we will have the privacy, because Clarissa will be gone till Sunday. But I don't think now is a good time to bring this subject up."

"Changed your mind?" Grace prodded.

"No, I don't think so. I just don't think the timing is good right now. I'll know when it is."

"Well, hey, look on the bright side—you won't be in Augusta, but you'll have your house to yourselves for the entire weekend. Champagne in the Jacuzzi, walking around naked, all that good stuff."

I threw my head back laughing. "Gracie, you're too much. You really *do* need a man in your life."

"Hmm, speaking of which, Mr. High and Mighty called me last night."

"No! No, please don't tell me you're considering seeing him again."

"Do you really think I'm *that* desperate for a man? Please! He did try, though. Gave me a bunch of crap, saying he was sorry, it really was never about trying to get my property, yadda, yadda, yadda."

"Do you believe him?"

"Not for a second. Just as I was ready to hang up he said I was a very foolish woman to turn down the amount of money he was still willing to pay me for this property. My parting words were 'go to hell and don't ever call me back,' then I slammed the phone."

I raised my hand to give Grace a high five. "Good for you."

"Some men think women are just so stupid. I'll never understand it."

"Well, he had no idea he was dealing with the likes of you. He saw those auburn curls and thought you'd be an easy pushover." I glanced out the window to Dock Street. "Oh, my God! There she is!"

Grace turned around to peer outside. "Oh, yeah, that has *got* to be the ex—maybe better known as *Miss* High and Mighty."

I tried to position myself in back of Grace just in case Carrie Sue peeked in the window. "Christ, do you think she'll come in here for coffee?"

Grace laughed. "The way she's dressed like a New York City fashion plate? I seriously doubt it. I don't think Coffee, Tea and Thee would be on her social register. Boy, she's a piece of work, isn't she?"

I leaned to my right and saw Carrie Sue was standing across the street at the railing to the Big Dock, looking out toward the water. Wearing a calf-length tan knit dress, a beige shawl wrapped around her shoulders, and tan heels, she looked completely out of place. "She looks a bit foolish in those clothes."

Grace shook her head. "You think?" she said, giggling like a teenager.

I found myself giggling right along with her, and a few moments later, Carrie Sue glanced toward the coffee shop and I swear she wrinkled up her nose before proceeding down the street.

36

Friday afternoon I was sitting on the deck working on Grace's scarf waiting for Adam and Clarissa to arrive home from school. We were having one of those glorious winter days on the island where the temperature hovered close to seventy. I couldn't seem to stop thinking about the fact that we had to take Clarissa to Carrie Sue's that afternoon. It just seemed so wrong. But to Clarissa's credit, she had been good about it even though it was obvious she didn't want to go. I glanced up to see my husband and stepdaughter walking into the yard.

"Hey," I yelled, putting my knitting down.

I watched Adam come up the stairs and noticed how tired he was looking. This situation with Carrie Sue was taking its toll on him.

"Good day at school?" I asked Clarissa as Adam leaned in to place a kiss on my lips.

She nodded. "We practiced for the Christmas play again. I knew all of my lines for Mary."

I smiled. "Of course you did." Adam and I were quite proud that she'd been chosen to play such an important part.

"And you won't forget it's Tuesday night?" she asked.

"Are you kidding?" Adam exclaimed. "I think we've marked it on every calendar in the house."

"And Grandma's still coming?"

"Absolutely," I told her. "And Aunt Dora, Saren, and Gracie will be there. They wouldn't miss it for anything."

She started to head to her room and stopped to turn around. "Do we have to invite Mama?" she asked Adam.

"Clarissa, that wouldn't be very nice not to include her."

"She probably won't come anyway," she mumbled under her breath before walking off.

Adam had been grading school papers, while I sat on the sofa knitting. Glancing up at the mantel clock, I saw it was already four.

"Oh, gosh, I'd better make sure Clarissa's all set to go to Carrie Sue's," I said, jumping up and heading to her bedroom.

She was sitting on the bed, Billie curled up beside her, reading a book. I looked around the room. "Where's your backpack?" I asked.

"Oh," she said, without enthusiasm. "I have to pack."

"Clarissa, you still haven't packed? I put all of your things on your bureau. There they are," I said, walking over to the neatly folded piles of clothes. "I'll put them in your backpack and you get your toothbrush and the stuff in the bathroom that you'll need."

Ever so slowly she slid from the bed. She returned a few minutes later with brush, comb, and her other essentials.

"Okay, put them in here. We have to get a move on. Carrie Sue is expecting you at four-thirty."

"Are you sure you'll pay attention to Billie while I'm gone? She's going to miss me."

She was right. "Of course, I will, Clarissa. We're going to your grandmother's for dinner this evening, and Billie's coming with us. We'll walk over with her so she'll get her exercise."

This brought a smile to Clarissa's face. "Thank you, and tell Grandma thank you for letting Billie come."

I zipped up her bag. "Okay, I think we're all set," I said, heading out of the room.

"Wait a sec," she hollered, holding up her knitting bag. "Can I take this?"

"Of course you can."

"But what'll I do if I have a problem? My mother doesn't know how to knit."

Hmm, good question. "You're knitting so well now I have a feeling you won't be making any mistakes."

I wasn't sure if I should accompany Adam and Clarissa to Carrie Sue's house, but Adam had insisted. "You have every right to be there," he told me.

We climbed the stairs to the condo with Clarissa between us. Finding the correct number, Adam knocked on the door. We waited a minute or two and when nobody answered, Adam knocked again, harder this time.

"Oh, for goodness sake, give a girl time to get outta the bathroom," we heard Carrie Sue holler from inside and a moment later she swung open the door.

Her eyes went directly to me. "Oh, I didn't know y'all were comin' too."

Without hesitating, I said, "Well, since this is where my stepdaughter's spending the weekend, I wanted to be sure the accommodations were adequate."

Tossing her head, Carrie Sue moved aside to let us enter. "Does this meet with your approval?"

We stepped into a small living room furnished with Key West furniture and décor. Shades of mauve and mint green covered the wicker sofa and chair cushions. Prints of pelicans and egrets hung from the walls. Stacks of newspapers were ready to topple off the coffee table where some dirty cups and dishes still sat, never making it to the dishwasher. A jacket and sweater had been tossed over the back of a chair and the distinct odor of cigarette smoke filled the room. My eyes went to the overflowing ashtray on the end table. Meet with my approval? No, not at all. But I remained silent.

"Carrie Sue, I thought we discussed that I didn't want Clarissa subjected to your cigarette smoke," Adam told her.

"Oh, for goodness sake. I've got a can of Lysol right here," she said, going into the kitchen. She returned and began spraying the room. "And yes, okay. While she's here, I'll only be smoking out there on the balcony." She pointed to a small covered area, accessed through sliding glass doors from the living room, where a small patio table and chairs were arranged.

"Well, come on, sugar, let Mama show you your bedroom," she told Clarissa and we followed her to a hallway that led to the room.

Nice enough, although not nearly as nice as the one she had at our house. Twin bed, bureau, end table, also in the Key West touristy décor.

"Isn't this nice?" Carrie Sue asked.

Well, it was certainly neater than the living room.

"Yup," was all Clarissa said.

"Okay," Adam told her, walking toward the front door. "We'll pick Clarissa up Sunday afternoon around three. She has school on Monday. What are your plans for tomorrow?"

"Plans?" Carrie Sue asked, like she'd never heard the word before. "Oh . . . well . . . um . . . I thought maybe we'd take a ride to Chiefland. To Super Walmart and do some Christmas shopping."

Super Walmart for the woman who was probably Neiman Marcus's best customer? And drive? I wondered how responsible she was on the road.

"Okay," Adam said, pulling Clarissa into a tight embrace and kissing her. "You be a good girl, and we'll see you on Sunday."

She nodded and immediately headed toward me. Surprised, I

opened my arms to accept her embrace and realized she'd made no attempt to hug her mother. Yet here she was displaying affection toward me. I kissed her cheek and held her back to look down into her face.

"You have a good time, and don't worry about Billie. We'll take very good care of her."

She nodded and we walked out of the condo. By the time we reached the bottom step, I felt moisture in my eyes. Dear God, I felt like I'd just dropped my puppy off at a pound—with no guarantee of the care it would receive.

"Well, I don't care about laws and judges," Opal stated, swinging her fork in the air as she spoke. "All I know is that Carrie Sue is the poorest excuse for a mother that I've ever seen."

For once, I had to totally agree with my mother-in-law.

"It's not right. It's just not right that that poor child should have to endure the likes of her. And all I can say is nothing better happen to my granddaughter when she's in the care of that lowlife."

Adam shook his head. "Mom, please. Enough. We all feel the same way, and there isn't a damn thing I can do about it. And I'm going to tell you again, do *not* say any of this in front of Clarissa."

Opal took a sip of her wine. "Oh, for goodness sake, Adam, give me more credit than that. I just hate the thought of that child being with Carrie Sue. And what's she going to do with her all weekend?"

Adam pushed roast pork around on his plate. "She said maybe they'd take a ride to Super Walmart tomorrow."

Opal sniffed. "Oh, she's going slummin'?"

I smiled. My thought exactly.

Poor Adam was feeling bad enough, and although Opal meant well, she didn't need to be badgering him, making him feel worse.

"Opal," I said, "this roast is delicious. I don't know how you always get it so perfect."

"Southern cookin' passed down for generations," she told me. "And we have my key lime pie for dessert, so eat up."

The rest of the dinner conversation centered on Clarissa's play and Christmas.

After we loaded the dishwasher, the three of us sat down to enjoy coffee and Opal's famous pie.

"Ya know," she said, shooting a glance across the table to Adam. "I have one more thing to say on the subject of Clarissa staying with Carrie Sue and then I'll hold my peace." When Adam remained silent, she went on, "I'd feel a whole lot better if that child at least had a cell phone with her. There's no telephone at Carrie Sue's house, is there?"

Opal was right. Since Carrie Sue had a cell, she didn't bother to turn on phone service.

Adam looked up at his mother. "Geez, you're probably right. I never gave that a thought. She should have a way to contact us if she needs us. I'll look into that right away on Monday. That's a good idea. Thanks, Mom."

I saw the self-satisfied grin that spread across Opal's face and smiled myself. Opal could be a pain, but she had a good heart and she was proving to be a very involved and concerned grandmother. Couldn't ask for more than that.

❦ 37 ❦

Somehow Adam and I managed to get through the weekend, but I won't lie, the house was terribly empty without Clarissa around. Poor Billie just moped and whined despite all the extra attention I lavished on her.

We even took Grace's suggestion, and Saturday evening we relaxed in the hot tub with a bottle of excellent champagne, which of course led to some excellent lovemaking. Knowing we had the house to ourselves, like before Clarissa had come to live with us, seemed to bring out a more frisky and passionate side to our sex.

But when I awoke Sunday morning and wandered into the kitchen to make coffee, Clarissa's absence was once again noticeable. While the coffee brewed, I put on my robe and walked outside to get the paper.

"Monica?" I heard my name being called and turned around to see Miss Tilly walking toward me.

"Good morning, Miss Tilly. How're you today?"

"Well, a bit upset if truth be told. Where's that lovely stepdaughter of yours?"

"Clarissa? Oh . . . well . . . her mother has moved to Cedar Key and will be taking Clarissa every other weekend. This was their weekend together."

"Is that so? Well, somebody needs to be keeping a closer check on that woman."

What on earth was she talking about? "What do you mean?" I asked.

"Well, I'm not one to carry tales, but . . . when it involves a child and especially one as sweet as that Clarissa, well, I don't think I should hold my tongue."

Irritation came over me. *Just spit it out,* I wanted to yell at her. "What exactly are you talking about?"

"I happened to be at Walmart yesterday afternoon." She adjusted her eyeglasses to stare directly at me. "There I was, in the cat section looking for some Christmas toys for my Fluffy, when all of a sudden it came over the loudspeaker that a little girl was at the courtesy desk at the front of the store. Clarissa Brooks was her name, they said, and could her mother please come and get her."

"What?" I exclaimed. Carrie Sue lost Clarissa in Walmart? "Oh, my God. Did Carrie Sue get her?"

Tilly pursed her lips and made a face. "Oh, yeah, she showed up—hobbling across the floor barefoot to the courtesy desk."

"Barefoot?" What the hell!

"Yeah, it was obvious she'd been getting herself a pedicure there at the front of the store. What kind of mother leaves a nine-year-old alone to get her toenails painted?"

The question of the century. "Was she okay? Was Clarissa all right?"

"She seemed to be. I was gonna walk up to them, but I stood in the aisle watching. Trying to mind my own business, ya know. So I hung around to see what was happening. She took Clarissa back with her to the salon, got her shoes on, paid what she owed, and walked out of the store. I followed them to the parking lot, just to make sure everything was okay, and I saw them both get in the car and take off."

"Oh, my God, anything could have happened to Clarissa." I could feel anger bubbling up inside me.

"Well, yes, exactly. That's why I thought I should tell you. Mind you, I don't like gossip, but as I said, when it involves a child. . . ."

I leaned over and hugged Tilly. "No, no, you did the right thing. Thank you, Tilly. I really do appreciate it."

I walked toward the house and dreaded having to lay this on Adam.

An hour later my anger still hadn't subsided. "Can you believe this?" I said to Adam after revealing Tilly's story. "What the hell kind of mother does something like that?"

His voice was controlled but I knew he was as upset as I was. "One who just doesn't *think*. Typical of Carrie Sue. Thank God Clarissa was smart enough to go the courtesy desk."

"She's a bright little girl," I said, placing French toast in front of him. "Now what? Are you going to have it out with Carrie Sue?" I wanted her punished. She didn't deserve the right to have Clarissa.

Adam stirred cream into his coffee. "I will, of course, but not in front of Clarissa. When we pick her up this afternoon, why don't we take Billie with us, and if you wouldn't mind, you could walk back with Clarissa and I'll stay and talk to Carrie Sue. I'll be instituting a new rule—no way is she to take that child off the island. She either visits with her here or not at all."

Didn't sound like much of a punishment to me, but I trusted Adam's judgment. "Okay. Are you going to discuss it with Clarissa?"

"I'd rather she tell us what happened, see what she says."

I waited in the parking lot with Billie on her leash. The poor dog had moped all weekend. A few minutes later Clarissa came running down the stairs and straight to Billie.

Scooping the dog up in her arms, she cooed, "Oh, Billie, I missed you so much! I'm sorry I had to leave you." She buried her face in the dog's fur.

"She missed you a lot too, but I gave her extra attention. How're you doing? Have a good weekend?" I asked as we started walking home.

"It was okay. Thank you for being so nice to Billie."

We walked along in silence the rest of the way home.

Walking in the kitchen door, Clarissa put her backpack and knitting bag on the counter, unclipped Billie's leash, and said, "Is it okay if I go check my e-mails? I haven't been able to talk to Zoe."

"Of course it is. I'll empty your backpack and put the dirty clothes in the laundry room."

Hmm, not one word about her escapade in Walmart.

After emptying the backpack, I peeked in her knitting bag and was astonished—the entire scarf was finished except for binding off. When on earth had she found the time to do all that knitting? Didn't Carrie Sue spend any time with her?

Adam arrived home about forty-five minutes later and I could tell by his face that the confrontation with Carrie Sue had only provoked his anger.

"How'd it go?" I asked. "Coffee? I just made a pot."

Coming over to give me a hug, he said, "Yeah, that'd be great. It went like I thought it would. At first she denied what happened—"

"Denied what happened?" I cut in. "How could she? Tilly witnessed it."

"She's a pathological liar, Monica. But I had her backed into a corner when I described exactly what happened. She wanted to know how I knew, and of course I wasn't about to tell her. According to her, she says she brought Clarissa to the toy department, told her to look around and then come to the front of the store to the salon."

"Even at that—you don't leave a nine-year-old alone in Walmart. Not with all the nuts out there today! Do you believe her?"

"Not at all, because knowing Clarissa, I think she would have preferred to sit in the salon and wait for her, rather than be alone in the toy department. Has she said anything to you about it?"

"Not a word, but I noticed her entire scarf is finished. How the heck did she manage that? Didn't Carrie Sue spend any one-on-one time with her?"

"Probably not. I told her she is never to drive Clarissa off the island. Actually, that didn't seem to faze her in the least. Where's Clarissa now?"

"On the computer, talking to Zoe."

"When she comes out, we'll discuss it and hear her side of the story."

We were finishing up our coffee when Clarissa wandered into the kitchen, Billie close at her heels.

"Clarissa, come sit down," Adam told her. "I want to ask you about something."

Her glance shot from me to Adam as she slid into the chair. "What?"

"Did you go to Walmart yesterday with your mother?"

"Yeah," was all she said, not volunteering any further information.

Adam gave her a few moments and then went on. "We happen to know that you got left in the toy department. How'd that happen?"

Clarissa's head shot up and then she began fingering the place mat in front of her.

"Clarissa?"

"Did Mama tell you?"

"No, she didn't. Somebody else did."

"Oh, the lady that helped me?"

I was sure she didn't mean Tilly, because Tilly would have told me if she'd gotten involved.

"Which lady?" Adam asked her.

"You know, the nice one. The one that always helps me."

Goose bumps formed on my body and I crossed my arms in front of my chest. Was she referring to Sybile?

"Tell us what happened," Adam encouraged her.

"When we got there, she asked if I wanted to look in the toy department with her and choose something for Christmas. So I said okay. I looked at different things and then we went into the book aisle. I had looked at a few books and I thought Mama was right there, in back of me, waiting. But when I turned around, she was gone. She wasn't there. So I went in the next aisle and all the other ones in the toy department—but I couldn't find her. I started to get a little scared. It was a big store and lots of people and I didn't know what to do. And that's when the lady came to me. She was standing in front of me and asked if I needed help and I told her yes, I couldn't find my mother. She told me to walk up front to where a big desk was and there'd be a woman there to help me. So that's what I did."

"You're a very smart and a very brave girl," Adam told her. "And then they announced your name on the loudspeaker and your mother came?"

Clarissa nodded. "Yup. She was getting her toenails done, because she came over barefoot with a funny, pink rubber thing between her toes. Then we came home—I never did get the toy."

I felt a lump in my throat. Carrie Sue had intentionally left her daughter in the toy department to keep her occupied while she got her pedicure.

"Don't worry about the toy, Clarissa," I told her. "Our tree will be overflowing with toys for you." I got up and leaned over to hug her and I saw a small smile form on her face.

Later that evening, I was sitting on the sofa knitting while Adam graded papers beside me. Clarissa was curled up in the chair reading.

He put the papers aside and stood up. "Time for bed, princess," he told Clarissa.

Carefully inserting her bookmark between the pages, she closed the book and set it on the table. "Good night, Monica," she said.

She walked toward me, leaned forward with arms extended, and gave me a huge hug. My arms automatically went around her as I kissed the side of her face, and I admit it—I melted. To have this child come to me of her own accord for a good-night hug said volumes to me—much more than the actual physical act. I glanced up over Clarissa's head to see Adam standing there, a huge smile on his face.

"Good night, Clarissa. Sweet dreams," I told her.

Watching them walk out of the room, I wondered again about the woman who helped Clarissa. Could it be possible? Could Sybile have designated herself my stepdaughter's guardian angel?

❦ 38 ❦

The following morning over breakfast Clarissa informed us, "Oh, by the way, Mama can't come to my Christmas play tomorrow night—because she has a date." This was related without an ounce of disappointment in her voice.

A *date?* Adam was right—this woman was hot to trot. She'd certainly wasted no time hooking up with somebody.

Adam looked up from his scrambled eggs and bacon. "Oh, okay. Well, you're going to have a lot of groupies there anyway."

"What are groupies?" she asked.

Adam laughed. "People who adore you and are anxious to see your stage debut."

Clarissa glanced at me with a smile and I sent her a wink.

"Are you at the yarn shop today?" Adam asked.

"Yeah, just till two, so I'll get Clarissa after school."

"When do we get to put up the tree?" she asked.

"Friday night," I told her. "And it's turned into a bit of a celebration. Your grandmother's coming, along with Aunt Dora and Saren. So I'm going to have Christmas cookies and eggnog."

Clarissa clapped her hands together. "Oh, wow, it'll be a tree-trimming party, just like in one of my books. Will Gracie come too?"

"I'll ask her when I see her today. I'm sure she will."

"That'll be fun," Adam said, getting up to clear the table. "Ten minutes, Clarissa, and we have to get going."

She headed to get her backpack as I began filling the dishpan with soapy water.

Walking back into the kitchen, Clarissa asked, "Do I have to go with Mama on Christmas?"

I'd been wondering about that too but hadn't brought it up with Adam.

"No. The new custody papers state that this Christmas is spent with me, but that your mom has you on Sunday because it's her weekend for visitation."

I could have sworn I heard her mutter "Good" as she walked out the back door.

Hearing the wind chimes, I glanced up from the computer to see Grace stroll into Spinning Forward, the usual two lattes in her hand.

"You're a lifesaver," I told her, raising my arms above my head and stretching.

"Lots of mail orders?" she asked, placing the cups on the coffee table.

"Yeah, must be that time of year. When Christmas approaches people begin to think how nice a personalized stocking would be for a child or grandchild. Dora and I can barely keep up, but I'm sure not complaining." I plopped onto the sofa and reached to uncap my coffee. "So what's up with you?"

"Well, I'm not sure I can top your news about Carrie Sue."

I laughed. I'd filled Grace in on the phone that morning before I left for the yarn shop.

"By the way, do we have to endure her presence tomorrow

evening at the Christmas play?"

"No—seems she has a date."

"A date? Damn. What? She's been here less than two weeks and that woman already has a date? Christ, how does she do it? *I* can't seem to get a date."

I shrugged. "Who knows?"

"Is he from the island?"

"Haven't a clue. I suppose she could have gone trawling in Gainesville. Might be somebody from there."

"Damn," Grace repeated. "Ah well," she sighed, "maybe I'm just destined to be a spinster."

I laughed. "Do they still call it that?"

"Actually, probably not. *Loser* might be more appropriate."

"Aw, Gracie, you're too hard on yourself. Look at you—extremely attractive, very intelligent, great sense of humor—Mr. Right will find you. It all has to do with timing."

"Yup, and my time will probably be when I'm in a nursing home, hobbling around with a walker."

Grinning, I said, "From some of the stories I hear, social life in a nursing home can be pretty active."

The wind chimes tinkled again and Miss Polly walked in.

"How're you gals doing?" she asked, joining us on the sofa.

"Great," I said. "I can make some coffee, would you like some?"

"No, thanks. I just popped by between customers to pick up that yarn you ordered for me."

"It's in the back room," I told her, going to find it.

"So he really sold it, huh?" I heard Grace say as I walked back into the shop.

"Who sold what?"

"Dick sold the bookshop," Polly explained. "Says he's been ready for retirement since he put it up for sale."

I totaled the amount for the yarn and slipped it into a shopping bag. "Oh, that's good. I know he was ready."

"Who's buying it?" Grace asked.

"Some fellow from Georgia. Seems he has a shop there as well. I heard he has somebody to manage that one for him while he gets this one set up."

"That's great," Grace said. "I'd hate to see the island without a bookshop."

"Yeah, that reminds me—I need to pop over there and pick up some books for Clarissa for Christmas."

Polly reached for the shopping bag. "Thanks. I need to get back for a color. See you gals later."

"Hmm," Grace said.

"What?"

"I'm just wondering if Mr. Bookshop Owner has a wife he'll be bringing with him."

I'd put chicken breasts in the oven for supper and Clarissa was sitting at the table doing her homework. I smiled as I recalled her dislike for chicken when she first came to us. Based on the way she ate it now, I wondered if it had had more to do with just being ornery rather than a true dislike for chicken.

"Do we leave for the play at six o'clock?" she asked.

I nodded as I picked up my knitting bag and headed to the great room. "Yeah, that's why we're eating at five tonight."

A few minutes later she joined me on the sofa, watching as I knitted.

I looked up and smiled. "Tomorrow I'll teach you how to bind off and then your scarf will be finished and ready to wear. What's your next project?"

"I thought maybe I'd do another scarf. But this time for Zoe, and I can mail it up to her."

"That's a great idea. It's good to keep practicing with your knit and purl rows, but I bet Zoe will love that. Plus it'll keep her warm up there. How's she doing lately?"

"Good," Clarissa said, leaning in closer to get a better look as I knitted. "She really likes Julie. She got to go shopping with her to pick out things for the baby's room, and the crib that they got—it was the one that Zoe liked best."

Smart woman, I thought. Including Zoe in the process. I was coming to understand children didn't require as much as I'd always thought. Attention, affection, and most of all love. The rest of it pretty much took care of itself. For a woman who a year ago considered herself maternally challenged, I was surprised with the daily insight that I seemed to be absorbing.

"Do they have any names picked out yet?" I questioned.

"Zoe says it'll probably be either Caleb or Zac. She likes Zac because then they'd both have a name starting with the letter 'z.' I like Zac better too."

"Me too. That's a very nice name."

"What's that you're doing there?" Clarissa questioned.

"This stitch is called knit two together. See, watch," I said, inserting my needle into the two stitches and knitting them together to slide onto the opposite needle.

"You ended up with one stitch."

"Right. It's pretty simple. You might want to try this on your next scarf."

"I like that," she said, gently touching the one stitch. "They were two—but they became one."

It wasn't lost on me that this could be a metaphor to describe the way my relationship with Clarissa was evolving.

❦ 39 ❦

Christmas evening I sat on the sofa beside Adam marveling at how incredibly different the holiday had been this year with a child around. I took a sip of wine and smiled at Clarissa. She was involved playing with one of the toys she'd received.

I'd been awakened that morning with shouts of "Santa came! He came!"

Adam and I had made our way to the great room to find Clarissa literally jumping up and down, unable to contain her excitement. Not to be outdone, Billie was running back and forth barking.

Despite not having my first cup of coffee, I laughed at the chaos that reminded me of my own Christmases as a child. The saying *Christmas brings out the child in all of us* took on new meaning for me.

"Look, look," she'd told us. "Santa brought me my very own TV and DVD player."

Adam and I had thought maybe Clarissa would like that for her bedroom, and it was an obvious hit.

Not at all familiar with Christmas-morning protocol for children, Adam had explained that the gifts that weren't wrapped were from Santa and the rest were from us.

"And he brought me all the Clementine books in the series, and look," she said, holding up cases of DVDs, "Movies to watch on my new player."

"I'd say Santa thought you were a very good girl," Adam had told her. "But remember the rule—now Monica and I get to have our coffee and then you can open the rest of the gifts."

All of it had been more fun than I could have imagined. It made me recall so many Christmases when I was single and working in Boston. Either I'd take off with a friend skiing or sometimes, exhausted from working so hard, I just slept the day away. Today was something I'd always remember—especially when Clarissa opened the box that held the sweater I'd made for her. Not only did that gift earn me a huge hug, she declared she loved it so much she had to wear it right away and promptly put it on over her nightgown.

Following the gift opening and breakfast, we had enjoyed a wonderful Christmas dinner at Opal's house with Aunt Dora, Saren, and Gracie. More gifts were exchanged and the true meaning of the day was when Grace sat at the piano and played Christmas carols, with the rest of us gathered around singing. Family and friends sharing love.

I glanced down at Clarissa on the carpet, still wearing the sweater I'd knitted her. I could be wrong, but I was willing to bet anything this was also one of her best Christmases.

The doorbell chiming interrupted my thoughts and I glanced at Adam, wondering who could be visiting on Christmas night.

"Oh, Carrie Sue," I heard him say at the front door.

After such a perfect day, my only thought was *shit!*

"Hey, y'all," she proclaimed in her singsong voice, breezing into the room. "Merry Christmas."

I looked up to see her stumble but catch herself before walking forward as she deposited brightly colored shopping bags in front of Clarissa.

"Y'all didn't think I'd forget my daughter on Christmas, did ya?"

Why not? I wondered. *You failed to acknowledge her birthday, and here it is 8:00 at night, with the holiday almost over.*

Adam was clearly flustered with the intrusion. "Oh . . . well . . . that's nice of you, Carrie Sue. Isn't it, Clarissa?"

With a bewildered look on her face, she glanced down at the bags and nodded.

Plunking on the sofa beside me, Carrie Sue said in a raised voice, "Well, go on. Open them."

It was then that I detected the strong odor of alcohol floating toward me. *My God, she's loaded,* I thought. *Comes here on Christmas night after probably drinking all day.*

Clarissa reached into a bag and pulled out a gaudy black velvet dress. Frilly red ruffles circled the hem, and from where I sat, the dipping neckline appeared to be inappropriate for a nine-year-old. Clearly, the dress wasn't Clarissa's style.

"Well, can't ya tell your mama thank you?" Carrie Sue urged. "Go ahead, open the other bags."

"Thank you," Clarissa mumbled, reaching for another bag. She pulled out an iPod. "What is it?" she asked.

"Oh, sugar . . . you need to get with it. All the kids have those. It's to listen to music."

"Oh," was all Clarissa said.

As she reached for another bag, Carrie Sue looked up at Adam. "Hey, handsome, where's your manners? Aren't ya gonna offer me a bit of Christmas cheer?"

Poor Adam looked ready to explode. "I'd say you've probably had more than your quota of *cheer* today."

Carrie Sue tossed her head as she attempted to pull down the skirt that was somewhere around her mid-thigh. "Oh, Adam. Always was Mr. Prim and Proper. And I think I'll be the judge of my intake. Christ, it's Christmas, lighten up."

"We have coffee, if you'd like some," he told her. "That's it."

"Well, never you mind. I'm headed downtown to meet somebody when I leave here—somebody not as stodgy as you."

"That's enough, Carrie Sue." Adam looked down at Clarissa. "Open the rest of the gifts, honey."

The next bag produced a DVD featuring a vampire movie.

"I don't like vampires," Clarissa stated, no apology in her tone.

"Oh, Clarissa Jo. For goodness sake, you really *do* need to grow up."

Grow up? The kid was barely nine! I had all I could do to keep my mouth shut.

The final bag held some sort of video game for the computer. By the looks of the cover, the violence it contained was better suited for a teen boy.

"Thank you," Clarissa mumbled again.

Carrie Sue stood up, wobbling a bit due to her four-inch heels and an excess of the cheer Adam had mentioned.

Without so much as a hug or kiss for Clarissa, she headed for the door. "Okay, y'all. I'm off to celebrate Christmas. Oh, and Adam, I meant to tell you—I have something going on tomorrow. Would it be all right if I don't take Clarissa as planned?"

I saw him shrug. "That's fine with me, but you can't take her the following weekend either. We have plans."

"Okay," she said, not an ounce of regret in her voice. "Then I'll call you. Looks like it'll be mid-January when I take her."

And with that, she was gone.

After we got Clarissa to bed, Adam and I were sitting on the sofa still trying to digest the scene we'd witnessed with Carrie Sue.

"I have to say, I know you'd always told me about her, but seeing her in action—wow, she's a piece of work. No wonder you couldn't stand living with her."

Adam sighed. "My only regret in that divorce was the fact I had to leave Clarissa with her."

"She's so unqualified to be a mother. I mean, really, did you see those hideous gifts she got? She has no clue what Clarissa likes or even what's appropriate for her."

"She never has. Between her drinking and her self-centeredness, she's clearly a woman who never should have had a child."

And I always thought that woman was me. Somebody just not cut out to be a mother. Based on what I'd witnessed with Carrie Sue, now I wasn't so sure. Over time I'd come to learn Clarissa's likes and dislikes. I'd come to feel how natural it was being in her company, how much I welcomed her laughter and her affection.

Maybe I'd been wrong. Maybe being a mother was about so much more than I ever realized. Simple things. Like just letting go and being yourself. I remembered hearing somewhere that people generally do the best they can in a given set of circumstances.

Looking back to April, when Clarissa had come to live with us, I was beginning to see how much I had known all along. Things I wasn't even aware of. And as a result, it now made me see that perhaps I was also *doing* better.

ᥲ 40 ᥲ

"My God," Grace said, wiping down the counter in the coffee shop. "That woman is a sandwich short of a picnic."

I laughed and shook my head. "Yeah, I have to admit, she's something. I just couldn't believe those gifts she got Clarissa."

"And then showing up three sheets to the wind. Nice. Very nice example to set for her daughter. What did poor Clarissa say about all of it?"

"I'm beginning to think that child has more intelligence than Carrie Sue could ever hope to have. When her mother left, she looked at Adam and asked if she had to wear that dress. He told her definitely not. Then she suggested donating all of it to Goodwill or something. I think I can understand why she really didn't miss Carrie Sue when she came to live with us."

"Exactly. A kid knows where the love is. Since she arrived, both you and Adam have shown an interest in her. From the sounds of it, something Carrie Sue never did."

"You know, after watching her in action, I've been thinking maybe my own mothering skills aren't as absent as I always thought."

Grace sat across the table from me. Leaning chin in hands, she said, "Hmm, you think?"

"Well, I don't know. All I know is that Carrie Sue has certainly proved she lacks common sense. Truthfully, she all but ignores Clarissa, and it's obvious she knows nothing about her. When she first arrived, neither did I, but now . . . well, gosh, I know her favorite color is purple, she adores dogs, her favorite TV show is *Hannah Montana,* she really does like chicken and—macaroni and cheese, well, she'd rather have that than anything."

I heard Grace chuckling and looked up at her. "What?"

"Listen to yourself. And think back to April. All those doubts that you had when Clarissa first came. I tried to tell you it would just take time, but oh no, you wouldn't listen. You were bound and determined to label yourself Mommie Dearest—and I do mean that in a derogatory way. It's never easy raising a child, but little by little you're catching on to what's important. Like teaching Clarissa to knit. Anybody can tell how much she enjoys that, but I don't think it's just the knitting—I think she likes the fact that it's something the two of you can do together and share."

The same thought had crossed my mind.

"You've been too hard on yourself, Monica. Personally, I think you've done a great job with Clarissa."

"You do?"

"Yes, I do," she said, getting up to come and pull me into a hug. "She's well adjusted, happy . . . what more can parents ask for?"

"That's exactly what Adam told me the other night. In addition to those things, he mentioned how well she's doing in school and said that's always a signal if a child feels stable."

"See? What have I been trying to tell you?"

Despite all the kudos from both Adam and Grace, one thing still nagged at me. I wouldn't admit it to them, but I still didn't feel that overpowering, fierce *love* that I knew most parents had for their children. We never even voiced those words to each other. Maybe a woman had to carry a child for nine months in order for that partic-ular emotion to surface? But then I recalled my mother being adopted and the deep love she shared with my grandmother, which once again left me with no answers.

The door to the coffee shop opened and both Grace and I looked at the man walking in. Not a local. Tall, slim but broad-shouldered, dark curly hair with a trace of gray at the temples, and olive-complexioned skin, dressed in casual slacks and navy pullover sweater. I wondered if maybe he was a substitute teacher at the school.

"Hi," Grace said to him, walking behind the counter. "What can I get ya?"

"I know it's a coffee shop," he said, speaking fluent English with an unmistakable French accent, "but I noticed your sign says you also have tea?"

"I do," Grace said with a smile and pointed to the board on the wall. "Actually, I have quite a good selection."

Walking closer to read the listings, he removed a pair of reading glasses clipped to the neck of his sweater. After a few moments he said, "Yes, I can see you have a wonderful selection. I think I'll have the chamomile, please."

He leaned over to inspect the baked goods Grace had in the dis-play case. "Oh, and one of those blueberry muffins to go with it."

Grace began preparing the tea. "Just visiting the island?" she asked him.

"Well, yes, for right now," he told her, his French accent becom-ing more pronounced. "I'm in the process of purchasing the book-shop downtown."

I sat up straighter in my chair. Ah, so this was the new owner.

"Oh, right. I'd heard somebody had purchased it." Grace placed the cover on the Styrofoam cup and extended her hand. "Well, wel-come to the island. I'm Grace Stone."

I watched as the man took her hand in his.

"Lucas Trudeau," he told her. "Very nice to meet you."

"And this," she said, pointing toward me, "is my best friend, Monica Brooks. Monica owns Spinning Forward, the yarn shop downtown."

He now shook hands with me and said, "Very nice to meet you, as well."

"Thanks. I hope you'll like it here."

Hmm, nice-looking guy. Well put together. Probably early forties, with a cosmopolitan look about him. Definitely looks like somebody who could own a bookshop, minus any nerdy qualities. A quick glance at his bare left hand told me there was also a good chance he was single.

"Yes, I believe I will. It appears to be a friendly town, and Dick assures me that it is."

"Oh, yeah," Grace said, laughing. "Cedar Key is definitely friendly. Everybody knows everybody." She passed the tea and muffin across the counter to him and rang up the sale.

"Do you mind if I sit here to have this?" he asked.

"No, not at all," I heard her say with a bit of enthusiasm in her voice. "Come join Monica and me. It's slow this time of day, so I was taking a break."

"So," I said as they both sat down, "how soon will you be opening the bookshop?"

"Well, I've also purchased the empty shop next door, so I'm going to be doing an expansion and remodeling. My goal is to have it open by the fall."

"Oh, what a great idea. I've always told Dick that bookshop was too small. He needed more space. Not like a chain, of course. There's something special about an independent bookstore. Did you see the movie *You've Got Mail?*"

Lucas threw his head back laughing, and it was difficult not to notice his attractive smile. "I did," he said, "and thoroughly enjoyed it."

"Weren't you just rooting for Meg Ryan?" Grace asked. "She had the greatest indie bookshop, and that stinker, Tom Hanks, wanted to put her out of business."

Lucas nodded. "Yes, I'm afraid with the poor economy the past few years a lot of shops like that one have failed. So I feel very fortunate to have done so well with my other one."

I recalled what Polly had told us and said, "Where's that one?"

"Brunswick, Georgia—about four hours north of here, just over the border."

I saw the look of surprise that swept across Grace's face. "Brunswick?" she said. "I was born and raised there. My aunt still lives there."

Now it was Lucas's turn to look surprised. "You said your last name was Stone? You're not by any chance related to Maude Stone, are you?"

Grace laughed. "I am. That's my aunt."

Lucas shook his head. "What a small world. Maude is one of my best customers. When I opened that shop five years ago, she's the one who was instrumental in forming the great book club that we have there."

"That would be Aunt Maude," Grace said. "She's always involved in one thing or another. With that accent and a name like Trudeau, you're French?"

"Yes, originally from the south of France and then about fifteen years in Paris. I had a bookshop there as well and sold it when I moved to Brunswick."

There was definitely some chemistry going on here, and I almost felt like I was intruding.

"But you won't be selling the shop in Brunswick?" Grace asked.

Lucas shook his head. "Not at the moment. I have an excellent staff I can depend on. This is what will allow me to spend a lot of time here getting this shop up and running. I had come here last year and fell in love with the island, so when I saw the bookshop was for sale, I couldn't help but make an offer."

"And you also purchased a house here?" Grace questioned.

"No, I'll be renting a small cottage over on Second Street. Very convenient to walk to the bookshop."

"I imagine your wife will like living here as well," Grace said.

I put my hand to my face, smothering a smile. Sly, Gracie, sly.

"I don't have a wife. . . . It's just me and Duncan. He's my Scottish terrier."

"Oh, they're adorable," I said. "My mother's best friend, she owns the B and B here, she has a Scottie, Winston."

"I got Duncan just before I relocated from Paris, and he's been a wonderful companion."

"I'm anxious to see what you do with the bookshop," Grace said. "I bet you have some great ideas."

"I think I do, yes." He glanced at the watch on his wrist and took the last sip of tea, then stood up. "It was so nice meeting both of you. Thank you for your hospitality and I look forward to seeing you again."

"Oh, same here," Grace said, watching him walk out the door.

The smile now formed on my face. "Interesting."

"Interesting? What do you mean?"

"Good-looking guy, don't ya think?"

Grace nodded. "Yeah, I guess so."

"Also single."

"Hmm, that's right, I think he did say that."

"Going to be here quite a lot getting the bookshop together."

"I suppose so."

I couldn't hold back the laughter any longer. "Oh, Gracie, 'fess up. You're attracted to him."

"God, was I *that* obvious?"

"No more so than he was."

"Get outta here!" she argued.

"I'm just telling you what I saw. And yeah, I'd say he was interested. Who knows, maybe you won't be that spinster in a nursing home after all."

⤳ 41 ⤳

Flipping the calendar to February on the kitchen wall, I was amazed that another month had zipped past. All things considered, it had been a pretty good one. We seemed to have settled into a routine, especially with Clarissa visiting Carrie Sue. Although I'd noticed that when she returned from her time with her mother, Clarissa seemed to be subdued, not talking much for a day or so and acting similar to when she'd first come to live with us.

I'd just finished running the vacuum through the great room when the phone rang and I answered to hear Opal.

"Hi, sweetie. Are you busy?"

"Just cleaning house. Why? What's up?"

"Well, I was wondering if I could stop by. There's something I'd like to talk to you about."

"Sure, I could use a break. Give me an hour, and why don't you come for lunch."

"Sounds good. See you then."

Hanging up, I thought *oh, damn*. I had a feeling maybe Opal was coming to tell me she'd decided to return to Georgia and wouldn't be able to keep Clarissa the weekend Adam and I were going to Augusta. If that was the case, I hoped that maybe Aunt Dora could take her.

I decided to dust and vacuum Clarissa's room before Opal arrived. Opening the door, I gasped. "Holy shit!" I yelled.

The room that had been kept perfectly neat for months now looked like a war zone. Clothes tossed here and there. A bath towel bunched up on the chair. Books scattered all over the unmade bed. And sprinkled on the carpet was glitter and tiny red foil hearts— everywhere. The empty tubes from these were on the desk.

Why would Clarissa leave her room like this before going to school? Well, I sure as hell wasn't about to clean it up.

I slammed the door behind me and walked out to the kitchen trying to calm down. Preparing two plates of crab salad, I kept shaking my head. What on earth had gotten into her? I thought we had the cleaning of her room under control.

Arranging lunch on the table, I looked up as Opal knocked and walked in.

"Oh, that looks yummy," she said, sitting down. "Can I help with anything?"

"No. Sweet tea?"

"That would be good. Something wrong?" she asked.

I let out a deep sigh before plunking in the chair across from her. "Yeah, plenty. I thought we were over Clarissa not keeping her room clean. Come with me," I said, leading the way.

Opening the bedroom door, I flung my arm forward. "Nice, huh?"

"Oh, my," Opal said, stepping over the threshold and looking around the room. "Obviously, the child is upset about something."

"*She's* upset? I passed upset about twenty minutes ago."

"Well, sure, honey. If she's been keeping her room clean, and then to have this." Opal gestured around the room. "Clearly, something's bothering Clarissa Jo."

How the hell did Opal know this? Was this something from Motherhood 102? An advanced level I hadn't gotten to yet?

"Seems to me Clarissa is testing you," Opal informed me.

"Testing me? But why?"

"Well, that I can't tell you. But yeah, testing to see your reaction to this. If I didn't know better . . . ," she began, and then stopped.

"What? What were you going to say?"

"Well . . . Adam said Clarissa's not real happy when she returns from Carrie Sue's place. Not that I can blame the poor child, mind you. But I'm wondering if this is her way of acting out—trying to get some control over a situation where she has *no* control."

"You mean because she really doesn't want to go to Carrie Sue's?"

"Exactly."

"That makes no sense. Just because she's back to not keeping her room clean, that doesn't mean it will stop the visits."

"Right," Opal explained. "But she's feeling lost and confused again. She could be looking for a way to feel secure. By not cleaning her room, she knows it will cause you and Adam to be angry with her."

"And that's what she wants?"

Opal smiled, put an arm around my shoulder and directed me back to the kitchen.

Sitting down at the table, she said, "What she *wants* is for you to give her some structure, something Carrie Sue has never done. By not cleaning her room, she's called attention to herself. This in turn forces you to address the problem. I'm not sayin' kids love discipline or being punished. However, it gives them the stability they crave. Lettin' a child run wild and do as they please doesn't show an ounce of love—what it shows is indifference on the part of the parent. Kids instinctively know this. Being a parent is the hardest job in the world—that's because it's so time-consuming. A parent who takes the time to discipline a child makes that child feel wanted and loved."

I poured sweet tea into our glasses and thought about this for a few minutes.

"So what you're saying is Adam has to discipline her. But she already knows Adam wants her and loves her."

Opal laughed. "Oh, Monica, sweetie, for such a smart woman sometimes you don't get it. It's *you* that she's looking to for the reassurance, not Adam. She knew you would be the one to see her room this morning. As I said before, she's testing you."

Which meant that it was up to me how I handled this. For the first time, I was on my own and had to make a decision about disciplining Clarissa.

Picking up my fork for a bite of crab salad, I said, "Thanks, Opal. How'd you get to be so smart?"

She threw her head back, laughing. "Comes with the territory, honey. Being a mama is trial and error, and it's all hands-on learning. Now—the reason I came here today is, I need *your* advice with something, and you can help me."

"Oh, I thought maybe you were coming to tell me you're leaving the island and can't take Clarissa next month."

Opal waved a hand in the air. "No, no. Actually, I'm not sure when I'll be going back to Naomi's. I just might have me a man in my life."

"A man?" I said with surprise. This was the first I was hearing about it. "Where'd you meet him?"

Opal patted her lips with a napkin. "Well, actually, I haven't. Yet. Not in person, anyway."

"What?"

"Well, see . . . um . . . I was on the Internet and . . ."

Now it was my turn to laugh. "You met him in a chat room on the Internet?"

"Well, yes. Anything wrong with that?"

"I'm not sure. Do you think he's really who he says he is? I mean, people can tell you anything in those chat rooms."

"Yes, well, I thought that too. But we've been chatting for a few months now. Even exchanged some photos. And now . . . well, he's coming to Cedar Key for a few months."

"He is? Hmm, then I guess if he's willing to meet you in person, he must have been truthful about who he is. Where's he from?"

"He's from Charleston, and I do think Hank's been truthful."

"Hank? Does he have a last name?" I kidded with her.

"Of course he does. It's Masterson. Hank Masterson. Has a nice sound to it, don't ya think?"

I smiled. It looked like my mother-in-law was smitten. "It does. Why's he coming here for a few months?"

"He's retired—worked in investments or some such thing. His wife died about ten years ago, children are grown and scattered across the country. He's never been to Cedar Key and thought it might be nice to come down here and spend a few months."

"Hmm, and get to know you?"

Opal pursed her lips. "Yes, that could be part of it. He's bringing his dog—has a Lab named Charlie. So he's rented a cottage at the Far Away."

"Interesting, but why do you need my advice about this?"

I swear I saw a crimson flush begin to climb up Opal's cheeks.

"Well, I've been out of the dating world for a while, ya know? Hank mentioned taking me to dinner in Gainesville one evening . . . and I was kinda wondering . . . what might be appropriate to wear."

My eyes went to the fuchsia-colored pantsuit she was wearing. The bright bluish red was something we'd all become accustomed to with Opal—showy, loud clothes that forced people to look. So here was Miss Key Lime Pie of 1960 asking *my* fashion advice? "Hmm, are you thinking of something more . . . subdued?"

"Subdued," she said, letting the word roll off her tongue while she thought about it. "Yeah, that might be what I'm looking for."

"Well, you can never go wrong with black or gray. Maybe an ankle-length gray skirt, charcoal gray turtleneck, and black blazer?"

"That certainly sounds subdued—even dull."

I shrugged. "Hey, you asked my advice."

"I did, and maybe you're right. Something like that would be appropriate for an evening dinner. Okay, got that. On to the next problem. . . ."

When she neglected to continue, I looked up from my plate. "And that would be?"

"Well, this is a delicate subject, but I don't have anybody else to discuss it with. Lord knows, I couldn't talk to Adam about it. But I was wondering . . . is a woman expected to kiss on the first date these days? And if so, does that kiss lead to . . . well, you know."

I had all I could do to stifle my laughter. Here was a woman who flaunted her sex appeal at every opportunity and she was worried about dating protocol?

Unable to resist, I said, "Does it lead to *sex?* Is that what you mean?"

The crimson on her cheeks deepened as she nodded. "Well, yeah—I hear so much about that Viagra stuff and all, I'm just not sure what to expect."

She struck me as a nervous teenager about to embark on her first date. Leaning across the table, I patted her hand. "Opal, I truly don't think much has changed in that department since you were out there dating. Nothing is ever *expected* of you, so just use your common sense and you'll be fine, I'm sure."

She nodded. "Okay, thank you." She took a gulp of tea. "Do you think I'm being foolish to meet him? I mean, gosh, at my age. . . ."

"Opal, don't be silly. What are you? Late fifties?"

"Sixty-three."

"Well, geez, that's far from ancient. What's wrong with having a gentleman friend? Look at my mom and Noah. It's nice to have a companion at this stage of your life. Somebody to go places with, have fun with. It adds longevity to your life."

"Yeah," she agreed. "You're probably right. Besides, guess they wouldn't have developed that Viagra if there wasn't a need for it."

I threw my head back, laughing. "Opal, you really *are* too much. That wasn't quite the longevity I was talking about."

✏️ 42 ✏️

I stood across the street from the school talking to Barb, the crossing guard, as I waited for Clarissa to come out the door.

"There she is," I said, crossing to meet her. "See you later."

"Hi," Clarissa told me, and then slid her gaze toward her shoes as we headed for home.

She knew I'd seen her bedroom. Well, if I was in charge, we were going to play this game *my* way. Both of us remained silent until we reached the end of G Street.

"Don't forget," she said. "I have to go to Chelsea's house this afternoon. We're working on a Valentine project."

"I didn't forget—but you're not going."

Her head shot up to look at me. "What? Why can't I go?"

"Did you see what your room looked like this morning?"

"Yeah, I'll clean it."

"That's right, you will, and then you'll remain in your room for the rest of the afternoon."

"That's not fair," Clarissa whined.

"Fair? I thought your dad and I made it clear to you that it was your job to keep your room neat and clean. I'm the one that does the dusting and vacuuming in there—and I can't do that with books and towels and glitter all over the place. I'd say that's not *fair*."

She remained silent for the rest of the way home.

Billie came running to greet us as we walked through the front door.

"Take Billie out in the yard," I told her. "Then call Chelsea and tell her you won't be coming over. Then you can begin cleaning that mess in your room. I suggest you get the DustBuster to clean up all that glitter."

I headed to the laundry room to fold clothes. There—I'd done it. I'd disciplined Clarissa for the first time. I wasn't sure what the aftereffects would be, but I knew I'd done the right thing.

By the time Adam returned home from school, Clarissa still hadn't emerged from her bedroom.

"Hi," he said, coming to put his arms around me as I stood at the counter peeling potatoes. "Have a good day?"

"It was okay. And yours?"

"Yeah, but you seem upset."

I was concerned about Adam's reaction to the incident and how I'd handled it.

"Not as upset now as I was this morning," I told him and went on to explain the situation.

Pouring himself a cup of coffee, he shook his head. "Geez, I thought we had that bedroom stuff all straightened out."

"Yeah, so did I."

"So I wonder what's really bothering her?"

That's exactly what Opal had said—that it could be about Clarissa not wanting to go to Carrie Sue's. How was it that they both knew that and I didn't?

"I had a message from Clarissa's teacher today," he went on to say. "So I stopped by to see her after school. It seems she's noticed a difference in Clarissa the past month or so. She's much quieter in class, not as willing to participate and volunteer answers. She also told me that Clarissa's grades are beginning to slip. We know she's certainly capable of doing excellent work, so something's wrong. Where's she at?"

"In her room. I punished her and told her she couldn't go to Chelsea's house this afternoon as they'd planned and that she had to clean her room."

Adam nodded and smiled. "Very good decision," he told me.

I let out a sigh and felt like I'd passed a pretty important test. "I'm glad you agree."

"Of course I agree. I told you when she came to live with us that we both had to be on the same page. You can't leave all the disciplining to me—you're her stepmom."

"But something is definitely bothering her. Now it's affecting her schoolwork. What're we going to do?"

"Well, I have a strong suspicion that all of this has to do with her not wanting to visit Carrie Sue. And I'm not sure what I can do about that, since it's Carrie Sue's *right*."

"But, geez, doesn't Clarissa have anything to say about all of it? It isn't *right* to force a child to go someplace she has no desire to be. Look at the problems it's creating."

"I know," Adam told me. "I think it's time to sit down with Clarissa and talk about it. Bring it out in the open and let her voice her opinion."

I was scooping bread pudding into dessert bowls following dinner and heard Adam say to Clarissa, "So what's up? You were very quiet while we were eating."

"Nothing."

I realized that recently she'd reverted back to her one-word answers.

"Well, Miss Carlson had a talk with me after school today."

Clarissa's head shot up. "About what?"

"About you falling behind in your grades. We know you can do much better. What's going on?"

"I don't know."

I placed the dessert on the table and sat back down.

Clarissa picked up her spoon and began moving the pudding from side to side.

"Something's wrong," Adam told her. "Let's talk about it."

"Nothing's wrong."

"Clarissa, if you're not going to talk to me, I can't help you. Does any of this have to do with visiting your mother?"

She kept her eyes focused on the pudding in front of her and shook her head. "No."

"Then you don't have a problem going to stay with her every other weekend?"

"Nope."

"Well, then I suggest you get your act together. Snap out of it, Clarissa. Keep your room clean and I'd better see an improvement in those marks—and mighty fast."

No comment from Clarissa.

"Understand?" Adam said.

Clarissa nodded. "Yeah."

"Okay, finish your dessert."

"I don't want it," she mumbled.

"Then leave the table and go back to your room. Monica told me you're being punished."

Without a word, Clarissa got up, pushed back her chair, and walked out of the kitchen.

Yeah, okay, I know I did the right thing, but gosh, I hated to see Clarissa so miserable. I didn't care what she told Adam, I was certain all of this had to do with Carrie Sue.

After Adam and I got the kitchen cleaned up, we went into the great room to relax. I picked up my knitting and curled up on the sofa. I had just started a lavender-colored sweater for Clarissa. She was probably so mad at me now she'd never wear it.

Adam sat down beside me. "Pretty," he said. "So anything else happen today besides Clarissa's bad behavior?"

"Yeah, your mother dropped by—for my advice."

"Really? What was that about?"

"Sex."

Adam turned to face me directly. "What?"

I laughed. "Well, not sex per se. However, she did want my advice and opinions on a few things. Seems she might have a gentleman friend in her life."

I went on to explain everything Opal had told me.

Now Adam was laughing and shaking his head. "Leave it to my mother. Well, she should have a male companion, if that's what she wants. And this guy, Charlie—where'd you say he's from?"

I was really chuckling now. "No, no. Her friend's name is *Hank*. Charlie's his dog. Now pay attention and get all of it straight."

"Okay, I'll take notes," he said, grinning.

"He's from Charleston and he'll be here for a few months. Booked a cottage at the Far Away. Sounds like a nice enough man and he'll arrive next week, so of course we'll get to meet him."

"That's great. We can always depend on my mother to brighten up an otherwise gloomy day. We'll have to have them over for dinner."

"Yup, I already told Opal we'd do that." I knitted for a few minutes in silence. "What are we going to do about Clarissa? She's due to go to Carrie Sue's this coming weekend."

"I know that. I'm going to have her go, but I'm also going to get in touch with Trent—tell him the situation and see if possibly anything can be done. I feel the same way you do. It's just not right to force a child to go if she doesn't want to."

Unfortunately, I was beginning to see how the court system could work when it came to children, and I felt disheartened as to what the outcome might be.

✁ 43 ✁

Friday afternoon I was at Spinning Forward working on the mail orders. Dora was knitting away on another Ewedora Stocking.

"Do you need to pick Clarissa up after school today?" she asked.

"No, Adam will get her. She has to go to Carrie Sue's for the weekend."

"Hmm, how's that going?"

"Not that well," I told her and filled Dora in on the current incidents.

"Such a shame," she said, attaching another ball of yarn. "Doesn't seem right, and it's always the child that suffers. You wouldn't mind if Carrie Sue was a loving and devoted mother, but we all know that she's not. And the worst part is so does Clarissa. Makes no sense why that woman would come here and demand that her daughter visit her when she clearly has no interest."

"I know. Adam's going to speak to Trent and see if anything can be done."

I turned toward the door as the wind chimes tinkled and saw Grace walk in.

"Hey," she said. "Twila Fay's covering my shop, so I thought I'd come over and bother you."

She passed me a cup of coffee. "And you came bearing gifts, so you're always welcome."

"I'm sorry," Grace said to Dora. "I wasn't sure you'd still be here and didn't bring an extra cup."

Dora put her hand up. "No, no. I'm just going to finish this row and then it's time for me to leave. You're closing up at four, right, Monica?"

I nodded. "Yup, and I'll be here ten till two tomorrow. I should be able to get these mail orders finished by then. I've done enough for today."

Walking over to the sofa, I patted the spot next to me. "Come join me, Gracie. I'll fill you in on the latest Clarissa/Carrie Sue news."

"That's always worth hearing. Somebody really needs to write a book about this island. The tales that could be told."

I laughed and proceeded to bring Grace up to date.

"I'm off," Dora called, walking toward the door. "And I'll be here two till four tomorrow. Y'all have a good evening."

Grace took a sip of coffee and leaned her head back against the sofa. "Well, I think I can top your news," she said, a hint of mystery in her voice.

"Really? What's it about?"

"Tony."

"Oh, God, Gracie, please don't tell me you're seeing him again."

"*Why* do you always say that whenever I mention his name? Will you please give me more credit than that?"

She was right. "I'm sorry," I said, reaching over to pat her hand. "I guess I just worry about you, and I only want you to have what's best."

"But . . . I do happen to know *who* is seeing him now."

"What? He's managed to hook another unsuspecting female on the island? She'd better watch out or he'll be after her property next."

"She doesn't have any property here on Cedar Key."

"Who is it?"

Gracie took another sip of coffee, making me squirm by taking her time with the answer. "Ready for this?"

"Stop it, Gracie, just tell me!"

"Carrie Sue."

Surely, I'd misunderstood her. "Carrie Sue?" I repeated. "Not Carrie Sue *Brooks?*"

Grace smiled. "One and the same."

I sat up straighter and leaned closer to see if Grace was kidding with me. Her face was dead serious. "Get outta here!"

"Nope. It's true. I saw them together last night. Twila Faye and I were going to go to the Seabreeze for dinner. So there we are, standing and waiting to be seated and straight ahead, there were Tony and Carrie Sue having dinner together. All lovey-dovey. Holding hands across the table, their eyes never left each other and then she leaned forward and he gave her quite a kiss. I wanted to holler 'get a room' and couldn't believe what I was seeing. But it was them. Twila Faye confirmed it and we hightailed it out of there."

"I can't believe it! *Her* and *him* together? Oh, my God!"

"Hmm, there *is* a God, isn't there? I'd say they damn well deserve each other."

I shook my head. "I have to agree with you on that one. Oh, wow, those two together is like . . . well, like a catastrophe waiting to happen. They're both so greedy and self-centered."

Grace smiled. "Like I said, they deserve each other."

"I wonder how long this has been going on."

"Haven't a clue, but just from what I saw, I'd say it's pretty intense."

"Geez, this could be a blessing in disguise. Intense enough for Carrie Sue to give up her visitation rights, I wonder?"

"Hey, if she feels Clarissa's cramping her style, I sure wouldn't doubt it. She's made it clear her daughter was never her top priority."

I nodded, digesting all of what Grace had just told me. "Maybe," I said, "just maybe Carrie Sue will get so wrapped up in Tony that she won't want to give up those two weekends a month."

Grace shrugged. "You could be right, and I'd bet anything she's spending half her time in Tony's apartment or he's over at her condo."

"Well, he sure as hell better not be there tonight when she has Clarissa."

The wind chimes tinkled again, and both Grace and I looked up to see Saren walk in.

"Hey, Saren," I said. "How've you been?"

"Good, real good, and yourself?"

Based on the news I just heard, I was feeling mighty fine. "I'm good too." I saw he was holding a gift-wrapped box in his hand.

Coming to place a kiss on my cheek, he handed me the box. "This here's for Valentine's Day tomorrow. Sweets for my sweet granddaughter."

I got up to give him a hug. "Oh, Saren, that's so nice of you. Thank you."

"It's them there French chocolates that you like so much."

"And I will truly enjoy them. Would you like some coffee? Gracie and I are just sitting around gabbing."

"Thanks but nah, think I had my coffee quota for today. Got an e-mail from your mom this morning. She's all excited about spending Valentine's Day in Paris."

I nodded. "Yeah, romantic that she is, she'll really enjoy that. She told me that she and Noah are booked for dinner at La Rotonde, where F. Scott and Zelda used to dine." I shook my head and laughed. "She's really in her element over there."

"And what's that nice husband of yours doing for Valentine's Day?"

"Adam made a reservation at the Island Room. Dinner at seven." Saren nodded. "Very good. I like to see my girls being pampered. If Sybile were here, why, I'd cook her a great meal and give her a bouquet of those gardenias she always loved."

Even though four years had passed since Sybile had left us, it hadn't diminished Saren's love for her one ounce.

"Well," he said, heading toward the door. "Guess I'll mosey on home."

"Thank you again, Saren."

He turned around quickly to face us and touched the side of his head with his palm. "Now see, I almost plumb forgot to tell you what I just saw."

"What was that?" I questioned.

"That fancy-dancy coffee place down the street—he's got a huge For Sale sign out front."

Grace and I both exchanged a look.

"What?" she said. "He's selling the coffee shop?"

Saren nodded. "Sure 'nuff seems that way. I reckon he's given up on making major changes to our island. Good riddance is what I say. Well, girls, y'all take care and I'll see you later."

"I'll be damned," Grace said. "So my business is safe after all, and if he has his place up for sale, he must be leaving town."

"That's what it sounds like. Hmm, I wonder if it also means Carrie Sue is going with him."

"Wouldn't that just be the icing on the cake? Getting rid of both of them at once. They sure as hell won't be missed—neither one of them."

"Well, it's obvious he's given up on his idea of a French restaurant. Probably came to finally realize he didn't have a chance up against the people of this island."

Grace laughed. "Yeah, I'd say we all did a pretty good job of running him out of town on a rail. Except for Carrie Sue, I don't think one person has been friendly toward him."

"That's one of the things my mother always loved about this island—how the people accepted her and made her feel so welcome."

"Yeah, well," Grace said, "your mother didn't come here trying to change things. She accepted Cedar Key for what it is and involved herself in the community."

I nodded and smiled. Raising my hand to tap Grace's in a high five, I said, "Here's to you, girlfriend. You may have lost the battle, but you won the war."

❦ 44 ❦

I turned in front of the full-length mirror in my bedroom to admire the red dress I was wearing—a clingy knit sheath, it showed off my slim figure to perfection. With a v-shaped neckline and cap sleeves, it was subtle, yet sexy. Casual was the normal style on the island and I enjoyed getting dressed up now and then with a bit of glamour. I still had enough choices in my wardrobe left over from my single days.

After slipping into black sling-back heels, I picked up the bottle of Chanel No. 5 Adam had given me for Valentine's Day and released a bit of spray to my neck. The perfume may be old-fashioned, but it had remained my favorite over the years.

Opening my jewelry box, I fingered a bracelet that had belonged to Sybile. Chunky links of gold, a small circular disc dangled from the center with two *s*'s intertwined. Sybile gave it to me shortly before she died. She explained that Saren had purchased it at a jewelry shop in Manhattan during his first and only visit there to see her—the visit that resulted in the conception of my mother.

I slid it onto my wrist and fastened the clasp. Wearing it on the most romantic day of the year seemed appropriate. My grandparents had shared a love that had lasted not only a lifetime, but even beyond.

Walking into the great room, I found Adam waiting, looking exceptionally handsome in a tan sport jacket, chocolate brown slacks, shirt and tie. I felt a ripple of desire.

Looking up from the newspaper he'd been reading, he let out a low whistle.

"You look stunning," he said, walking over to bury his face in my neck. "And no wonder you love that perfume. Talk about a turn-on."

"Ah, does this mean I've managed to seduce you?"

"You've seduced me from the first moment I laid eyes on you in that yarn shop."

I felt Adam's hand slide down my back and laughed. "Hey, if you keep that up, we'll never make the Island Room."

"My plan exactly," he said, joining my laughter.

"We have the entire night to ourselves," I told him, picking up my white knitted shawl and handbag.

"And I intend to take advantage of it," he said, reaching for my hand and leading the way to the door.

Enjoying coffee following a wonderful dinner and wine, I smiled as Adam related a story to me about an incident at school. After all my uncertainty during my dating years, it had reached a point where I wondered if I'd ever meet the right guy. I'd begun to think I wasn't cut out for a long-term relationship, and unlike many of my friends, I refused to settle. I wasn't naïve enough to think I'd find the perfect guy, but I also wasn't willing to endure some of the flaws and traits my friends seemed to think were fine when they were dating and once they married, those same flaws became constant irritations and the cause of much unhappiness. And then Adam walked into my life, and while nobody's perfect, he sure came mighty close.

When he finished his story, I reached across the table and took his hand. "I love you, Adam. I will always love you."

His face softened as he squeezed my hand. "And you—you are that one great love of my life and always will be."

"We're fortunate to have found each other. Do you realize how many people go through life and never know what it's like to love and be loved so deeply? Look at poor Grace."

Adam nodded. "Yeah, but I have to say, the women in your family seem to somehow find that special love—Sybile and Saren, and your mother and Noah, and now you. Maybe in time it will happen for Grace. She's not your family, but possibly some osmosis will be at play there."

I laughed. "Right. From hanging out with me, it'll eventually rub off on her. I know one thing, she's pretty relieved that Tony's selling his place and probably leaving the island. So Carrie Sue didn't mention anything to you yesterday about him?"

"Not a word, but I'm not surprised. She's never been one to keep me in the loop."

"I can't help but wonder if she'll take off too. How do you think that would affect Clarissa?"

"To be honest, I think she'd be relieved."

"I think Clarissa's still ticked off at me for punishing her the other day."

Adam stroked my hand. "Don't take it personally. Kids are smart, Monica. She knows she deserved that punishment. You have to know how much she likes you."

"I thought she did these past few months—but now, I'm not so sure."

"Kids get angry at their parents all the time. She'll get over it. Wait and see. Hey, has Grace heard from that fellow that's buying the bookshop?"

"Lucas? Well, I guess he's come back to her coffee shop a few times, but he only talks to her briefly about the construction work that's going on. She said he was in this past week and told her he won't be back till the summer. He has things to tend to in Brunswick."

"That's a coincidence that Grace's aunt lives there and they know each other. Wonder if Grace will be paying her a visit? She never seems to go up there."

"Yeah, I know. They're very close, but there has to be a reason Grace stays away from that town. She hasn't shared any of this with me and I don't want to pry."

"Well, it'd be nice to see Grace have somebody in her life that she cares about."

"I agree," I said and leaned over to kiss Adam's cheek. "I'm sure glad I have you in my life."

Adam stood up and reached for my hand. "The bill is all set. Why don't we go home so you can show me how glad you are?"

"Now, that sounds like the perfect way to end a perfect evening."

Somewhere in the distance, I heard a bell ringing. Turning over, I snuggled deeper into my pillow, and that's when I heard Billie barking. I opened my eyes to see Adam getting out of bed, hopping from one foot to the other to pull on a pair of sweatpants. Glancing at the bedside clock, I saw it was two-thirty in the morning, and the bell I'd heard was our doorbell ringing.

Jumping up, I threw on a robe. "What the heck? Who's at our door at this hour?" I called after Adam, following him to the great room.

Both of us got to the front window at the same time and saw the blue and white golf cart belonging to Officer Bob parked on the road. This couldn't be good.

Adam flung open the door and we both gasped to see Officer Bob standing on our porch with Clarissa.

"What's wrong?" Adam exclaimed, pulling the door wider for them to come in.

Clarissa was wearing pajamas and sneakers and clutching Raggedy Ann in her arm. She bent down to receive Billie's excited kiss.

"Well," Officer Bob said. "I was doing my patrol on Second Street and I saw this little one walking along in front of the library."

Adam pulled her into his arms. "My God, are you all right? What on earth were you doing wandering the streets alone at this hour?"

"Come sit down," I said, walking into the great room.

My heart went out to Clarissa. Her eyes were droopy from sleep and her hair was a tangled mess. She looked like an orphan.

"Well," she said, settling herself on the sofa with Billie in her lap. "I woke up and Mama was gone."

"What?" I exclaimed. "What do you mean she was *gone?* Where is she?"

Clarissa shrugged. "I don't know. I checked her bedroom and the other rooms and she wasn't there."

"Was she there when you went to bed?" Adam questioned.

"Yeah, but she was all dressed up."

"All dressed up? My God, did she go out and leave you alone there?"

"Probably," Clarissa mumbled. "But when I couldn't find her, I got scared, so I got Annie and we were walking home when Officer Bob found us."

Officer Bob shook his head. "I couldn't imagine why she was out alone at this hour. Do you have any idea where her mother might be?"

I could see the anger spreading across Adam's face. "Monica, why don't you take Clarissa and get her off to bed," he said. I knew he didn't want to talk in front of his daughter.

"Come on," I told her. "I think Billie needs to get back to sleep too."

We walked into Clarissa's room and I closed the door to allow Adam privacy. I pulled down her spread and fluffed up her pillow. Clarissa hopped in with Billie beside her.

"Oh, wait," she said, jumping out of bed and going to her backpack on the desk. Reaching inside, she pulled out a piece of paper and handed it to me. "I'm sorry. I forgot to give it to you yesterday."

I looked down to see a gigantic red heart sprinkled with what I was sure was the glitter on her carpet from a few days before. In perfectly formed large letters she had printed: Be My Valentine—Love, Clarissa Jo.

Moisture stung my eyes as I stared at the handmade card. Pulling Clarissa into my arms for a tight hug, I said, "Thank you, and of course I'll be your valentine."

Her face lit up with a smile as she headed back to bed. Reaching up, she put her arms around my neck. "Good night, Monica."

"Good night, Clarissa. Sleep tight."

I closed the door to her room and realized Adam had been right. Kids are very forgiving.

"Yes," I heard him say as I walked back to the great room. "Yes, I do want to press charges."

Officer Bob nodded in understanding and began writing information on his clipboard. After he completed the forms, he said, "And I'll make sure your attorney gets a copy of this."

Just as he was about to leave, the phone rang and Adam grabbed it.

"You're damn lucky she's here, Carrie Sue. How dare you take off and leave a nine-year-old alone all night! I've seen mother dogs that take better care of their pups." There was a pause and he raked his hand through his hair. "What? So what are you saying? That Clarissa's lying! If you'd *been* there, she wouldn't have left in the middle of the night. I know my daughter better than that."

I could make out Carrie Sue's raised voice coming from the phone but didn't catch what she was saying.

"Why should I believe *you?* My lawyer will be in touch."

With that, he slammed the phone into the base. "She's home. Claims she's been there all night and she woke to find Clarissa gone. I don't believe a word she's saying."

"Okay," said Officer Bob. "I'll mosey on over to her place now. See what she has to say. You folks take care. I'll be in touch."

Adam turned around after closing the front door and took me in his arms. "Thank God she's all right," he whispered.

I nodded and didn't allow myself to think what could have happened. "I can't believe she'd claim that Clarissa is lying about all of this."

"I told you before that Carrie Sue's a pathological liar, so it doesn't bother her at all to put the blame on her own daughter."

"Come on," I said, going to turn out the light. "I've got her all tucked in safe and sound. Let's try and get some sleep."

45

"Are you sure?" I said to Adam the following Wednesday evening as we cleaned the kitchen following supper.

"Yes, I want you to go to the yarn shop tonight and join the ladies. It'll be good for you. You need a girls' night out."

Adam was right. It had been a stressful few days. "Okay, I'll go," I said, putting the last glass in the dishwasher. "After I say good night to Clarissa."

I found her curled up on the sofa working on another scarf. This time it was a blue and white one and meant to be a gift for Zoe's new brother when he was born in two months.

"That looks great," I told her. "It'll be perfect for Zac next winter."

Clarissa nodded, not taking her eyes from her needles. "Yeah, I thought so too. I think Zoe will like it."

"I'm sure she will. Okay, I'm heading over to the yarn shop for a couple hours, so I'll see you in the morning."

I was glad I'd listened to Adam. It was fun being surrounded by females, catching up on island gossip.

"So what's this we hear that Opal has a man in her life?" Polly asked, looking up from the sweater she was working on.

All of the needles stopped clicking as four faces looked at me expectantly.

I laughed and shook my head. "You gals are terrible. It's not up to me to discuss Opal's love life."

"Oh, come on," Twila Faye said. "You know what's going on. Did she really meet him on the Internet?"

"Yup, she did."

"Isn't he here on the island now?" Dora asked.

"Yeah, he is," I said, concentrating on my pattern.

"And so . . . ," Polly said. "Have you met him yet?"

Grace nudged my elbow with her hand. "Cripe, Monica, tell us what's going on."

I placed my knitting in my lap as I tried to suppress a smile. These ladies thrived on the current gossip, especially if a hint of romance might be involved. "There isn't much to tell you. His name is Hank, he arrived the other day, he's staying at the Far Away with his dog . . . and we've invited him and Opal to dinner Friday evening. There. Satisfied?"

"Hmm," Polly said. "Imagine that. Leave it to Opal to get involved with technology and snag herself a man."

"Yeah," Dora said. "Years ago we met fellows at church or were introduced by friends and family. We did have blind dates, but they were, well—recommended. Not a complete *stranger*. Has Opal seen him since he arrived here?"

I nodded. "Yes, he went to her house for coffee yesterday, and according to her, he's exactly as she thought he'd be. Don't forget, they've been talking and getting to know each other for a few months now on the computer. Opal said she felt like she'd known him forever."

"That's become quite popular," Grace said. "Couples meeting

that way. Might not be a bad idea. They start off being friends and can find out a lot about each other by exchanging e-mails."

Polly shook her head. "I agree with Dora, it's sure not like it used to be. I see something advertised on TV all the time—something to do with signing up on the computer with a dating company and they match you with somebody who has your exact interests. Seems to me that kinda takes the fun out of getting to know a person. You ever do anything like that, Grace?"

"Me?" she said, shaking her head. "Nah, guess I'm an old-fashioned kind of girl. I like that instant chemistry that might occur the first time you meet somebody. Going through a dating service seems a bit too contrived for me."

"Speaking of that chemistry," I said, "seen any more of Lucas?"

"Oh, would that be Lucas Trudeau? The new owner of the bookstore. Are you two seeing each other?" Polly leaned forward, waiting for Grace's answer.

"Yes, Lucas is the new bookstore owner, and no, we're not seeing each other. He's just dropped by the coffee shop a few times."

"I saw him at the post office the other day," Dora said. "Seems like a nice fellow. Introduced himself and said he plans to be ready to open the shop by October."

"I heard he's originally from France and has another shop in Brunswick," Twila Faye said. "Isn't that where you're from, Grace? Did you know him before you moved here?"

"I've been gone from Brunswick almost ten years and he only moved there from Paris five years ago, but it seems he knows my aunt Maude. He said she's a frequent customer in his shop."

"And so . . . ," Polly said, a smile covering her face. "Does he have a *wife?*"

"No, he does not," Grace told her. "However, he also doesn't appear very interested in me. Stops by for coffee, chats a bit, and that's it. Besides, after that recent fiasco with Tony, being committed to somebody isn't high on my list right now."

"Is it true that he really left the island with Carrie Sue?" Twila Faye asked.

I nodded. "Yup, the dynamic duo left together yesterday morning. After the crisis over the weekend with poor Clarissa, that's probably the kindest thing Carrie Sue's ever done for her daughter. She swore up and down that she hadn't left Clarissa alone Saturday night—of course we don't believe her. But when Officer Bob got to her place, she was there, so we had no proof. However, Adam had reached the end of his rope with her. He told her if she'd voluntarily sign the papers and give up her visitation rights, then he wouldn't press charges."

"And did she?" Twila Faye questioned.

"Without a moment's hesitation. Why she even came here in the first place, we have no clue. She's always been a poor excuse for a mother. Once she met Tony, she found a means to get herself out of here. Adam probably did her a favor forcing her to sign the papers."

"And she had no qualms about giving up rights to visit her daughter?" Dora asked.

"Not in the least. Everybody else is always to blame, so this way she can say that Adam *forced* her to give up her rights. Makes her look like the injured party."

"Sure, when everyone knows she never wanted the responsibility of motherhood to begin with," Grace said.

I nodded. "Exactly. Finally, I think we can safely say we've seen the last of Carrie Sue Brooks."

"How does that make Clarissa feel?" Polly asked. "Does she feel rejected at all?"

"Quite the opposite," I told her. "In all honesty, I think the poor child feels relieved. We've had some problems with her these past few months since Carrie Sue got here and Clarissa had to visit her twice a month. Her grades slipped in school, some behavior problems, and it's obvious she just hasn't been happy."

"I can understand that," Dora said. "You and Adam are her

family. She knows how much you both love her and kids know when people are being phony. I'd say she knew Carrie Sue pretty well."

There was that word *love* again—an emotion I couldn't honestly say that I felt for Clarissa. While I was far from a phony, I still questioned if I truly *loved* the child.

"You've got that right," Grace said. "By the time I came along, I think my parents had outgrown parenthood. They were into living their own life, and a kid infringed on that."

Grace had never discussed her parents much with me, but I knew they were in their late forties when she was born and her sister, Chloe, was twelve years older.

"When I was twelve and my parents were killed in that car crash in the south of France, I was fortunate that Aunt Maude was willing to raise me. And that was the difference between her and my parents—I always felt she deeply loved me. Never once did she make me feel that taking me in was her *obligation*. She always made sure that I knew she truly enjoyed having me with her."

I remained silent as I focused on the knitting in my hands, but I hoped that Clarissa knew that I honestly did enjoy having her with us.

⤞ 46 ⤝

Since Carrie Sue had left the island a month before, we'd seen a marked improvement in Clarissa. No further behavior problems. Her grades at school returned to As and Bs, but best of all was her happy attitude. She smiled more, laughed more, and appeared to be a more well-adjusted child.

With the arrival of Hank on the island a new happiness had also come over Opal. Both Adam and I were fond of him, and it was easy to see why she delighted in his company. Distinguished looking with a crop of white hair, he had a way of making people feel at ease, and his wonderful sense of humor provided lots of laughter.

I had just zipped the second piece of luggage closed when Clarissa came into the bedroom.

"Are you excited about going to Augusta?" she asked.

"I am," I told her. "Is there anything in particular you'd like me to get for you while I'm there?"

"No, but when you get back could you teach me that knit two together stitch?"

I smiled. "Of course I will. We'll find you a pattern for a scarf where you can use that stitch. And I tell you what, you're getting so accomplished, pretty soon I think you'll be able to begin a sweater."

Clarissa's eyes lit up. "Really? Could I make one for Billie to wear?"

"I don't see why not," I said, walking out of the bedroom. "There are lots of patterns now for doggie sweaters. She'd like that and it'll keep her warm in winter."

Adam looked up from the crossword he was working on and smiled. "All packed?"

"Yup, and your mother should be here shortly to get Clarissa."

"I'll go get my duffel bag," she said.

A few minutes later Opal knocked on the kitchen door and walked in. "Is my favorite girl ready to spend a few days with her grandma?"

Clarissa ran over to give Opal a hug. "Yeah, and Billie's ready too," she said, clipping on the dog's leash.

"Okay." I reached for the tote bag containing Billie's food and treats. "Here's everything you need for Billie. I did give you the phone number at the Partridge Inn, right?"

Opal waved a hand in the air. "Yes, you did, and I have both your cell phone numbers and we'll be just fine." She ruffled the top of Clarissa's hair. "Now your job is to go and have a wonderful time. Hank is escorting the two of us for dinner this evening to the Island Room and we have a full weekend of activities planned for Clarissa."

I smiled as Clarissa jumped up and down. "Oh, goody. I like Hank, and maybe Billie can play with Charlie in your yard."

"I think that can be arranged," Opal told her.

Clarissa ran to hug Adam and then me. "Have fun," she hollered, following Opal out the back door.

"You too," I hollered back.

*   *   *

As soon as Adam negotiated the curve on the hill, I saw the Partridge Inn situated majestically at the top. Six stories high, pale yellow in color, with white verandahs and balconies. The front façade was partially hidden by looming dogwood trees in full bloom.

"Oh," I uttered, "It's just lovely."

Adam placed his hand on my leg. "It's considered one of the grand hotels of the classic South."

He pulled the car into the small, attached parking garage.

We removed our luggage from the trunk and walked into the cobbled brick courtyard with a small pool at the center. The door from the courtyard led us to the lobby. Victorian décor and furniture gave the feeling of stepping back in time.

While Adam got us checked in, I looked around and understood why my mother loved staying here. It had a warm and inviting ambience.

"All set," Adam said, turning to the bellhop. "Room three-oh-two."

The man was placing our luggage on the cart. "Very good, sir. I'll be right up."

We took the elevator to the third floor and made our way along the thickly carpeted corridor. I could now see the building was tiered on different levels. Down three steps, a short walk along another corridor and up a few more steps. Our room was at the end and Adam inserted the key.

Stepping into a spacious area, I took in the king-sized bed and elegant furnishings. Long, full-length windows allowed the sun to stream through, creating a golden glow.

"Oh, how pretty," I said, and felt Adam's arms go around my waist.

"I'm glad you like it. I think we'll have a nice four days."

We both turned at the knock on the door.

Adam opened it, the bellman removed our luggage from the

cart, accepted his tip, and said, "Enjoy your stay at the Partridge Inn," before quietly closing the door behind him.

"How about some champagne?" Adam asked.

It was then that I noticed the silver bucket on the coffee table in front of the sofa, with the bottle cooling inside.

"Sounds wonderful," I said, going to sit down. "You've thought of everything."

"I thought we'd relax here for a while. I made an eight o'clock reservation for dinner at the Verandah Grill downstairs."

I laughed at the pop when Adam removed the cork. "What a great sound."

Filling both flutes, he joined me on the sofa. "Here's to us," he said, lightly touching the rim of my glass.

"To us," I repeated before taking a sip of the delicious bubbly. "Hmm, very good."

"It is," he said, after taking a sip. Placing the glass on the table, he reached for both of my hands. "Do you know how much I love you, Monica? I can't even imagine my life without you."

I leaned forward and my lips found his. "I love you more than I thought possible," I told him. "You're everything to me, Adam. There was a time in my life when I doubted I could love somebody like this, but then I met you and I knew I'd been waiting all my life for you."

"This sure hasn't been an easy first year of marriage for us, and it's been the hardest on you, what with Clarissa coming to live with us and then Carrie Sue showing up. I just want you to know how much it means to me that you've hung in there and not given up."

"Given up?"

"I know what your history has been in the past. When the going gets tough, you had a habit of running."

I pressed my lips together and looked down at the flute in my hand, but didn't say anything. He was right. I knew that. I wasn't known for having the tolerance for working things out. It was always much easier to simply walk away. But with Adam it was different—I couldn't conceive of spending my days without him. No matter what.

I took another sip of champagne and then sighed. "I guess maybe that's what *real* love is all about. When you've found your soul mate—that one person in the world you don't want to be without—well, there isn't anything that you can't get through together, and it's you who made me realize that."

Adam took my champagne glass and placed it on the table. Standing, he reached for my hand and pulled me up beside him.

I felt his lips crush mine as my arms went around his neck and I was instantly filled with desire.

"Come on," he said, his voice husky, as he led me toward the bed. "Let me show you how I love you."

Sitting in the beautiful dining room of the Verandah Grill, I felt a happiness that had seemed to be missing the past few months.

Following a passionate session of lovemaking, I also felt sexy and very desirable.

Adam looked across the table and smiled. "God, Monica, you look exceptionally beautiful tonight."

"You make me *feel* beautiful." I was glad I'd chosen the sleeveless black dress. Simple, yet classy.

"Oh, it doesn't have a thing to do with me. I saw the heads that turned when we stepped off the elevator."

I laughed. "Hmm, it must be my afterglow still radiating. God, when was the last time we made love in the afternoon?"

"I don't know, but it's been much too long, and we'll have to be sure to fix that when we get home. Send Clarissa to my mom's after school for cookies and milk and I'll come home early."

I laughed again. "You're terrible, but not a bad idea."

The waiter arrived with our entrees and smiled. "Bon appétit. Special occasion?"

"Yes," Adam said without hesitating. "Actually it is. We're celebrating our love for each other."

The waiter inclined his head. "And *that* is the best possible thing to celebrate. Enjoy."

"That was so sweet. You really *are* quite the romantic."

Adam smiled. "For you, always."

"Oh, this duck looks delicious," I said, picking up my fork.

We savored the wonderful food and followed the meal with coffee.

I exhaled a breath as I tried to formulate thoughts in my mind before speaking.

Adam looked up. "Anything wrong?"

"No," I said, shaking my head. "There's just something I want to discuss with you. Actually, it's been on my mind since we were supposed to come here in December."

"And you've waited three months to talk about it?"

"Yeah, I guess I just wanted the time and privacy for us. And maybe the subject is better discussed on neutral territory."

Adam's face registered confusion. "What is it?"

"Well," I began and found myself nervously fingering the spoon beside my coffee. "I've just kinda been wondering . . . what would be your thoughts . . ." I stopped to be sure I phrased my question properly. "What would be your thoughts about possibly having a baby. Together. The two of us." My eyes shot to Adam's face to gauge his reaction and I saw his dumbfounded expression. "I know, I know," I rushed on. "We had kinda agreed not to have children before we married, but . . ."

Adam was shaking his head. "No, Monica, you have that wrong. *We* didn't agree not to have children. *You* indicated that you were pretty sure you didn't want any—and I supported your decision."

"Oh," was all I could manage to say, and I looked up to see a smile cross my husband's face.

He reached across the table for my hand and gave it a squeeze. "Are you saying you've changed your mind? You'd like to get pregnant?"

"I think so. Maybe."

"What changed your mind?"

"I'm not really sure. Maybe Clarissa did."

"Clarissa?" Adam said with surprise.

"Yeah, ever since she found out that Zoe's getting a baby brother, she's been dropping hints about having a brother or sister of her own."

"I did catch a few of those hints, but I didn't think you were paying any attention to them."

"I guess I was paying more attention than I thought. Both of us had no siblings. While that's certainly not the worst thing in the world, being an only child can be lonely. You have nobody to share your history with—only childhood friends, if you stayed in touch."

"Very true," Adam agreed.

"I think too my change of feeling might have to do with the fact that I'm not such a bad stepmom after all. I'm beginning to think that everyone was right—kids don't come with a manual, so you learn as you go along. Now, of course, I understand that a baby would be a whole lot different than raising a nine-year-old, but . . . since I haven't done too badly with Clarissa and I've really enjoyed learning to be a mom to her, well, there just might be some hope that I could be a *real* mom. Maybe I was wrong when I thought I might be one of those women who just shouldn't attempt motherhood."

"Like Sybile?" Adam said softly.

I nodded. "Yeah . . . and like Carrie Sue."

A huge smile now covered Adam's face and he squeezed my hand again. "I love you so much, Monica. I always respected your possible choice of never having a child with me. You were honest from the beginning on how you felt about this, and I accepted that. I loved you way too much not to. However, if you would like us to have a child together, my answer is yes, definitely *yes*."

In that moment I didn't think I could possibly love Adam any more than I did, and I also hadn't realized how much I desperately wanted to create a new life with him—a part of both of us.

I swiped at the moisture in my eyes and smiled. "Okay. Okay, then. I will not be starting my next cycle of pills in two days. That's the end of those."

Adam brought my hand to his lips. "And think of all the fun we'll have making this happen," he said, winking at me.

ᦞ 47 ᦞ

Monday afternoon Adam and I were sitting at an outdoor coffee shop. The weather had been spring-perfect during our stay. Dogwoods and azaleas were in full bloom all over Augusta, creating a riot of color.

I felt the warm sun on my back and smiled. All was right in my world. Now that Adam and I had had the discussion about pregnancy, it was like a weight had been lifted from me. I was still surprised by the fact that getting pregnant was something I wanted even more than I realized. For so long I had convinced myself that like my grandmother, I just wasn't cut out to be a mother, but when Clarissa came into my life she made me see I was wrong.

"So what other shopping do you want to do this afternoon?" Adam asked, pulling me from my thoughts.

"I just wanted to get something for Clarissa. Maybe we could browse the shops along Broad Street."

"Sounds like a good idea," he said, taking the last sip of his coffee. "All set?"

I stood up and reached for his hand. "Yup."

A shop called Once in Time caught my eye. "Let's try there," I said, pointing to a display of antique dolls in the window.

Stepping inside, I inhaled the wonderful scent of lavender. The small shop had tables with artfully arranged lamps, potpourri, lace tablecloths, and assorted antique items. Dolls with bisque faces perched on swings that hung from the ceiling.

"Hello," a woman said, walking toward us. "Looking for anything in particular?"

"Just browsing," I told her. "You have a lovely shop."

"Thank you. All of the items have come from estate sales and many have a history or story behind them."

"Oh, that's interesting," I said as my gaze caught a table at the back of the shop with music boxes and I walked toward them.

I was immediately drawn to a porcelain egg-shaped design. A base of white was surrounded with a perimeter consisting of four rows of pearls and gold braid. The open egg shape was attached to the base with gold filigree, and more pearls and gold decorated the egg top. But it was what was inside the oval egg that drew my attention. A young girl, dressed in a period Victorian frock, a large lavender bow holding back her hair, and standing beside her looking up with adoration was a cream-colored dog that was a replica of Billie.

"Oh, Adam, look," I whispered, reaching out to gently touch the top of the music box.

"That certainly looks like Billie with Clarissa, doesn't it?"

"That's exactly what I thought." I picked it up, found the turnkey beneath the base, and wound it a few times. The haunting melody of "Amazing Grace" filled the shop as shivers ran through me. That was the song Sybile had insisted we play at her funeral—about being lost and then found. "Oh, my God," I said.

Adam must have remembered me telling him this, because he nodded. "A coincidence?" he questioned.

"I don't know, but it's certainly uncanny." I turned around to find the shop owner watching us. "Do you know the history on this piece?"

"I do," she said. "It's one of my favorite items, but let me get the book and read it to you."

She went behind the counter and produced a large, leather-bound journal. Skimming through the pages, she nodded. "Here it is. This particular piece has been here since I opened four years ago, and I've never understood why it hasn't sold. It's a bit pricey, but not outrageous. I obtained it from an estate sale and always felt bad that there was no family left from the original owner, because it really was an heirloom and should have been passed on."

"Is that all you know about it?" I asked.

"No, when I purchased it from the owner's attorney he gave me this paper that went with it." The woman removed the paper from an envelope and began to read. "Given to my beloved daughter, Abigail, age ten, September, nineteen twenty, when we almost lost you to pneumonia."

My hand flew to my face. "That's terrible and so sad."

The woman smiled. "Actually, it's a very nice story. The woman's attorney explained to me that what had been related to him was that the outcome for the daughter didn't look good. However, within a few days of purchasing this music box and placing it at the child's bedside, she began to improve and had a full recovery."

"Are you saying it has magical qualities?"

She shrugged. "Who am I to question? I can only pass on the story that was told to me and the history that goes with the music box."

I looked up at Adam and saw him nod.

"Well, it's found a very special home now," he said. "For our daughter. Could you wrap it for us, please?"

A smile crossed the woman's face. "Certainly, and call me silly, but I can't help but feel it's been here all this time just waiting for you."

*   *   *

After we left the shop we decided to stroll through the River-walk. We had gone there the day before and I loved the quiet beauty. It was a two-tiered park that ran along the Savannah River, filled with leafy trees, flowering bushes, and benches to sit and gaze at the water.

Holding Adam's hand, I watched a boat lazily make its way down the river. "Let's sit on that bench up there for a while. It's such a gorgeous day and I really like this place."

After we'd been sitting for a few minutes, Adam said, "So I take it you're enjoying your stay in Augusta?"

I felt his arm go around my shoulder and leaned into it. "This has been such a wonderful time. I love the town itself, but being here with you is what's made it so special. So yes, I'm really enjoying Augusta."

He kissed the top of my head. "Good, because we still have another full day tomorrow—our last one."

I sighed, drinking in the goodness of what we shared.

At that moment, Adam's cell phone rang and he flipped it open. "Mom? Is everything okay?"

I glanced at my watch—just past three. Clarissa would be finishing up a program that the library had arranged for the children for the week of spring break.

"What? When did this happen?"

I saw him grip the phone tighter and I knew by the worried expression on his face that something was wrong.

"What is it?" I whispered.

Sliding the phone away from his mouth, he said, "Clarissa's sick."

"Okay, go ahead, Mom. I'm listening. Right, well, of course you did the right thing. Oh, dear God, ICU?"

I saw his face crumple, and all of a sudden I got a queasy feeling in the pit of my stomach.

He stood up and indicated we were leaving as he continued to listen to Opal on the other end of the line. "Yes, yes, put him on."

Keeping pace with Adam, I walked beside him toward the parking lot.

"Yes, hello," I heard him say before he paused again. "Of course, whatever you think is best. Absolutely. Is she awake?" Another pause. "I see. Okay, well, as you know, we're in Augusta, Georgia." Adam swung his wrist up to look at his watch. "We'll need about an hour and we'll be on the road, and the drive is about six hours. Okay, thank you. Mom? Okay, we're heading back to the Partridge Inn now to check out. I'll call you on your cell once we get on the road to get an update. You're not there alone, are you? Oh, good. Okay. Love you too."

I held my breath waiting for Adam to explain what had happened. He leaned against the car, dropped his face into his hands, and began to sob. My arms went around him.

Attempting to compose himself he said, "Clarissa wasn't feeling well yesterday. Just a headache and complained of feeling tired. This morning she complained of a stiff neck and she had a fever, so my mom didn't let her go to the library. She called the pediatrician and he said to bring her to Shands right away." He stopped to take a breath and shook his head. "The doctor thinks it could be bacterial meningitis."

The bottom suddenly fell out of my world.

He zapped the remote, unlocking the doors, and we jumped in.

"Oh, God, Adam. What are they doing for her? Is she awake?"

"He said it was good that my mother got Clarissa there so fast. They started IV antibiotics on her right away, because he suspected meningitis from the symptoms. No, she's not awake. He explained they've sedated her to keep her quiet. She's in intensive care and he needed my permission to do a spinal tap, which will tell us for sure if it's bacterial meningitis."

The next hour passed in a blur. Adam checked out while I threw our clothes into the luggage. When we got to the lobby with the bellman pushing the cart, the manager came from behind the desk, extending his hand.

"I'm so terribly sorry about your daughter's emergency. Please know I'll have her in my prayers."

Both Adam and I mumbled a thank-you and headed to the car.

We were on I-16 heading toward I-95 when he passed me his cell phone. "Could you dial my mom's cell number, please?"

I did and then passed the phone back to him.

"Okay," he said. "We're on our way. Any change there?" He was silent listening to Opal's voice on the other end of the line. "Oh, they think it's bacterial meningitis? Now what?" More silence. "Okay, I'll call you in a couple hours, but if there's any change whatsoever, you call us."

I placed my hand on his leg. "They did the spinal tap?"

He nodded. "Yeah, and it looks definitive. They're now doing other tests to identify the bacteria. They'll culture the fluid and have those results in about two days. This will determine which antibiotics are effective against that particular bacterium. Then they'll be able to adjust the antibiotic they've already started if they need to."

I was having a hard time digesting all of this. My mind seemed foggy and I refused to let myself think any further than the next moment.

"Who's with your mother at the hospital?"

"Hank. He's the one that drove them. After the pediatrician said they needed to get Clarissa there right away, she called Hank. And Dora took Billie back to her house."

I felt Adam give me a squeeze as his hand encircled mine, and for the first time that I could remember I didn't feel the warm security his touch had always given me.

❦ 48 ❦

Forty-five minutes later we were merging onto I-95 following the signs for Brunswick / Jacksonville when my cell phone rang. I answered to hear Dora's voice.

"Monica? Are you and Adam okay? Where're you at?"

"We're scared to death about Clarissa. Just got onto I-95. Any update?" I wished that my mother wasn't in Paris. I knew how confusing medical jargon could be, and it would have been nice to have a registered nurse at hand to fill in the gaps.

"No, I just spoke to Opal. Clarissa is still sleeping."

"My God, Dora, this all happened so fast. Do you think she'll be okay?"

"I called your mother, Monica, to let her know what's going on. She said meningitis comes on that quickly, that's why it's so important to get treatment right away, but the problem is that we have to wait for culture and blood results to be certain of the correct antibiotic."

I repeated my question. "Do you think she'll be okay?"

There was a pause before she said, "Monica, I can't truthfully answer that. It's serious. Very serious. It can lead to death within hours, and that's why treatment is started right away without waiting for the results of the tests."

I gripped the phone tighter. She was right about how serious this was, and it was something I'd never experienced before. "I just thank God Opal was with her and knew exactly what to do." Would I have known under the same circumstances or just brushed it off as a minor flu?

"I want you to know she has an excellent doctor and she's in an excellent hospital. I have Billie here with me and we've set up a phone tree to keep calls to a minimum. I'm the one who checks in with Opal, and then I call Saren and Grace to give them updates."

"Thank you. Thank you for everything. Is Billie okay?"

"She's confused, of course, wondering where Clarissa is, and I'm sure she can't figure out why she's here with me, but she's fine. Only ate a little supper this evening, but that's to be expected."

"Right. Okay, thanks again, Dora. I'll be in touch."

I disconnected and filled Adam in on what she had to say—but I neglected the part about how serious this was. I figured he'd find out soon enough.

After stopping briefly at a rest area on I-95 for the bathroom and vending-machine coffee, we pulled into the parking lot of Shands Hospital at exactly 10:37.

We raced to the emergency room entrance and asked directions for intensive care. Stepping off the elevator, we saw Opal and Hank huddled together side by side on a sofa in the waiting room. Opal jumped up when she saw us walking toward her and pulled Adam and me into her arms.

"Oh, thank God you're here. There's still no change since we spoke an hour ago." She dabbed at her eyes with a crumpled tissue as Hank came up and put his hand on her shoulder.

"Can we see her?" Adam asked.

"Yes, of course, come on," she said, leading us to the desk at the nurses' station.

Opal introduced us to the nurse in charge.

"I'm Regina, the charge nurse for this shift. Let me get Clarissa's nurse."

She returned with an attractive brunette wearing blue scrubs and a black stethoscope dangling from around her neck.

"Hi, I'm Tara. I've been with Clarissa since seven this evening. There hasn't been much change since I came on duty. Her last temp was still a hundred and three, we're running in some IV antibiotics, and she was having a little difficulty breathing earlier so the doctor ordered some oxygen to make her more comfortable. I'm afraid at this point, that's all I can tell you. But I want you to be aware when you go in to see her that she's hooked up to lots of monitors and there's lots of tubes, so don't be alarmed. Dr. Sutter is still in the building and he wanted me to page him when you arrived so he could speak with you. Do you have any questions?"

I stood there mute while Adam shook his head and said, "No, not right now. Thank you very much. You'll let us know when the doctor arrives?"

Tara nodded. "I'll come and get you. Just go through these doors and Clarissa's bed is the first one on the left."

Adam turned around to Opal. "Mom, you've been here all day and night. I want Hank to take you home now. Monica and I will be staying."

Opal dabbed at her eyes again. "Are you sure, Adam? I can stay."

"No, I'm positive. You look exhausted. You'll get her home, Hank?"

"Absolutely. Don't you worry. Come on, Opal."

My mother-in-law embraced both Adam and me and then allowed Hank to lead her to the elevator.

"Ready?" Adam said.

I reached for his hand and nodded. We pushed the double doors open and walked into a large, semicircular room. In the center was what I assumed was the nurses' station. A U-shaped area, with office chairs on wheels, lots of counter space and many screens that blinked as lines and numbers ran past. Five nurses sat at the counter looking through paperwork. Tara saw us and nodded, then resumed watching the monitor in front of her.

My gaze panned the unit and that's when I saw what looked like about eight individual cubicles, white curtains arranged to prevent anybody from seeing beyond. I felt Adam tug my hand and followed him to the first one. He quietly slid the curtain back, allowing us to enter the cubicle. My legs began to tremble uncontrollably and I gripped his hand tighter. We stood there for a few moments taking in what was before our eyes.

A dim fluorescent light cast an eerie glow on the area. Monitor screens, IV machines that beeped as green numbers glowed, plastic bags of fluids resting on the bedside table, and what looked to be miles of plastic tubing—all of it snaking its way into some part of Clarissa.

I finally forced my eyes to her, and for a second I thought I might faint. She lay in the middle of a bed that looked way too large for her, white sheet and blanket up to her neck, her face as pale as the linens, and covering her nose and mouth, an oxygen mask that hissed and released a steam vapor. Her eyes were closed and in that moment I wasn't even certain she was breathing.

"Oh, dear God," I whispered, letting go of Adam's hand as he walked to the bedside. My legs were trembling like somebody with hypothermia and I gripped the iron bedrail.

I heard Adam murmuring to Clarissa as I stood there staring at what seemed to be a scene from my worst nightmare, and in that moment an emotion surged through my body that was both familiar and unfamiliar. It consumed my entire being because I knew without a doubt that it had come from the depths of my very soul.

Tears flowed down my face as I walked to the other side of Clarissa's bed and allowed the emotion to envelop me. I gently reached under the blanket and held Clarissa's small hand in mine. With my vision blurred, I whispered, "I love you, Clarissa. God, how I *love* you. Please be all right."

I felt Adam step behind me and put his arm around my shoulder as the tears I couldn't control continued to fall. Staring at Clarissa so fragile, so vulnerable, and so terribly ill made me understand what it meant to deeply love a child and feel like your heart was being ripped out.

Neither Adam nor I spoke. We just stood there looking down on our daughter, clinging to each other until we heard Tara say, "Mr. and Mrs. Brooks? Dr. Sutton is out here to speak to you."

I swiped at my eyes and reached for a tissue from the box on the table.

A tall, distinguished-looking man who appeared to be in his early fifties held his hand out to us as we approached the nurses' station. The pocket of his white lab coat had *Dr. Sutton* stitched in blue thread.

"I'm Clarissa's doctor," he told us without a trace of a smile. "Why don't we go sit in a room over here so we can talk? Would either of you like coffee, a soft drink?"

"No, thank you," Adam and I said in unison and followed him into a small room with a desk and three chairs.

The doctor sat behind the desk and placed paperwork and file folders in front of him.

"I won't lie," he told us. "We have a serious situation, but we have Clarissa on the antibiotics and as soon as we get all the results back we'll have a better idea if they're the correct ones. If not, we'll know which ones to switch her to. You were fortunate your mother wasted no time in getting her in here. That will probably be in

Clarissa's favor. I'm afraid I don't have much more information for you right now. Do you have any questions?"

"Is she unconscious?" Adam asked. "Can she hear us speak to her? Does she know we're here?"

"It's very important that we keep her quiet and calm, so we have her pretty well sedated right now. I can't say for sure, but yes, she probably can hear you and feel your touch. She drifts in and out of sleep, and when she was awake earlier she was having some difficulty breathing, that's why I ordered the oxygen. Are you familiar with bacterial meningitis at all?"

Adam shook his head. "Not really. What could the complications be? What might happen?"

"I don't mean to alarm you, but there're some complications we need to watch for. That's why she has to be in ICU. She could possibly have seizures, go into shock, or she could even lapse into a coma. Now, none of these things might happen, but you do need to be prepared, and of course if she went into a coma we'd have to place her on mechanical ventilation for her breathing."

I gripped the arms of the chair and glanced at Adam. His face was the whitest I'd ever seen it and I knew he was struggling to hold on to his emotions.

Dr. Sutton gave us a few moments to digest what he'd told us and said, "Any other questions?"

"Yes," I said in a voice that sounded foreign to my ears. "What exactly *is* bacterial meningitis? And how did Clarissa get it?"

"It's an inflammation of the subarachnoid space, which is located within the layers of tissue covering the brain and spinal cord. People who get this have been exposed to the organism, and it's most common among infants, children, adolescents, and people over fifty-five."

Adam shook his head as if trying to comprehend all that was happening. "So now, all we can do is wait?"

"I'm afraid so," Dr. Sutton replied. "I'd suggest you go home for the night and get some rest. We'll be in touch if there's any change."

"No," Adam said, without hesitating. "We're staying here all night. We'll be in the waiting room and go in to see Clarissa when we're allowed."

Relief came over me and I reached for Adam's hand to squeeze it in agreement. There wasn't any way I wanted to leave Clarissa here all alone without us nearby.

Dr. Sutton stood up and nodded. "That's not a problem. That'll be fine. I'm leaving shortly, but Dr. Wilson will be on duty until I return in the morning. If you have any questions or concerns, tell Clarissa's nurse to page him."

Adam and I both thanked him and returned to the vinyl sofa in the waiting room, where we were about to spend the longest night of my life.

ᔟ 49 ᔟ

I felt Adam stir beside me and opened my eyes, feeling momentarily disoriented. My gaze took in the dimly lit waiting room. Dread washed over me as I realized why we were there.

"Are you okay?" I heard Adam say and felt his arm tighten around my shoulder.

I nodded and saw the large round clock on the wall read 6:25.

"Did you sleep at all?" I asked, feeling guilty for the hour or so I must have gotten.

"A bit. There's no change. Clarissa's still sleeping. How about I get us some coffee?"

I sat up and stretched. "That would be great."

"A doughnut or something to go with it?"

"I couldn't eat a thing. Just coffee."

I watched Adam walk toward the elevator. In the dim lighting and hushed quiet everything that had happened since the previous afternoon seemed surreal. I wouldn't even allow myself to think about the possibility that we could lose Clarissa, and my mind drifted back to the day she'd arrived at our house. Such a sullen and withdrawn little girl. Not at all the same girl who was now so seriously ill. Clarissa had flourished living with us—she'd become happy, well-adjusted, and secure.

And how about me, I thought. I'd also had quite a transformation in the past eleven months. Little by little, all of the doubt I'd ever had about motherhood had slipped away, until suddenly one day being a mother to Clarissa had felt like the most natural thing in the world. So much so that I even looked forward to giving birth to my own child.

But this sudden and frightening situation with Clarissa was making me rethink my decision. To lose a child had to be the most painful and traumatic event that a parent could go through. I wasn't sure that I had the strength to endure something like that.

"Monica?"

I looked up to see Grace standing in front of me. Jumping up, I threw my arms around her and broke into sobs. "Oh, God, thank you for coming."

I felt her squeeze me and then move me away from her as she swept the hair back from my face.

"Any change?" she asked.

I shook my head. "None. She's still sleeping and we're waiting on the final test results. God, I'm so glad you're here."

She gave me a bag, saying, "Now, where else would your best friend be during a time like this? Here, I brought you some muffins from the coffee shop. Your favorite—blueberry ones."

I smiled through my tears. "Gracie, what would I do without you? You're the best."

"Hey, Grace," we heard Adam say and turned around to see him carrying a cardboard container filled with half a dozen cups of coffee. "I figured you'd be here before long." He passed a cup to each of us. Spying the logo on the bag, he said, "Ah, blueberry muffins?"

Grace nodded. "I'm so sorry about Clarissa, Adam, but all of Cedar Key is praying for her, so she's in good hands."

"Thanks," he said, and took a sip of coffee.

"When do you think you might know something?" she asked.

Adam shrugged. "We're waiting on those final results. Dr. Sutton comes back on duty at seven, so maybe we'll hear something then."

"I'm going to head into that restroom over there. One of the nurses gave us an admitting bag with toothbrush and stuff. I'll be right back."

By the time I returned to the waiting room, I had to admit that physically I felt a bit better. When Adam returned from freshening up we went in to see Clarissa again. She was beginning to stir but still was not awake. My heart turned over at the sight of her—so helpless, and I was powerless to do anything to make her better.

Adam and I went back to the waiting room to find that Grace had set up the table with juice, muffins, and bagels.

"I ran down to the cafeteria," she told us. "Y'all have to eat something. It's eight in the morning and I bet you can't remember the last time you ate."

She was right. "Thank you," I said, sitting down to nibble on a muffin. I had no appetite, but felt it was the least I could do for Grace's kindness. I saw that Adam was doing the same.

About ten minutes later, Dr. Sutton entered the waiting room and both Adam and I jumped up.

"Good morning," the doctor said, sounding a bit more congenial than the night before. "Well, I think I have some good news. I don't want you getting your hopes up quite yet, but we've isolated the bacterium and we started Clarissa on the proper antibiotic."

There was no way to describe the relief I felt hearing his words. Adam pulled me into his arms and I felt his tears mingling with mine.

Dr. Sutton put up a hand. "Now, look, we're not over the hump yet, but it's a good start."

A good start was good enough for me. A good start gave me hope and allowed me to feel that maybe, just maybe, Clarissa would be okay.

"Thank you, Doctor," Adam said. "Now what? Will she be waking up?"

"Well, we still have some waiting ahead of us. It'll take about twenty-four hours to see a dramatic improvement with the new antibiotic. I think by this evening we can begin decreasing her sedative and she'll be more awake. We'll be doing more blood work and monitoring that. My hope is that within forty-eight hours she'll be on the road to recovery. I know you've been here all night and I strongly suggest that you go home, get some rest, and then come back late this evening. By then, Clarissa might be awake for short periods of time."

Adam nodded. "Thank you again, Doctor. If we go home, you do have our home phone number in case there's any change?"

"Yes, it's in the records, and I would personally call you, but I don't anticipate that happening at this point."

We watched him go back inside the ICU and turned around to receive a huge hug from Grace.

"It sounds good," she said. "Now we just have to keep thinking positive and sending out lots of prayers."

I nodded. "What do you think?" I asked Adam. "Do you think we should leave for a while?"

"I'll stay," Grace said. "I know I'm not a family member and I can't go in to see Clarissa, but I'll stay out here to keep an eye on things." She lifted a tote bag. "See, I even brought my knitting, so I'm all set."

Adam's cell phone rang before he could answer me. I heard him say "Hi, Mom" and knew it was Opal calling for an update.

A few minutes later he disconnected and said, "Yes, I think we should go home and try to get some sleep, or we'll really be useless in the days to come. Grace, if you could stay for a while that would be great. My mom and Hank will be here by one, she said, and they can relieve you. If you'd like to go in to see Clarissa, I can arrange it and tell them you're her aunt."

I caught a look of alarm crossing my friend's face. "Oh, that's really nice of you, Adam, but if you don't mind, I'd really rather not see Clarissa like that. You know, so sick. But if there's anything going on and she needed somebody, I'd be right here."

I could understand Grace's hesitation and pulled her into an embrace. "That would be great. We really appreciate it, Gracie, and I love you for being such a good friend."

"I love you too," she said.

"Okay, well then, we'll head home and be back this evening. All set?" Adam asked me.

"Call us if you need to," I told Grace, following Adam to the elevator.

Just as he pushed the button, I exclaimed, "Oh, no! The music box. I can't leave Clarissa here without the music box I bought for her. She *has* to have it."

I think Adam saw a touch of panic on my face and he patted my arm. "Okay, wait here. I know which bag it's in. I'll run out to the car and bring it back."

I saw Grace look at me questioningly as Adam got on the elevator and I proceeded to tell her the story behind the music box that I'd found in Augusta for Clarissa.

"What an amazing story. I mean, really—could you call it coincidence? The dog resembles Billie, the box plays "Amazing Grace," which Sybile wanted played at her memorial service, and it was originally given to this other little girl when she had pneumonia and they almost lost her. It sounds like this music box has magical qualities."

"That's exactly what I thought when I found it, and I felt compelled to get it for Clarissa."

We both saw Adam coming toward us from the elevator, gift bag in hand.

"I had wanted her to unwrap it," I said, gently removing the paper and satin bow. "But I want to leave it at her bedside before we go."

Holding it up for Grace to inspect, I said, "Isn't it gorgeous?"

She touched it gingerly with her fingertips. "It is," she said, softly. "It's very special. I can tell—because it has a good *feel* to it."

Adam and I walked to Clarissa's bedside and I wound the music box. The haunting melody of "Amazing Grace" filled the small cubicle.

I leaned over and kissed Clarissa's forehead. "Get well," I whispered. "Get well and come home to us, where you belong. I love you so *very* much, Clarissa."

❦ 50 ❦

As we approached the Number Four Bridge onto Cedar Key, I glanced out the car window to see the sun shining on the water like glittering jewels. Smaller islands dotted here and there for as far as the eye could see. Pelicans swooped and dove into the water, their clumsy antics causing me to smile.

Thank you, I silently whispered. *Thank you for this beautiful slice of paradise where I call home and thank you for Clarissa coming into my life. Please let her get better and come home to us.*

Adam pulled into our driveway and I let out a deep sigh. Our house had never looked so good to me. Walking inside, it felt like we'd been gone much longer than just four days. So much had happened in that short time.

Putting down our luggage on the kitchen floor, I found a note from Dora written that morning.

Dear Monica and Adam,
Billie is fine with me, so when you get home, get some rest and call me when you get a chance. I put a seafood casserole in

the fridge for you. All you have to do is heat it in the mi-
crowave. And there's fresh-baked biscuits to go with it on the
counter. I love you both.
    Aunt Dora

I smiled as I turned and saw the basket covered with a tea towel.

Adam read the note over my shoulder and gave me a squeeze. "That was nice of her. I'm going to hop in the shower and then we can have a bite to eat."

"Good idea, and I'll shower when we're done. Then I guess we should listen to Dr. Sutton and try and get some sleep."

Although I wasn't sure I'd be able to sleep, I must have drifted off as soon as Adam and I got into bed and I curled up in his arms.

I awoke and saw the bedside clock read five-thirty and was surprised that I'd actually slept for six uninterrupted hours. That was a good sign, I thought. No phone calls about Clarissa. She must still be okay. I glanced over to see Adam still sleeping and carefully got out of bed, not waking him.

After getting on my robe and using the bathroom, I tiptoed out of the room, quietly closing the door behind me.

I prepared the coffeemaker and then dialed Dora's number.

"Oh, Monica, it's so good to hear from you. Did you and Adam get some sleep?"

"Yes, I managed to get six hours and Adam's still sleeping. Thank you for the casserole and biscuits. They were delicious. You didn't hear anything about Clarissa, did you? Nobody's called here."

"Opal called to tell me they got her started on the correct antibiotic this morning and then she called around four o'clock to say that Clarissa was awake for a little while."

"She was? How is she?"

"Opal said she was a little groggy, but other than that, she seemed okay. Opal told her that you and Adam had been there all night and you'd gone home for a while but would be back this evening. She said Clarissa smiled, asked if she could hear the music again, and drifted back to sleep. Opal said you left a music box there for her?"

"Yes, I bought it for her in Augusta and I wanted her to have it now."

"Well, she seems to really love the music from it. If she keeps improving like this, I think she's going to be okay, Monica."

"God, I hope so."

"By the way, I left something at your house. It was entrusted to me before Sybile died."

"What?" I said with surprise. "What on earth is it?"

"It's a letter, from Sybile to you."

"A letter? What's it say?"

"Oh, I don't know. It's sealed and your name is on the envelope. I was specifically told by Sybile to give it to you—when you became a mother. That's exactly how she said it to me, not when you had your first child or when you were pregnant, but when you *became a mother* and she said that I would know when that time was. I think that time is now, Monica. I've watched you with Clarissa for almost a year and there isn't any doubt in my mind—you have truly become a mother and I think you need to have Sybile's letter."

Tears burned my eyes as I recalled my doubts of that morning at the hospital. "Oh, I don't know," I said. "I was beginning to think maybe I had the strength after all, but going through this with Clarissa, I've been so frightened. I just don't know. . . ."

"Well, *I* know. Being frightened for your child does not make you any less of a mother. If anything, it increases that ability. It's only natural to fear losing your child, but you can't let that fear consume you to the point where you turn aside from motherhood. And that fear, Monica—it never goes away. But you learn to let go of it a little at a time, especially when your children are small. Because that letting go is what enables them to grow and become who they're supposed to be. But the worry—I won't lie. A mother never stops worrying about her child. That goes with the territory. So you may as well get used to it now."

I smiled. Leave it to Aunt Dora to set things right. "I see what you're saying. Where's the letter?"

"I put it on your desk in your studio. I hope whatever Sybile has to say will comfort you."

"Thanks, Dora, and thanks for giving it to me now. I love you. I'm going to go read it."

I poured coffee into a mug and took it to my studio. Sitting at the desk, I saw the cream-colored envelope with Sybile's familiar bold handwriting.

For my granddaughter, Monica she'd written on the front.

Picking it up, I sat holding it for a few minutes, recalling the first time I'd met her at the Lighthouse. She'd made it clear immediately that I was not to call her *Grandma,* and within a short time I'd come up with the nickname of Billie for her, which she loved. I also remembered how she'd questioned me about the fellow I was dating at the time, asking very pointed questions, and when I finished, she'd asked with a straight face, "Yeah, but is he good in bed?"

I smiled as I reached for the letter opener to unseal the envelope. Sybile was a character, no doubt about it. She gave off a crusty exterior, but inside there was a mellowness that drew me to her from the moment we'd first met.

Removing the cream-colored pages, I began to read.

My dearest Monica,

If you're reading this letter then it means you are now a mother and that I have a great-grandchild. I was very specific to Dora about when to give this letter to you. As your other grandmother so aptly proved, one does not have to give birth in order to become a mother. So no matter how it occurred, you now have a child as you read this.

When you learned the story concerning your mother's adoption, you never once held it against me for making that choice. And for that, I thank you.

However, I also got the feeling that perhaps you thought, like me, motherhood wasn't to be part of your life. You could have been right, because I do strongly believe that not every woman is cut out to be a mother. But if you're reading this letter, something changed your mind to make you feel otherwise and for that, I'm very grateful.

No, I still do not have any regrets for giving your mother up for adoption. It was the right thing to do for me. However, with my days now limited, the one thing I do regret is not having enough time to spend with both you and your mother.

I know how independent you've always been—a trait that we both shared. And I know that you admired this trait in me. Perhaps that was why you were so easy to accept my decision about your mother's adoption. However, I need you to know the truth. I need you to know that while I may have been independent and followed my own path, I was never brave about it.

Perhaps a quote from Mahatma Gandhi will help you to better understand what I'm saying. "A coward is incapable of exhibiting love; it is the prerogative of the brave."

I allowed a deep and true love with Saren to be wasted because I was a coward. I wasn't willing to take a chance, even after my modeling career failed. If I was alone, I couldn't be hurt. I wasn't brave enough to show love and risk the pain that might go with it. Instead, I chose to spend many lonely years both without my daughter and without the love of my life.

But you, my darling granddaughter, not only are you inde-

pendent, but you have the wonderful trait of being brave. And because you're reading this letter, you have proved that. You have chosen to risk the pain and exhibit love by becoming a mother. And I am so very proud of you.

So hold on to the strength that you possess, grow from your mistakes, love like you've never been loved before, and every now and again—think of me. Because I will always be with you, Monica, and I will always love you.

Billie (your grandmother)

I wiped the tears from my eyes and let out a deep sigh. My grandmother was a very wise woman, and even in death she was sharing that wisdom with me. She was right. If you don't open yourself up to love, you can never be hurt. Is that why I ran from so many relationships? And is that why when I met Adam I knew I couldn't run anymore, because if I did, I'd be giving up that one great love of my life? And was it easier for me to claim I had no mothering traits because I certainly wouldn't be subjecting myself to possible heartache and pain if I remained childless?

And then Clarissa walked into my life and changed the way I felt about everything. Just like her father had done.

I slipped the pages back into the envelope and left it on the desk as I heard Adam calling from the kitchen.

"Hey," I said, walking into his embrace. "Get enough sleep?"

"I did. I feel like a new person. No calls about Clarissa?"

"No, but I take that to be good news. It's six-thirty. Let's get dressed and head back to the hospital."

Adam nodded. "Don't you want something to eat before we go?"

"I'm not that hungry, but let me get you a cup of coffee. We can get something at the hospital cafeteria."

"Good idea."

* * *

We walked into the ICU to see Dr. Sutton talking to Clarissa's nurse at the nurses' station. He turned, holding up a finger to us, and then resumed going over a chart with the nurse.

Coming toward us, he actually had a smile on his face. "Well, you two certainly look a bit more rested, and I think you'll be very pleased with the difference in Clarissa. That antibiotic seems to be doing the trick. She's not being sedated anymore and has been awake for a few hours now." He looked at Adam. "Your mother's been in there with her, and she and her friend just left a few minutes ago to grab something to eat in the cafeteria."

I felt Adam reach for my hand and give it a squeeze. Hearing the doctor's words sent a jolt of happiness through me.

"God, that's wonderful news. Does this mean Clarissa's going to be okay?" Adam questioned.

"I'd say yes. She's over the hump now. Still pretty weak, but that will just take time. She'll only continue to improve with the antibiotic, and I think by Friday we'll be able to move her to a regular floor."

Adam put out his hand. "Thank you. Thank you so much for everything you've done."

"Yes," I said. "God, we can't thank you enough."

"Well, that little girl is very much loved, and I'd have to say that love played a huge part in getting her through this."

"Is there anything we could have done to prevent her from catching it?" Adam asked.

"You mean like a vaccine? Actually, there's a fairly new one out called Manactra. But I'm afraid it wouldn't have helped in Clarissa's case. The CDC recommends it be given to children ages eleven to eighteen, and at nine, Clarissa wasn't a candidate to receive it."

Adam nodded. "And once she comes home, is there anything we

need to be watching for? Symptoms or anything that might cause a problem?"

I saw a brief look of concern cross Dr. Sutton's face. "I'll go over all of this with you in more detail before she's released, but you will have to have routine hearing tests done on Clarissa for a while. Unfortunately, deafness can be a residual effect of meningitis. But you don't need to concern yourself with this now. Chances are she'll be fine. You'll just want to keep a check on it."

"Can we go in to see her?" Adam asked.

"Absolutely. If you have any other questions, just call me and I'll see you here over the next few days to give you updates."

Hand in hand, Adam and I walked into the ICU and paused at the cubicle where Clarissa was.

The doctor was right. Already she'd begun to look better. The oxygen mask was no longer on her face. Her bed had been raised to a semireclined position and even her face seemed to have more color. Her eyes were closed and we stood there watching, each of us lost in our own thoughts.

Almost as if she could feel our presence, her eyes fluttered open and she saw us. A smile crossed her face as we went to the bedside, each of us taking a turn to lean over and kiss her.

"So," Adam said. "You've had a time of it. How're you feeling, sweetheart?"

"Tired. How long have I been here?"

I brushed her bangs back from her forehead. "Since yesterday morning. It's Tuesday evening."

"Oh, no, because I got sick you had to come back from Augusta early?"

I reached for her hand and gave it a squeeze. "You silly goose. We wouldn't have been anywhere else."

"Monica's right. As soon as we got the call from Grandma yesterday afternoon, we were on our way back here. Are you having pain anywhere?"

Clarissa shook her head gently. "Not anymore. I had a real bad headache the other day and then a stiff neck, and I was so tired. When I got the fever, Grandma thought it might be the flu so she called the doctor and he said we should get to the hospital right away." Clarissa paused for a second before going on. "I was scared."

My heart went out to her and once again I could feel tears welling in my eyes. I leaned over to kiss her and said, "Of course you were scared, but for being so scared, you've been a mighty brave girl."

A hint of a smile returned to her face. "Do you think so?"

"I know so, and now you'll just be getting better every day."

"How's Billie? I miss her."

"I know you do. She's fine, but she misses you too. Aunt Dora is keeping her at her house and I know Billie will be very happy when you come home."

"Now, this is what I like to see," I heard Opal say and turned around to see her with a huge smile on her face. "Quite a difference in our little girl, huh?"

"A huge difference," Adam said. "Thank God."

Opal passed a gift bag to Clarissa. "Just a little something I found that I thought you might like."

Clarissa pulled out a buff-colored stuffed dog that bore a close resemblance to Billie. Hugging it to her chest, she exclaimed, "Oh, thank you, Grandma. I love it." Then she looked directly at me. "And I love my music box, Monica. Thank you so much. Grandma said you got it for me in Augusta."

"I did. I thought with the little girl and the dog it was perfect for you."

"Every time the nurse comes in she winds it up for me so I can hear the music."

As if on cue, Tara poked her head around the curtain. "It looks like you're all having fun in here, but I'm afraid you should take five more minutes and then let Clarissa rest for a while."

"Good idea," Adam said and I noticed that Clarissa's eyes were beginning to droop a little.

"Will you be back tomorrow?" Clarissa asked.

"We're not going anywhere tonight," Adam told her. "We're sending Grandma and Hank home now and it's our turn to stay. We're all taking turns doing shifts so you won't be alone."

"Really?" The look on Clarissa's face told me she was happy about this.

"Really," I told her. "Your dad and I are going to go to the cafeteria now to have something to eat, but we'll be in to check on you throughout the night."

"And we already have it arranged," Opal said. "Hank and I will be here tomorrow morning at nine to relieve you to go home. And Dora, Saren, and Grace have worked out their shifts as well."

I shook my head. *Leave it to all of them,* I thought. *That's what family and good friends do—they take care of each other. Because of the love that binds them together.*

❦ 51 ❦

I had just finished dusting and vacuuming Clarissa's room when the phone rang.

"So tomorrow's the big day, huh?" I heard Grace say.

"Yes, after ten days in the hospital Clarissa's finally coming home. God, this house has been empty without her."

"Are you busy right now? I was going to pop over for coffee."

"Not at all. I'm cleaning Clarissa's room and just have to get fresh sheets on her bed. Come on over."

"Be there in five," Grace said, hanging up.

"Gosh, it feels like forever since we just sat and gabbed like this," I told Grace.

"I know. I've missed you, and now that Clarissa's coming home tomorrow—I won't lie, I've been scared to death about her."

"You weren't the only one. When I think how close we came to possibly losing her—I'm just so glad it's all behind us now. Do you know that Adam left three messages for Carrie Sue on her cell? Three. And she hasn't even called back."

"She's in her own little world. I have a feeling that after going through this, you don't doubt your mothering ability any longer."

"You're right, I don't. I think for the first time in my life, I feel comfortable where I'm at. Being a mother to Clarissa, I mean. Unfortunately it took something as serious as this to make me realize how much I truly *do* love Clarissa. Not just in words, but deep inside me. I'll never forget walking into ICU and seeing her in that bed. All of the love I felt for her just gushed to the surface and overwhelmed me. I think maybe it was always there. I just didn't want to acknowledge it."

Grace nodded. "Yeah, sometimes the simplest things in life are the toughest to figure out."

"And," I said, holding up my coffee cup in a toast, "It might not be much longer till we'll be calling you Aunt Gracie."

"What?" she gasped. "Are you pregnant?"

"Not yet, but Adam and I did have that talk in Augusta. I'm off the pill. So we're trying. We'll see what happens."

Grace clinked her coffee cup against mine. "Here's to your success. Oh, Monica, I'm so happy for you."

"Thanks. Hey, what's been going on with you? Bring me up to date. Hear any more from Lucas?"

"He did stop in the coffee shop last week before he left the island. He's gone back to Brunswick to square things away there. He said he'll be back here around August."

"Oh, not till then? And he didn't ask you out?"

"It's really strange. I got the feeling that he wanted to, if that makes sense. But no, he didn't. Like he thought better of it for some reason. I don't know—I think I should just chalk it up to having rotten luck with guys. But . . . I might be taking a trip to Brunswick myself."

"Really?" I asked with surprise. She still hadn't shared with me why she was so reluctant to visit that town. Since she was so close to her aunt, I figured it must have something to do with a guy.

"Yeah, I spoke to Aunt Maude the other day. She's begging me again to come and visit. Not that she's old at seventy-two, but she's not getting any younger, and now macular degeneration prevents her from driving here anymore. I'm thinking maybe I should go for a few days and bring her here for a visit."

I nodded. "Might not be a bad idea, Grace." I took a sip of coffee. "Look, you can tell me it's none of my business, but I consider you my closest friend and I think I'm yours. If you don't want to tell me, okay, but why do you resist going to Brunswick? You're very close to your aunt, so it can't have anything to do with her."

Grace was silent for a few moments, fiddling with the handle on her coffee cup. "Oh, gosh no, it doesn't have a thing to do with Aunt Maude and she knows that. And I guess she's always loved me enough to understand." Grace let out a deep sigh. "It has to do with a guy, Monica. Somebody I was heavily involved with. He lives on St. Simons Island, very close to Brunswick, and I never wanted to risk seeing him again."

I now recalled how she'd shared with me about her miscarriage and figured he must have been the father. I waited for her to explain more, but she didn't.

Running a hand through her curls, she said, "I don't know, maybe the time has come for me to return there and face my demons."

"Very often time has a way of healing things and allowing us to do that," I told her, not wanting to press for more information.

"Yeah, maybe," was all she said.

We had decided to surprise Clarissa when we picked her up at the hospital and had Billie waiting in the backseat of the car. Watching their reunion, I couldn't stop smiling. Clarissa was beside herself with joy as Billie cried and whined and wouldn't stop licking Clarissa's face during the drive home. The quirky little noises that Billie made almost sounded like she was talking and telling us how happy she was to have her beloved Clarissa back again.

We got her settled on the sofa to rest with Billie curled up beside her. Adam returned to the family room carrying a cardboard box filled with brightly wrapped presents.

The look of astonishment on Clarissa's face made me laugh. "These are for you," I told her. "Gifts from my mom and Noah that she sent from Paris, Aunt Dora and Saren and Gracie. And some of the kids from school dropped by to bring you something."

"Oh, wow, these are all for me?"

"They are," Adam said. "You're a very special girl. Go ahead, start opening them."

We sat and watched as she opened pajamas, dusting powder, books, and games, along with assorted other things to keep her busy while she recuperated.

"Everybody was so nice to me," Clarissa said.

"Well, you deserved it," I told her, picking up the wrapping paper scattered around the sofa. "But you still have one more gift. It's not wrapped, but I think you'll like it."

"I do?"

"Yup," I said, nodding to Adam.

He went into our bedroom and returned carrying a large wooden sign with the wording hidden.

I saw the look of interest that crossed Clarissa's face and smiled. "Well, as the new proprietor of the yarn shop, I recently made an executive decision." I went to stand beside Adam. "Spinning Forward was the name my mother had chosen for the shop, and since I'm the new owner, I thought maybe that required a new name. And because you've turned into such a proficient little knitter, I'd like you to be my assistant there."

Excitement covered Clarissa's face. "Really? You mean like Aunt Dora?"

I nodded. "Yup, just like Aunt Dora, and when we begin doing the knitting classes for kids, you can be right there with me helping. And so," I said, waving my hand toward Adam with a flourish, indicating he could now turn the sign around, "I wanted the new name to show that you and I are a twosome."

Adam turned the sign around with the words YARNING TO-GETHER burned into the wood. A pair of long bamboo needles and a shorter pair were entwined below the wording.

Clarissa's hand flew to her face as she gasped. "Oh, my goodness! That's what I always used to call knitting."

I laughed. "That's right. I thought it was so cute, and the term is appropriate for you and me. So I think it's the *perfect* name for the shop. What do you think?"

Clarissa got up from the sofa and pulled me into a tight embrace. "I love it! I *just* love it," she exclaimed. "I don't know why I always called it yarning instead of knitting—but I'm glad I did."

Adam smiled. "I think Monica is too."

He propped the sign against the wall so that Clarissa could stare at it from the sofa.

"When you're feeling better, we'll go to the yarn shop and get it hung outside. We'll have a little ceremony, like when they christen a boat," I told her. "And everybody will come."

"That'll be so cool!"

"Oh, gosh, I almost forgot—Zoe called this morning before we left to get you. She's been calling every day to check on you and said you should receive her gift in the mail soon. Her baby brother was born late last night, two weeks early, but he's fine."

"He was? Zac is here? Oh, that's so cool. Can I call Zoe later?"

"Of course you can," Adam said. "How about some lunch now and then you can rest for a while?"

"Okay. Gee, so now Zoe's a big sister. Lucky her."

Adam and I exchanged a glance.

"You think?" Adam said. "She's not an only child anymore. She'll have to share everything now that she has a new brother in the house."

"Oh, I don't think Zoe will mind that at all."

"Hmm, maybe not," I said. "But gee, she'll have to be pretty responsible now. You know, helping out to do things around the house. Maybe being quiet while the baby is sleeping, not playing her CD player really loud—that sort of thing."

"Well, right. That's what a big sister does, you know. It must be a great job to have."

"Would *you* like to be a big sister?" Adam asked.

Clarissa's face shot up to look at him, filled with excitement. "Oh, would I ever! I'd love to be a big sister. It's lonely being an only child, you know. Are we getting a baby?" Her glance swung from Adam to me.

We both laughed. "Well, not right at the moment," he told her. "But it just might be possible in the near future."

"Oh, wow!" she exclaimed, happiness oozing from her. "Wait till I tell Zoe. Then we'll both be big sisters. Oh, thank you," she told us. "I've always wanted a baby brother or sister."

Now that I was off the pill, Adam and I had discussed whether jealousy might be a problem for Clarissa. She'd just proven to us we needn't have worried.

By the time we'd finished dinner, the light shower we'd gotten had stopped. The sun was back out, just in time to begin setting in the western sky.

Adam and I were on the deck enjoying a glass of wine while Clarissa spoke to Zoe on the phone inside.

He reached over to take my hand. "Do you know how much I love you? I'm an incredibly lucky guy to have you in my life."

I smiled. "But I'm the lucky one. And I love you back even more."

"I don't think that's possible. We have so much to be grateful for, don't we?"

"We do. And so much to look forward to ahead of us."

I turned as Clarissa joined us on the deck.

"Everything okay with Zoe and her brother?" Adam asked.

"Yes, he's coming home tomorrow. Zoe got to hold him in the hospital today. I was a little jealous when she told me, but then I remembered you said we might be getting our own baby soon. I told Zoe and she was so excited for me."

Adam and I both smiled.

"You know," Clarissa said. "That lady was right. She said I had to stay here because so many good things were going to happen to me."

Despite the warmth of the air, goose bumps covered my skin. "What lady?" I asked softly.

"That lady that's been with me since I got here. She's gone away now, though. When I was so sick in the hospital, she was right there the whole time next to my bed. Didn't you see her?"

I saw Adam shake his head as we both continued to listen.

"Well, she was. And then she told me it was time for her to leave and I wouldn't see her again. But she said that would be okay because so many good things were going to happen to me and I'd be all right now."

I felt a chill go through me. Dear God, was Clarissa referring to Sybile? Had Sybile's spirit been here protecting Clarissa, looking out for her, waiting until I understood what it meant to deeply love this child? Waiting for *me* to become a mother in every sense of the word?

"So the lady is gone now?" Adam asked, like what he'd just been told was the most natural thing in the world.

"Yeah, I think so, because I haven't seen her for a few days now. But that's okay. I have you and Monica and Billie. And maybe a new sister or brother coming."

Clarissa felt secure in the love that surrounded her. Had *the lady* simply been a figment of her imagination? Something a lonely child had required and something that had soothed her?

"Oh, look," Clarissa said, going to the edge of the deck.

Adam and I got up to follow. Hovering above the water was the most vivid rainbow I'd ever seen. Deep pastel shades of pink and green and blue merged into an arc above Cedar Key.

"You know what?" I said, putting my arms around Clarissa who was standing in front of me. "They say there's a pot of gold at the end of the rainbow. A treasure."

Clarissa looked up at me with awe. "There is?"

"Well, that's what they say, but I'm not sure I believe that." I leaned forward and kissed her forehead. "Because *you* are my treasure, Clarissa. I love you *so* very much, with all my heart. I hope you know that."

She turned around to face both Adam and me, putting an arm around each of us. "Oh, I do," she said. "Because I love you just as much, and I always will."

I rested my chin on Clarissa's head and smiled as the rainbow seemed to intensify over my slice of paradise.

ACKNOWLEDGMENTS

Being a writer is an isolated profession, but being surrounded by family, friends, and fans allows me to be connected to the "real" world when I'm not busy creating new characters and plots.

Every single one of you has given me support, encouragement, humor, and a huge amount of loyalty, which I treasure.

I deeply appreciate all of the CRMs at Barnes & Nobles across the country who showed such huge support for *Spinning Forward*. One in particular was instrumental in setting up a fan base for me in the Atlanta area. For Carla Wilson at the Norcross, Georgia, Barnes & Noble . . . thank you! You're the best!

For each and every knitter who purchased my first book and continues to support my writing career, I hope you know how grateful I am. Keep those needles clicking and keep turning those pages.

Another group that I owe a huge thank you is the wonderful librarians across the country. You know how special and rewarding reading is, and to carry my work in your library is the ultimate compliment to me. A very special thank you to our own Cedar Key librarian, Molly Jubitz.

For my friend of over thirty years in Nova Scotia, Rose White, who first became my friend as a pen pal. Thank you for encouraging me way back then and insisting I would someday be a published author. I'm glad I listened to you, and I value our friendship.

Another thank you to Mary Ann Packer, my friend of over fifty years since we met in second grade. We've both fulfilled our passion and our dreams . . . you became the artist, and I became the writer. Aren't we proof that great things are possible!

And to my more recent friends, what would I do without you?

Our visits to Cedar Key, before relocating, were always made more special by Doreen and Oliver Bauer, owners of the Faraway Inn. Staying there with our Holly created memories that were the beginning of my love affair with this slice of paradise.

For Edie Zaprir, owner of Kona Joe's Island Café . . . thank you for friendship and the opportunity to chill out, when I'm not writing, with your great coffee on your deck overlooking the Gulf.

Joyce Aycock (my neighbor) and Marge Webber (who discovered me because of my blog about Cedar Key) . . . your support is deeply appreciated and I'm certainly glad our paths have crossed, all because of the island we love.

For Savannah Howard, my ten-year-old next-door neighbor. Thank you so much for allowing me the chance to get "inside" the head of Clarissa Jo. Asking you questions helped me create her character even better.

To my wonderful editor, Audrey LaFehr, thank you so much for making this story even better with your suggestions. You're a joy to work with! To Martin Biro and the rest of the Kensington team, a huge thank you for all of the assistance you provide getting my work on the bookshelves.

For my very good friends Alice Jordan and Bill Bonner. Your enthusiasm and support for my work has no bounds. I hope you know how much I value this! And once again, thank you both for reading this manuscript and offering your insights and input.

For my daughter, Susan Hanlon, and my two sons, Shawn and Brian DuLong . . . your support and pride mean everything to me.

Thank you to my husband, Ray, who makes this sometimes difficult career easier. Being my own personal chef and a caregiver to the dogs and cats when I'm on deadline and all of your support allows me to focus on the make-believe world, creating characters and stories that fulfill my passion.

And to you, my readers . . . my deepest gratitude for your feedback via e-mails, but most of all, thank you for granting me a space on your bookshelf.

CASTING ABOUT

Terri DuLong

ABOUT THIS GUIDE

The following questions are intended to
enhance your group's reading of
CASTING ABOUT.

DISCUSSION QUESTIONS

1. Why do you think Monica was insecure about motherhood?

2. Discuss Adam's reaction and feelings when he was granted full custody of Clarissa Jo following his ex-wife's accident.

3. In the beginning, how supportive do you think Monica was toward Adam? Toward Clarissa Jo?

4. Following Carrie Sue's accident, did you agree with the judge's ruling in favor of Adam? Why or why not?

5. Do you feel Grace was a positive or negative influence on Monica with regard to becoming a new stepmom? Discuss her impact on Monica as a friend.

6. Discuss Saren's feelings about Sybile's spirit still hovering over them. Did you feel she could be sending Monica a message, and if so, why?

7. How would you describe Monica's behavior toward Clarissa Jo in the beginning? Withdrawn, uncomfortable, fearful, angry, loving, involved? Explain your reasons.

8. What do you think Clarissa Jo's feelings were on leaving her mother? How do you think she felt about relocating? How do you think she felt toward Monica?

9. Did you feel "Billie" was a figment of Clarissa Jo's imagination? And if so, how did you account for the "coincidences," like knowing about Atsena Otie, naming her dog Billie, etc.?

10. Regarding the incident when Clarissa Jo broke the glass bowl that had belonged to Sybile . . . Did you think Monica overreacted? Did you feel there was any possibility the child could have let the bowl slip out of her hands on purpose? Explain your reasons.

11. Did you think Monica overstepped her bounds as a friend when she told Grace what she had discovered about Tony? Why or why not?

12. Where, in the story, did you feel was the beginning of the turning point in Monica and Clarissa Jo's relationship?